WHERE
THE
RIVER
ENDS

Also by Charles Martin

Chasing Fireflies

Maggie

When Crickets Cry

Wrapped in Rain

The Dead Don't Dance

WHERE THE RIVER ENDS

Charles Martin

BROADWAY BOOKS
New York

Copyright © 2008 by C. Martin, Inc.

Published in association with Yates & Yates, LLP, Attorneys and Counselors, Orange, CA

Reader's Guide copyright © 2009 by Broadway Paperbacks, an imprint of the Crown Publishing Group, a division of Random House, Inc., New York.

Excerpt from *The Mountain Between Us* copyright © 2010 by C. Martin, Inc.

Originally published in hardcover in the United States by Broadway Books, an imprint of the Crown Publishing Group, a division of Random House, Inc., New York, in 2008, and subsequently published in paperback in the United States by Broadway Books in 2009.

Library of Congress Cataloging-in-Publication Data
Martin, Charles, 1969–
Where the river ends / Charles Martin.
    p. cm.
1. Married people—Fiction. 2. Terminally ill—Fiction.   I. Title.
PS3613.A7778W48 2008
813'.6—dc22
2007042819

ISBN 978-0-307-88829-7
eISBN 978-0-7679-3083-3

PRINTED IN THE UNITED STATES OF AMERICA

Book design by Lee Fukui and Mauna Eichner

10 9 8 7 6 5 4 3 2 1

First Mass Market Edition

For my grandparents, Ellen and Tillman Cavert
. . . who have loved well for sixty-seven years

PROLOGUE

I don't have good memories of growing up. Seems like I knew a lot of ugly stuff when I shouldn't. The only two things I remember as beautiful were my mom and this riverbank. And until I knew better I thought they'd named the river after my mom.

The man who lived in our trailer was always angry. Always smoking. Don't know why. He lit one cigarette with the glowplug end of the other. Touched them like sparklers. They matched his eyes. He never hit me, least not very hard, but his mouth hurt my ears. Mom said it was the devil in the bottle, but I don't think you drink meanness. You can try and drown it, but, in my experience, it's a pretty good swimmer. That's why it's in the bottle. To escape it, she and I, we came here. She told me it'd help my asthma. I knew better. Dying was about the only thing that'd help my asthma.

With a brick sitting on my chest, I pulled every breath through the length of a garden hose. That made it sort of difficult to get what I thought or felt out my mouth. Mom was always wanting me to talk about my feelings, trying to pull me out of me. I told her, "Forget feelings. I can feel later. Throw me some air." Between bottle-man, the albuterol and the spastic cough I couldn't shake, there was a disconnect between my mouth and my heart. Something in me had been severed.

I lived in pieces.

Maybe *islands* is a better word. Whenever I crept inside myself and took a look around, I didn't see one whole. Or one main. I saw a continent cut and quartered with each section floating aimlessly on some far corner of the globe. I've seen pictures of ice sheets near the pole that do the same thing.

From the ages of five to eight, I wore a helmet even when I wasn't on my bike and grew up with the nickname "Smurf"— adopted from my occasional lip color. To occupy me during my forced sedentary and mostly sucky childhood, my mother bought me some paints, and in them I found escape—painting the world I wished I lived in.

We had this bench down by the river where we used to sit nights. Mostly when the cigarette haze and verbal dribble drove us out of the trailer. Our butts had worn it smooth. One night, when I was about ten, I'd picked up on the trailer park chatter and I said, "Momma, what's an 'easy' woman?"

She'd heard it, too. "Who you been listening to?"

I pointed. "That big fat woman over there."

She nodded. "Honey, we all lose our way."

"You lost yours?"

She touched the tip of my nose with her finger. "Not when I'm with you." She put her arm around me. "But that's not what really matters. What matters is what you do when you find yourself lost."

She walked me through the woods, sat me on the bench and panned her hand across the view in front of me. "Doss, God is in this river."

It was one of those copper-colored evenings when thunderclouds blocked out the sun. The edges were red and the underside dark blue and bleeding into black. In the distance, we could see the wave of rain coming. I scanned the riverbank, the ripples on the water, remembering all the times I'd felt my tongue thicken and turn numb, right before I blacked out due to oxygen deprivation.

I frowned. "That explains a lot."

She pushed the hair out of my eyes while I stole two quick puffs on the inhaler. "What do you mean?"

I held my breath and thumbed over my shoulder. "Well, He ain't in that trailer."

She nodded once. "He was when I made you."

I had just learned to cuss, so I was testing my boundaries. "Maybe." I hacked and spat. "But he sure as hell ain't now."

She squeezed my cheeks between her fingers and jerked my head toward the water. "Doss Michaels."

"Yes, ma'am."

"Look at the surface of that river."

I nodded.

"What do you see?"

My voice sounded thick and garbled. "Black water."

She squeezed tighter. "Don't get smart with me. Look again."

"A few minnows."

"Closer—at the surface."

I waited while my eyes focused. My teeth were cutting into my cheeks. "The treeline, some clouds . . . the sky."

"What's that called?"

"A reflection."

She let go of my mouth. "I don't care what trash the world throws at you, don't let it muddy your reflection. You hear me?"

I pointed at the trailer. "Well, he does and you don't say nothing."

"True. But I can't fix him. And you're not broken."

"Why do you let him stay?"

She nodded, then said quietly, " 'Cause I can only work so many hours in a day, and"—she held up my inhaler—"he's got benefits." She lifted my chin again. "Band-Aid, are you hearing me?"

"Why you call me that?"

She pressed her forehead to mine. " 'Cause you stick to me and you heal my hurts."

I didn't know squat about life, but I knew one thing for certain: my momma was a good woman. I nodded back up the street. "Can I go tell that big fat woman that she can just suck on a lemon?"

She shook her head. "It wouldn't do any good."

"Why?"

Lightning spiderwebbed the sky. " 'Cause all that fat just represents pain." She brushed the hair out of my eyes. "Last time . . . you hearing me?"

"Yes, ma'am."

A few minutes passed. The air grew damp, charged with electricity and smelling of pungent rain. "What you got—what you can do with a pencil or a brush—that's something special." She pulled me close. "Any dummy with half a brain can see that. I didn't teach you to do what you do. Couldn't have, 'cause I don't know the first thing about it—can't draw myself out of a wet paper bag. What you got comes from some place none of the rest of us know nothing about. That makes you special."

"I don't feel special. Most the time, I feel like I'm dying."

She hiked her skirt up over her knees to dry the sweat off her legs. A rusty razor had cut the rough skin above her heel. She waved her hand across the world. "Life ain't easy. Most the time, it's hard. It seldom makes sense and it ain't never wrapped up in a neat little bow. Seems like the older you get the more it trips you up, breaks you down and bloodies you . . ." She tried to laugh and then fell quiet a minute. "People come to this river for lots of reasons. Some of us are hiding, some of us are escaping, some of us are looking for a little peace and quiet, maybe trying to forget, anything to ease the pain we carry, but . . . we all come thirsty." She pushed the hair out of my eyes. "You're a lot like this river. In your fingertips, you got what people need. So don't hold it back. Don't dam it up. And don't muddy it." She flipped my hand over and spread her palm against mine. "Let it flow out, and one day you'll find that people from all over will dive in and drink deeply."

She laid a sketchbook across my lap, handed me a pencil, then aimed my eyes downriver. "You see that?"

"Yes, ma'am."

"Now close your eyes." I did. "Take as deep a breath as you can." I coughed, sucked it in and held it. "See that picture on the back of your eyelids?" I nodded. "Now . . ." She placed the pencil in my fingers just as the first raindrop fell. "Find the one thing that makes you want to look again . . . and let it out."

So I did.

That evening, she studied my sketch. Her nose was running. Eyes too. "Promise me one more thing."

"Yes, ma'am?"

She stared out my bedroom window, where the river floated beneath a cloud of steam. She tapped my temple and laid her hand across my chest. "What you got inside you is . . . is a well that bubbles up from way down deep. It's sweet water, too. But"—a tear dripped off her face—"sometimes wells run empty. If you ever get to hurting and all you feel is ache—you reach down and find your well empty, nothing but dust—then you come back here . . . dive in and drink deeply."

And I did.

1

I climbed the final step into my studio, sniffed the dank fire-place and wondered how long it would take an errant flame to consume everything in here. Minutes I should think. Arms folded, I leaned against the wall and stared at all the eyes staring back at me. Abbie had tried so hard to make me believe. Even taken me halfway around the world. Introduced me to Rem-brandt, poked me in the shoulder and said, "You can do that." So I had painted. Faces mostly. My mother had planted the seed that, years later, Abbie watered, nurtured and pruned. In truth, given a good flame and a tardy fire department, I stood to make more money on an insurance payout. Stacked around me in layered rows against the four walls lay more than three hundred dusty works—a decade's worth—all oil on canvas. Faces cap-tured in moments speaking emotions known by hearts but spoken by few mouths. At one time, it had come so easily. So fluidly. I remember moments when I couldn't wait to get in here, when I couldn't hold it back, when I would paint on four canvases at once. Those all-nighters when I discovered Vesu-vius in me.

The last decade of my life was staring back at me. Once hung with promise in studios across Charleston, paintings had slowly, one at a time, returned. Self-proclaimed art critics pontificating in local papers complained that my work "lacked originality," "was absent of heart" and my favorite, "was boring and devoid of artistic skill or understanding."

There's a reason the critics are called critics.

On the easel before me stretched a white canvas. Dusty, sun-faded and cracked. It was empty.

Like me.

I stepped through the window, along the side of the roof, and climbed the iron stairs to the crow's nest. I smelled the salt and looked out over the water. Somewhere a seagull squawked at me. The air was thick, dense and blanketed the city in quiet. The sky was clear, but it smelled like rain. The moon hung high and full, casting shadows on the water that lapped the concrete bulkhead a hundred feet away. The lights of Fort Sumter sat glistening in the distance to the southeast. Before me, the Ashley and Cooper rivers ran into one. Most Charlestonians will tell you it is there that the two form the Atlantic Ocean. Sullivan's Island sat just north, along with the beach where we used to swim. I closed my eyes and listened for the echo of our laughter.

That'd been a while.

The "Holy City," with its competing steeples piercing the night sky, lay still behind me. Below me stretched my shadow. Cast upon the roof, it tugged at my pants leg, begging me backward and pulling me down. The ironwork that held me had been fashioned some fifty years ago by local legend Philip Simmons. Now in his nineties, his work had become the Charleston rave and was very much in demand. The crow's nest, having ridden out the storm, had come with the house. In the thirteen years we'd lived here, this nine square feet of perch had become the midnight platform from which I viewed the world. My singular and solitary escape.

My cell phone vibrated in my pocket. I checked the screen and saw the Texas area code. "Hello?"

"Doss Michaels?"

"Speaking."

"This is Anita Becker, assistant to Dr. Paul Virth."

"Yes?" My breathing was short. So much hung on her next few words.

She paused. "We wanted to call and . . ."—I knew it before she said it—". . . say that the oversight committee has met and decided on the parameters of the study. At this time, we're only accepting primary cases. Not secondary." The wind shifted and swiveled the squeaking vane. The rooster now pointed south. "Next year, if this study proceeds as we hope, we're planning on adding a study on secondary . . ." Either she faded off, or maybe I did. "We're sending a letter recommending Abbie for a study with Doctors Plist and Mackles out of Sloan-Kettering . . ."

"Thank you . . . very much." I closed the phone.

The problem with a Hail Mary pass is that it hangs in the air so long, and most are dropped in the end zone. That's why they invoke God.

Because it's impossible to begin with.

The phone rang a second time, but I let it ring. A minute passed and it rang again. I checked the faceplate. It read, "Dr. Ruddy."

"Hey, Ruddy."

"Doss." His voice was quiet. Subdued. I could see him, leaning over his desk, head resting in his hands. His chair squeaked. "The scan results are in. If you two could get around the speakerphone, thought maybe we'd talk through them."

His tone of voice told me enough. "Ruddy, she's sleeping.

Finally. Did that most of yesterday. Maybe you could just give them to me." He read between the lines.

"I'm with you." A pause. "Umm . . . they're uhh . . ." He choked. Ruddy had been our lead doctor since the beginning. "Doss, I'm sorry."

We listened to each other listening to each other. "How long?"

"A week. Maybe two. Longer if you can keep her horizontal . . . and still."

I forced a laugh. "You know better than that."

A deep breath. "Yep."

I slid the phone back in my pocket and scratched my two-day stubble. My eyes stared out over the water, but my mind was a couple hundred miles away.

Empty-handed and lungs half full, I climbed down and back through the window. Running my fingers along the trim tacked to the wall, I crept down another flight. The staircase was narrow, made of twelve-inch-wide pine planks, which at nearly two hundred years old, creaked loudly—tapping out a story of age and the drunken pirates who once stumbled down them.

The sound lifted her eyelids, but I doubted she'd been asleep. Fighters don't sleep between rounds. A cross breeze slipped through the open windows and filtered across our room, raising goose bumps across her calves.

Footsteps sounded downstairs, so I crossed the room, closed the bedroom door and returned. I sat next to her, slid the fleece blanket over her legs and leaned back against the headboard. She whispered, "How long have I been asleep?"

I shrugged.

"Yesterday?"

"Almost." While we could manage the pain with medication, we couldn't deter its debilitating effects. She would lie still, motionless for hours, fighting an inner battle in which I played helpless spectator. Then for reasons neither of us could explain, she'd experience moments—sometimes even days—of total lucidity, when the pain would relent and she was as normal as ever. Then with little warning, it would return and she'd begin her own private battle once again. It is there that you learn the difference between tired and fatigued. Sleep cures tired, but it has no effect on fatigued.

She smelled the air, catching the last remnants of aftershave that still hung in the air. I lifted the window. She raised an eyebrow. "He was here?"

I stared out over the water. "Yup."

"How'd that go?"

"About like normal."

"That good, huh? What is it this time?"

"He's"—I lifted both hands in the air making quotation marks with my fingers—" 'moving you.' "

She sat up. "Where?"

More quotation marks. " 'Home.' "

She shook her head and let out a deep breath that puffed up her cheeks like a blowfish. "For him, it's my mother all over again."

I shrugged.

"How'd you leave it?"

"I didn't. He did."

"And?"

"He's sending over a team of people in the morning to . . . 'collect you.' "

"He sounds like he's taking out the trash." She pointed at the phone. "Give it to me. I don't care if he is four heartbeats from the President."

"Honey, I'm not letting him take you anywhere." I flicked a piece of paint off the windowsill.

She listened to the sound of footsteps downstairs. "Shift change?"

I nodded, watching a barge slowly putter up the Ashley.

"Don't tell me he talked to them, too."

"Oh, yeah. Really put everybody at ease. Basically read them the riot act disguised as an 'attaboy.' I just love the way he gives you what he wants you to have under the pretense of your best interest." I shook my head. "Sleight-of-hand manipulation."

She wrapped her leg around mine, using it as leverage to push her head up, allowing her eyes to meet mine. The once fit thighs now gave way to bony knees, thin veins and sticklike shins. Her left hipbone, the once voluptuous peak of the hourglass, pointed up through her gown, which hung loosely over the skin. After four years, her skin was nearly translucent—a faded sun-drenched canvas. Now it hung across her collarbone like a clothesline.

The shuffling downstairs faded into the kitchen. She stared at the floor. "They're good people. They do this every day. We've only got to do it once."

"Yeah . . . and once is enough."

Our bed was one of those old, four-poster, Southern things that Southern women go gaga over. Dark mahogany, it stood about four feet off the ground, was bookended by steps on either side and Lord help you if you rolled off it at night. There were two advantages: Abbie slept there, and when I laid on my side, my line of sight was above the windowsill, giving me a view of Charleston Harbor.

She stared out the window where all the world rolled out as a map, the green and red channel lights blinking back. Red right return. She slid her fingers into mine. "How's she look up there?"

I loosened the scarf and let it fall down across her shoulders. "Beautiful."

She rolled toward me, placed her head on my chest and ran her fingers inside my button-down where both my chest hairs grew. She shook her head. "You need to get your head examined."

"Funny. Your father just told me the same thing." I stared back out across the water, blindly running my finger along the outline of her ear and neck. A shrimp boat was working its way out to sea. "Actually, he's been telling you that for almost fourteen years."

"You'd think by now, I'd listen." The boom lights of the shrimp boat rolled slowly east to west, seeming to skim the ocean's surface as it reached the larger swells.

Her eyes lay sunken, the lids dark and dim, as if eye shadow had been tattooed in. "Promise me one thing," she said.

"I already did that."

"I'm being serious."

"Okay, but not if it involves your dad." She pressed thumb to index finger, snatched down and plucked out one of my chest hairs. "Hey"—I rubbed my chest—"it's not like I've got a surplus of those things."

Her fingers, like her legs, were long. Now that they were skinnier, they seemed even longer. She pointed in my face. "You finished?" She fingered a circle around the opening in my shirt. " 'Cause I see one more."

That's my Abbie. Thirty pounds lighter and still making jokes. And that right there is what I held to. That thing. That finger in the face—the one that threatened strength, promised humor and said "I love you more than me."

She scratched my chest and nodded at the picture of her father. "You think you two will ever talk?" I studied the picture. We had taken it last Easter as he christened his new darling, *Reel Estate*. He stood, broken bottle held by the neck, champagne dripping off the bow, white hair ruffled by the sea breeze. Under other circumstances, I would have liked him, and sometimes I think he would have liked me.

I glanced at his picture on her dresser. "Oh, I'm sure he'll talk."

"You two are more alike than you think."

"Please . . ."

"I'm serious."

She was right. "He still rubs me the wrong way."

"Well, me too, but he's still Daddy."

We laid in the darkness listening to the footsteps of well-intentioned and unwelcome strangers shuffling below us. "You'd think," I said, staring at the sound coming up through the floor, "they'd come up with a better name than 'hospice.' "

She rolled her eyes. "How's that?"

"It just sounds so . . ." I trailed off.

We sat awhile longer. "Did Ruddy call?"

I nodded.

"All three?"

I nodded again.

"No better?"

I shook my head.

"What about the guy at Harvard?"

"We talked yesterday. They're still a few months out from starting that trial."

"Sloan-Kettering?"

I shook my head.

"What about the website?" Two years ago, we'd created a

website for people with Abbie's condition. It had become a clearinghouse of information. We gleaned a lot from it. Got to know a lot of people who led us to a lot of really knowledge-able people. A great resource.

"No."

"Well, that just sucks."

"You took the words right out of my mouth."

Silence again, while she studied a fingernail absent of polish. Finally she looked at me. "Oregon?"

The Oregon Health & Science University, or OHSU, was on the cutting edge of developing some new systemic therapy that targeted cancer at the cellular level. Real front-lines stuff. We'd been in contact with them for several months, hoping for some sort of clinical trial in which we could participate. Yesterday, they had established the parameters for the trial. Because her disease had moved out of her organ of origination, Abbie didn't qualify. I shook my head.

"Can they make an exception?"

I shook my head a second time.

"Did you ask?"

It had taken so much. And yet, all I could do was sit back and watch. While I held her hand, fed her soup, bathed her or combed her hair, *it* had no quit. No matter what you threw at it.

I wanted to take it back. Wanted to kill it. Slice it into a thousand painful pieces, then stamp it into the earth, grind it into nothing and eradicate its scent from the planet. But it didn't get here because it was stupid. It never shows its face and it's hard to kill something you can't see.

"Yes."

"And M. D. Anderson in Houston?" I didn't answer. She asked again.

I managed a whisper. "They called and . . . they're still two, maybe three, weeks from a decision. The uhh"—I snapped my fingers—"oversight committee couldn't meet for some reason. Some of the doctors were on vacation . . ." Looking away, I shook my head.

She rolled her eyes. "Another holding pattern."

I nodded. A single piece of yellow legal paper lay folded in thirds on the bedside table. Abbie's handwriting shone through, covering the entire page. Beneath it sat a blank envelope. A silver Parker ballpoint pen rested at ten o'clock and served as a paperweight.

Eyes lost out over the harbor, she was quiet a long time. She said, "When was the last time you slept?" I shrugged. She pulled on me and I leaned back where she placed her head on my chest. When I opened my eyes again, it was 3 a.m.

Her whisper broke the silence. "Doss?" Her gown had fallen off one shoulder. Another reminder of what had been stolen. "I've been thinking." A horse-drawn carriage rolled down the cobblestone beneath the window.

I'm not a vengeful person. I don't anger easily and most will tell you I've got a rather long fuse. Patience is something I have a good bit of. If you have asthma, you understand. Maybe that's why so many people ask me to take them fishing.

She stared at the framed newspaper article, hanging on the wall, yellowed from the sun.

~✱

It was six months ago. The Charleston paper was writing some feel-good stories about local celebrities and their New Year's resolutions. Thought it might jump-start the rest of us. They called and asked Abbie if they could interview her.

The reporter came to the house and we sat out on the porch watching the tide roll out. Pen in hand, he expected her to rattle off the fantastic. Her responses surprised him. He sat back, studied his writing and turned up his list. "But . . . ?"

She sat up and leaned toward him, backing him off. "Did you ever see the beginning of the *Jetsons* cartoon?"

He looked surprised. "Yeah, sure."

"Remember when George and Astro hop on the tread-mill?" He nodded. "That's been us for four years." She tapped his legal pad. "This list is my best shot at cutting the leash."

He shrugged. "But there's nothing . . ."

"Extraordinary?" She finished his sentence. "I know. In fact, it's entirely normal. Which is the point. 'Normal' is a memory." She looked at me. "The last few years have purged us of extraordinary." She slid on her sunglasses. "You spend enough time flailing just to keep your head above water and you'll discover what you truly care about. This list is my way of fighting back. That's all. It doesn't include climbing Mount Everest, running with the bulls in Pamplona or circling the world in a balloon."

She sat back and palmed the tears running off her face. "I need"—she grabbed my hand—"to sit on a breeze-swept beach, sip from little drinks decorated with umbrellas and worry about color combinations for somebody's kitchen."

She thought for a second. "Although, I would like to do a loopty-loop in an old plane."

He looked confused. "What's that?"

She waved a large circle in the air with her hand. "You know . . . a loopty-loop."

"Can I add that to the list?"

I spoke up. "Yes."

Rather than calling it Resolutions, she called it her Top Ten

Wishes for the year. Something about it struck a chord with readers. Maybe it was the simplicity, the gut-level honesty. I'm not really sure. For the last five months, she'd been getting letters and a lot of traffic on the website. Wanting to remind her that she had once hoped and wished, I'd framed the article and hung it next to the bed. Only problem was that with all that we'd been through the first part of this year, we hadn't really checked off any. She pointed at it. "Hand me that."

She dusted off the glass with her gown, her reflection staring back at her, then loosened the tabs on the back, pulled off the cardboard and slid the article from beneath the glass. Half laughing and mostly smiling, she reread the article then shook her head. "Still wishing."

"Me, too."

She lay back. "I want to give you your anniversary present."

"Five months early?"

"I'm surprised you remembered the date."

"I don't want anything."

"You'll want this."

"I don't need anything."

"That's what you think."

"Honey . . ."

"Doss Michaels." She pulled me to her. "I'm not doing this here. Not like this." She fingered my hair off my brow. Her game face had returned. "I won't do it."

You see that? That right there? In the nearly fifteen years I've known her, Abbie has possessed and exhibited a trait that I've never been able to put my finger on. A prisoner on the tip of my tongue, no articulation gives it justice. Every utterance falls flat. But while the name escapes me, its power does not.

I protested, "But . . ."

"Not here."

There was no use arguing with her when she got this way. Sick or not. And although she'd argue the point, she got that from her dad. The only response was "yes, ma'am." Strange how two words can change you forever. I laid the article across the bedspread in front of her. "Pick one."

She pointed without looking. "All the way from Moniac."

Number ten. Of the list, it was the most impossible. I raised both eyebrows. "You realize that we're two days from the first of June?" She nodded. "And that officially marks the beginning of hurricane season?" She nodded again. "And the Jurassic-sized mosquitoes are just now hatching?" She closed her eyes and nodded a final time with a sly smile.

I pointed to her parents' house a few blocks down the street. "What about him?"

She tapped the single yellow legal page resting on the bed-side table.

"And when he gets it, he'll call out the National Guard."

"Maybe not." She sat up, more focused now. "You could talk to Gary. He can prescribe something. Something to—" She pressed her fingers to my lips. "Hey." She wanted my eyes. The edges were blurring and I knew that added to the weight she already lived under. I turned. "Have you ever broken a promise to me?"

"Not that I know of."

She folded the article and stuffed it in my shirt pocket. "Then don't start now."

Neither option was very good. "Abbie, the river is no place to—"

"It's where we started."

"I know that."

"Then take me back."

"Honey, there's nothing but a bunch of hurt down there. It won't be the same."

"You let me be the judge of that." She gazed south out the window.

I tried one last time. "You know what Gary said."

She nodded. "Doss, I know what I'm asking." She tapped me in the chest. "They say we have reached the end." She shook her head and pressed her lips to my face. "So let's start over."

And so we did.

2

Rain pelted the windshield in sheets. Every few seconds, golf ball–sized hail smacked the hood and rooftop, thundering like firecrackers. I leaned forward and rubbed the backside of the glass with my palm, but that did about as much good as the wipers. Ninety miles ago, a semitrailer dragging a broken hydraulic line passed us in the left lane and sprayed the front of the Jeep with brake fluid and sparks. The oil-and-water smear, mixed with headlights and early-morning darkness, gave the world a Coca-Cola tint. The region was suffering a drought. The aquifer was down and people from South Georgia to North Florida were subject to watering restrictions. Few areas felt the effects more than the river. She was eight to ten feet below normal, and while this deluge was needed, most of it would never reach the river.

In the 1950's, before the federal interstate highways cut the U.S. in six-lane precision, wonder, efficiency and freedom, their smaller and less efficient two-lane twin brothers politely meandered through and around small-town America—careful not to upset the balance of pecan trees, live oaks and fourth-generation chicken farms. Dotted with concrete-block, mom-and-pop motels, full-serve gas stations and all-u-can-eat buffets, U.S. 1—something like an east coast Route 66—was the life-

21

line of every traveling salesman and vacationing family from Maine to Miami. Between the free orange juice stands, junk stores, alligator farms and state-line souvenir stores brimming with stale Claxton fruit cakes and Mountain Dew, the route represented Americana in its heyday.

Trying to stay awake, I clicked on the radio. A weatherman was in mid-report and hard rain smacked his microphone. He was yelling above the sound of the wind: "Four weeks ago, a tropical depression moved across the southern portion of West Africa. For the next seven days, the tropical storm system continued across the coast of Africa and the tropical Atlantic. After moving through the Caribbean Sea, satellite pictures on May twentieth showed an organizing cloud pattern over the south-central Caribbean Sea. And on May twenty-third, Tropical Storm Annie—so named as the first storm of the year—strengthened and moved northward. And at six a.m. this morning, Annie spun herself into a hurricane." I turned it off and stared through the windshield. River guides, by default, become closet weathermen. We have to. It's just the nature of the job. I wiped the backside of the windshield again. Towering pines now lined both sides of the road. I crossed her off. The rain we were experiencing had nothing to do with Annie, and given her location, she'd fizzle long before Florida.

Stretching southward from Waycross, Georgia, to the Florida border, sits a seven-hundred-square-mile peat-filled bog that hovers like a poached egg inside a saucer-shaped depression that was, more than likely, once part of the ocean floor. When plants die, they fall to the swamp floor where they decompose—a process which emits both methane and carbon dioxide—producing peat. And because decomposition is a slow process, it takes fifty years to add another inch of peat to the base of the swamp. The thick web traps the gas, building pressure and forcing the islands upward—like corks floating to the surface. As they rise, the gas is released where it glows like Northern Lights in its rise to the surface. In the mid-1900's, visitors claimed the existence of UFOs, established tours and sought to sell tickets until scientists showed up and proved otherwise. Since their formation, the peat masses have been unstable and trembling—sort of like the earth's plates but a bit more fluid—causing the Choctaw Indians to so name the place "The Land of Trembling Earth."

In English, it sounds like "Okee-fen-o-kee."

On the surface, it's primeval and untouched. Uninhabitable to most men. For all practical purposes, it serves as the drain for the southeastern part of Georgia and northeastern section of Florida.

Drain is the key word here. Like all drains, there's a limit to what they can get rid of in a given period of time.

When the swamp fills up, the overflow spills out in two places. It's a lot like New Orleans but with only two holes in the dike and with a lot less murder, gambling and prostitution. The larger pipe, called the Suwannee River, winds its way about two hundred miles southwest across Florida and dumps into the Gulf of Mexico. Her 130-mile little sister, the St. Marys, first snakes south to Baldwin, hovers across the top of Macclenny, turns due north toward Folkston, then makes a hard right eastward, where she finally spills her crooked self into the Cumberland Sound and the Atlantic Ocean.

Given its tea coloring, the St. Marys is called a blackwater river. Two hundred years ago, sailors used to venture into the Cumberland Sound and run upriver some fifty miles to Trader's Hill, filling their casks to overflowing because the tannic acid kept the water potable for long periods—like transatlantic voyages.

In times of drought, the St. Marys River can be a few inches deep and a few feet across. At its headwaters in Moniac, it can be little more than a trickle. But prolonged rains—the lifeblood of the swamp—can swell the river's banks, closer to the ocean, to more than a mile wide with "holes" thirty or forty feet deep. Normal flow rate might be a half a mile an hour, while flood flow might be as much as six or eight. Maybe even ten.

Flooding here is a sneaky thing. When it floods, it does so from the ground up. Because the rain comes in from other places, the water rises beneath your feet without warning. One minute you're asleep, moon bright, not a cloud in the sky with the bank sitting thirty feet from your tent. Six hours later, you wake to find your sleeping bag soaked and your tent three inches under water. Floods here don't fall down around you. They rise up beneath you. Out of nowhere.

Folks who live on the river usually ask two questions before building a home: where is the hundred-year flood plain and how do I build above it? Given that no insurance company in its right mind will write flood insurance for the St. Marys Basin, most homes are built on stilts.

Even the churches.

Despite this, the banks are dotted with homes, fish camps, swimming holes, marinas, rope swings, zip lines, whiskey stills, mud bogs and even one well-hidden nudist colony. Activity bustles along the banks like ants beneath the surface of their hill. From headwaters to sound, she is one of the last virgin landscapes in the South.

THE RAIN HAD SLOWED ME to a crawl so I pulled off beneath an overpass and pushed the stick into neutral. Abbie lay in the back, half asleep. Every few minutes she'd mumble something in her sleep that I couldn't understand.

The treatments are the worst. They whittle away at your core, strip you of everything and leave you with fleeting memories. She'd tried so hard for so long to hold on, but like water, it had slipped through her fingers.

I crawled into the back of the Jeep and lay down next to Abbie. She curled inward toward me. I pulled the plastic bag holding the yellowed and wrinkled newspaper article from my shirt pocket. I'd learned a few years ago to use whatever I could to stoke her hopes—keep her thinking out beyond the present moment. Because if she concentrated on the here and now, she'd spiral down fast. It was how I'd learned to get her from there to here.

Her eyes cracked long enough to recognize it. She smiled and nodded—meaning she'd play along. "I'd like to . . ." The whisper was hoarse and distant. It was the drugs. Her pain threshold was rather high. She'd had a lot of practice. Her face told me she was fending it off as best she could.

Abbie had always suffered with migraines. She internalized most everything, and in her case the tension had to go somewhere. Maybe her dad had something to do with it. They came on quickly and left slowly. By the time we met, she'd tried a dozen different medicines, yoga, acupuncture and deep-tissue massage, but all with little to no relief.

When we were alone, she'd place my index finger just above her ear. That was Abbie-speak for "Trace me." From her temple, my fingertips followed the lines of her ears and neck, her collarbone, the rise and fall of her breast, her arms, wrist, fingertips, the mound of her hips, the descent of her thigh, the little knot on her knee, the curve of her calf and the arch of her foot. Often, she'd fall asleep and when she woke the migraine was gone.

I traced her. "Number one?"

She swallowed. "Ride an antique carousel."

I prodded, "Number two."

She read the list off the backs of her eyelids: "Do a loopty-loop in an old plane."

The items were printed in no particular order. When one didn't make sense to him, he'd inquire and she'd explain. To keep the simplicity of her list, he printed it the way she said it, but the clarification became a parenthetical note in his article. "I just love the way you say 'loopty-loop.' Say it again. One more time."

She licked her lips. Her tongue was cottony white. The first *l* stuck to the top of her mouth. "Loopty-loop."

"Keep going."

"Sip wine on the beach."

"We're not even halfway." She placed her head on my chest and breathed deeply. "Number four."

She paused. "I've forgotten."

It was good to know she'd not lost her sense of humor. "I highly doubt it." She almost laughed. I shook the ziplock bag holding the article. "Still waiting."

She raised an eyebrow. "Go skinny-dipping."

"And number five?"

The vein on her right temple had appeared blue and bulging. Meaning her head was throbbing. She pressed her palm to her forehead and held it there.

I asked, "Scale of one to ten?"

"Yes."

That meant nine point eight. I flipped open both the latches on the Pelican case and dug through the contents. River guides call them "otter boxes." They're watertight, they float and are crash proof. Chances are good you could load it with your mother's china dinnerware, fling it off Niagara Falls and when you found it at the bottom, you could eat dinner off the plates. I found what I needed, popped the safety tip on the syringe, squeezed out the air and injected the dexamethasone into her arm. She didn't even flinch. After four years, I was better than a lot of nurses at giving Abbie her shots.

Minutes passed. Slowly, she spoke, "Swim with dolphins."

"Keep going. You're on a roll."

"Wet a line."

"Number seven."

"Pose." She chuckled.

"Number eight."

She spoke without reading. "Dance with my husband."

"Two to go."

"Laugh so hard it hurts."

"And? Last but not least." I mimed a drum roll with my fingers and made a trill sound with my tongue.

"Ride the river . . . all the way from Moniac."

She pushed my hat back. It was felt. Called a Banjo Paterson hat. Made in Australia by Akubra. A 4½" crown, 2¾" brim. I bought it about eight years ago because I thought it made me look like Indiana Jones. Now it was faded, the brim rose and fell like a roller-coaster track and my thumbs had worn a hole where I pinched the crown. As much as I wanted to look dashing and heroic, my reflection looked more like Jed Clampett.

"You're not gonna actually wear that silly-looking hat, are you?"

I nodded. "My head spent five years just breaking it in."

She laughed, "It's broken alright."

The problem with a wish list was what it told you about the person who wrote it. If it's honest, it's a rock-bottom, bare-bones, clear shot all the way to someone's soul.

Hats can do the same thing.

3

Most said it was a match made in heaven. Those who didn't were just jealous.

William Barclay Coleman had been born with "presence." Tall, handsome, well-spoken, he commanded attention and even those envious of him treated him like E. F. Hutton. His gentleman's pedigree was flawless. The Citadel, Harvard Law, European summers abroad. A young political up-and-comer, he grew up with a speaker's gavel in his hand and was the youngest candidate ever elected to the South Carolina legislature. But that was just the beginning.

Ellen Victoria Shaw was the poster child for Emily Post and Gloria Vanderbilt. A fifth-generation Charlestonian, she attended Ashley Hall and then, as a freshman at Randolph-Macon women's college, no less than eight suitors asked her to accompany them to Fancy Dress—Washington and Lee's annual formal. By her junior year, most every Kappa Alpha in a hundred-mile radius invited her to the Confederate-themed Old South Ball where the whispers and jealous mutters of the Hollins, Sweet Briar and Mary Baldwin girls voted her the unofficial belle of the ball.

She graduated—a double in French and Art History—returned home and then a chance meeting at the Hibernia Society ball.

He was twenty-five. She, barely twenty-two. They courted, appropriately, for nine months and then married in a wedding that shook most of Charleston with jealousy and unending speculation and gossip. For a wedding gift, he gave her a convertible Mercedes 450 SL Coupe.

After an Austrian alpine honeymoon topped off with a Tanzanian safari and a trek up the lower slopes of Kilimanjaro, they returned to his family home on the Battery in Charleston where he strategized for a run at the governor's mansion. Eighteen months later, she bore him a daughter, Abigail Grace Eliot Coleman—the sixth generation. During the inauguration ceremony the following January, Abigail Grace smiled through her bonnet at every camera flash and drank up the attention like chocolate. Even then she had a knack.

But life took a turn.

Abigail turned two, and Ellen fell ill. Bruises that wouldn't go away. Tests confirmed ovarian cancer run rampant. It didn't take long. The widowed father placed Abigail Grace in Miss Olivia's arms, put the car in cold storage, hid his mourning and focused his aim. He gave himself to "the people," and after two terms as governor, he ran for Senate—where's he's been ever since.

When Abigail was ten, the then junior senator remarried. Like her predecessor, Katherine Hampton was everything Charleston. She could trace her lineage to one of the founders of Charleston and signers of the Declaration. In his search, he had done the unimaginable—he had found a woman who could dance on glass. She was strong enough to step out of Ellen's shadow while not dishonoring her memory.

ABBIE GREW UP A DEBUTANTE, a graduate of Ashley Hall, the only daughter of the senator from South Carolina and the poster girl for the social elite. She had more class in five minutes than I had all day. Or all week. While I tripped over a crack in the sidewalk, stepped in dog crap or spilled mustard across my white button-down, she dabbed the corner of her mouth with a lacy napkin, made friends with stray dogs and levitated down sidewalks like Mary Poppins. We were as different as two people could be, and why she chose me is still a mystery. If you could see me, I'm scratching my head.

Christmas break my freshman year at the College of Charleston. I was working the late shift at the Charleston Place Hotel bar, located just off the Gone With the Wind double staircase that led upstairs. It was near midnight, I was bussing a table and four girls walked in. Everything about them said "Charleston." Their walk, their clothes, the way they held their mouths. It's not a snobbish thing, it's upbringing. Sure, it could get snobbish, but in that moment, it was a seamless fusion of culture and class.

They ordered cappuccinos, lattes and a sampler plate of finger desserts. I screwed up the espresso, burned the milk with the steamer and squirted runny whipped cream across the top of their cups only to have the canister erupt and splatter my apron—which at the end of the day is a pretty good description of me.

They whispered and laughed 'til nearly 1 a.m. It used to be that when I saw a group of girls like that, my mind would sort of lump them all together. I'd see the group while no one person really stood out.

Except her.

She was one part Julie Andrews and two parts Grace Kelly.

She was unlike anyone I'd ever seen, and trust me, I've spent some time studying pretty faces. With her, it wasn't the high cheeks, the lips, chin or nose. It was her eyes—and something behind them.

At Charleston Place, we catered to a lot of famous people. From Arab sheikhs to Hollywood A-listers, the only thing uncommon is the absence of commonality. I knew she was famous, I knew I'd seen her face before, but I'd been on my feet for fourteen hours and things were a little fuzzy.

Finally, the most giggly girl in the group waved me to the table. I tried to act all waiterly, refilled their water glasses and stood back, towel hanging across my forearm. Her friend, Elizabeth I would later learn, raised both eyebrows and said, "You keep looking, and I'm gonna charge admission."

Busted.

I stammered, "Do I . . . do we . . . have we met?"

"I don't think so," she said quietly, "but sometimes I'm mistaken for someone else."

I should've quit before I shoved my foot down my throat. I nodded, tried not to smirk, couldn't and walked back to the bar where I wiped it down—again. They left cash on the table and walked out into the lobby of the hotel.

I thought to myself, I know her from somewhere.

When the four of them walked past the Scarlett stairwell, she ran up the stairs—her long legs covering two at a time—and then straddled the railing like a horse and flew down on her butt. It was as out of place as McDonald's in Japan, yet as I watched her, I witnessed a rarity—a woman who had taken what she wanted of Charleston, and not let it take her.

They disappeared out the front door under the amused chuckle of the doorman. His white-gloved hand tipping his hat, he said, "'Night, Miss Coleman."

She patted him on the shoulder. "'Night, Mr. George."

I leaned on the bar and poured myself some club soda. Ten seconds later, George sauntered into the bar, palmed off a table and said without looking at me, "Don't even think about it."

I pointed. "Who was . . ."

He shook his head and turned his back on me. "You're not even in the same universe."

He was right. But that's just the thing about those stars that light up the universe. They reach you wherever you are.

4

JUNE 1, 4 A.M.

The rain let up so I stuffed the article back into my pocket, climbed back into the driver's seat and eased off the clutch. At 4 a.m. we pulled into the parking lot of the St. Marys Sportsman—a combination pawnshop and river supply store for every paddler, fisher, skier and hunter in a sixty-square-mile area. Gus wouldn't open for a couple of hours but chances were good that my key still fit the gate and warehouse, so we pulled around back and I left the car running. Gus, the owner and my former boss, had told me to make myself at home whenever I came back to town, so that's what I intended to do.

One of the great things about small South Georgia–Norman Rockwell towns was how little things actually changed from decade to decade. Gus had never been too big on alarms or changing locks because the crime rate in St. George was usually limited to cow-tipping kids or truckers attempting to avoid agricultural inspection stations, so I slid my key into the lock and turned it, unlocking the gate.

I grew up in a trailer park not far from here. From midway through the eighth grade to the year I left for college, I worked and guided for Gus. Conservative estimates would suggest that I logged more than three thousand kayak or canoe miles on the

St. Marys—more than anyone I ever knew or heard of. Including Gus.

I decided I'd try the honest approach. I knocked on the door of Gus's trailer. A few seconds later the light clicked on and Gus cracked the door. One eye was shut, the other barely open. "Hey, Doss."

"Hey."

"Gimme a second."

Gus was maybe fifty now. Sun-battered and river-weary but he was fitter than most college kids. He stepped out looking more weathered and pruney, yet his smile was unchanged. Gus knew me, my story and had been the first to sign his name to the documents that got me through high school. I extended my hand, said, "Gus, I need to do some shopping."

He glanced at the car. "You want to talk about it?"

I shook my head. "Not really."

"You sure?"

"Yeah."

"Whatever you need. Make yourself at home."

I backed up to the door—the engine running—while Gus unlocked the bolt and rolled open the door above me. I pulled down two eighteen-foot Mad River canoes—one tan and one mango-colored—off the rental racks, three paddles and a couple of life vests and we tied them to the roof racks atop the Jeep. Gus noticed Abbie asleep inside but said nothing. I walked through the warehouse cramming a duffel bag with whatever I thought I needed.

Inside the store, I threw some food and canned goods into a cooler, along with a stove and some small green propane tanks, two large blue tarps, a tent, a spinning reel along with a few Beetle Spins, and whatever else I could carry. Opening the glass of the display case, I lifted a small waterproof handheld Garmin GPS unit. The GPS used satellites to locate position. I didn't grab it to tell me where I was, although it would do that within about three feet. I knew the river well enough. But I needed it to tell me how far we'd traveled and distance to future points. It would help me plan breaks, overnights and help me anticipate shelter. The problem with the river, even for someone like me, is that it is constantly changing. And in changing, it can look different with little notice. Also, with the tidal influence we'd encounter at Trader's Hill, it would be nearly impossible to judge how fast we were traveling and, as a result, how far we'd traveled. Two miles an hour makes a world of difference. Lastly, the more tired I became, and I was sure I would, the less I'd be able to judge speed or distance. The GPS would guard against that.

Gus picked up on my shopping and began laying a few things on the countertop that he thought I might need. He scratched his chin. "You going to the sound?"

I nodded.

"You going alone?"

I looked at the car and shrugged.

About that time, somebody knocked on the front door. Gus frowned, and spoke to himself. "It's the middle of the night." He stared through the door and saw two men standing in the shadows. He hollered through the glass, "We're closed."

The first man spoke up. "Don't look like it."

Gus smiled. "Why don't you come back tomorrow morning? We're doing inventory."

The second man pressed his face to the glass. "We're going gigging and just needed a few things. Wondered if you could help us out."

Gus glanced at the computer screen where the radar showed

Annie swirling herself into a spinning red mess. He looked at me. "If they knew what they were doing, it'd be a good time to go gigging, with the change in the barometer and all, but I got a feeling these guys don't know the first thing about gigging." He shrugged and waved. "Sorry, fellows. I just work here. Good luck to you."

Gus turned and walked into his office. One fellow gave him the finger while the other limped to their Tahoe. When he opened the door and stepped into the driver's seat, it looked like two other guys sat in the backseat. We were entering hurricane season and it would not be uncommon for four down-on-their-luck losers to see opportunity in the aftermath of a hurricane.

They disappeared out the drive while Gus reappeared from his office. He laid two items on the counter. Gus had never been an alarmist, but he'd lived in these woods a long time. This was not his first rodeo. He was a realist, and as a result, I suppose I was, too. "You're liable to bump into more than just snakes out there." The first was a Smith & Wesson model 22-4. A revolver with fixed sights, chambered in .45 ACP. The second was a Remington 870 twelve gauge with an eighteen-inch barrel. Which needed no explanation. I grabbed both along with a few boxes of shells.

"Thanks." On the wall of his office hung an oil on canvas piece that I'd made nearly a decade ago. It was a Christmas gift—a way of saying thanks. I'd painted it from the perspective of someone just poking their head up through the water, looking up. Gus was sitting in a kayak, smiling, paddle in hand, midstroke. He was at home there. I suppose we both were. The picture depicted movement and the creases in his cheeks suggested a deep-down easiness that came with a paddle. I had named it *The Paddler's High*.

He nodded at the picture of himself. "People ask me about that all the time. Want to know if I'll sell it."

"What do you tell them?"

"Not yet."

"What're they offering you?"

"Let's just say I could pay cash for one of those new Ford diesels."

"Take the money."

He stared into the painting. "No. I think I'll hold on to it awhile."

Arms full, I tucked the holstered pistol behind my back, threw everything into the back of the Jeep, then made one last pass through the store. Gus's computer homepage had been set to the local Doppler radar screen of the Weather Channel. He did this to keep an eye on river conditions for his clients and people wishing to rent equipment. It showed everything from the Okefenokee Swamp to the Cumberland Sound. At the bottom of the screen, like a running stock ticker, ran double-digit numbers depicting river level heights sent by automatic sensors placed along the river's 130-plus-mile length. Between the two I had a pretty good picture of river conditions. He pointed at the ticker. "If the storm turns this way, that will change a good bit."

"I remember."

Several sizes of waterproof map cases hung along the check-out counter. Guides use them to keep the maps dry until their minds knew the river better than the map—which occurred after a few seasons on the river. I needed the map less than I needed the bag, but it had been a while so I took both. The map would confirm the GPS readings and vice versa. I pulled the newspaper article from my shirt pocket, slid it into the map case and sealed it shut.

With the car loaded, I turned to Gus. I owed him a bit of an explanation. "How you been?"

"Well, I'd prefer to be standing in an eighteen-foot Hewes flats boat somewhere in the Keys where cell phone reception was nonexistent, but"—he waved his hands across the store—"stores don't tend themselves."

"Sell the painting. Buy the boat. Take a vacation."

He nodded. "Maybe one day." He shook a pebble out of his Teva. "You sure you don't want to talk about it?"

"The doctors sent us home." I pulled a paddle tether off a hook on the wall and began playing with the slipknot. "Whatever you hear in the coming week, it's probably only half true."

I tore a sheet of paper off a pad I kept in the car, listed everything I'd just loaded into the Jeep and wrote my credit card number on the bottom. "It'd be better—for me—if you'd wait a week or so to run my card."

"You need some money?"

"No, it's just that there will be some people paying attention and I don't want them to know where I am yet. They'll know soon enough."

"You in trouble?"

"Not the kind you're talking about. Least, not yet."

He folded the invoice and tucked it in his shirt pocket. "Next month."

"Thanks, Gus."

I stepped into the Jeep and buckled my belt. Gus hung on the door and stared down the highway. "I was thinking about your mother the other day."

"Oh yeah?"

"That was one lovely lady. I ever tell you I asked her to marry me?"

I shook my head and laughed. "No."

"Said she'd been married and it didn't take. Besides, she liked me too much. Said once I got to know her, I'd take off." He was quiet a minute. "I think she done right by you."

"She tried."

Gus used the parking lot as a staging area for all the folks that rented from him. After outfitting everyone with life jacket, paddle and kayak, we'd load the kayaks and canoes into the river from the side of the parking lot. A short walk downhill to the beach and put in. It was shallow enough to launch but not so deep that if someone tumped or capsized they couldn't stand up. He stared down over the water. "She loved this river. Thought it was something special."

"That, she did."

He put his hand on my shoulder. "It is, you know."

"Some would say it's nothing but a low spot in the earth's crust—where all the junk drains out."

He slipped his hands in his pockets. "That's one way of looking at it."

"You got another?"

He nodded. "Yup, but you'll remember soon enough. She can remind you far better than I." He shook his head. "The river never changes. It may alter its path a bit, but it never changes. It's us who change. We come back here and we're different. Not it."

"When I was a kid, Mom told me that God lived in the river. I used to lay on the bank, real still, waiting for him to surface."

"And when he did?"

I laughed. "Jump on his back and choke him until he answered a few questions."

"Careful what you wish for."

A breeze rattled through the treetops bringing a coolness with it. "Gus, I'm sorry to come to you like this."

He shook his head and picked at his teeth with a toothpick. "This river's taught me a good bit. Probably why I don't leave here. It winds, weaves, snakes around. Rarely goes the same way twice. But, in the end, it always ends up in the same place and the gift is never the same."

"Meaning?"

"It's the journey that matters."

5

One of the great things about growing up in the sticks was the ignorance. Country people aren't dumb and certainly not stupid. We pride ourselves on common sense and more than one of us have aced the SAT, but there are certain things we know very little about and, admittedly, some of that comes from a prideful unwillingness to either ask a few questions or want to know. Don't worry, it's not a regional disease. I've found it exists in New York, too. They just call it by another name.

In my education, art was one of those things. For most of my friends, art was a class you took or something you made when you spray-painted your girlfriend's name on the side of a water tower. It wasn't that we didn't appreciate human achievement. We did and do. It was more the high-browed conversation that surrounded it. We didn't have time for all that foolishness. We just saw beauty in different places and forms and then we surrounded it with a different conversation and language.

So when others saw what I could do with a pencil or brush, they immediately thought I was Picasso—although they had no idea who he was or why they said I was like him. They just liked his name and it made them sound important. I knew better and wanted nothing to do with Picasso. Maybe I "saw" differently. I don't know. I suppose fish think the same thing of swimming and breathing water. They don't think they're anything special until you pitch them up on land.

Before my mom left this world, she made it a practice of taking me to the library. We went two or three times a week. It was air-conditioned, smoking was not allowed, admission was free and they stayed open late. We spent hours looking at art books and talking about what we liked or didn't. Our conversations were not educated. We said things like, *I like his smile, I like those colors, That makes me laugh,* or *That looks like it hurts.*

I would learn later that what we were really saying was, *That speaks to me.* Because that's what art does. It speaks to us, and if we speak the same language—and if we've learned how to listen—we either hear it or we don't.

We "studied" the classics of Greece and Rome and then wondered what in the world happened during the medieval period. I didn't know much but I at least knew that the world had taken a step backward if we were judging it by its art. Mom would spread the book in front of me, lay a clean sheet of paper across the table and I'd draw what I saw.

I never tried to make sense of the whole of the world of art. I took only what I wanted. Only what I needed. My purpose was rather singular. Unlike some artists who could transition seamlessly between various forms, subjects and styles, I couldn't. Still can't. So I concentrated on what I thought I was good at—and what I needed. That meant faces. Specifically, emotions. Those library visits taught me that emotions included the angle of the shoulders, the height of the chin, the interweaving of fingers, the extent to which a chest was expanded with air, how legs were crossed, angled or spread, how a toe curled up or down, how much light reflected off the eyes.

While my mouth had a hard time getting out what was on

the inside of me, my hands knew instinctively how, when I got up close and saw how the masters did it, I intrinsically understood. I just knew, I can't explain that.

Most were total screwups. Few, if any, had it together. They painted out of brokenness, out of despair, and often out of poverty. Hence, the skinny artist.

But I learned something. Something I'd need later. Fallen, broken men can make great art.

When I got older, I learned that I was attracted to realism, not idealism. Had no use for expressionism that sought to increase the impact of images on the viewer by distortion or oversimplification. I had no use for modernism, cubism or surrealism. Picasso did nothing for me. That's not to say he won't one day, but he didn't then and doesn't now.

I wanted to touch the viewer. Deeply. No tricks. With what is real, not with what isn't. I cared nothing for sleight of hand.

I made it through high school with little competition. My advisor placed some of my pieces in a regional art show and, by chance, I caught the eye of an art teacher and won an art scholarship to the College of Charleston. That's when life opened my eyes. I elected to double in Art and Art History. I knew my craft needed work, but I also wanted to understand the lives of those who made it. Not only *how* but *why*. The craft without the reason didn't mean as much. The reason added context to the gift. None of us create ex nihilo.

I read biographies of artists, studying their lives as much as their work. Most led tormented, broken lives. Many of them brought it on themselves. I never could understand why the most screwed-up people make some of the best artists. Time and time again, great art rose out of a cauldron of torment, fueled by eccentrics who lived on the fringe of society, who seemed to care little for that which society cares greatly about and vice versa. Of course, there are exceptions, but they are just that—exceptions.

Most operated on the periphery. One foot in their world, one foot in ours. Wealthy nobles sought their talent, bringing them out of their world and into this one.

Fortunately, my wealthy noble had been the good people at the College of Charleston, which meant my classes were half paid for. The other half I scrounged together from tips or loans.

My apartment in Charleston was basically a one-room studio with a loft where I slept. Showers were cold more often than not, wharf rats were common attic perusers and I kept a list on the bathroom wall naming the biggest roaches I'd captured in a clear plastic Solo cup. I named them much like hurricanes, one for each letter, and I'd been through the alphabet twice. The biggest to date was Merlin. Once I trapped him, it took twenty-seven days to go belly-up. But other than that, it was cozy, clean and the perfect place to work when I wasn't working.

It was a two-story storefront on King Street wedged in between Beaufain and Market. My display window was ten feet wide, as was my entire studio. Fifty years ago, someone had bricked in the grassy space between two buildings and sold the space to a dentist. He used to park his chair right up front where everybody could see him working. Problem was, his patients didn't like being on parade for all of King Street, so he sold out to a printer who spent thirty years printing and when he lost his business market to the Internet, he rented it to me. I had hoped that location would give me a chance at selling something. Anything. So I leaned what I thought were my three best pieces up against the window. Not real sexy but I'd been eating Ramen noodles for three weeks and couldn't quite afford easels. I seriously considered stealing a few from the art lab, but deep down, I had a feeling that presentation was not my problem. Even the Christmas rush didn't bring a sale.

There was an exception to this. About once a month, sometimes more, and usually at night, a woman would stand at my window and stare. She was tall, wore a scarf or baseball cap, jeans and something long-sleeved, and big round sunglasses that covered half her face. Once she stood there for an hour, leaning against the glass, studying the three pieces in the display and then trying to see past them at my other work leaning against the wall. Several times I motioned her in, even opened the door once and invited her, but she turned and disappeared without a word. From then on when she appeared, I just waved. Once, she waved back. I figured she liked looking so I let her look.

LIKE AN IDIOT, I had enrolled in early-morning classes thinking it would give me all day and night to work or paint. Mostly paint. When I wasn't tending bar, chances were good I was covered in paint, charcoal, or slipping along the Battery in my running shoes.

Having pitched my asthma medication years ago, I did something the doctors told me I couldn't. I grew my lungs. Maybe *stretched* is a better word. It had become my escape, helping me stay on a relatively even keel. Gone were the hacking, sputtering, passing-out days. Somewhere in the past fifteen years, it had morphed. What I have is called EIB. Exercise-induced bronchospasm. Put my lungs under duress, without adequate warm-up, and they actually clamp down, causing more duress, causing more clamping, and so on. A downward spiral. Add to that dry, cold air and I'm a basket case. But let me warm up, ease into the idea that I might need to eat mass amounts of oxygen and my lungs loosen up nicely. Further, warm damp air acts like a lubricant. I love running in a summer rain. I've even known moments of relative speed when I can run a long time. Hours. I'm not setting any land-speed records, but I've known the runner's high.

Usually, when I clocked out at work, I'd grab a tea bag or two, either Constant Comment or Earl Grey—kind of like you do when you're checking out of a hotel and you grab the individual bottles of soap and conditioner. You've got a hundred at home, but for some reason, you take two more because you never know when you might actually use it. In my case, the caffeine helped fend off the hunger. The restaurant was pretty good about turning a blind eye when it came to eating leftovers once the kitchen had closed.

One night I clocked out and then sucked down a bowl of French onion soup, some clam chowder, a few chicken strips and an entire loaf of French bread. I was full for the first time in a few days so I ambled out onto King Street and, for reasons I cannot to this day make sense of, turned hard left onto Market, en route to Waterfront Park. It was a clear night, or morning, and I wanted to smell the water and stare out over Fort Sumter.

I strolled along, angry over my tips, complaining about my inability to sell anything even remotely resembling art and sick and tired of Chinese noodles. In truth, I was having a pity-party—and those are always better alone. All I was missing was a bottle, but I couldn't afford one.

I reached the park, and strolled around the fountain to one of four granite platforms placed along the waterfront. Their bases were constructed with the idea that statues would be placed on them in the future. At the moment, they looked like miniature helicopter landing pads, three feet off the ground and half surrounded in semicircle walls of granite. The locals called them echo chambers, because if you stood in the center and spoke exactly at twelve o'clock you could hear your own echo. Quite loudly, actually.

I hopped up on the base, whispered and heard something clank against metal, then a muffled scream followed by a painful grunt. I looked up, saw nothing and then looked again. Along the walkway, I saw the outline of a man's back. He was leaning over something or someone and was raising his hand as if to hit them. I'm no hero and there's no *S* on my chest, but next thing I knew I found myself running across the grass. I glided off the granite wall, sprung myself airborne and caught the man in the chest. He was enormous. Broad-shouldered, as thick as he was wide, bearded and reeking like the Dumpster outside the hotel along with a pretty heavy dose of alcohol. My chest collided with his shoulder and I thought I'd just been hit by a Mack truck. The person beneath him scurried off to one side as he turned his attention to me. I stepped backward in between him and whoever he was beating. The perfume told me it was either a girl or a guy who wanted to be. I held out both hands. "Wait, sir—"

He laughed, lunged like a cat, grabbed me by the throat, cut off my air and threw me backward like a rag doll. He looked like the guy in *The Green Mile,* only meaner. I hopped up, hands shaking like stop signs, heard somebody crying behind me, felt a hand shaking as it was pressed against my back, and then I smelled that smell again.

I stuffed my hand in my pocket and pulled out $67 in one-dollar bills. His teeth shone white as his hand wrapped around the money. His other hand tightened around my throat. I reached into my back pocket and handed him my wallet, which held my license, student ID and two maxed-out credit cards. What he didn't know wouldn't hurt him. He palmed the wallet and stuffed it in his back pocket. Unfortunately, neither of those two had any effect on his grip on me or his advance on the girl. He pushed me—therefore us—back into one of the granite semicircles and backhanded me hard across the mouth. The world went squirrelly, and the streetlights hazed over then reappeared. When I could focus, I saw him back on top of her, one hand around her neck, the other up her shirt. This had gone from bad to worse, so I tried the only thing I had left. I reached into my front pocket, pulled out the pocketwatch I'd carried since my uncle gave it to me at my mother's funeral and held it out. He eyed the dangling gold thing in front of him and then held it to his ear. "Keep it. It's yours. All of it . . . just please don't hurt the girl."

She was frantic, but he was nearly three times her size. I tried one last time. "Sir . . . please, you're hurting the girl." He stuffed the watch in his pocket, backhanded me and began tearing at her jeans.

He had her pinned down now. The crack of his butt was showing, he had exposed himself and he was pulling her by her long hair, threatening to snap her neck like a twig. The coughing told me she was having a hard time breathing. I took four steps, jumped on his back, dug my heels in and rammed both index fingers one knuckle deep into his eye sockets. He reached for his face, uttered some guttural thing that told me what I'd done was painful and turned on me.

The good news was that he let go of the girl, allowing her to stand up and run. The bad news was that with her gone, and him knowing this, he was now left with me. His facial expres-

sion changed sort of like the Hulk, he was foaming in both corners of his mouth and I'm pretty sure I shouted something I
wouldn't have repeated in the presence of my mother.

You ever see those videos of college pranks where fraternity
brothers—hoping to imbibe a sense of brotherhood—dump
pledges in those large tumbling dryers at the coin laundry and
then laugh while their butts turned orbits around the room? For
the next sixty seconds, that's about how I felt—absent the fabric
softener. Having rubbed me into the concrete, blackened both
my eyes, busted my lip, and broken my nose, he lifted me over
his head and threw me out over the handrail like some WWF
wrestler. I helicoptered through the air and landed in the marsh
where a blue crab was munching on the head of a mullet.

Wrestling man's eyes narrowed as I floated hip-deep in a
bed of wiregrass, muck and what smelled like sewage runoff.
He grunted, shoved himself back in his pants, turned and
walked off—evidently he couldn't swim. For the next twenty
minutes, I wallowed and concentrated on the next breath. With
no sign of him, I scraped my way to the railing, pulled myself
out and hobbled home. Twenty minutes later, I locked my
door, sat in the shower and calculated the cost of a trip to the
emergency room. Absent health insurance, the numbers were
a bit high. My head pounding, I swallowed four aspirin and
looked in the mirror. My nose had turned sideways across my
face and now looked more like a lightning bolt. I grabbed it
between my right thumb and forefinger, pulled downward
quickly and woke the next morning, a butt-naked snow angel
sprawled across the first floor of my studio.

Looking out between the slits that had become my eyes and
then around the bulbous thing that was once my nose, I stared
through the glass—some four feet away—and into thirty sets of

rather wide eyes, three rows deep, staring, but not at my art-work. Thanks to the three 60-watt bulbs I had dangling from an extension cord above the artwork, I was lit up pretty well.

I climbed the stairs, fell into bed and woke somewhere in the afternoon to a blood-crusted face, a pounding migraine and a note taped to the door. It read: "If you're interested in a dis-creet yet artistic black-and-white photo shoot, call the number below. I have my own darkroom and studio. Philip."

I threw the note in the trash, swallowed more aspirin and called one of my classmates to find out what I'd missed. James Pettigrew was a street-smart kid from the streets of Detroit who wrote poetry when he wasn't sculpting clay. When he picked up the phone, he was scanning the news online and not real interested in talking with me. Smacking gum, he cut me off. "You hear about last night?"

"No."

"Senator Coleman's daughter got singled out on the board-walk while walking home. Some drunk behemoth jumped her and was trying to make her his wife when some unidentified stranger objected to the wedding and messed up his plans. Little while ago, the cops caught a guy that fits the description she gave of the attacker. He was carrying some cash and a pocket-watch that both jell with her story. No ID yet on Superman. Senator held a press conference this morning from the steps of the Capitol then flew home. Landed in Charleston just a bit ago."

"She okay?"

"Whenever a six-foot, ten-inch man repeatedly backhands the face of the spokeswoman for one of the major cosmetic lines in the country—who also happens to have been voted by the *New York Times* as one of the hundred most beautiful faces in the United States—whose face, by the way, made the cover of three of the most highly read prime-time magazines in the country—well, what do you think?"

Scenes from the night before flashed across my eyelids but the details were fuzzy.

"Doss. Where you been? What rock you been living under? Abbie Coleman goes by the professional name of Abbie Eliot."

I knew I'd seen her somewhere before.

I hung up, called in sick to work and hung the Closed sign across my front door. I'd collect my watch and wallet when the pain subsided.

Financial problems aside, I needed a "subject" of my own. My senior project was due in two months and I had yet to land on a subject. Most students had been working on theirs for weeks. Further, it was well known around town that senior art majors paid their subjects by the hour. That, too, was a difficulty for me.

Compounding the problem was the "nude" assignment. To graduate, every senior was required to present a portfolio of twelve pieces showcasing their best work—one of which was to be a nude piece. Some of my classmates acted like they had joined the art program for this very reason: they got to hang out a sign that read something like, "Hey, I need a nude subject for my senior portfolio." To make it seem more official and more legitimate, they'd rent out a swanky studio, drape a sheet across a wire forming a backdrop, hang a spotlight, play some new-age music and buy a bottle of wine with a screw-off cap. Then they'd schedule several "sittings" that lasted a couple of hours and included a lot of serious looks and casual small talk. Some of my classmates milked this thing for all it was worth because it was the only way they'd ever get a girl to take her clothes off.

Two types of girls showed up: the first was the adventuresome freshman—sometimes a sophomore—who was stretching her wings, wanting to try something new and usually angry at her dad. She usually showed up with a friend, a little giggly and the smell of alcohol on her breath. The second was the experienced senior or first-year graduate student who showed up alone, angry at an ex-boyfriend and armed with thoughts of finding herself. Nice girls and cover girls just didn't come knocking.

So, in truth, the problem was not finding someone, but finding the right someone. And then there was one other thing. I just had a problem with someone I didn't know walking in and taking their clothes off. I mean, who does that? What kind of person walks into a room with a stranger, strips down to her birthday suit and stands there while you walk all over her with your eyes. I realize we're supposed to be focused on our subject and studying the "form" but that's just the problem: I've yet to meet a woman who can be reduced to a form. Form can't be extracted from the essence like some broth reduction.

In the history of mankind, no single person yet has learned to swim by having the strokes explained. At some point, they dive in. In art, that diving has nothing to do with holding a brush, pencil or chisel. It's something your heart does and only then will your hand follow. You, me, any artist, cannot take the beauty that is woman and transfer it to any medium, be it canvas, stone or, least of all, film. Problem was, my art teachers had no idea what I was talking about. They thought art started in the hand and traveled up the arm and into the heart. They had reversed the process. Art flows out, not in. Though, I will say, if you're empty, not much will flow out. Which might have been their problem to begin with.

In my education, every assignment was run through some Cartesian filter in which we sat back, scratched the stubble on our chin and "thought" about the art before us. We used that filter to reduce the work to a series of strokes, shades and hues. What kind of nonsense is that? Whatever happened to "Wow! That's beautiful." I'm not slamming the process of perfecting a craft, I'm slamming the idea that you perfect a craft solely by studying the craft. It's a sickness that I've been trying to avoid since I first picked up a brush or pencil.

'Course, all this philosophical conversation never got me very far with my professors. Especially when it came to the nude. There was no getting around it. They just looked at me and raised their eyebrows. *Paint the sucker!* They thought my objections grew out of a dislike for hard work. So I invited them over, and those same eyes grew wide. My work ethic was intact. By the age of eighteen, I had produced a larger volume of work than most of them had in their entire life, proving that my mom was the second-best teacher I ever had. I had come to art school having already learned most of what they hoped to teach me. Most of them had no idea what I was talking about. Was I an idealist? Absolutely. But once they saw the amount of work I had produced, and was producing, they could not argue with my work or craft. For me, the craft wasn't the point. The point was the point. And most never understood that. Most of them were infected with a sickness they didn't know they were carrying. And worse yet, didn't know they were transmitting.

Despite my soapbox rantings and self-righteous indignation, I needed to graduate and they stood between me and that walk across the stage. Had it not been for the fading memories of my mother, I'd have told them to shove their sheepskin. Which brings me back to the nude.

In defense of my stubbornness, I had been looking for two things: the right face and the right figure. That's all I wanted. One face. One figure. And preferably, the two went together. I had always felt that God made a few perfect ones, so I was waiting to find her and then have that face sit still long enough for me to fumble through my inadequacies and capture it and her on canvas.

Okay, in truth, I was afraid. Afraid that whoever sat there would see right through me, would see that I didn't know what I was doing, that I was intimidated, and when they stood up, walked across the floor and stared at my work—at themselves—they'd laugh at my attempt. In the psychology books that's called a fear of failure, and when it came to my art—more specifically, the nude—it paralyzed me.

Completely.

6

We pulled out of Gus's and passed through St. George on our way to Moniac. St. George is made up of one railroad track, one grammar school, one gas station, one restaurant, one four-way stop and one post office. I stood in the intersection, scratching my head, trying to remember where they'd put the post office when I heard what sounded like a prop plane flying low above me. It buzzed overhead and I thought, What crazy nut is flying in this weather? Then I could have sworn I heard singing. The lights on the wings shot straight up, turned, barrel-rolled and spun earthward. About a hundred feet off the highway in front of me, it leveled out, righted itself and landed. It was an open-cockpit, bi-wing plane and reminded me of the Red Baron. Its fuselage was a gleaming sky blue and its wings yellow. It crossed the railroad track like a car, and then pulled to a stop at the intersection. The pilot waved, lifted his goggles and then pulled into the gas station directly up to the twenty-four-hour, self-serve pump. He cut the engine, ran his credit card through the machine and started pumping gas. When finished, he threw a piece of hail out of the cockpit, pointed upward and hollered, "It's hell up there. Think I'll take the long way home. You mind giving me some help?" I crossed the street and he said, "Just push," so I leaned against the wing. Surprisingly, it rolled rather easily. He nodded, said, "She's pretty light." He pulled down his goggles and said, "Thanks much," then took a long look at the car where Abbie lay sleeping. Then he started talking to someone I couldn't see. He cranked the engine and, just like he was driving a Cadillac on a Sunday afternoon, rolled east down the highway. After nearly a mile, he rocketed heavenward where the two blue wing lights disappeared into the darkness.

~᠊᠊᠊᠊᠊᠊

ABBIE WANTED HER DAD to know where we were, but didn't want to call him. A letter would tell him what he needed to know without giving him a chance to control the outcome. She licked the back, slid the letter inside, sealed it and handed it to me—it was the single sheet of yellow legal paper that had been sitting on the bedside table. I pulled into the post office, and was peeling a stamp out of the book when it hit me. We needed time. The problem with the post office is that they were efficient, which meant he'd get this letter in a day or two. I needed them to deliver it next week. Preferably, late next week. I turned to Abbie, "You mind if I buy us a few days' time?"

She shook her head and forced a smile. "Just as long as it gets there."

I walked around the building to the drop box and reversed the addresses. Meaning, I addressed it to us, at our house, and wrote the return address as his. Then I peeled off the stamp and dropped it in the box. Without the required forty-one cents postage, it'd spend a few days in post office wonderland while they took their sweet little time tossing it around, angry that it didn't have a stamp and enacting justice—or rather revenge— on whoever sent it. Further delaying its inevitable return. Then they'd stamp it "Insufficient Postage" in bright red ink and finally, out of sheer mercy to the poor miscreant soul who had mistakenly sent it, return it to the address in the top left-hand corner—which is exactly what I wanted. When Abbie's father saw this, he'd know I'd bought myself some time, because he's not stupid. And he'd know that I knew this about him and then he'd cuss me for being too cheap to buy a stamp, but given the list of faults he kept on me, this wouldn't make the top fifty.

Twenty minutes later, we pulled onto County Road 94 heading west to Moniac—a map-dot left off of most maps.

Moniac is called a "community" because it'd be ridiculous to call it a town. It sits due south of the Okefenokee swamp, twenty-seven miles east of Fargo and twelve miles west of St. George, which puts it smack in the middle of nowhere. It's little more than the intersection of highways 94 and 121, Lacy's Country Store, a bridge and a dead pecan orchard. With a little tailwind, Tiger Woods could probably hit a ball with his driver from one end to the other. Around here more people talk on CB radios than cell phones.

Most folks drive through without every knowing they've been here. Despite this, it's the bridge that's significant.

Below it flow the headwaters for the St. Marys and the first put-in outside of the Okefenokee. Most paddlers will tell you the river isn't navigable for another thirty miles until she rounds the bend at Stokes Bridge and heads due north, but skip it and you miss something beautiful. Sort of like giving birth to a teenager. You might be glad you avoided the diaper stage and the terrible two's but you'd miss a lot.

We crossed the bridge, swung back around and ambled down the side road to the underside of the bridge. Residue of an old campfire, charred logs, cigarette butts and shards of brown bottles littered the bank.

The ground beneath the bridge looks like something out of a *Mad Max* film. When the construction team finished with the overpass, they dumped all the used concrete and rebar into the river. Discarded beer cans and Sprite bottles floated between the jagged edges of busted, Buick-sized concrete chunks and waterlogged cedars caught in the cracks.

Then there's the river herself.

You ever walked into one of those seventies bars, something you'd see in an Austin Powers movie where long strands of beads are draped from every doorway? To get in, you have to slide your hands through, push them aside with your forearms and slip in without snagging your shoulders on the beads. Getting into the river is a lot like that. Scrub oaks, twenty feet tall, sewn together with itchy vines and Spanish moss swimming with red bugs, hang over the river forming a nearly impenetrable canopy. The exceptions are air and pinholes of light. The gnarled trees rise up out of the bank, lower their branches, span across the bluff like a fence row and interlock their leaves with prickly pointed palmetto bushes.

She is protective of herself—and those who enter her.

The river trickles more or less southward out of Moniac across fallen deadwood, through beaver dams and around cypress stumps. At Moniac you can jump across, and she's rarely more than a couple feet deep.

I turned under the overpass, parked beneath the bridge—out of sight of searching helicopters—and unloaded. The rain let up, sun broke through and began burning the mist off the water. But that was short-lived, because the sheets of rain returned about the time I started carrying Abbie across the grass to the canoe.

I stepped down into the river and slipped on a slimy rock—bouncing Abbie like a Raggedy Ann doll. As many times as I've stepped into this river, I should've known better. I laid her in the bottom of the canoe atop a sleeping bag. Using the tent poles, a blue tarp and some nylon parachute cord, I rigged a makeshift tent from the bow to midway down the canoe. Her feet might get wet, but the angle of the canoe in the water would keep her face elevated and the opening in the rear would shed the rain and allow me to keep an eye on her. I changed her fentanyl patch, giving her a constant medication feed for seventy-two more hours. The patch was a lot like those worn by people who are trying to quit smoking. It was waterproof, allowed her to shower, bathe and even swim. In Abbie's case, though, the patch contained a pain medication called Duragesic that helped knock the edge off. It was what I called a base-layer medication, because if the pain escalated, we'd need other layers. I locked the Jeep and stood beneath the overpass. As I stared out into the rain, a daddy longlegs walked across my foot. Few know it, but it's one of the most poisonous spiders known to man. Only problem is that its mouth is too small to bite a human.

I filled the trailing canoe with everything I'd piled into the back of the Jeep, then covered it with the second tarp. I made one final run to the Jeep and grabbed the bright yellow Pelican case. Next to Abbie, it was the most important item in the canoe.

~❧~

I DON'T THINK GARY had been all that happy to see me when I'd knocked on his door. It was the middle of the night. He appeared in a robe and sleepy haze. "Abbie okay?"

I explained what we were doing while he made coffee. He blew the steam off his cup. "You know you're nuts."

He scribbled three prescriptions and handed them to me. I shook my head. "Gary, I can't fill these."

"Why?"

"Because the folks at Walgreens will be on the phone for three hours making sure you meant what you wrote and by then, the senator will have gotten a whiff and he'll know something's up. We'll never get out of Charleston. Don't you have this stuff in your office?"

"Yeah, but I can't give you this much narcotic without someone else in my office assisting. Wait a few hours."

"I don't have a few hours."

"Doss, there's a reason the law requires us to keep this stuff under lock and key. It's a check-and-balance sort of thing." He dangled his keys. "I have the key. My office manager has the combination."

"Come on, Gary. I know you better than that."

"I won't do it. If we're audited, I'd lose my license."

"Then tell it to me."

"What?"

"The combination. I'm no dummy."

He took a deep breath. "I'm going back to bed." He laid his keys on the countertop next to him and stopped on his way out of the kitchen. "First drawer to the left of the cabinet. Left side. Written in pencil. It's backwards, so start on the right side and work to the left. And don't look at the cameras over your left shoulder. We have twenty-four-hour video surveillance. Better yet, put some panty hose over your head." He walked out, so I grabbed his keys, drove to his office and let myself in. I found the combination, wrote it in reverse, unlocked the cabinet and on the second try, the safe door clicked open.

I dug through the inside, found what I needed, dropped it into a plastic bag and was about to walk out when I saw the unopened box of Actiq—raspberry-flavored pain lozenges on a stick that come in doses from 200 to 1,600 mcg. They were lollipops prescribed a lot for kids and older folks who needed fast-acting, ingestible medication to combat breakthrough pain. In the last several months, they had become Abbie's candy of choice. She ate them as needed. I grabbed the entire box. I never looked at the camera over my left shoulder, but since I had turned on the light and wasn't wearing panty hose, my identity would be rather obvious. The combination of all the drugs in my possession was basically weapons-grade pain management—and enough to guarantee prison if caught.

I drove back to Gary's house, handed him his keys and he rummaged through my bag. He handed it back, speaking in his doctor's tone of voice. "Now, listen. This is important. You've got six dexamethasone syringes, two dopamine syringes and enough fentanyl patches to last a month. The dexamethasone injections will reduce the swelling in her brain, giving her a few hours of clarity and returning her to a nearly normal playing field. If the pressure grows too much and begins pressing on her brain stem, it'll do one of two things. If it raises her blood pressure, there's nothing you can do. Probably won't bother her much anyway. If it lowers it, it'll hinder her body's natural desire to breathe and probably send her into shock. The dopamine counteracts this by elevating her heart rate and pressure. In more practical terms, the dexamethasone is a nuclear bomb to her adrenal gland. Each injection will be like burning jet fuel in a car engine. It'll run great while the fuel lasts, but chances are also good that it'll blow it altogether. High-altitude climbers on Everest and K2, working in the death zone, pack it in as a last-ditch effort in the event that they need to counteract the effects of edema, which compresses brain structures. If you've ever been congested to the point that you could not breathe through your nose, then squirted some Afrin nasal spray up your nose, then you have a pretty good idea of how it works."

He placed a finger in the air. "Oh, and both dopamine and dexamethasone, while effective when used alone, can cause a problem when used together. They counteract one another. Using both together can be a bit of a balancing act."

He was right. Abbie had been using various forms of these and other drugs for so long that she'd become desensitized to their effect. Meaning, she needed more narcotic to achieve the same benefit. Which would have been fine if the pain had stayed the same. Problem was, while the pain ramped up, our ability to combat it spiraled downward.

He folded his arms. "As her doctor, I'm obliged to tell you. Over the long term, dexamethasone causes ulcers, bleeding of the organs, euphoria, water retention, heart insufficiency, blurred vision and wide-angle glaucoma. Other than that, it's a peach."

I shrugged. "I guess the good news is that we needn't be too concerned about the long term."

He shoved his hands in his pockets and turned toward the street. "And . . ."

"Yeah?"

"You won't see it coming and it won't be pretty. In truth, you'll hear it before you see it. Once you do, it's a ticking time bomb. Problem is, you can't see the fuse."

He pointed at my bag of goodies. "The dexamethasone . . . one will ease the pain, two will knock her out for most of a day . . . three will . . . well . . ."

I knew what he was trying to say. "Thanks, Gary."

"If you have anything left to say, say it now."

I walked back up the steps. "Close your eyes."

"What?"

"Just close your eyes. I have a present for you." He did and I backhanded him about as hard as I could in the left eye.

He hit the floor. "What'd you do that for!"

I helped him up. "You need a story to go with the lie that you're going to tell the office manager in a few hours." I pointed at his swelling eye. "Now you've got one."

"You could've warned me."

"Sorry." I handed him an Actiq. "Here, this'll help with the pain."

"Very funny." I turned and started walking down his steps. "Doss, you know what you're doing?"

I shrugged. "Not really. I just know I can't stay here."

He shook his head. "I don't envy you."

"I'll be seeing you, Gary. Sorry about your eye."

"One more thing."

"Yeah?"

"One of the conversations right now in the medical community is how much is too much narcotic. With all the conversations about euthanasia, we are constantly asking ourselves, whether out loud or quietly to ourselves, when we, as physicians, have crossed the line from fighting pain to . . . helping someone go quietly into that long night. You following me?" I nodded. "Given Abbie's desensitization to the medication, she'll need a lot of it. If . . . if you give her what she needs . . . at the end of the day, you could be charged with, well . . . between what's in that bag and what would be in her bloodstream, they'd just build the prison on top of you."

"Thanks, Gary."

I TIED THE CASE to my seat and shoved it behind me. I could lose everything else but it. And maybe the revolver. I stepped in and shoved off, dipping the paddle tip in the water. My cell phone rang in my pocket. Caller ID read "SIR." This was not unexpected. I shoved it back in my pocket and let it ring. When we first married I managed to fly beneath his radar. Now, not so much. A few minutes later, it rang again. And again. Abbie whispered from beneath the tarp, "You better answer it. You know how he hates to be kept waiting." The fourth time he called, I flipped it open. The tone of voice reminded me of the one he used while in the Chamber as he was speaking to members on the other side of the aisle. The booming one heard on C-SPAN, FOX and CNN. "Where is Abigail Grace?"

⚓

DOUBLE NAMES IN CHARLESTON are a way of life. Most blue bloods decree at least one. It's an oral remnant of Scarlett's Camelot days and a not-so-gentle reminder of their ancestral link to nobility. When he first enrolled her at Ashley Hall, then Governor Coleman had insisted on it—intending to elevate her above the fray and distance her from her competitors. One of the youngest governors in the history of the Union, he expected people to jump when he barked, so he surrounded himself with people who asked, "How high?" Propped in pigtails and pearls, she cared nothing for the sort. She did not work for him, had no ambition other than being his daughter and didn't give two bits about his title.

Thus began the tug o' war.

Ever since, they'd lived with this private uneasiness. In public, they shared a necessary truce. She gave him that. That, too, was Charleston. Appearances must be kept. But if you listened to the way she said "Daddy," it was there.

From the moment I'd met her, Abbie had been nothing I expected. On the surface, she was a senator's daughter, birthed in lace, raised by "help" and K-thru-12'd at Ashley Hall, where the echoes of the Gullah nannies hung in the air. *I'm Charleston born and Charleston bred and when I die I'm Charleston dead*. Steeped in society and cured in culture, her first word had been *deb*—as in *debutante*. Beneath the surface, where we swam, she was as at home there on a beach wearing a bikini top and frayed cutoffs as at the Hibernia Society ball decked out in pearls and shoulder-length white gloves. Somehow, she moved seamlessly, and effortlessly, between both worlds.

Miss Olivia, who changed her diapers and gets a good bit of the credit for raising her while Dad was trying to get reelected, said that somewhere in the first grade, Abigail Grace Eliot Coleman put her hands on her hips, stamped her foot and said, "What's wrong with 'Abbie'?" Over the years, in direct proportion to their escalating battle, she chipped away at her name. From third to sixth grade, she clipped it from "Abigail Grace" to "Abbie Grace." Cute, while still respectable. It also fit with her starring role in the musical *Annie* at the Dock Street Theater. In junior high, as her modeling career began to take off, landing her jobs in national mail-order clothing catalogs and local commercials, her name survived another cut to "Abbie G." A butchering that narrowed her father's eyes, but technically it was two names and only used in informal settings—which meant never around him. She'd outgrow it. As a junior, several would-be beaus, prom hopes high, rang asking for "Abbie." He responded with a dial tone. No matter, sixteen-year-old Abbie went anyway and just to add insult to injury she accepted jobs from two of the largest swimsuit makers in the country. Those two-piece photos quickly earned her a first-class ticket to New York where she and her agent—an attorney sent along by her father—met with cosmetics lines, shampoo and perfume companies, a sports news company with a rather famous swimsuit edition and one well-known lingerie monopoly. Midway through her senior year, he discovered that her teachers were addressing her as "Abbie." Which was bad, but it would get worse. Much worse. One Saturday morning, after two cups of coffee and a bran muffin spurred his daily constitution, he was flipping through the swimsuit edition and stumbled upon her picture. That magazine went in the trash—along with his subscription. Abbie graduated and he brokered a peace with a gift. He pulled the Mercedes out of cold storage and gave her the keys. But the cease-fire was short-lived. Speaking at her commencement ceremony, Senator Coleman fired what he thought was a final volley across her bow, announcing her full name in a tone that sought to return her to legitimacy, reestablishing her bloodline. Owners spoke of horses in much the same manner. But the smug smile was premature. A year later, "Abbie Eliot" sealed her rebellion when she quit Georgetown and signed an exclusive New York contract. Within weeks, her travel schedule included Europe and the Far East. By the age of nineteen, her travel schedule included New York and London and her glossy picture stared back at him from the glass-topped table in the dentist's office. Establishing a professional and public name that did not link her to him was a blow he could not counter.

She'd made a name for herself. Which was just fine with her.

A DEEP BREATH. "She's right here."

"Where is 'here'?" He could be direct when he wanted.

"Sir, I can't tell you that."

"Can't or won't?" See what I mean?

A pause. "Won't."

"Son . . ." He laughed uncomfortably. Senator Coleman did not like *not* being in control. Now that he'd been appointed chairman of the Finance Committee, he liked it even less. "At the wiggle of my finger, every law enforcement officer in the states of Georgia, North Carolina and South Carolina will be looking for my daughter. And don't think for one second that I won't call out the National Guard."

"She mentioned that."

"You doubt my resolve, son?"

"Sir, I don't doubt your love for your daughter, if that's what you're asking. But . . . this is something I've got to do."

"Son, you're deranged. You'll bring her back here right—"

"Sir, there's a part of me that would really like to do that, but . . . with all due respect, you don't know—"

He was screaming now. "Don't tell me what I don't know!"

While his public persona was all poise, polish, cuff links and Hermès ties, his backroom manners were more brass knuckles, Dickies and Carhartt. When he lost his temper, spit collected in the corners of his mouth, spewing like venom the louder he spoke. "You can't run far enough. Hide and I'll find you . . . I'll have you buried beneath the jail."

I guess you picked up on the fact that our relationship had not been smooth sailing. Despite his disdain for me, I'd always admired him. Even voted for him. He'd come from little and done much. And while getting elected is one thing, staying elected is another. He'd managed to do both. From the governor's mansion to now his fourth term as senator, he'd never lost an election. His tentacles stretched far and wide in Washington. A blessing and a curse—because what they say about power is true. I think in his other life, that one that included the good-old-boy farmer from South Carolina with the piece of hay sticking out his mouth, we'd have gotten along pretty well.

I swallowed and stared out across the water and at Abbie's pale frame tucked beneath the tarp. Senator Coleman detested the thought of dying for one simple reason. It was beyond his control. Others' deaths reminded him of this. The fact that his daughter showed no signs of fearing it might have been his singular weakness. It had always struck me as odd that someone so powerful, so accomplished, could be so easily derailed by something that no human, save one, had ever beaten. Because of this, we'd not seen much of him the last few years. Notice I said we hadn't seen much of him, not that he wasn't much help. He was. It's complicated. He got us into places we'd have never gotten in alone and on more than one occasion bumped us to the front of the line. If we didn't fly first class, he sent a jet. He helped from a distance because being too close hurt too much. Except once. That's how I knew he loved her. She knew this too, but that did little to make it any easier.

I needed to hang up before he traced the call with some NASA satellite. As a ranking member and chairman of several committees, the least of which was Armed Services, they were probably triangulating me now. "Sir, I'm sorry. I'm real sorry for a lot of things, but I"—I spoke softly—"this is for Abbie."

"She should be here. With us."

"With all due respect, sir. You've had four years. You couldn't have asked for a much more captive audience. If you wanted to be with her, you could have."

"Just what is that supposed to mean?" His anger was palpable. He was not used to, nor did he tolerate, discussion that was not geared toward total agreement. I had never fallen in line with this so our conversations had been short and usually started and ended by him. It has its roots in the moment I asked him if I could marry his daughter. Also another short conversation.

"Sir, I don't expect you to understand."

He was screaming now. "You're delusional . . . a dreamer who never would have amounted to anything had it not been for Abbie."

"I agree with you, sir, but—"

"But, what!"

I stared at Abbie. "Please understand . . ." He started to say something else, but I flipped the phone closed and tossed it in the river, where the water swallowed it. Tiny bubbles rose up around its edges as the light on the faceplate dimmed to dark.

I climbed back to my seat, my hands remembering the feel of the paddle, and fought to find that one description that just nailed my wife. You'd think after fourteen years, I'd come up with something, anything but "Honey." I admit, it's rather weak.

I tapped the article in the map case. "You would have to pick the most difficult one."

"I'm not here to check off just *one*."

"I figured. Guess we better get busy."

"Uh-huh."

"You rest. I'll paddle."

She cracked a smile. "Just the way it ought to be."

I sunk the paddle in the water, pulled hard, reminding my muscles, and slipped beneath the moss-draped arms over the river. The ocean lay 130-plus miles beyond—an hour in a car or a week on the river.

On the outside, everything had been taken. Abbie's professional life, her beauty, the welcoming softness of her bosom, the rounded curves, the confident smile. But that was just the external stuff. We could live without that. What about the stuff you couldn't see? Her unbridled passion for life, her intimate desire for me, her childlike hope in pretty much anything, her incomparable dreams. Abbie was a shell of her former self. A feeble skeleton dressed in a ghost's clothing. The only thing left was time.

I'm no sage. I don't pretend to have this all figured out, but I know this: some live well, some die well, but few love well. Why? I don't know if I can answer that. We all live, we all die—there is no get-out-of-jail-free card, but it's the part in between that matters. To love well . . . that's something else. It's a choosing—something done again and again and again. No matter what. And in my experience, if you so choose, you better be willing to suffer hell.

I didn't look back and wouldn't look ahead. So I stared at Abbie, sunk the paddle in the water and pulled.

7

I woke up hungry, face tender and one eye swollen completely shut. My lip was busted and looked out of proportion to the rest of my face. Somewhere along my right rib cage, a knifing pain told me that I'd either broken a rib or bruised it rather severely.

I put on some water to make some Ramen noodles, when I heard a tap at the door. I pulled some jeans over my boxer shorts and opened the door.

It was her.

I stood there like a deer in the headlights.

She looked up and down the street, then without invitation, stepped past me and into my studio. She was wearing a baseball cap, sweatshirt and jeans and looked sort of like one of those Hollywood A-listers who's shopping in the mall and trying not to be noticed. I stuck my head out the door, looked up and down the street and then back at her. She motioned to the door, which I shut, and then moved toward the back, near the boiling water, and out of the streetlight.

Hands in pockets, she looked around, taking in what little there was to take in. When she looked up, there were tears in her eyes. "I didn't get to thank you. I just ran and . . ." She wiped her face on her shirtsleeve.

"Would you like some tea?"

She smiled. "Yes."

I might not have had much, but tea I had. I reached into a drawer stuffed with tea bags and she started laughing. "You like tea?"

I shrugged. "I umm . . . I steal it from work. A bag or two a night. Sometimes three. It's easier than stealing coffee."

She laughed again. I poured two mugs of tea and pointed to a chair in the corner. Since I didn't have a table, I often ate in that chair with my dinner on my lap. She sat and I leaned against the wall, the tea bag string draped across one finger. She sipped and eyed the hundreds of pieces of my work either leaning or hanging around my studio. She stared up at the loft. "You stay busy."

I picked a dirty T-shirt off the floor, turned it right side out and pushed my head and arms through it. As soon as I did, I realized my mistake. Somewhere in the last week, I'd run out of deodorant and since then, I'd apparently worn that T-shirt. I held out a stop-sign hand and said, "I'll be right back." I hobbled up the stairs, put on a clean T-shirt, washed my underarms with a rag, sprayed them with cheap aftershave, then came back down and resumed my tea-steeping dip with the tea bag. She pointed and said, "You forgot . . . one thing."

I looked down and found my zipper wide open. While I fumbled with it, she set down her tea and began studying my art. Slowly, she eyed each piece. Really taking them in. I sat quietly. After the third or fourth piece, she stopped and looked around. "Where's the piece of the Gullah woman?"

"What?"

She pointed to an interior wall. "It used to lean over there. She was working at the slave market, weaving a wiregrass basket."

Somewhere in my first week at school, I was walking

through the market, getting my bearings, when I came upon this woman. She looked mid-seventies. She was leaning against the brick of the slave market, a hundred baskets at her feet, a single piece of grass sticking out of her mouth, no teeth, no dentures, knotty hands, dirty dress, tattered hat, bronze skin and yet there was something about her eyes. With the woman's permission, I spent a week—every afternoon for an hour when the light fell soft behind the trees—and captured her.

Abbie said, "Everybody paints the Gullah"—she shrugged—"they're easy targets. But you've done something not normally seen. Not even in New York. You captured the eyes. And Miss Rachel"—she tapped the center of the woman's frame on the canvas—"has some of the kindest and most beautiful eyes God ever made."

"You know her?"

She looked over her shoulder. "I grew up here."

I was confused. I scratched my head. I had never put her on display in the window. "Where have you seen it?"

She crossed her arms and pointed at the window. "We've never actually met, but from time to time, I window-gaze. See what's new. What you're working on." She lifted her sunglasses back over her eyes and I saw her again for the first time.

"That was you fogging up my glass?"

She nodded.

"Why didn't you come in? I don't bite."

She shrugged. "Sometimes it's nice not to be known."

She spent twenty minutes looking at my walls. The more she looked, the more I felt like a nude subject beneath the spotlight.

Finally she turned to me. "When do you graduate?"

"Technically, this summer."

She waved her hand across the room. "Problem?"

"Well . . . no, not really."

She read my hesitation and stepped closer. "We have a Christmas party. An annual thing. I'd like it if . . . if you'd come."

"Yeah? I mean . . ." I tried to sound like I attend these things all the time. "Yeah. Sure."

"Saturday week? Around seven. I'll send a driver."

Driver? "Yeah, sure." I pointed toward the street. "Mine's parked right down the street. I don't like him blocking my view."

She scanned my studio one last time, her eyes landing on the only photograph I owned.

On June 13, 1948, Nat Fein was sent to Yankee Stadium. The usual photographer had called in sick. Nat, a thirty-three-year-old from Manhattan's east side, usually shot human interest images for the *New York Herald Tribune;* i.e., he once took a picture of a cemetery with a one-way sign in the foreground. But June 13 was different. It was the twenty-fifth anniversary of the famous park in the Bronx and in that ceremony they would retire number 3. Babe Ruth. It was his house and everyone was there to see him. At fifty-three years old, he was the greatest player in baseball history, but for the last two years had been in and out of hospitals. A sportswriters agreement meant no one had ever used the word *cancer,* but when Nat first saw him in the locker room Babe was too weak to tie his own cleats. A male nurse did it for him. Nat watched him, saddened. The Babe, skinny, his uniform hanging off tilted shoulders, slipped on an overcoat and shuffled to the visitors' dugout. When his name was called, the place erupted. Babe slipped off his coat, grabbed a bat and walked to home plate—leaning on the bat. When he reached home plate, he took off his hat with his left hand and stood there, facing the house that he built. Every photographer had staged himself along the first and third base lines—in front of Babe. To get a shot of one of the most photographed faces in history. But not Nat.

Nat had seen his face and it wasn't the one he wanted to remember. Also, the only place "3" could be seen was from behind home plate. So that's where he stood. And while most of the other photographers used flashbulbs, Nat used available light. He shot low, near the ground, up across Babe's shoulders and out into the upper deck.

The result was one of the most famous pictures in sports history.

The next day, it appeared on the front of the *Herald Tribune* and then the AP picked it up and it ran on papers around the country. Two months later, Babe Ruth died. And in 1949, Nat Fein received the Pulitzer Prize for the photo.

She pointed at the picture. "Seems sort of out of place."

I shook my head. "Not really."

She seemed intrigued. "How so?"

"Take a long look at it." She did. "Now close your eyes." She looked at me. "Just close them." She folded her arms and closed her eyes. "Now, tell me what you see."

She opened her eyes. "His face."

"Exactly. Except you can't see it by looking at that photo." I walked to the wall and slid a large canvas out from behind another. I had filled most of the canvas with the Babe's face.

"Wow." She studied it a minute. "Have you shown that to your professors?" I shook my head. "You should."

I slid it back into its place. "I'm . . . well, I do faces. At least I'm trying."

She stared at me. She didn't want to leave. "Why?"

I folded my arms and shrugged. "Because of what they say without ever uttering a word."

She nodded. "I'd better get back. He's probably worried. Flew all this way and I'm not even home."

"Who's *he*?"

"Daddy." She checked her watch. "About seven, then?"

I glanced at my watchless arm and said, "Sure. When the freckle gets past the hair."

She laughed. "Thanks for the tea."

"Yeah . . . there's always more. And if not, I know where I can steal some."

She pulled the baseball cap down over her eyes. Her tone when she spoke was quiet and soft. "And . . . for last night."

I set down my tea. "Anybody would have done the same thing."

"Yeah?" She shook her head and pointed over one shoulder. "One man with binoculars was watching us through a window. Another, a jogger, crossed the park and pretended not to see."

"How'd you see them?"

"It was hard not to. I was on my back."

I shoved my hands in my pockets, trying to look like James Dean. "Well, next time, pick somebody bigger. Make it a challenge."

"Do you always make jokes when someone else is trying to be serious?"

Long pause. "I rented this place eight months ago with the hopes that the storefront would allow me to sell my work." I waved my hand across the room. "I've yet to sell the first piece. Making jokes helps me . . . in truth, it's the curtain I hide behind so folks like you won't see that the emperor's food taster has no clothes."

She bit her lip. "From what folks are saying, you don't wear them much anyway."

"Yeah, it's a new marketing campaign to get people to the window."

"Too bad you can't keep them there."

"Ooh . . . that cuts deep."

She walked across the room, grabbed Miss Rachel and placed her in the window. "Each piece should have a name. It'll help people identify with them. Buyers, that is." She thought a minute and pointed at Miss Rachel. *"Contentment."* She looked at me. "Because she is."

She untied the dusty $300 price tag off an existing piece and hung it over the corner of Miss Rachel's canvas. Then she carefully placed a 1 in front of the 3 and stood back, chewing on a fingernail. She tilted her head, considered it a moment, then wrote over the 3, creating an 8 in its place. She stood back. "Folks around here like to feel they are buying something of value. If you don't value your work, why should they? In New York, this would be a bargain, and"—she waved her hand across the shoppers milling along the streets—"that's where most of these folks shop when they're not"—she shaded her eyes with her hand—"fogging up your window."

She tugged on the bill of her baseball cap and disappeared around the corner. She had yet to tell me her name.

8

JUNE 1

I steadied the boat and began paddling just as a muted voice rose up from beneath the tarp: "Hey, good looking." I leaned in. "You have done this before, right?"

"Once or twice."

She shifted to one side. "That sounded like it went well."

She was smiling beneath the adrenaline rush brought on by the combination of fentanyl and Actiq. I knelt, sweat dripping off my face and nose. "Yeah, well, I never really liked Charleston anyway."

She rolled her eyes closed, then open.

"We can still turn back."

She shook her head. Her tongue was thick. "I'm with you."

I felt her feet, which, despite the seventy-five-degree heat, were cold and clammy. "How you feeling?"

She shifted uneasily. "Never better."

"Headache?"

She nodded and tried to smile. When the headaches had first started, she said it was like riding a roller coaster that never stopped while sitting next to someone who kept banging you in the head with their elbow.

Rigged with a stern-to-bow towline, the second canoe tracked behind, slipping serpentine across the water. Knotted and twisting, ancient live oaks rose up on either side and reached out across the water forming a canopy that spoke of Pat Smith's forgotten land and maybe the ghost of Osceola. Cypress stumps spiked up through the river's surface, while deadwood fell across, forming raccoon bridges and fishing-line snags. At this early point in the river's life, where she was less than fifteen feet across, portage was a necessity. At her deepest the river was a foot and her shallowest an inch, so every few minutes, I'd step out, pull both canoes across a log or sand bar, then hop back in and shove off only to hop out once again and start all over. During one three-hour stretch, I fashioned a makeshift harness and sloshed ankle-deep along the bank and river bottom.

Unlike rivers out west that cut canyons down into and through rock walls, the edges of the St. Marys ebbed and flowed depending upon rainfall—making it difficult to establish a state line within a few feet. One day the river might be ten feet wide at a given point, but throw some rain in that equation and that can widen to thirty or forty feet in a day, only to recede back to ten or expand to fifty before the next day's end. In the last few decades, home buyers and builders made sure they bought or built above the hundred-year flood line.

Once out of the swamp, the river travels through Moniac at Highway 94, then according to the map, some thirteen miles to State Road 121, but that's a lie. Whoever made the map was smoking crack. Probably more like twenty-five. Riding her is brutal, tough work and yet a beautiful, mysterious, even somewhat prehistoric passage. To miss it is to miss some of the heart of the river. Abbie knew this. That's why she'd said, "All the way from Moniac." Taking a helicopter's view north of Glen St. Mary, the river turns hard left, or due east, and runs across the northern tip of Macclenny. From there she bends north, where the winding river makes a crooked run up to Folkston—meandering some two miles for every crow mile. At Folkston, she bears hard right, and zigzags east by southeast to the coast. Crow distance from swamp to ocean is a little more than sixty miles. Total river distance is nearer 129 miles, give or take. Usually, more give than take.

But if you trace her lines, things are different. While the headwaters bubble only sixty crow miles from the ocean, she is in no hurry to get there. And while she may run under one name, she is, in actuality, four rivers. The first runs from Moniac, under Highway 121 to Stokes Bridge—maybe thirty-one miles. Think drainage ditch inside a bridge tunnel. It's narrow, overhung with trees that interlock like fingers, crisscrossed by elevated railroad trestles, crawling with frogs, hanging with Spanish moss, slithering with snakes and given the nearly impenetrable maze of pick-up-stick trees that have fallen across her, nearly impossible to paddle for very long. You can swim it, pull through it, push over it, walk around it or cut through it, but she will regulate your speed and it will not be fast. She has her own rhythm. Chances are, unless you've spent much time around here, hers is a good bit slower than yours—physically and emotionally. Her flow is unregulated, so while some corners are fast, others—given the topography—are slower. Maybe the water pools up, maybe her banks widen, maybe she has cut through the bed to the limestone and sped up, or maybe she U-turns and whips you around like a water-skier. Whatever the case, there is little consistency other than that she is moving toward the ocean. Whether you live or die matters not, but don't think her impersonal and don't doubt her. She is far more in tune with you than you are. Having cut all the way to the limestone, some of her banks are bluffs some forty feet high, others are root-webbed sand hills, while others are cow pastures whose grass and mud roll into the water. Doing so has left holes that are teeming with warmouth, perch, smallmouth bass and water moccasins. When the sun can break through the canopy, her sides are dotted with Buick-sized white sandy beaches; leaning, tin-roofed, vine-covered barns; and screen-enclosed tree houses—but trickling down the middle is a copper blanket of sweet bronze liquid that in most places is also cool.

Part two of the river runs from Stokes Bridge to Trader's Ferry—forty-four miles. Here she widens, offers stretches of paddle-ability, and runs nearly the entire length with bleached white beaches. Because she is constantly eroding her banks and floor, the ancient trees that line her inevitably fall inward. First they lean, almost bowing as she passes by, then they cross like swords in a military-dress procession, then they topple as she undercuts their roots in her way to the limestone. She ranges from a foot deep to maybe ten in a few of the deeper spots. Beneath her surface is an intricate and invisible spiderweb of branches, or arms, that pull at boats and those who wish to float her. Beyond the branches, tucked into the shadows, are white-tail deer, black bear, feral hogs, quail, turkey and horseflies with an attitude. It is also here that people have begun to populate her banks, built homes on stilts, swim in her shade, bask in her coolness, swing from ropes hung high in her towering arms, ride zip lines and litter her with beer cans, bobbers and bathing suits. From copper bronze, her color has darkened to that of iced tea. Depending upon the sun, maybe weak coffee. But don't let the color fool you. Black does not equal bad. Or evil. Her sandy bottom filters her every hundred feet. Like everything on the river, appearances can be deceiving.

Leg three runs from Trader's Ferry to the Coastal Highway, or Highway 17—a distance of thirty-six miles. From the railroad trestle at 17, the ocean is only another eighteen miles downstream, which means that tides begin to affect her. Her flow will actually reverse every six hours. Like a flushing toilet, she empties quickly and fills slowly. Her banks widen to some two to four hundred yards across. She brims with otter, beaver, water moccasins and alligators. Some ten feet in length, their heads nearly three feet long. Boat ramps, fish camps and long since rotted docks have replaced sandy beaches. Her banks now roll down into the water with pine trees and palmetto bushes making a nearly impenetrable wall. Approaching the bank is like petting a porcupine—you must pick your way in. And not quickly. Residents have sunk pilings into the bank, poured and fortified concrete walls and built getaways where they sit on the porch, sip mint juleps and listen as the river rolls by. Below, she has opened herself to recreation—motor boats haul skiers, fishermen, poachers or wildlife officers and Jet Skis buzz like hornets. Beneath them all, she has morphed once again. Here she hides her secrets and flows Starbucks black.

The final leg runs from the bridge at Highway 17, past the town of St. Marys to the Cumberland Sound where she empties into the Atlantic. Here she might reach a mile wide, maybe wider, and some forty feet deep—deep enough for the submarines at King's Bay. Her brackish water has turned cloudy brown, stinging with salt and running with dolphins, sharks, redfish and trout. Her pluff mud banks crawl with fiddler crabs, razor-edged oysters and sporadic piles of English cobblestone once used as ballast. Here, her pace quickens, swirling undertows—water tornadoes that spin beneath the surface—can pull ducks below the surface, and while she winds and meanders, don't let her crooked self fool you—her speed is deceiving.

While her landscape changes with every mile, so does her rhythm. Her cadence. And she will not let you get in a hurry. At first she slows you, allowing little more than a crawl. Once she has nursed you, she opens, allowing you to stand and walk.

When she finds you willing, she grants you open water and lets you stretch your legs. Finally, if you're worthy, and because you've lasted through the worst she could throw at you, she opens her arms, takes you into her bosom and mothers you. But she is a jealous mother. If you hesitate, if you doubt her, if you blink and take your eye off her, she will spit you out of her mouth, cast you out to sea and bury you in the deep.

Once the water hits the ocean, the sun lifts it to the clouds, only to spill it once again across the continent. In that cycle, certain molecules of water have made this journey from swamp to river to ocean thousands of times.

DOWNED TREES, stumps and beaver dams made the first five hours mostly miserable as paddling goes. The harness began cutting into my shoulders because I spent as much time out of the canoe pulling and portaging as I did inside and paddling. Abbie lay there and laughed. A little after noon, the rain let up, then stopped altogether and the sun poked a hole in the clouds. Steam burned off the water, which had begun moving slightly faster, and the heat jumped into the upper seventies. The change in barometer did strange things to animals—including snakes. They'd be looking for higher ground, which meant they'd be out of their holes and moving.

The river made a hard right turn, leaving a sandbar, so I took advantage of both the topography and the sun, beached the canoe and carried Abbie to a spot where she could soak in the sun and sink her toes in the river. She was feeling pretty good, so she sat up when I set her down.

One of the gadgets I'd bought from Gus was a little gizmo called a Jetboil, developed by high-altitude climbers. It was a self-contained, self-lighting propane unit, about the size of a coffee can, that could boil two cups of water in less than ninety seconds. I clicked it on, started peeling a hard-boiled egg and then poured the tea while Abbie licked the chocolate off a Snickers bar and fed the rest to the minnows nibbling on her toes.

She scanned the underside of the canopy, her skin white against the sun and her veins blue against the surface. "I think I remember it here."

I nodded. "This canopy runs a few more miles and then the river widens, spreads the trees and lets in the sun, warming the water."

She sniffed the air and pointed with half a Snickers. "And somewhere along here, a pasture runs down to the water's edge. Seems like I remember something about some cows."

"You do." I thumbed a fleck of eggshell off my thigh. "There's a chicken farm not too much further. Depending on the wind, we'll either get the cows or the chicken. Sort of a hit-or-miss thing."

She chewed slowly. "How long before you'll remarry?"

Abbie was far more comfortable with her not being here than I was. "What kind of a question is that?"

"Come on, this is not a news flash. You've had four years to get used to the idea."

"That doesn't mean I am."

"So?"

"So what?"

"Have you?"

"Have I what?"

"Gotten used to the idea."

"Yeah, honey. Just peachy."

"Seriously. You could live another fifty or sixty years."

"And?"

"What're you gonna do?"

"To begin with, I figured I'd start smoking and drinking like a fish to cut the time in half."

She saw she wasn't getting anywhere. A minute passed. "You should, you know." It was a statement, not a question.

I handed her a mug. "Next time, you can make your own dang tea."

She hovered above the steam. "Seriously. We need to talk about this. Now"—she batted her eyes—"here are the names of five people I think you should consider."

"I'm not talking about this with you."

"Mary Provencal. Pretty, smart, probably keep you out of trouble. But you'd have to learn how to make a better martini."

"I'm not believing this."

"Karen Whistman."

"Honey, she's married."

"Yeah, but she won't be for long. She's tall, outdoorsy, knows a thing or two about art and has more money than God."

"Would you stop it?"

"Three. Stacy Portis. A little short but always the life of the party and from what I hear, great in bed. Which"—she laughed—"she'll need to be after you've been married to me."

"You're killing me."

"Fourth. A stretch, but . . . Grace McKiver."

"Have you lost your mind?"

She pitched the remains of her Snickers in the river. "Probably, along with most everything else. Now, Grace might seem cold at first, but once you get to know her she's sincere, loyal to a fault and, thanks to a very good plastic surgeon, a goddess with her clothes off."

I watched the Snickers float like a short turd in the water. "That answers a lot."

"Lastly, Jeanne Alexander."

"I'm not listening."

"She's probably the most like me, so you'd have to unlearn very few of your bad habits."

"What bad habits?"

"Well, since you brought it up."

"I didn't. You did."

"You leave your underwear on the bathroom floor. Toilet seat too often up. You squeeze the toothpaste in the middle. Never make the bed. Hate yard work. Haven't cleaned your studio in ten years."

"That's 'cause I haven't been in there in nearly three."

She stopped and tilted her head, a practiced move. "Which brings me to my point."

"This is your father coming out in you."

"You should marry. I mean, not right away. Play the mourning widower and give it a year. Maybe eighteen months. Besides, it'll get them competing."

"Abigail."

She didn't look at me, but stared off into the trees. "You should. I hate the thought of you living alone." She licked the chocolate off her front teeth. "But more than that. You must promise me that you will sit at your easel—"

"Abbie."

"I'm serious. Promise."

"No."

"Why?"

"Because . . ."

She tapped me in the chest. "I know you. You can't keep it all bottled up in there. Sooner or later, you'll have to let it out."

"You sound like Mom."

"You're trying to change the subject."

I packed up the canoe and then scooped my arms beneath her, lifting her. She wrapped her arms around my neck. "Promise?"

I looked her in the eyes, fingers crossed. "I promise."

"Uncross those fingers and say it."

"I promise . . . I will always remember the way you burnt your first pot roast to a crisp."

"Are you finished?"

"Okay . . . I promise I'll always wish I could make the art you've always thought that I could."

She nodded. "Fair enough."

I looped the harness around me and began my snow-dog pull. She lay in the boat, staring at me. "You can, you know. It's in you."

"Can what? What's in me?"

She pointed her 800 mcg lollipop at me. "Don't start that crap with me."

I didn't have to turn around to see her windshield-wiper finger cutting the air. "Honey . . ." I stopped pulling, letting the lines fall slack. "Face the music. I fish better than I paint. I even helped your dad catch fish and he sucks. But in terms of art, other than a portrait here and there—which I'll admit, I do seem to have some talent for—I'm a hack for hire. Just look at our house. Garage to attic, it's full of stuff we can't sell."

"You're not a reject to me."

"Well, you'd be alone on that one."

The Actiq often did this. Made her chatty and defiant. Not that she needed help on the defiance part.

"Band-Aid."

A deep breath. Her adopted nickname for me. "Yes."

"Come here."

I untangled myself and sloshed backward, kneeling beside

the gunnel. She rested her head on her palm. "I've seen art in Rome, London, New York . . . even Asia." She touched my nose. "No one moves me the way you do."

Despite my dashed hopes and her continued embarrassment, that right there is the singular reason I've not burned everything I've ever painted and continued to keep my studio. Because she believed long after I'd quit.

"I love you Abigail Coleman Michaels."

"Good. Glad we settled that. Now, *mush!* It's hot in here with no breeze." I turned, lifted the straps across my shoulders and began pulling. As the tension pulled back, she said, "You know you might also consider Wendy Maxwell, her family's got that place—"

"Would you shut up and go to sleep?"

She paused and her tone changed. "Not until you set my feet on Cedar Point."

Her voice echoed with a sense of finality. I leaned into the harness, dug my feet into the sand, and the ropes cut into my shoulders.

9

The driver of the car was wearing a black hat and white gloves. I walked out wearing faded jeans—a hole in the right knee—a black T-shirt and my only sport coat—which was blue and missing a button on the right sleeve. "You think she'll notice?" I asked. The driver stared at my sleeve and shook his head but said nothing. "Great," I said, stepping into the back-seat, " 'cause I'd hate to overdress."

Pushing the door closed he said, "I doubt that will be a problem."

He drove me down King Street to South Battery and stopped before an imposing three-story crowded with people. Classic Charleston. All the women wore pumps and pearls while all the men were wearing the same brand of four-eye, lace-up leather shoes, the same shade of khakis, same style of blue button-down and slightly varied versions of striped ties.

I stepped out of the car and nearly choked on my own tongue. To my left, the sidewalk looked dark, desolate and inviting. I stared up at the porch, which held up the four huge columns in front of the house. She stood at the banner, engaged in conversation, looking at me.

I straightened my coat and the driver whispered behind me, "Don't worry, sir. Most of them are just compensating. If the story about you, and what you did for Miss Coleman, is true, you'll be fine."

"And if it's not?"

He studied the scabbing cut across my right middle knuckle and the purple under and around my left eye. "I imagine it is."

"Thanks."

I climbed the stairs into the aroma of designer perfumes married to Bermuda aftershaves. I'd never seen more diamonds in my life. Ears, neck, fingers. If these people were compensating, they had spent some money doing it. Mink, cashmere, camel hair and starched oxford broadcloth created the texture where high-pitched laughter echoed above the low hum of conversation.

She slid through the crowd like water. "Thanks for coming."

"You know all these people?"

"Most." She looped her arm in mine. "Come on, I want to introduce you."

We walked through the front door, into a grand entry where five layers of trim accented the fourteen-foot ceilings and the crystal chandelier looked to weigh a ton. Along one wall a tall man in a white coat dipped a ladle into a silver punch bowl and filled china teacups with something that smelled of apple cider, cinnamon, clove and citrus. He offered me a cup, "Suh?"

"No thanks."

Abbie took the cup from him and said, "Thanks, George." She offered it to me. "It's wassail. I made it."

I sipped it. "Interesting, but . . . but good."

She set the cup down, turned right and walked into a den where the firelight was glowing off flush faces and dark mahogany. A white-haired, distinguished, handsome man in a striped suit stood surrounded by forty or fifty people. Some swirled brandy, others sipped Chardonnay, all held a glass. He was the epicenter of attention and conversation. When the crowd parted to make way for her, which meant us, I recognized him. He was broader than I had anticipated and sounded taller on TV.

She led me forward, looping her other arm through his. Looking back, that was the moment I joined the tug-of-war. And he sensed it. "Daddy, I'd like you to meet Doss Michaels."

I extended my hand. "Senator, sir."

His handshake was firm, practiced and cold, and his cuff link was sharp and pointy. He had sized me up before our hands touched. "So, I have you to thank for saving my daughter."

"No, sir. Given a few more minutes, I think she could have taken him."

He smiled. "Well spoken. Well spoken." The crowd laughed and then quieted. He addressed them. "Everyone, may I introduce Doss Michaels to you? A man I have just met and yet to whom I am forever indebted following the events of last week." They clapped and made me wish I could jump through a trap door. She looped her left hand back through mine, interlocking our fingers, and spoke to all the women who'd gathered about—waving her right index finger like a windshield wiper through the air. "Not yet, ladies. He's mine, you can just wait your turn."

I had never seen one person more comfortable with and more in command of her surroundings. She had a gift. She led me outside to the porch and around another table where a lady was serving okra soup. Below us, near the center of the yard, two men stood over an open fire and roasted oysters. The backyard was well lit and looked like an English garden. The perimeter was an eight-foot-tall hedge that had been trimmed at perfect ninety-degree angles. She poured me a lemonade and said, "Here, drink this. It'll take the edge off." I sipped while she reached high and rubbed her fingers on a plant hanging above her. She sniffed them and then held them below my nose. It reminded me of roses.

"That's a funny-looking rose."

She laughed. "That's 'cause it's not. It's a rose-scented geranium."

"Are you one of those people who really knows plants? Green thumb and all that?"

She pointed across the backyard. "Would you like to see my garden?"

"If it'll get me away from all these people, I'll help you dig in it."

We walked through the maze that was her garden while she pointed, named and explained. "That's pittosporum . . . that's my rose garden . . . twenty-seven different kinds . . . this is my citrus. Eighteen different trees from Dancy tangerines to satsumas to Duncan grapefruit." We turned another corner. "That's a loquat tree."

"A what-quat?"

Her laugh melted me. "Loquat."

It was an odd-looking little fruit—round and maybe half the size of an egg. I picked one off a limb and smelled it. "It reminds me of those little things we used to throw at cars when I was a kid."

"You sure those weren't kumquats?"

"Well . . . it was some sort of quat."

She rolled it in her palm. "They're also called Japanese plums. You can't buy them in a store 'cause they have no shelf life, but they're sweet. You had one when you came in."

"When?"

"Loquat liqueur. It's in the wassail."

"Where do you get it?"

"You don't. You make it."

My suspicion was growing. "You're one of those people, aren't you?"

"I don't know," she said smiling. "What kind of person is that?"

"Martha Stewart meets Julia Child. You probably sleep two hours a night and make your own wrapping paper at Christmas."

She turned away, smirking. "What's wrong with making your own paper?"

I looked back toward the house and the growing crowd of people. "You're good at this."

She snapped a dark red rose off a bush and slid the end of it into my coat pocket. "I've had a lot of practice." She waved to an elegant older woman across the yard. "Born into it. Then adopted by it." She smoothed my jacket collar and stepped closer, into my personal space. "By the way . . . it's Abbie. But"—she waved her hand across the crowd—"most of these folks call me Abbie Eliot."

I sipped and swallowed, letting the lemonade warm my throat. "I spent some time at the library this week. You . . ." She'd been written about in every magazine and paper you could mention.

"Don't believe everything you read."

"Which parts do I believe?"

She smiled, pulled on my hand and led me back across the grass. "You'll have to ask me that."

I followed. Her in one hand, the lemonade in the other. "Okay."

I spent the evening walking in her wake, growing addicted to the smell of her perfume and the gentle pull of her touch.

Whether by the smell of her or the taste of that lemonade, I grew more intoxicated by the minute.

After she'd introduced me to twenty-five people whose names I couldn't and wouldn't remember, she led me across to the other, grassier side of the yard where tents were set up and people were nibbling on appetizers. She eyed the buffet. "You feel like grazing?"

I lifted a near-empty glass. "Yeah, my lips are feeling fat. I need something to soak up the lemonade."

We filled a single plate and then sat alone on a bench in a darkened corner of the yard, overlooking the party. With no utensils in sight, I asked, "What do we eat with?"

She fingered a chicken leg and bit into it, talking with her mouth half full. "Fingers."

I lifted a chicken leg and the barbecue sauce dripped down my fingers. "Doesn't make sense to cover the women in diamonds and the tables in white linen but leave Charleston's finest sucking on their fingers."

"Welcome to Charleston."

"By the way"—I chewed, mouth full, the corners covered in sauce—"I owe you a commission."

Another bite. "Huh?"

"A lady came in this week and actually bought Miss Rachel. Asked me if I'd take seventeen hundred."

"What'd you say?"

"I asked her if she wanted me to gift wrap it."

She laughed. "So you paid rent this month?" I nodded, brown smear spreading across my face. "Good, it's nice to know I'll be able to find you and won't have to play stupid, snooping around the art school again."

"That how you found me the first time?"

She waved at someone across the yard and then stared out

across the crowd. "People will tell you most anything if you know how to ask the right questions."

"In your case, I'd say it had less to do with how you asked, and more to do with the fact that you asked at all."

She looked at me, her voice growing soft. "Doss Michaels, you flirting with me?"

"That bad, huh?"

She shrugged. "I don't know. Refreshing, actually."

"I thought it sounded a bit rehearsed. Sort of like I rushed it."

She set my glass on the grass, out of reach. "I'm cutting you off. No more lemonade for you."

My tongue felt thick and the sides of my lips were tingly. "Good idea." An iron gate marked the corner of the backyard and an exit for me. "You feel like walking?"

"You had enough culture for one night?"

"I'm not too big on parties. Never know how to act."

She hooked her arm inside mine and led me through the gate. "Can you keep a secret?"

"Probably not."

"That's why they make the lemonade."

We walked across South Battery, through White Point Gardens and onto the high battery overlooking the split of the Cooper and Ashley rivers. Named after Lord Anthony Ashley Cooper, the twin rivers once served as the cotton highway of the Confederate South. Plantations floated their white gold downriver on barges, parked them in Colonial Lake—just a few blocks away—and waited on a buyer and export to the rest of the world. Which explains why most felt the Atlantic Ocean started at their doorstep.

The breeze was cool so I slipped my jacket over her shoulders. A well-lit yacht motored inland, returning to the marina.

I waved my hand across the wake, making small talk. "A lot of history has passed through these waters."

She considered that a moment. "Tell me about you."

Her tone caught me. The playful woman at the party had been replaced by a serious, real and curious girl. I dangled my feet off the concrete wall. "So much for small talk, huh?" She shrugged. "I grew up on a . . . a river south of here. A paddle in one hand, pencil or paintbrush in the other." I waved my finger like a wand over the landscape around us. "This is beautiful, but Charleston, for me, can't hold a candle to the St. Marys. She's . . . well . . ." Feeling foolish, I trailed off.

"What brought you here?"

"Art scholarship."

"How's that going?"

"Not sure. I don't know if I'm learning how to make better art or forgetting that I once could." She raised an eyebrow. "I used to think it was pretty simple. Being here, different teachers, different motives, it's gotten complicated. Confusing. I'm not sure I look at a canvas the way I once did."

"But your stuff is selling."

"Well, let's be honest. One piece sold. Thanks to you, but more importantly, I don't make art simply to sell it."

She stared at me. "But you're selling it."

"Sure, I hope it sells like hotcakes, but that's not what I'm thinking about while I'm making it."

"So you're an idealist." While she leaned against the concrete wall, I sat further back, dangling my feet. This placed her just inches in front of me. Lights from the marina lit the right side of her face, highlighting the lines of her cheek and the short wisps of hair just above her ear. My eyes traced the contour of her ear, the softness of her hair, then glided along the rim of her cheek, skating between the shadow of her eyelashes and the recess of her cheek. Moonlight bounced off the ripples of the water where it bled seamlessly into the edges of her face. In the distance, Fort Sumter sat twinkling between the rim of her lips and the lines of her nose.

"I was fourteen when my mom's car slid off the road, broadsiding a concrete barrier. She was driving back from the store on bald tires in a light rain. On the front seat the paramedics found new paints and a roll of canvas. After the burial, I went home, lined up each of my inhalers on the fence and shot them with a stolen shotgun. Then I slipped beneath the cover of the river and disappeared. I had a lot of questions I couldn't answer and was tired of living inside a plastic bag. For an entire summer, I paddled from the swamp to the ocean. No medicine. If I couldn't breathe, I wouldn't. I stole enough to eat and learned to duck and dodge people who asked too many questions. Sometimes early in the morning or late at night, when the mosquitoes hatched and the mist rose off the river, I'd lay on my stomach, my nose inches from the water, and squint my eyes trying to catch a glimpse of Momma's God in the river."

She interrupted me with a smile. "And if you found Him?"

"I was going to grab Him around the neck and choke Him until He answered me."

"Did He?"

"If He did, I never heard Him. 'Course, it's hard to hear when you're hurting." I shrugged. "I turned fifteen, swam to the surface and convinced enough folks in the trailer park to forge enough papers to help me finish school. Mom would have wanted that. At least that's what I told myself. Besides, the school couldn't argue with what I could do with a brush. It was somewhere in there I first remember hearing the term *realist*. I didn't even really know what that was. I used to tell them, ' 'Course it's real. I painted it.' "

"While technically my work was good, it was also devoid of emotion. Hollow. Even I could see that. That river summer had changed me. I had learned how to hold my breath. To live half alive because it kept the pain away."

"Pain of what?"

"The present. Beyond all the coughing, sputtering and hacking, in between the moments when the light around the edges of my eyes narrowed and the tunnel closed in, I have held on to the inkling that I was made to breathe. That my lungs actually serve a purpose other than suffocating me. All they need is a reason.

"My mom helped me see beauty when I thought there was none. She'd steal me away to the river and then dip me in the sunlight as it dripped through a weeping willow. Then she'd set me in front of the canvas, hold my hand in hers, tell me to close my eyes and then rub my fingertips across the texture of the canvas. 'Doss,' she'd say, 'God is in the details.' I told her, 'Momma, that may be but'—I'd touch her temple or point to the bruises on her neck—'he ain't no place else.' "

"I'd like to have met her."

"I can take you to her grave."

"I'm sorry."

"Me, too." A minute passed.

"And your dad?"

I shrugged. "Word around the trailer was that my mom was 'easy,' so I'm not quite sure if the guy who lived with us was my dad. I haven't seen him since before the funeral."

She stared at me, letting the sound of the wake from the yacht roll across the top of the river and spill across the rocks. "So when you paint, you're painting for your mom?"

Between her father's power and her own success, everybody wanted something from Abbie. Given this, she was guarded.

Not unkind, not insincere, but careful. It didn't take a genius to see there was more behind her question.

I shook my head. "I grew up in . . . in pieces. Mom saw this and it hurt her. Oil and canvas were her gifts to me. And sometimes, even if for the briefest of moments, they were the glue that put me back together. I can't explain that. It just did."

"An aspirin for your anger?" Another question.

"Anger?"

"I watched you fight a man twice your size."

I nodded. "Yes, sometimes I become angry. But then there are moments when I lose track of time and when I look up and the canvas is staring back at me."

My tone softened. "It's a welling-up. I can't *not* do it." I tapped the side of my head. "When God wired my brain to my mouth, I think he might have crossed a wire. What's supposed to go to my tongue, runs out my fingers. I think and my fingers move. So I paint." I stared at my hands, trying to poke fun at myself. "If you want to know what I think, talk to the hands." She rolled her eyes. "I came here, art school, thinking they knew more than I. That they could teach me more than some battered woman along the river." I shook my head. "They're just painting by numbers." She said nothing. "But . . . I'm also a realist and I'd like to graduate, so I'm keeping my mouth shut." I put my hand on her shoulder, then realized I had and pulled it back. "It felt good to sell that piece to that lady. The thought that she might hang it where it can be seen fills my need." I picked a pebble off the wall and tried to skip it across the water.

After a moment she asked, "What's the need?"

I shrugged. "Take a deep breath."

She frowned.

"Go ahead. Take as deep a breath as your lungs will allow."

She inhaled deeply.

"Now hold it."

Thirty seconds passed.

"Keep holding it."

Her face began to turn red. At a minute she let it out and sucked in a long breath.

I nodded. "That's the need."

10

JUNE 1, EVENING

We slid onto the beach around dark. I checked the GPS. "Distance traveled" read 9.6 miles. Not good. I needed to rethink how we did this. I could travel half again as fast with only one canoe. Problem was, we needed that second one to make it to the ocean. I would just have to walk and paddle faster, which was going to be difficult given that I was out of practice and out of shape.

I spread a bed on the beach for Abbie, propped her up and then started searching for wood. I built a small fire to warm us and fend off the mosquitoes and gnats. Night on the river can be tricky. It's Africa-hot during the day, but mountain-cool at night beneath the trees.

Riding in the canoe had worn her down. A lot. She closed her eyes and lay perfectly still. Around nine, she said, "You need to eat something." Her mouth was cottony dry and her breath had a weird metallic smell.

The thought hadn't crossed my mind. "I'm not too hungry." I held a mug to her lips and she sipped.

"You just pulled two canoes and me ten miles down this river." I straddled a log, pulled the lid on a can of peaches and ate slowly. She opened one eye. "That's not going to cut it."

I finished the peaches, zipped open the tent and lifted her

slowly off the beach. I laid her inside, then boiled water in the Jetboil. While it cooled, I zipped us inside, then slowly slid off her clothes. She whispered, "You're getting good at this."

"Practice." Her fentanyl patch needed changing so I peeled off the old, swabbed the skin on her arm, dried it and applied a new one. I slowly wiped down her arms and legs, toweled her off, slipped her head and arms through a T-shirt and zipped her inside a single-layered fleece bag. In the last several months, she'd quit sleeping in anything that placed pressure on her skin—said it felt like it was cutting into her. I tied the scarf loosely around her head and pointed. "I'll be outside." She squeezed my hand and turned on her side.

I stoked the fire, dragged a dead limb from behind some palmetto bushes, laid it across the fire and then sat on a log, swatting mosquitoes and counting what few stars I could see through the canopy. An hour later, I heard a stick crack. Having spent enough time in the woods, I could hear the difference between a small twig under the foot of a squirrel and something larger, broken under the weight of a larger foot. This far out in the boonies, it wasn't uncommon to bump into feral hogs, deer, armadillos, raccoons, wild dogs, even a bear, so I slung the shotgun and scanned the bushes with the flashlight. When I saw nothing, no two eyes staring back at me, I worked the slide action on the shotgun—loading the number 8 birdshot into the chamber—thinking the sound alone might deter something looking for a meal. I had loaded the first round birdshot, the second two as buckshot and the last two as rifled slugs. My thought process was deter, stop and kill. Number 8 would kill most anything in these woods, if close enough, as would the buckshot. The slugs were insurance because they'd pass through most anything—like an engine block. Nothing moved so I clicked the safety back on and set the shotgun beside me.

I grew up in or around the woods so I'd grown accustomed to the sights, smells and sounds. Especially the sounds, since my nose has never been that reliable. While it may get quiet at night, it is seldom silent. Birds, crickets, frogs, gators, dogs, you name it. And often they will feed off each other. Little sounds here and there that create some sort of animal-chain reaction. If one chirps or croaks, often the others will assume it's okay to do the same. The reverse is true as well. If one goes silent, the others will fall silent long enough to figure out why. I sat back down on that log and noticed how deathly quiet the woods had become.

I started thinking about old movies. Especially those scenes in which some character named Festus, Stumpy or Lefty scratches the back of his neck and says, "I can't see them, but I got a notion we're being watched." Usually, he's right. Because the next scene we see is filled with Indians wearing war paint.

I can't explain it, but I had that feeling. I went over it in my mind: I heard a stick crack. Under weight. Probably more than a squirrel or raccoon. Also, the sound appeared muffled. Deer and hog feet don't do that 'cause they're hard. But people feet and bear paws do. To be honest, I wasn't too concerned about bears. Black bears are more curious than dangerous. But it's that other possibility that had the hair up on my neck.

I unzipped the tent, lifted Abbie—still in her sleeping bag— off her mat and pressed my finger to her lips. "Shhh." She hung her arms around my neck. I looped my arm through the Pelican case lanyard and then the sling of the shotgun and slipped down the bank out of the fire's reflection. I crossed the river—ankle-deep—and walked up a sandy beach on the Florida side. Abbie whispered, "What's wrong?"

I scanned the river, listening. "Not sure."

I set her down on the bank beneath a few overhanging

trees. Twenty minutes passed. While we waited, I found myself plotting tomorrow's path in my mind, thinking about where we could lunch and where we might take on more water. Where we might encounter people, where we could hide. While the river was cleaner than most, and you could drink it if you had to, I tried not to given the runoff. Too many pesticides I couldn't see and too much manure I didn't want to risk tasting. Artesian wells fitted with hand pumps dotted the riverbanks if you knew where to look.

I was about two seconds from carrying Abbie back to the tent when the first man appeared in the river. He was tall, skinny, barefooted, wore cutoff jeans and a T-shirt with no sleeves. He had stepped out from behind some trees, dipped his feet into the river and walked slowly to the canoes. He picked his feet up slowly, and then slipped them back in the water without a sound. Deer walk the same way when they don't want to be noticed. A second man appeared behind him and walked directly to the tent with a third man close on his heels. The first man picked through the canoes while the second and third tore the tent apart. I could only hear snippets. They whispered in harsh tones.

The two at the tent got in a shoving match and then threw the whole mess—tent, my sleeping bag, our clothes and everything else I had stowed—into the fire. The flame-retardant tent smothered the fire, filling the campsite with smoke, causing more shoving and all three to cough. Finally, the heat won. The flames caught, climbed chest-high and lit the riverbank.

By the time the smoke cleared, the quiet man picking through the canoes had packed most everything we had into one canoe and began pulling it back upriver. A hundred yards or so later, he pulled it up the riverbank and slid it into the trees. For several minutes I could hear him sliding it through the

CHARLES MARTIN

woods. The fire roared and crackled, showering the bank in heat and light. The two that remained were getting more aggravated. Their faces glowed golden. I saw enough to know I didn't like them but not enough to pick them out of a lineup.

We edged back under the trees. I placed my finger on Abbie's lips again and lay down beside her, staring through the grass toward our campsite. Growing angrier, the two that remained gathered up everything they didn't want and threw it in the campfire turned bonfire. The flames were now fifteen feet high and licking the underside of the tree limbs. They slung whatever else remained over their shoulders and began carrying it back across the river, following the lone man who'd just stolen our canoe. That left one canoe and little else.

I placed my hand on the shotgun. Abbie put her hand on mine and said, "Everything over there is replaceable. You're not."

11

With her parents' party still in high gear, Abbie hopped off the concrete wall, tucked her arm inside mine and said, "How much do you know about Charleston?"

"I know how to get to work, school and a few places where the fish occasionally bite."

She raised both eyebrows and shook her head. "That won't do. Won't do at all."

The roads in Charleston are wide—designed that way in 1680 to avoid the congestion typical of London's narrow streets. So we walked up East Bay, along Rainbow Row, took a left on Elliott to Church and down Cabbage Row. She pointed up and down the street. "You ever seen *Porgy and Bess*?" I shook my head. "Well, when you do, *this* is Catfish Row."

We crossed over to the Dock Street Theater. "This is where I learned to stand in front of a bunch of strangers." She smiled. "And like it." She led me a few doors down to the Pirates' House built out of blue granite quarried in Bermuda. "Rumor has it," she said, pointing at her feet, "there are secret tunnels leading from beneath the house all the way to the wharf."

"You believe the rumors?"

She nodded.

"How come?"

She looked left, then right and leaned in closer. " 'Cause I've been in the tunnels."

We U-turned and then righted on Chalmers—Charleston's longest remaining cobblestone street. British ships in the East India Trade Company used England's cobblestones as ballast in their transatlantic voyage. Landing here and filling her stores with cotton, rice or lumber meant she left us her rocks. Frugal colonists used them to pave the streets, filling in the cracks with crushed oyster shell that, due to its high lime content, naturally filtered the runoff. Turning left on Meeting, we passed under the Four Corners of Law—so named after the four buildings that line each corner: the federal courthouse and post office, the county courthouse, City Hall and St. Michael's Episcopal Church. After another right on Broad, she steered left on King—culminating our walk through and around the visual library of architecture that is Charleston. Abbie explained, "Charleston has the largest number of original eighteenth- and nineteenth-century homes in the country. In the renaissance that resulted after Hurricane Hugo, a fever spread. Everybody wanted a piece, sending home prices skyrocketing to nearly a thousand dollars a square foot. Rarely does someone post a for-sale sign in the front yard. They aren't needed. The owner merely mentions to a friend or realtor that they are thinking about selling and before day's end they'd have answered eight or ten calls. Bidding wars are not uncommon. Most homes around here are what they call the Charleston single house. One room wide, with its narrow end bordering the street. The porches—or piazzas—often run the length of the house, and face south or southwest to catch the prevailing sea breeze. Colonists learned long ago it's better to plan for the long, oppressively hot summers than the brief winters." Abbie knew more about Charleston in five minutes than I knew at all. She ducked in one alley to show me a bricked herringbone drive-way. At another, an original Philip Simmons ironwork, or a garden growing something unique: "That wisteria is thought to be a hundred and fifty years old." I'd studied art most of my life, but Abbie's eye was as developed, if not more so, than mine. She saw beauty in the smallest of details. At another gate, she leaned over and pointed up. "That's called Kiss Me at the Gate or Breath of Spring." It slid through her fingers. "It'll grow six to eight feet, and its blossoms dangle, but mostly its known for its fragrance."

I was amazed. "How do you know all this?"

"I'm a Charleston girl." She smiled. "We're raised to know this stuff."

It was after midnight and we had come full circle, just a few blocks from her house. She looked at me. "You tired?"

I shook my head. "No, I think the walk did me good. I don't know what you people put in that lemonade but it ought to come with a warning."

She laughed, grabbed my hand and we walk-jogged a few blocks back toward the water. Pulling me along she said, "They close at one, so we might get there in time."

"Who closes at one?"

The streets were quiet, lit by the occasional passing car or gas streetlamp. A couple of cats fought over a Dumpster and somewhere in the distance a high-pitched dog bark was fol-lowed by a low-pitched response. We ran back out onto Rain-bow Row and crossed over to a corner liquor store. She pushed open the door, where we found an elderly black gentleman wearing a crimson sweater-vest. He sat behind a counter, one long leg extending beyond the counter, a penguin wingtip tap-ping in rhythm to the jazz coming out of the solid-state radio above him. One eye was cloudy but his beard and mustache were trimmed and his pink shirt had been pressed and starched. Abbie crossed the floor and he stood, beaming. "Must be some party if they sent you shopping at this time of night."

She pulled my hand. "Mr. Jake, this is my friend Doss Michaels."

He looked at me through his one good eye, sizing me up. Abbie turned to me. "Mr. Jake used to work at the theater. He taught me how to dance."

He laughed an easy laugh but never took his eyes off me. He was quiet a minute then extended his hand. "You that boy I heer'd about the other night that helped Miss Abbie?"

I nodded. "I am."

He waved his hand across the store. "Then anything you want is yours."

She stepped closer and wrapped an arm around his waist. "Mr. Jake, I wanted to show Doss the cellar."

He walked around the corner, pulled on a recessed handle at the floor level and lifted a large door. She flicked a light switch and the three of us descended some old wooden steps into the basement.

It was cool, and some water dripped somewhere. From what I could tell, the basement had been made entirely of large, hand-cut bricks. Mr. Jake explained, "This here is one of the tunnels out of the original old city of Charleston." He waved his hand across the room like a buzzing bee. "They runned the len'th of the city. During Hugo, they filled up with ocean water . . . that flushed out all the rats." He laughed again, something he did a lot of. "Some have collapsed. Some remain. Few know about them."

I ran my hand along the wall and listened. He continued, "When I was a kid, I used to come in through a city drainage pipe out near the wharf, walk a couple of blocks through these tunnels with a candle in my hand and pop up inside the theater. They wouldn't let me in the front door, so I come up underneath. I've seen more shows there than . . . anyone living I s'pose."

Abbie turned toward me. "Mr. Jake is being modest. He started his acting career at Dock Street, then took it to New York where he starred in more than one on and off Broadway show."

He nodded, remembering. She grabbed his hand. "Mr. Jake, you still remember our first dance?" She kicked off her shoes and turned to me. "I was six. Dock Street needed a fill-in and doing so involved a very complicated number with Mr. Jake." I leaned back against the wall while Abbie led and Mr. Jake remembered. His heels scuffed the brick floor taking two steps while the man in his memory took one. His face told me everything I needed to know.

They finished, his breathing was heavy but his smile had grown. She stood on her toes, kissed him on the cheek and said, "Mr. Jake, you're still the best."

"Miss Abbie"—he pulled a handkerchief from his back pocket, shook it loose and wiped his brow and neck—"you do an old man good."

We climbed out of the basement and stepped out of the liquor store underneath a single streetlight. Returning home, she talked more about the homes we passed, their history and those who owned them. I listened, walked off the buzz and felt something strange. I had spent my life swimming between the islands inside myself but had never seen one from another. That night, I stared across the ocean in me and saw, for the first time, a distant shore.

12

We passed the night on the beach beneath a crepe myrtle. Abbie laid her head on my lap and slept in fits while I listened, thought back through the last four years and grew angrier. Watching three idiots rifle through our life was, in football terms, piling on. I was downright pissed. She mumbled, talked in garbled sentences and her arms and legs twitched in short violent strokes. Given the pain, she'd not known deep sleep in months. Maybe a year. She floated in and out of consciousness—resting just beneath the surface. It was like watching someone who slept with one eye open.

I ran my fingers down her temple, ear, neck and along her shoulder. The shadows around her eyes were dark and sockets sunk deep. Her fingers trembled. I cupped them inside mine and tucked them beneath her chin.

She'd hoped for so much, so many times and for so long but each scan, each new devastating report had chipped away at her. Doctors told me that the restlessness was a function of the illness—the deterioration of her central nervous system, the medicines that poisoned her. I think there was more to it. Deep down, Abbie knew that if she let her guard down she'd never wake up.

I'm a sucker for the Rocky movies. I've watched each some twenty times. I can't explain that other than there's just something about a man who refuses to go down. Who stands toe to toe, time and time again and says, *I am*. Don't take that the wrong way. I'm no Rocky. Hardly. But my Abbie is. Look at her. Here lies the most beautiful, most precious, most magnificent woman on the planet who, despite the baggy skin and that little voice sitting on her shoulder telling her she's not even a shadow of her former self, is still swinging. Still throwing blows. Still reaching deep.

In the weeks and months to come, people will look at what I've done and ask me why. Why'd I do it? I'm not sure I can put that into words. If they have to ask, then they really won't understand the answer. At least, an answer they can accept or will understand.

Nobody fights forever, so I prepared myself for two battles. The first was fighting alongside her. We've done that. As well as two can. But as the years have ticked by, I've seen a second front coming—and it's the tougher of the two. Abbie might still be swinging but she was beat. To be honest, I think she was still in the ring fighting, simply for me. Lately, the thing that had been keeping me up nights was wondering what would happen if I told her that she could let her guard down—that she could stop fighting. What if she was just waiting on me?

WHEN SUNRISE FINALLY BROKE through the treetops, I was ready to shoot somebody. She woke, lifted her head off my lap, rubbed the sleep out of her eyes and said, "How you doing?" I turned downriver, thumbed away the tears, my right index finger tapping the trigger guard of the shotgun. She raised an eyebrow. "That well, huh?"

She sat up. "Don't let them rob us of this. Got it?" See what I mean?

"Wait here while I go see what's left." I slipped down into the river and headed back to the campsite.

My reconnaissance didn't take long. They'd thrown everything into the fire. The fire must have been hot because only ashes littered the riverbank. The second canoe was empty but it would float. In short, we had no food, no shelter, and no GPS. Abbie had her sleeping bag and the T-shirt she was wearing but nothing else. I had the long-sleeved shirt I was wearing, the shorts I had on, a pair of Tevas, a shotgun, a revolver and the Pelican case. None of which we could eat or drink.

We had to get going.

I pulled the mango-colored canoe back down to Abbie, laid her in the middle and said, "In a few miles, we'll start coming upon some cabins and that . . . resort. Maybe we can find a few things there."

She smirked. "Resort, huh? I should fit right in."

The Bare Bottom Resort was a nudist colony populated by all manner of society—from the older and more comfortable to the younger and more experimental. They usually stayed back from the river and didn't draw attention, but if you didn't know what to expect, you might find yourself surprised.

She tapped me in the chest pocket and raised her eyebrows. "What're we checking off today?"

"Honey, we're going to try and find some water and, if we're lucky, some clothes for you."

She slipped her leg outside the zipper of her sleeping bag. Several small bruises polka-dotted her thigh. "Cheer up . . . It's not every day you get to paddle your favorite river with a naked woman."

"Good point."

I reached behind my seat for the map case, but it, too, was gone. I patted my chest hoping to hear the rustle of the plastic bag. No rustle.

She read it on my face. "That too, huh?" I nodded. The sides of her lips turned up. "I think I can remember."

It was a familiar place. I scratched my head. When everything is gone, what remains?

I hadn't been paddling twenty minutes when I pushed the bow of the canoe through some overhanging limbs and pulled through into a deep pool on the other side. The bank rose twenty feet on either side, nearly straight up. Downed trees formed a spaghetti junction so I stepped out, threw my arms through the straps and leaned into their weight. It was like walking on a beaver dam for a hundred yards. With every step, I'd break through one layer of twigs and sticks, only to be temporarily stopped by another layer submerged between the surface. I pulled on the limbs, ducked below others and stepped over still others. The problem was not me but the canoe—and not breaking every one of Abbie's ribs. I was pulling the canoe over a log, sweat pouring off my face, my hands cut and bleeding, and Abbie's hand came up over the edge. She was starting to laugh. "Honey?"

I set my feet and pulled. Then set them again and pulled harder. Finally, the canoe slid over the log and glided across the water about four feet until it hit another log. Standing hurt. "Yes?"

"When we get home, let's get this thing serviced. I think the shocks on this baby are shot."

"I'll take that under advisement."

"Good." She lay back down. "Wake me when we get out of this mess."

I walked around to the bow, grabbed the ropes again and stared at the river in front of us. There were another fifty such trees—horizontal hurdles—just within eyesight. When Abbie had said all the way from Moniac, this is what she meant. The impossible part where there is no rhythm other than some off-beat thing that only the river hears. Here, the river owns you. It breaks you down, holds you at its mercy and you don't stand a chance. It is here that she stops you. Makes you look around. Forces you to measure . . . and be measured.

Forearm-thick muscadine vines, starting on opposite banks, had climbed up the live oak trunks and then crossed over the river using the limbs as a trellis. Having met in the middle, they interlocked, wove together and created a patchwork through which little sunlight passed but, come September, would hang thick with grapes. Currently, they were thick with leaves and little green flowers and crawling with lizards.

The vines often exceed a hundred feet in length and flourish in warm and humid conditions where the soil is sandy. Hence, the river. The tough-skinned, five-seeded grapes grow to two inches in diameter and range in color from greenish bronze to bronze, to pinkish red, purple and almost black.

When they ripen, folks will lay a tarp across the ground and shake the vine. Sugar content of the grapes can reach twenty-five percent, so they'll make good jellies and jams, but down here the preferred use is wine.

I slid over a log, heaved on the canoe and it slid over and down, resting in the water. I was spent. I leaned on the bow, gorging on air. Somewhere behind me, I heard a hammer cock.

A broken, raspy voice—thick with mucus—broke the stillness. "You ain't got a lick o' sense."

I turned and stood nose to barrel with the business end of an old rusty shotgun that looked about five feet long. Behind it stood the most hideous woman I'd ever laid eyes on. Toothless gums, mouth half full of snuff, the brim of her hat was pushed up flat over her forehead where it touched the crown, and her hands were gnarled and her fingers crooked in all the wrong places. She wasn't white or black but some faded shade between. Her face was covered in freckles and the top half of her right ear was missing. She wore denim overalls, a tattered denim shirt and knee-high rubber boots. She slid the barrel off center and sized me up. Now if she pulled the trigger, she'd just blow off the right side of my head rather than the whole thing. Her left eye was clouded over and a large cataract had dimmed her pupil. She closed her mouth, pushed all the spit to one side, then pursed her lips and shot it in a practiced stream out the side of her mouth. Over to the right, some fifteen feet away, a scratchy noise caught her attention. With swiftness, she swung, aimed and pressed the trigger. Four feet of flame rose out of the barrel and somewhere across the river, a rodent with a long tail caught the entire load and was launched airborne in a hundred disconnected pieces. She ejected the shell, slid another in and slammed the receiver shut. Eyes narrowed, she studied me and the canoe. The blast had brought Abbie upright and bright-eyed. The woman pointed the barrel down and raised one eyebrow. She shook her head. "Rats! They gnawin' at my vines. I don't like that."

Abbie nodded. "I see that."

The woman waved the barrel at me. "You with him?"

Abbie pointed at me. "He promised me an Alaskan cruise,

you know one of those whale-watching deals, and . . . this is what I get."

The woman broke the receiver open, hung the shotgun across her arm like a boomerang and laughed. She spat a dark stream out into the river. "I like you."

Abbie shrugged. "Gee, that is sure better than the alternative."

The woman laughed again. The mucus hung on her vocal cords and made me gag just listening to it. "What you doing with him?"

"He's my husband."

She waved the bent barrel toward me. "He's an idiot."

"You know, my dad has been telling me that for fourteen years."

The woman laughed a hyena-howl that rose up through the trees. The force of the laugh dislodged the tickler in her throat. She cornered it with her tongue, cocked her cheeks and rocketed the oyster-sized loogie out over the river. "I like you."

Abbie followed the arc of the spittle. "I'm glad we've established that." When the spit landed, the fish nibbled at it, popping the water with suction.

The woman walked down into the water and waded up next to the canoe. She stood waist-deep, eye to eye with Abbie. Swaying to one side, she said, "You sick?"

Abbie nodded. "Yes, ma'am."

"What's wrong with you?"

"Well . . ." Abbie looked at me and shrugged. Then she did the knock-on-wood thing on her head. "I've got this thing in my head that's growing. Seems to have a mind of its own."

The woman tongued an enormous wad of snuff from one cheek to another. "What's gonna happen?"

"Well, according to the doctors, it's kind of like having a miniature bomb in my head."

"When's it gonna go off?"

"That's the question."

The woman pulled on Abbie's arm, edging her closer to Abbie's head. She studied her face and neck. "Don't see nothing."

"Me either, but take my word for it." Abbie smoothed the scarf. "There's something in here."

"Well, what happens when it blows up?"

Abbie smiled. "That's sort of a good news–bad news sort of thing. The good news is that it won't hurt anymore."

The woman rested the shotgun on her right shoulder. "And the bad news?"

Abbie pointed at me. "He gets to marry one of my rich friends."

The woman slammed the shotgun closed and waved it at me, nodding. "It's always about the money, ain't it? Son of a—"

Abbie put her hand on the woman's shoulder. "It's okay. Really."

Evidently, she heard another rustle on the far beach because she swung one hundred and eighty degrees and spewed another four feet of flame out the barrel. This one didn't so much go airborne as it just disintegrated, leaving a red stain on the beach. The woman nodded and spat. She broke the receiver, ejecting the shell, and thumbed in a third round, hanging the gun back across her right arm. She sniffed the air then turned back to Abbie. "You need help with him?"

Abbie shook her head. "No . . . I got it." She waved me off. "He's a pansy beneath all that sweat and muscle."

The woman waded over next to me and tilted my hat back, exposing my eyes. "Look right tough to me." She touched my right temple with a calloused thumb, corkscrewing it slightly. "If the bomb goes off, I might come calling."

Abbie choked down a laugh. "Oh please do. I will sleep so much better knowing he's not shacked up with one of my best friends."

The woman nodded and walked back through the water to the bank. There was a hole in the rear of her overalls exposing the fact that she wasn't wearing underwear and that her butt hung like her cheeks. Abbie covered her mouth and stifled another laugh. When the woman reached the bank, she waved her barrel across the trees and then turned to Abbie. The smile had faded, bulldogging her wrinkles. She sucked through her teeth. "In some places, this here river is wide. Other places, it's deep. In others, the trees all fall across it, making one 'mell of a hess.' Still others, it snakes around its elbow to get to its thumb. But it pours out long distances. And nothing never stops it. You can't dam it. You can try but it'll run around. It'll make a way. That's what she do. She always makes a way." She spat and pointed the broken barrel in my general direction. "I reckon it's a lot like him." She walked to a wooden box on the beach and pulled out a bottle. It was old and its surface was dim with scratches. She bit the cork, pulled it out, then swigged from the bottle. She swirled it around her mouth, sort of gargling with its contents, and nodded. She rammed the cork back in and handed me the bottle. "Last year's. Jis' 'bout right."

I pointed at the vines above me. "You make it?"

She nodded. "I did. My recipe. Round here, we call it scuppernong, southern fox wine, joy juice and"—she shook her hips in a dance move I hope to never see again—"dance lubricant."

Abbie looked at me and raised both eyebrows. "Oh my."

The old woman folded the shotgun back across her arms. "You two go easy." A rustle and scurry in the leaves on her left brought the shotgun up and cocked the hammer all in one motion. She aimed and held it, her eyes growing wide. Satisfied, she uncocked the hammer and returned the shotgun to the cradle in her arms. When I turned, a water snake was swallowing a still-shaking rat. The only thing sticking out of its mouth was the tail.

I pulled my hat down, stepped into the harness and began walking.

That's the river. Beneath all this, beneath the worst she can dish out, she will rise up, ugly and disgusting, hideous enough to gag a maggot, and yet if you dive in, crack the surface, and swim where others won't, she will surprise you, amaze you and remind you.

13

It'd been two days since the Christmas party. A single bulb lit the canvas before me and it was now near midnight. I sat on a bar stool in the loft, a paint-tipped brush bit between my teeth. Eyes narrowed, head tilted like a dog, I was trying to make sense out of a shadow. On the canvas in front of me was her face, seen from close behind her right ear, down along her cheek line, over the angle of her lips and the lines of her nose, which pointed to Fort Sumter and separated the Ashley from the Cooper. Her face covered nearly half the canvas. Wisps of hair in the top left corner, her ear just below and right of that, which led down her face to the fort, which floated in the water in the bottom right-hand corner. The piece led your eye from the top left corner, downward to the bottom right-hand corner and the fort, the lights of which led upward to the moon that hung brilliant in the top right-hand corner, only to lead you left again—a complete circle of perspective.

A rap at the door broke my concentration. Brush in mouth, I walked down to the door expecting to shoo some drunk cadet and tell him that my door was not his dorm. Cigarette smoke and rowdy, bellied-up, bar noise met me as I cracked the door. I pulled it wider and she stepped from the shadows—a mink coat and pearls. I heard myself step back and suck in air. She smiled, shook her head and stepped past me. "You working?"

I looked at my watch and spoke around the edges of the brush. "Not anymore."

She rolled her eyes. "Good."

I shut the door and she let her eyes adjust to the dim light. The single bulb in the loft caught her attention. She craned her neck, spotted the canvas and began climbing the stairs. I followed, keeping my distance. She studied it several minutes, stepping closer, turning her head and then moving away.

"You mad?" I asked.

"No," she said without looking at me. "I'm used to people stealing my picture."

I handed her the canvas. "Sorry."

She shook her head. "Why me?"

" 'Cause you're . . . you're you."

She shrugged. "Maybe." She was quiet a minute and looked like she had something else she wanted to say. Finally, she said, "It usually takes somebody with Photoshop to make me look like that."

I asked a second time. "You mad?"

"No, but I'm an easy target. Anybody can paint me. Don't be like everybody else." Her intensity surprised me. "People are always telling me I'm beautiful. Okay, so what. I've spent most of my life in front of cameras. People use my image to sell a product. That's all. At the end of the day, they've used me—my face or figure, which by the way I had nothing to do with—to tell everyone else how they are *not* like me. Hence, *you're not beautiful.* Or, *you're not pretty.* Or, *you don't measure up.*" Her eyes were glassy. She waved her hand across my studio. "If you want to make great art, something that can reach beyond time and space, find someone who isn't and show them that they are. Paint the broken, the unlovely . . . and make them believe."

A TIGHTLY WOUND spiral staircase led to the roof. At night, depending on the moon, streetlights and breeze, I'd often work up there. It was quiet, usually blanketed in a breeze and gave me a bird's-eye view of the world. "Rooftop?" she asked. I nodded. "Can we?"

I climbed the stairs, pushed open the door and helped her up. The brick facade of my studio rose up above the flat roof and stood waist-high, separating us from the exhaust and noise of King Street. Fat pigeons, comfortable in their perch, sat cooing on the brick. I shut the door and they flushed, rising like Red Barons spiraling above us. She pointed at the closest, most daring purple pigeon. "Look, you little squirt. My daddy collects shotguns. You poop on this mink and I will personally hunt you down myself." He arced hard right and flew off into the night.

She was a complexity unlike any I'd ever met, much less known. Serious one moment, laughing the next. But it was an ability whose transition that came at a price. She leaned against the brick and closed her eyes. "You better get me downstairs."

"You okay?"

She nodded like a seasick sailor. "Migraines. Not much warning."

We shuffled back down the stairs and by the time we reached the first floor, I was carrying her. I laid her in my bed, filled a ziplock bag with ice and placed it beneath her neck. My only set of sheets was dirty so I'd been sleeping on my sleeping bag laid out across the mattress. She palmed the mattress. "Nice sheets."

"Sorry. After the other night and my WWF debut, they were a little bloody." I pointed to the crumpled pile in the corner.

I took her shoes off, slid a pillow under the backs of her knees and laid a blanket across her legs. Then I spread her mink across her arms and shoulders. She whispered, "You've done this before?"

"Yeah, my mom."

She slept hard until sunup when the recycle truck brought King Street to life. I sat on a stool, my fingertips covered in ten shades of dried paint, a brush stuck between my teeth like a pirate's knife, another in my hand. Throughout the night, I'd finished the picture.

She sat up on the bed, rubbed her eyes and stared past me to my work. "You've been busy." I nodded, unsure of her reaction. She patted the bed. "If you were going to take advantage of me, you missed your chance."

I smiled over my brush. "Don't think I didn't think about it, but then I remembered that your daddy collects shotguns."

She stood and walked to me, putting her hand on my shoulder. "Yes, he does." With my brush still in my mouth, she kissed me. "Thank you."

I spit the brush out. "You're welcome."

She laughed. "Will you do me a favor?"

"Is it legal?"

"Yes, but"—she eyed the canvas—"it'll take some time. And"—the seriousness, returned. Another seamless transition—". . . it might test you."

"Name it."

She pointed to my paints, brushes and easel. "Is this portable?"

"It can be."

"You busy this afternoon?"

"Just work, but I can call in sick." She slipped on her shoes, grabbed her mink and kissed me a second time. "That was better without the brush." She walked to the door and slid on her glasses. I pointed to the street. "People might start to talk if they see you leaving here at this time. Around here it's called the walk of shame."

"They'll talk anyway." She pointed at my canvas and the picture of her. "You priced it yet?"

"It's . . . it's not for sale."

"About five then?"

"Five."

14

Reynolds Bridge is a single-lane bridge of poured slabs of concrete and iron. It has no railing, no lights and, given that the river has cut deep into the sandy bluff beneath, it sits some twenty-five feet above the river. This doesn't sound like much, but the bridge is flat. Mature trees have grown up underneath it—their roots protected and their branches arching out around the edges of the bridge and reaching toward the sun.

Confederate flags decorate river shacks built on stilts and tucked back in the trees. A discarded Pepsi machine rested faceup and upside down on the Florida side. The plastic was cracked and somebody had shot it a dozen times with what looked like a large-caliber bullet.

Down here—between the bluffs—you hear little sound. It's like walking on snow. Muffled echoes mostly, but even then, you're not sure. The only smell is the decomposition and an occasional bloom. Paddling through, you feel like you're living beneath the earth's surface.

The Bare Bottom Resort owned several acres on the downriver side of the bridge. One naked person might be little attraction, but fifty is not. Every third tree held a bright orange or yellow POSTED—NO TRESPASSING sign. The owners hoped it would ward off the unwanted, and create a buffer to keep Peeping Toms at a distance. But telling South Georgia rednecks they weren't welcome in their own backyard only made matters worse. The woods were usually swarming with local kids hoping to see their first naked woman. I know, I used to be one of them. Problem is that many of the people who join nudist colonies aren't, and never were, members of the Swedish bikini team. So while we crept through the woods hoping to get a glimpse of the cover girl for *Sports Illustrated,* that first peek probably did more damage than good. When I was a kid, the POSTED signs should have read, "This ain't all it's cracked up to be. Look at your own risk, 'cause when you have, you'll wish you hadn't."

'Course, I'd been away a long time and it'd be my luck that the only constancy is change.

Trees overhung the river forming a thick canopy and the river actually pooled in several places, making good swimming holes. I beached the canoe beneath an old rope swing and said, "Hang tight. Be back in a bit."

She laughed. "Normally, I'm a size four, but I might could squeeze into a two. And get something that matches my eyes."

"Don't get your hopes up."

"Remember," she said, starting to laugh, "think like them. Blend in."

"Very funny."

I slipped through the woods a couple hundred yards and came upon a row of cabins. I could smell breakfast cooking and hear televisions playing various versions of the news but nobody was outside and no clotheslines were draped in clean clothing. Certainly, these people had to wear clothing sometimes. They did go to the store.

Across a large lawn, maybe four football fields in size, sat the public pool. It looked like a dozen or so people were milling around it. On the far side, I read the words *Spa* and *Laundry*.

Bingo.

I stepped out of the woods but remembered what Abbie had said. The point was to *not* draw attention to myself. I turned around, hopped behind a tree, stripped to my birthday suit, pulled my sunglasses down over my eyes and began strolling across the lawn like a regular. Then I thought through the process of carrying something back, so I backpedaled, grabbed my shirt and threw it around my neck like a towel.

I'd never been so self-conscious in all my life. I tried to whistle but couldn't get my lips to cooperate.

I made it halfway across the lawn when an older woman stepped out of her cabin maybe fifty yards off. She wasn't wearing anything either, and hers was a wrinkled and sagging image I could have done without. She waved, turned her back—another image that will haunt me to my grave—then began watering flower boxes across her deck, paying me no more mind.

These people are weird.

'Course, then I thought about me, walking across their backyard, naked as a jaybird, and figured I was probably weird too.

I made it to the pool and tried not to make eye contact with the eleven other people either stretched out around the pool or swimming in it. There were three kids, a couple of teenagers and four adults. Looked like two families. Feeling more self-conscious than I'd ever felt in my life, I strode across the pool deck and stepped into the spa where I was met by a women's yoga class.

You've got to be kidding me.

Looking at no one and yet everyone, I walked down a

hallway and into what sounded like the laundry room. I didn't draw any attention, which was good in an odd sort of way. The women were all focused somewhere between a downward dog and rising moon. In the laundry, twelve sets of washers and dryers were all running. Evidently, the women brought their laundry to yoga. *Jackpot!*

I looked over my shoulder, then started quietly rifling through each dryer. I found a bathing suit bottom and top, a towel, and some cutoff shorts that all looked like they would fit Abbie. Then I thought, Feet. I grabbed a pair of socks and a bar of soap off the sink. I rolled everything inside the towel, slung it back around my neck and walked back out through the yoga class trying to think about taxes, the square root of pi or tinkering with a Rubik's Cube.

I skirted the pool deck, waved at one man reading a book on the far side. The woman next to him raised her nose out of a book and said, "You new here?"

"Yeah." I turned sideways, pointing to the far row of what looked like rental cabins. "Just in. We try and get down once a year."

She sat up and pointed to a row of cabins opposite the pool house. "You ought to come up tonight. Number fourteen. George here is grilling burgers and we're inviting the neighbors. Just a get-together."

"Sure. Uh . . . 'bout what time?"

"Sixish. You bring your wife?" It was a question.

"Yes. Thanks. We'll see you then." George waved and the lady returned to her book, smiling.

I walked back across the lawn where two men and one other woman waved at me from their porches. *This is just shameless exhibitionism. Men are not made to walk around naked. It's not comfortable.* I stepped into the woods and found T-shirt-only Abbie doubled over. Tears were running off her face. She was laughing as hard as I'd ever seen her laugh.

I handed her the clothes. "That's not funny." She couldn't even talk. I grabbed my shorts, looped my arm into hers and we strolled butt-naked through the woods.

She looked behind me and slapped me on the right cheek. "You got a cute butt."

"Well, it's not my best feature."

We reached the river where a rope swing hung above us. Swingers could perch themselves on the bank, fly out across the beach and land in a pool that, given the water's dark color, looked to be several feet deep. Abbie unrolled her clothes and found the soap. She stared at me, that sneaky look in her eye. "When in Rome . . ." She slipped off her shirt, untied the scarf and hovered across the white sandy beach. After everything, she still gets to me. She is still the most beautiful woman on the planet. The water was knee-deep and coppery bronze. The sun dipped behind dark clouds, which pushed out the rain that then fell in large drops that smacked the water and trees. The rain was cold but the river was warm, so we slipped down to our shoulders, our chins skimming the water's surface. It was one of those moments. Blink and you'll miss it. Water dripped off the lobes of her ears and tip of her nose, steam rose off the water in miniature twisters that spiraled up through the trees in quiet dissipation while the clouds emptied themselves. If there's glory in the heavens, it was being poured out on my wife.

I grabbed the bottle of scuppernong, pulled the cork and let her lay in the cradle of me. I leaned into the river and we sipped silently, watching the moisture spin upward. The rain slowed and she said, "Bathe me." So I did. When the sun cracked back through the clouds, I spread the tarp on the beach, zipped us into her sleeping bag and we slept off the wine. It was an hour's worth of sleep that felt like a week.

After we woke, I was folding up the bag and she slapped me on the butt. "Three down. Seven to go."

She was right. We'd just checked off numbers 3, 4 and 9. Abbie had a way of making me forget the hell we were living in. This moment was no exception. I loaded the canoe, laid her down in the center and cut the paddle into the water. Only then did I realize that the shotgun was gone.

15

A few minutes after 5 p.m., a 5 Series BMW with dark windows parked at the meter in front of my door. She rolled down the window and waved at me. I locked up and set my easel, a blank framed canvas and two fishing tackle boxes filled with paints and brushes in her trunk. Another woman sat in the front seat so I hopped in the back. Abbie turned around and introduced me. "Doss, this is Rosalia."

Rosalia was heavy-set, maybe mid-fifties, probably South American and had evidently spent a good bit of time in the sun. She turned toward me, offered a calloused, dry hand. Her eyes were baggy, she had no eyebrows to speak of, her nose was crooked, one ear was missing and she had no teeth.

We drove across town, toward some docks and large warehouses. Abbie talked while shifting gears. "We set up this studio for last-minute shoots. It's not perfect, but it'll do."

The warehouse was cool, expansive and, thanks to the concrete floor, every whisper echoed back at you. In the center, a gray curtain hung across a cable stretched taut between two poles. Studio lighting, comprised of dozens of different types of lights, angled toward the curtain. Some shot up from the floor, some were direct, others filtered down onto a black mat and small stool.

Rosalia wore a long dark brown skirt, a large dirty white apron and old running shoes—one of which was untied due to a broken lace. Her top was a baggy lavender uniform shirt that most "house help" had been either told or conditioned to wear. Something about her struck me as off, but I couldn't quite place it. Something was off balance.

Abbie sat Rosalia on the stool, whispered something, then moved to a control box and began flipping lights on and off. Rosalia sat on the stool wiping her hands on her apron. Abbie spent several minutes considering the lighting. She'd turn one on, add another to it, turn a third off, only to immediately add accent with a fourth. She turned to me. "What do you think?"

"I like it, but if you add something soft at her feet, it might get the feel I think you're looking for." She flipped another switch, chewed on her lip and then swigged from a water bottle. Finally, she nodded.

She grabbed my hand, led me to Rosalia and spoke in Spanish. "Rosalia, this is the artist I told you about." Rosalia smiled, did not look up at me, and nodded. Abbie patted her knee and looked at me. "Doss, some of my first memories include this lady. She would comb my hair and tell me I was pretty long before I knew the meaning of the word." She turned to Rosalia. "It's okay. Go ahead."

Rosalia straightened her apron, then began to unbutton her shirt. When she'd loosed the last button, Abbie stepped behind and helped her slip it off. Quickly, as if she was afraid she'd change her mind, Rosalia reached behind her and unclasped her own bra. Then, without pulling her arms through, she let it fall, exposing the imbalance.

Abbie knelt next to her, patted her on the arm and spoke to me. "Rosalia fled her country when I was just a baby." She pointed at a crooked and wide scar—nearly an inch and a half in width—that ran from the nipple of her right breast, across her sternum, across where the left breast used to be, under her armpit and around onto her back. "But not before a man with a machete got ahold of her." Rosalia's right breast sagged nearly to her waist, held up only by the roll of fat pushed up by her apron. Abbie stood behind her, untied Rosalia's jet black hair streaked with white and let it fall across her shoulders. It came nearly to her waist.

I looked at Abbie. Searching. Abbie kissed Rosalia on the cheek and lifted her chin. Then she spoke to me. "Rosalia has always wanted a portrait. I told her you could do it."

I stepped back to my canvas, made it look like I was prepping pencils and paints, wondering how in the world I was going to do that when Abbie walked behind me and put her arms around me. She whispered in my ear, "Doss, look with your eyes." She covered my eyes with her hand. "Not these." She slid her hand down onto my chest. "These. Look through here and show her what she's always wanted to see." She slid her hand into mine. "Show her that she's beautiful beyond measure."

I stared at the horror staring back at me. "How?"

Her breath was warm on my ear. "Search what you see and find the one thing that makes you want to look again."

Rosalia sat on her stool, staring back at me. I shifted uneasily on mine, my palms sweating, mouth dry, thinking, What do I do when she discovers that I can't do what she hopes I can do? Abbie walked around us, talking on the phone with her agent, booking flights, managing her career. She could multitask on a level I'd never comprehended. Before me, sat Rosalia. Quietly waiting.

With nothing to hide, and nothing to hide behind, she lifted her chin, pulled one shoulder back, looked down her nose and out of the corner of her eye at me.

In three seconds, she went from pitiful and broken to towering and magnificent.

Four hours later, I had the bones of a sketch. Abbie flew to New York, but I spent the next eight days sweating and hyperventilating. Abbie flew home, called me at 2 a.m. and I held her at bay. "Not yet." Okay, yes, I was afraid. So I spent another two days tweaking it, getting my courage up, then finally, because she nearly beat the door down, I let her in and clicked on the light.

The light hit the canvas and Abbie stepped back. She sucked in a chestful of air, dropped Indian-style onto the floor and covered her mouth, crying. I stepped back into the shadow, wondering. Worried. Growing sicker by the second. Abbie pulled the light closer, then lightly brushed her fingertip across the texture of the scar on the canvas.

She turned to me, her lip quivering. Tears were pouring off her face. "Oh . . . I don't know how to say this."

Me either. I started backpedaling. "This is just one option. I can start over. Maybe try it from a different angle or—"

She began shaking her head. "No . . ." She stood, placed her palms on my face and pressed her lips to mine. I remember her face was wet, her mascara had smeared like a raccoon and my knees buckled like the Tin Man.

That kiss traveled down my face, through my throat, it parted my shoulders and cut into the deeper places in my soul before coming to rest. She placed her head on my shoulder and just shook her head. "Magnificent."

Standing in my loft, staring at Rosalia, with Abbie pressed to my chest and the taste of her tears on my lips, Abbie taught me to breathe again.

Oh, and with Rosalia's permission, I graduated.

16

South of the Bare Bottom, the river makes a head-fake east and then darts back south again. She does this until the St. Marys Bluff road. The level of the water allowed me sporadic moments of paddling. Other times I stepped out, walked along the bank or in the water and slid the canoe through the shallows.

Midafternoon, I stopped to adjust the straps on my shoulders, looked down and a pine snake had coiled about five feet away. Pine snakes are long—like five or six feet—skinny, light brown in color and make an awful hissing noise if you hack them off. I had, so he was hissing at the top of his lungs. Abbie asked, "What's that noise?"

I studied the ground around me and realized he wasn't hissing at me. At my feet, maybe twelve inches from the toes sticking up out of my Tevas swam three pygmy rattlers. Usually less than a foot long, pygmy rattlers gnaw on you more than strike but they're no less venomous. Give them enough time and they'll chew on your toes, turning your foot a bunch of weird colors. Antivenin works but it'd mean a trip to the hospital and it wouldn't be fun or pretty.

Abbie's not too fond of snakes. I don't like snakes either, but if you're going to travel this river, especially this far up, you better get used to them. Normally, I'd shoot them, because the only kind of snake I like is a dead snake, but I didn't want to risk the noise. I splashed the three at my feet and they skittered across the top of the water. Then I splashed the pine snake. He made a U-turn and slithered up the bank and into a tree. That's one of my least favorite visuals—a snake going away. Snakes and disease have much in common—they are far better at sneaking up on you than you are on them.

~~~

RIVER BLUFF ROAD parallels the river for a mile or so. It's the first river frontage road we'd come to and it's on the Georgia side where the bluff is noticeably higher. Most homes are old farmhouses with tin roofs and porches that run the length of the house. Nearly every house has a row of dog kennels and a garage nearly as big as the house. We passed beneath a stolen Winston Cup Series banner that stretched across the river behind a house whose yard was lined with a dozen or so stripped and rusting parts-cars sitting on blocks in various forms of disarray and dysfunction. Sun-faded plastic chairs were scattered across the lawns and three plastic pools sat above ground bulging at the seams. The sign above the door read, PROTECTED BY SMITH AND WESSON.

RVs complement most large garages. Mangy, collarless dogs roam free. Most sleep in the middle of the road and snap at the bumper of the rural mail carrier as he drives by. Pink flamingos are a common yard decoration, as are bald tires, old bass boats, burning trash piles and SEE ROCK CITY mailboxes and birdhouses.

Down here, everybody goes to church. And while there are many buildings, they all fall under one banner. It's one of the largest denominations in the world—it's called the First Holy

Congregation of NASCAR. Most worship outdoors. During rainouts, they wear ponchos or poke arm holes in the sides of black plastic can liners. It's a come-as-you-are, pretty free-flowing place. A lot of hand waving, screaming and cheering with two hundred and fifty thousand of their closest friends. To say these people are evangelical would be an understatement. Their hats, T-shirts and jackets outline the tenets of their faith. The flags hanging off their garages identify their particular arm of the church while their bumper stickers give the name of their favorite pastor. Services can run several hours, which is why most folks bring coolers with food and refreshment. Some attendees even camp out in the parking lots on Saturday waiting for the doors to open. Most services conclude with a combination communion and baptism. Surrounded by his deacons and other staff, the pastor of the day—always a flashy dresser—stands on the podium after he's whipped everybody into a pretty good frenzy and then he just sprays them with the elements. Folks up front can drink or swim—it's up to them.

We slipped beneath the banner as a knee-high, mangy, collarless, mostly white dog walked down the bank and sunk her muzzle in the water. She had one black eye and a hungry litter somewhere, because her freckled teats were engorged and the milky tips were dragging the sand. A half mile further down, we passed three pit bulls with spiked collars rolling in the mud. Two of them had cuts above their eyes while the third was missing an eye entirely. The fence beyond them held a spray-painted sign that read "Forget Dog, Beware of Owner." Behind them, cows ambled through a pasture flanked by pesky cowbirds and horseflies the size of half dollars.

We paddled through the wafting smoke and pungent smell of a burning trash pile as six more pit bulls raced across the yard aimed at us. They crossed the hundred-yard distance before I had time to fumble for the revolver. When they reached the river's edge, they stood ten feet off the bank in a perfect row and bared their teeth. They growled, spewing spit across the river, and a few even barked, but they did not cross the imaginary line. Each wore a collar with a small black box and a little antenna that suggested an electric fence for which I was grateful. I hoped the inventor of that gizmo was enjoying his retirement on some beach served by cabana girls carrying little umbrella-decorated drinks. He'd earned it. I made no sudden movement and slowly push-poled us through the shallows. Abbie cracked one eye and said, "Am I about to be eaten?"

I shook my head slowly but didn't take my eyes off the bank. "Not as long as the power stays on."

"And if the power goes out?"

"Well . . . I'm bigger, so they'll probably chomp on me first. You should have time to reach the top of the bluff before they pick me clean and come looking for dessert."

"That's comforting."

WE MADE FOUR MORE miles by sundown. The river began to open a little, requiring less portage and more paddling. Long white sandy beaches paralleled us on either side. Palm trees shot up like rockets and palmettos bent over the sides of the bank, dipping their fronds in the water like tender fingers. Redwood-sized pine trees, anchored into the banks, towered like skyscrapers along with sprawling scrub oaks.

Mom was right.

Sundown came and found me looking over my shoulder. It wasn't like I could go running to the police. I thought maybe we could outrun them, but I had a feeling they knew this river about as well as I did. A gentle breeze picked up and the river made a hard right turn. Almost a complete 180 degrees. This was Skinner's Beach. Up the bank was a small screened-in outdoor kitchen and an artesian well fitted with a rusted old hand-pump that used to work. Church youth groups, Boy Scout troops and Friday-night tailgaters regularly frequent here due to its many campsites, availability of water and the large grill, tables and covered area in the event of rain.

I beached the canoe, slid it beneath the shade and lifted Abbie into my arms. She didn't open her eyes or move—the pain had returned. I carried her up the bank, pushed open the screen door and laid her on the table that was long enough to seat some twenty people. I propped her head up and then started priming the pump to bring the water up. It finally gurgled out, rusted and stained. Three minutes of pumping and the water was clear, cold and sweet. I washed out a stainless-steel mug and carried water to Abbie. She sat up, sipped and then lay back down. I grabbed the Pelican case from the canoe, uncapped one of the dexamethasone syringes and then turned Abbie on her side. I swabbed her skin with alcohol, then slid the needle into what remained of the meat of her left cheek.

I returned to the pump and bent next to the spout, letting it rain down over my head. It was cold, clean and helped open my weary eyes. When my right arm grew tired of pumping, I stood and let the water run off me.

Dusk fell around us. I returned to the outdoor kitchen and pried the locks off the wooden storage bins beneath the table. Scout groups and churches used them to keep paper goods dry and away from the mice, but oftentimes they'd leave canned goods because they didn't feel like hauling them out. The first box held nothing but paper plates, some plastic Solo cups and three rolls of toilet paper. The second one contained a tarp, a box of unopened but stale saltine crackers, two cans of sardines marinated in Louisiana hot sauce, three Swiss cake rolls and some matches. In the third, I hit the jackpot—graham crackers, marshmallows and a few Hershey bars.

The fireplace was more of a pit, open on four sides, and the metal chimney hung from the roof, drawing the smoke and heat upward. It was a safe way to let kids cook s'mores.

A dozen or so straightened coat hangers had been laid across the rafters. I pulled one down and placed it into the fire, burning off the rust. Once hot and sterile, I stabbed it through two marshmallows and pulled a bench up close to the fire. I wasn't too crazy about lighting a signal fire, but I had a feeling that whoever was following us already knew where we were. Besides, the warmth felt good. A minute or so later, Abbie appeared next to me. I placed two chocolate squares on top of one of the crackers, then slid a gooey marshmallow on top and capped it with the other graham cracker. Abbie smiled. "Honey, you shouldn't have." Melted chocolate and marshmallow goo squeezed out the sides of her mouth as she bit into it.

I pointed the poker downriver. "Tomorrow, a few more miles and we'll start coming upon the weekend getaways. Most have outdoor kitchens and refrigerators. Until then . . ."

She smiled, marshmallow dabbed in the corner of her mouth. "If I didn't know you better, I'd say you'd done this before."

"What? S'mores?"

She shook her head. "No, dummy, the stealing."

"Admittedly . . ." I glanced out over the river. "I've had some practice."

The fire died down and coals turned white while we ate every crumb, including the saltines, but Abbie turned up her nose when it came to the sardines. I set aside the Swiss cake rolls for breakfast. The quick energy would help get me going. I was tired and I had a feeling I wouldn't get much sleep tonight either.

The night passed with little excitement. A light rain drizzled around midnight, cooling the air, so I stoked the fire, and then unfolded the tarp and towel and laid both over Abbie. About two hours before daylight, I lifted her off the table and laid her cocoonlike in the bottom of the canoe. She was sleeping fitfully, so I gave her a lollipop; she flew to la-la land and stayed there until daylight.

At Highway 121, the Okefenokee Trail turns due east for six miles until Stokes Bridge where she makes a hard left and bends due north in a relatively straight shot to Folkston and Boulogne. In topographic terms, it is here that the river has begun rolling off Florida's shoulders.

The river widens here to eight car lengths—give or take. ATV tracks cut the banks along with bog holes, and several trash piles, tucked up in the palmetto bushes, are used as regular dumps by the locals. A waterlogged mattress, the corpse of a bullet-riddled refrigerator, half a motorcycle, several dozen *National Geographics*, and a myriad of Budweiser cans and bottles had melted into the mud and sand. Below the bridge, a three-wheeled, rusted shopping cart sat upside down, its once-chrome basket clogged with sticks and plastic bags. A newer model—shiny red plastic—lay in a mangled pile atop the concrete chunks having not survived the drop from the bridge.

17

For the record, I did ask his permission. The key there is *ask*. His schedule was always tight. It was tough getting an audience with him—even for five minutes. He was seldom alone. It was Thanksgiving weekend. He'd come home to cut the turkey. Abbie had been working all over. She'd been gone weeks at a time. I'd graduated and was working two jobs: For rent money, I was guiding fishermen off the flats for redfish. I could make a couple hundred bucks a day when the fish were biting. When they weren't, I painted.

Rosalia's portrait hung in Abbie's parents' house in the foyer. When asked about it, they would credit a "local artist" which infuriated Abbie, but the fact that it was one of the first things you saw when you walked in suggested that even they couldn't deny the power of the image. Whenever Abbie was home, she'd eavesdrop on the dinner-table conversation, waiting for just the right moment to circumvent her parents. She'd pop her head around the doorjamb, say hello to their guests then point nonchalantly. "I know the artist if you'd like him to consider you. He's very busy, only takes a select few clients a year, but"—she'd smile and raise her eyebrows—"I can get his attention."

Over her parents' objections, Abbie arranged meetings with prospective clients. We'd arrive at their house, I'd agree to paint his or her portrait, then talk about specifics and schedule the first of a couple sittings. In my first consultation, the husband, an oil executive, asked, "What do you charge?"

I was about to say a thousand dollars when Abbie said, "Normally, he charges ten, but because of me, he's agreed to lower his fee to seventy-five hundred." The man nodded as if she'd just taken his order at a fast food restaurant and given him his total at the register.

My jaw nearly hit the floor.

In nine months, I had paid off my school debts and bought my first car. But, in truth, I'd have done it for free, because for the first time in my professional life, I felt valued. Valued because that person in front of me, that "subject," was trusting me with one of the most valuable things they owned—their reflection.

I could not have been happier.

Conversely, her parents could not have been more unimpressed. Her stepmother was the more vocal of the two. Thanksgiving morning, I walked up onto the back porch and was two inches away from knocking on the door when I heard, "You two are running a racket and when people find out, Doss will never paint in this city again." I pulled my hand away and sat on the bench next to Rosalia, who was shelling peas.

"Mother . . ."

"Don't 'Mother' me."

"Have you seen any of his work other than Rosalia?"

A reluctant pause. "Yes."

"And?"

Katherine picked up the paper and turned to the obits. "I suppose, it's . . . fair."

"Fair?"

She set down the paper. "I don't like you seeing that boy."

"You don't say."

"Abbie, he grew up in a trailer."

"And your point is?"

"He's not your type."

"You mean, 'my kind.' "

"He'll never be one of us."

"Mother, he's not trying to be one of us."

"My point exactly."

"Sort of refreshing, don't you think?"

Abbie climbed upstairs, and I heard the shower cut on. Rosalia leaned against me, pressing her fleshy shoulder to mine. She looked at me out of the tops of her eyes, patted me on the thigh and nodded me onward. I kissed her on the forehead, knocked lightly on the screen door and pushed it open. "Good morning, Mrs. Coleman."

"Oh, hi, Doss. Do come in. You look hungry. Can I get you some breakfast?"

Painting portraits has taught me something about people. All my clients have two faces. The one they live with and the one they want me to paint. Mrs. Coleman was no different.

Thanksgiving night, after the house emptied, Senator Coleman was holed up in his office. I knocked on the door. He looked up, expressionless. "Hello, Doss. You lose Abbie?"

"No, sir, I wanted to speak with you."

He leaned back in his chair. "About?"

"Well, sir, about Abbie." He rocked slightly, leaning on a pencil that was pressed into his chin. "Well, then, I'll just get to it." I couldn't figure out what to do with my hands so I finally just shoved them in my pants pockets. "Senator Coleman, I'd like to ask your permission to marry your daughter." He quit rocking and put the pencil down. There was an empty chair across from him but he made no mention of it. In the span of a few seconds, a lifetime passed. Finally, he shook his head and simply said, "No."

I didn't know what to say. Just where do I go with that? "Any chance I can talk you out of that position?"

A practiced smile. "No."

There was a lot I wanted to say at that moment, but wasn't sure how to get it out and even less sure that it would do any good. In his mind, I was an impetuous, twenty-one-year-old starving artist. He'd made up his mind long before I walked in that door. "Yes, sir." I turned, walked out and pulled the door closed quietly behind me.

While I was hurt, Abbie was livid. I'd never seen her so mad. After an hour she had yet to cool off. We stood down by the water. Actually, I stood and she paced. "Just who does he think he is?"

"He's your father."

"That doesn't make him God."

"Not in his mind." We stood there, deflated and angry. "Maybe if I made something of myself and came back in five years he'd change his mind, but I heard him the first time. No means no. Forever."

She stared out across the water, shaking her head. I knew that anything less than total compliance was akin to a declaration of war—one more shot across Fort Sumter. I didn't want that for Abbie and I had no desire to separate her from her family. I knew that what I was about to do would be painful for a long time to come, but I also knew it was best.

I needed to give her an out. I turned her toward me. "Please forgive me for what I am about to do." She began slowly shaking her head. "Abigail, your father is right." I took one step back. "I'm the product of a trailer park. You are Southern royalty. I'm a dreamer, a loner, and I seldom get what I think or feel out of my mouth. I'm more suited to work the parties at your parents' house than attend them." Tears filled her eyes. "You're a national phenomenon who can talk with kings and queens or sweetgrass basket weavers."

"Doss . . ."

"I'm good at one thing. Everything you touch turns to gold."

She began to shout. "Don't you dare do this to me. Not because of him."

"Abigail, your mom was right. I'm not your kind."

She placed her right index finger to my lips. "I'm a girl, in love with a boy."

Somewhere a ship's horn sounded. In the river, a boat planed and started skimming across the water. Beyond the Battery, a horse and carriage ambled down cobblestone. Overhead in the midnight darkness, seagulls were squawking, and in the park behind us, a girl threw a tennis ball for a slobbering chocolate lab beneath a streetlight. I took both her hands in mine. "Will you marry me?"

It was the Friday after Thanksgiving, 1992.

She stamped her foot. "Doss Michaels! You just scared the crap out of me."

"Abigail . . . will you marry me?"

She pounded me on the chest. "Not until you say you're sorry."

"I'm sorry."

"You didn't really mean that."

I knelt. "Abbie, I can't give you the life your father has given you and your mother. I don't know how I'll make it in this world so I can't promise you much of anything. Except this: I will give you all of me. No pretensions, no walls, no lies. There's never been and will never be another man on the planet who will love you the way I do. When I'm not with you, it hurts. And when I'm with you, it still hurts 'cause I know somewhere in the next few hours I'll be without you again. I've been hurting most of my life and I don't want to hurt anymore. Please take me . . . and the islands inside me . . . and make me whole."

She looked at me out of one corner of her eye. "You ever do this to me again and I'll—"

"Abbie?"

She chewed on her lip. "I have a confession." She half turned and pointed. "I have a mole on my butt."

"Can't wait to see it. It'll be our little secret."

She shook her head. "Doss. I'm not the woman on the magazines. No one is that woman. She's a figment of—"

"I'm not in love with the woman at the checkout counter."

"Yeah, but . . . I'm just the outline. They put me in a computer, erase the wrinkles, shrink the nose, pull in the chin, draw in the cheeks"—she cupped her hands beneath both breasts— "make my boobs bigger."

I shook my head. "I'm in love with the Abbie that's standing in front of me."

She knelt, eye level with me. "And when I'm old and ugly, sagging in all the wrong places?"

"Abigail Coleman, I'm not marrying the idea of you. Or even the memory of you. I'm marrying you. So don't worry about what you might become. I'll love her, too. Even more. I'll take the bad because that means I will have lived to know the good."

She pressed her face to my chest, the sobs bubbling up quietly. When they grew too strong to hold back, she threw her arms around my neck, let out a cry that sounded like it started near her belly button and then pressed her tearstained and snotty face to mine. "Yes."

18

On the afternoon of the third day, we passed under the bridge at Highway 121. That meant we'd come twenty-three miles. Six more to Stokes Bridge—the quarterway mark.

This far up, the river isn't used recreationally—as it is south of Trader's Ferry. That meant the river would offer us cover up here, but further north, then east, it would open up and we'd start bumping into joyriders on Jet Skis, Bubbas in johnboats fishing the banks and federal wildlife officers patrolling in their twenty-two-foot Pathfinders mounted with FM radios, satellite phones and two-hundred-horse Yamaha four-stroke engines. Once spotted, you might duck and dodge your way around the engine, but not the radio.

The river narrowed again, the sandy bottom poking up through the water, making the river only a foot deep. A long expansive beach opened on our left. The sticky afternoon sun pressed down on my shoulders, making me sleepy, so I slid the canoe quietly beneath a tree, careful not to wake Abbie. Above us, on the Florida side, an enormous house was under construction. Its owners must have known what they were doing, because they'd bought the highest bluff on the river. The sheer topography of it placed them above any flood—except maybe Noah's. Beyond us, the river turned hard right. I closed my eyes and saw every square inch of the riverbank. Within eyesight hung the stub of a rope swing where I learned to do a back flip. The rope was frayed, green and swayed slowly.

Below it sat the remnant of a bench.

I beached the canoe and shook Abbie. She raised an eyelid. "We there yet?"

I nodded. "Yeah, we're here."

She stood, weak-kneed and wobbly. "Good, 'cause I was thinking we had like another hundred miles to go or something."

Concrete steps led from the riverbank, up the bluff and into the backyard of what looked like a ten-thousand-square-foot house. The high-pitched roofline came down over an expansive concrete back porch that would hold fifty rocking chairs and provide a spectacular vista of the river snaking below.

I carried Abbie up the steps and through the knee-high grass of the backyard. The house had been studded, the roof had been shingled and dried in and the brick had been laid but there were no windows, no Sheetrock and no interior finish work. It looked like they had just started working on the inside and only a few windows had been set in the front of the house. A Port-O-Let sat near the back porch, so I helped Abbie onto the seat and let her lean against me while her body emptied itself of more poison.

The doors were locked but I crawled through a window and brought her in. The vaulted ceilings in the den were nearly twenty feet high and a fireplace large enough to lay in grew out of the far wall. Cold ashes piled in the bottom. I checked the flume, which was open, rummaged through the lumber scrap pile and built a small fire. Abbie lay on the ground and turned toward it. I found some drop cloths in the laundry room along with a working sink. I brought Abbie a cup of water, then

searched the remainder of the house. The second floor was no
less small and when it came to views on the river, this might be
about as good as it gets. The house was pretty clean, meaning
there wasn't much to be had. Back in the laundry room I discovered a Mr. Coffee and a half-full can of Maxwell House. I
plugged the coffeemaker into an orange extension cord that ran
in from the garage and the red light flashed on. While the Mr.
Coffee sputtered, I pulled one of the aluminum foil–sided insu-
lation boards out of the garage and laid it on the ground in front
of the fire. It was the stuff they nail to the studs before they lay
the brick. I covered it with a painting tarp and then we spread
across it and listened to Mr. Coffee. Abbie put her head on my
chest, twirled a chest hair and said, "You've been kind of quiet."

"You feel like going for a walk?"

"You think there's a wheelbarrow around here?"

"Might be." I found one leaning against the house. It was
one of those large plastic kind with two wheels in the front
making it more stable. I hosed it clean and set Abbie in it, facing
forward. "Your chariot, madam." I handed her a bottle of water
and said, "And drink this." The more fluids I could get into her,
the better she would feel. It'd keep her blood pressure up and
help flush out the toxins caused by all the poisons we dumped
into her.

She tucked the bottle between her legs and held on to the
sides, making a whipping motion with her arm. "Mush!"

"Cute. Very cute."

I rolled her along the rim of the bluff—the river flowing on
our left, thigh-high grass waving on our right. I pushed her
maybe a half a mile, stopping every few minutes for me to get a
better grip. Sitting up and sipping seemed to do her good. It put
color in her face.

We rounded the bend beneath the stub of the rope swing.

Further to our right, some hundred yards into the woods, stood the first row of trailers. Long since abandoned, vines covered most every square inch like long, fraying strands of wet hair.

We pushed through, ferns brushing our shins, and walked out into the open. Before I was born, twelve ragged trailers had been arranged in a circle—tucked up against each other with all the order of derailed train cars. In the middle, out by the bonfire stain, everyone parked their cars, threw the trash, flicked cigarette butts and spun the bottle. Made for a rather unhealthy environment. At the time, the trailers were all owned by one man—a landlord of sorts—who believed in upkeep as much now as he did then. I pushed Abbie into the center and turned in a slow circle. It felt like someone was stepping on my chest.

The trees had grown and now towered over the park. Doing so had created a canopy of sorts with lots of shade and little direct sunlight, keeping everything relatively cool and damp. She sipped her water. "Which one was yours?"

I pointed. Huge vines of poison ivy climbed up every side. Three leaves, red stem, just touching it would make me blister and itch for two weeks. It formed an intricate web that closed itself somewhere on top. What wasn't covered in vine was discolored due to mildew and black mold. All the glass had been broken, the front door was gone, the three steps that led up to it were nowhere to be found, and like most of the rest of them, it was riddled with shotgun pellet holes.

"Where was your room?"

I rolled her around the back side and stared at the window frame where my window air conditioner once hung. The gaping hole suggested that somebody had stolen it. "My air conditioner used to be right there. It didn't cool too well, but it rattled a lot. I'd switch it to high to drown out the sound—inside and out."

Abbie nodded and said, "What about the bench?"

The path had grown tall with weeds, downed trees and palm-sized banana spiders—who's six-foot webs stretched across the path. I picked up a long stick, pulled down the webs like I was making cotton candy and threw the stick aside. Abbie watched the spiders and pulled her legs in tight to her chest. We bulldozed through the grass and twice I had to lift her over a dead tree. While Abbie nervously ran a branch along the top rim of the wheelbarrow, I pushed her out into the clearing atop the sandy bluff.

Made out of an oak log, cut in half and resting on two pilings, the five-foot bench sat in the middle beneath the spindly arm of a live oak that reached out across the river. Wood rot had collapsed the pilings and worms had eaten through most of the bench seat. I rested my foot in the middle and it crumbled, too soft and soggy to crack.

I stood there staring at the anchor in my memory. Abbie climbed out of the wheelbarrow, wrapped her arms around my waist and rested her head on my shoulder, eyeing what was once the bench. She was about to say something when I heard it.

Around here it's known as "the hatch." It sounds like a car in the distance driving toward you with squeaking brakes. You know the high-pitched sound that makes your skin crawl? The hatch occurs regularly here because this is where the mosquitoes lay their eggs. Up here, where the water is slow-moving and the still pools are many, the larvae are safe. Then, whenever they've done whatever it is that they do, they hatch, sending tens of thousands of mosquitoes into the air at once where they swarm and make that high-pitched sound that only a mosquito makes. Normally, you can't hear it until they're buzzing around your ear, but fifty thousand is another thing entirely. You can hear that nearly forty yards off. The swarming is an indication that they are hungry, and mosquitoes really only eat one thing. Abbie heard it, too. "Are we near a highway?" I shook my head while considering our fastest escape. "Then, what's that sound?"

About then, they reached us. Most of my skin and hair turned black. I grabbed Abbie, put her into the wheelbarrow and started running down the bluff. Every inhale brought bugs down my throat. Abbie was screaming and slapping herself, while the bugs flew into my nose, my ears, my eyes and bit me through my clothes or on bare skin. Within seconds, my skin and face were on fire. We barreled down the hill, up through the long grass, across the open area next to the house and into what would become the garage. Most of the mosquitoes had flown away by the time we reached the house, even fewer followed us in, but there was still a cloud in the house hovering around me. I lifted her out, climbed the steps into the house and when we reached the den, I set her down and rubbed and patted her legs while she slapped my shoulders and face. She slapped me six or eight times in the face, each slap growing harder each time. Abbie hated mosquitoes. She was about to slap me again when I grabbed her hand. "Honey . . . you're not helping." Blood was dripping out of the corner of my mouth where she'd hit me. "Oh . . . oops." That's when she started laughing. I brushed the few remaining bugs off her right leg and sat down. Since those guys on the river threw most everything we had into the fire, I didn't have any antihistamine, which meant that I was in trouble if Abbie started to swell up. I searched her arms, legs, neck and face for any sign of rising welts, but found nothing. Not a single one. I, on the other hand, was swelling and starting to look like somebody had shoved an airhose up my nose and inflated my face. I took my shirt off and Abbie started to count the red bumps from my waist up. She quit when she got to a hundred. Finally, she sat back and chewed on a fingernail. "Oh, Doss. Does that hurt? It looks painful. Is that painful?"

Her adrenaline was pumping and she was talking fast. I closed my eyes and laid down on the concrete floor with enough bug juice flowing through my veins to kill a small animal. I sneezed, clearing my nose of the last of them. "No, honey . . ." My lips were growing numb and fat. "It feels good."

"Well, I've always wanted to know what you looked like as a baby. Now I know." She stared at her arms and legs, marveling at the absence of bites. "I guess mosquitoes can sense the difference."

"Difference in what?"

"Between blood that has been poisoned . . . and blood that hasn't."

⚓

MY SWEET LITTLE REUNION was over. My face was on fire and both my left ear and left eye were nearly swollen shut. The tops of my hands and fingers were so fat that the paddle felt twice as thick as it had an hour ago. If I could have come out of my skin, I would have. I packed up the canoe, shoved off and shook my head.

While the view downriver had changed, the framework had not. The trees—swaying with Spanish moss—had spiraled taller and leaned in further across the river, but the bend still swept right in a slow easy arc disappearing some four hundred yards into the distance where the horizon merged into one unbroken treeline. The broken bench passed high on my right. I didn't look. Two more paddle strokes and I inhaled deeply, holding it. I scanned the view before me, closed my eyes and focused on the one thing that I couldn't live without.

She held me there a long time. Maybe three minutes. When I exhaled, I didn't feel a thing.

19

The sun poked its head up over Fort Sumter, then crawled up the Battery as we talked and dreamed and tried to figure out what we were going to tell her parents. I could take or leave the big Charleston wedding—I wanted whatever Abbie wanted. But it didn't take a rocket scientist to know that she and her mother would need a mediator to navigate the details of a wedding—especially one they hadn't agreed to. They would have come to blows. And heaven help us if her father got involved.

A city bus slowed to a stop behind us, its brakes metal on metal, and picked up a young mother and pigtailed girl wearing a pink backpack and pink shoes. The air brakes hissed, the bus pulled off and Abbie placed her palms on my face. "Let's leave right now."

"What, today?"

"Right this second."

"Don't you want to plan something?"

"Doss, I've wanted to marry you since I first laid eyes on you. Now marry me right this minute."

"Honey, no minister or priest in his right mind will just up and marry us on the spot."

"Doss, I don't have to marry in a church. God knows my

heart." She laughed. "He's probably tired of hearing about you—I've been asking Him for you most my whole life."

The thought of that struck me. "Really?"

She held my face in her hands. "And I loved you long before I met you."

There it is again. That thing that is my wife. "Where, then? Who?"

"I don't know, but you'd better get creative." She tapped her watchless left wrist. "The clock is ticking."

"But, Abbie, I don't have a ring."

She put her hand on her hip. "Well, you should've planned ahead." She chewed on her lip. "I have plenty. We'll use one of mine."

"I'm not marrying you with one of your own rings."

"You got any other options?"

"Well . . . this is Charleston. And it's the Friday following Thanksgiving. National holiday. Biggest shopping day of the year."

"If we go shopping around here, word will spread and we wouldn't make it out of the first store before my folks met us at the second."

"What about someplace where we could sort of look without really looking?"

"What do you have in mind?"

"Slave market."

"Perfect."

We walked up the Battery and north to the slave market where the women were already busy at work on their baskets. Several blocks long and maybe a half a block wide, today it serves as something akin to an outdoor mall. Vendors were unlocking their cases and spreading wares across their tables.

Inside was a combination flea market, craft store, antique shop and sports memorabilia bazaar. It was the last place in the world that a lady like Abbie should have been shopping for a ring. The brick walls were those see-through kind that let the breeze through but still housed the bazaar inside. We walked in hand in hand. "You know," she said, "slaves were never actually sold here."

"Then why do they call it the slave market?"

"Because it's the market where slaves were unloaded off the ships before they were hauled off to the auction blocks elsewhere. Later, it was used by slaves to sell their goods." She thought a moment. "Although, I suppose from the slaves' point of view, it's merely a matter of semantics. A transaction took place somewhere."

"How do you know all this?"

She twirled and sang softly, " 'I'm Charleston born and Charleston bred and when I die . . .' "

"I know, I know."

She pulled on my arm and led me to a display where a lady was selling sterling silver flatware. Most of it was called Old Orange Blossom. In a case on the far end of her display, she had a dozen or so old, plain silver bands. Abbie pulled her sunglasses down over her eyes and began looking.

The lady asked, "Can I help you?"

Abbie pointed. "Are those silver?"

The lady shook her head. "Platinum."

"May I?"

The lady nodded and slid the ring tray out of the display. Abbie tried on several until she found one that fit. The price tag read "$280." Abbie asked, "Do you have any men's sizes?"

The lady smiled and pulled another tray from the display. She looked at me. "Do you know what size you wear?"

I shook my head.

She glanced at my finger. "You're either an eleven or something pretty close to it. Try this." She slid a ring on my finger. It was a little stubborn going over the knuckle but I couldn't sling it off.

I turned to Abbie. "Will this work until I can buy you a real ring?" I shot a glance at the lady. "No offense, ma'am."

She laughed. "None taken."

Abbie spun the worn ring around her finger. "Doss, I don't need a diamond."

"Abbie, every girl deserves a diamond."

"Well, then, I'll just keep this one until that day comes. And even when it does, I'll wear them both."

"How much for the pair?" I asked.

"Four hundred dollars, normally, but today we're having a spur-of-the-moment sale that's twenty-five percent off."

"Sold."

"You want me to gift wrap?"

She had no real intention of gift-wrapping these rings. She was prying and we all knew it. "No thanks. They wouldn't stay in the paper very long."

I gave the lady my credit card, signed my name, slid both rings into my pants pocket and steered Abbie toward the jail.

It was the Friday following Thanksgiving. A national holiday. Which meant the courts were closed and most of the judges were off fishing or golfing. Surrounded by so much history, I remembered my twelfth-grade history class. The Magna Carta mandates that an arrested individual must see a judge within twenty-four hours of being incarcerated. Charleston was no hotbed of criminal activity, but certainly at least one person had to get stupid on Thanksgiving Day.

We glanced through the window into Judicial 1 where the

Honorable Archibald Holcomb Fletcher III was holding court. Abbie smiled slyly. "Follow me. I've got this covered." We waited quietly while Judge Fletcher dealt with three kids who got caught painting a carriage driver's horse with blue spray paint and then two DUIs. When the courtroom cleared, he looked up over his glasses at Abbie. "Abigail, what are you doing in my courtroom with that young man?" I got the feeling he didn't really need to ask.

"Getting married."

He laughed. "Not in my courtroom. You're daddy'll have my hide. As will the rest of Charleston."

"Your Honor, I'll make this easy for you. You can either marry us"—she smirked and raised one eyebrow—"or not."

He paused, not knowing exactly what card she was about to play. The tone in her voice told him that she knew something about him that few others did, but he didn't want to suggest he had anything to hide by asking what she was talking about. "You got a license?"

Abbie shook her head. "Nope."

"You'll have to wait 'til Monday morning when the office opens. Eight-thirty a.m. Once you apply, there's a twenty-four hour"—he spread his hands across the air like a fan—" 'cooling off' period. It's called that so impetuous young kids don't do something"—he stared at me—"stupid. In the meantime I'll just call your dad and make sure he's comfortable with"—he waved his finger through the air at me—"all this." He folded his arms.

"Judge Fletcher? Has my daddy been pretty good to you? Helping you get reelected a couple of times?"

He nodded. "And that's exactly why you're not getting married in this courtroom."

"I don't want to marry in this courtroom. I want to get married down there under that little arbor."

He stood up. "Abbie girl." He pointed with his gavel. "That thing is cheesy as hell. You need a proper wedding. St. Michaels, white dress, bagpipes . . . a priest."

Abbie crossed her legs and looked at her fingernails. After a minute she looked up at him. "Two things. First, anywhere I get married will be in the sight of God, so I'm not worried about His blessing. Secondly, Your Honor, over the years I've come to know quite a few reporters. Many here in town. And seeing as how they need you in their corner, they'll probably turn a blind eye to your Tuesday-night poker games. Although I imagine the South Carolina bar would love to hear about it. But I think it's those circuitous and long trips home that will grab their attention. Just how long does it take to drive a mile? Mrs. Cather's house lady says sometimes it can take four or five hours. Even longer when Mr. Cather is out of town." She smiled earlobe to earlobe. "And to think he's actually home when you're snooping around his pool house. Now, I'm no reporter, but I imagine that will make the front page of every paper in South Carolina."

I whispered out of the corner of my mouth, "Remind me never to play poker with you."

He looked at me. "Son, what is your name?"

"Doss Michaels, Your Honor."

"You do realize that if you go through with this her father will skin you alive, draw and quarter you and then cut off your head and post it on a stick at the city gate."

That pretty much sums it up. "Yes, sir."

"How old are you?"

"Twenty-one."

"And Abbie?"

"The same, sir."

He threw his gavel down. "Follow me." His heels made a clicking sound on the tiled floor. We reached a door that read "Marriage Department" and he said, "Wait at that window." Then like a sliding door in a doctor's office, he pushed it open.

I gave him our driver's licenses and birth certificates and he said, "Seventy dollars. And we don't take credit card or check."

I handed him seventy dollars cash and he filed our application for us. Five minutes later, we stood beneath the arbor, where wilting silk flowers draped around our heads. The arbor stood in the corner of a small, paneled room. A couple of benches led up to a two-by-four frame covered in ribbon and decade-old Christmas lights. The arbor was rounded like a tunnel and the lights flashed sporadically. Abbie looked around her and laughed. Judge Fletcher held a printout of the vows in one hand and looked at Abbie over the tops of his reading glasses. "You realize what this is going to do to your mother?"

Abbie looped her arm inside mine. "Judge Fletcher, with all due respect, my mother's not getting married here."

"I don't have to do this, you know." What he was really saying was that just because he was doing this didn't mean he was admitting guilt, which of course he was. It was a weasel statement.

She pulled her cell phone out of her pocket and smiled.

He turned toward me. "You know, she gets this from her father."

"Yes, sir."

"You seem like a smart kid. Don't start thinking with your plumbing. Take her home, drop her at her parents' house and run the other way."

Abbie put her hands on her hips. "Like you're one to talk—a model of discretion. Your Honor, this is one of the only guys I've ever met who doesn't think with his plumbing. You might take some lessons from him."

I whispered out of the corner of my mouth again. "Well, maybe I have been a little."

She whispered back, smiling. "A little's okay."

He cleared his throat. "We are gathered here today to witness this man and this woman joined together in matrimony, which is an honorable estate and therefore *not* to be entered into"—he glanced at us over his glasses; it was more of a frown than a smirk—"unadvisedly or lightly, but reverently and discreetly, into which estate these two persons present come now to be joined.

"Doss Michaels and Abigail Coleman, if it is your intention to share with each other your joys and sorrows and all that the years will bring, with your promises, bind yourselves to each other as husband and wife."

I heard him say the words *joys and sorrows,* but I really had no idea what he was talking about.

"Doss."

"Yes, sir."

"Will you take Abigail Grace Eliot Coleman as your wedded wife?"

"Yes, sir."

"Not yet, son. Just hold on." I nodded. "Will you take Abbie as your wedded wife. Will you love her, comfort her, honor and keep her, and forsaking all others keep only unto her, as long as you both shall live?"

"I will."

"Abbie, will you take Doss as your wedded husband? Will

you love him, comfort him, honor and keep him, and forsaking all others, keep only unto him, as long as you both shall live?"

Abbie said, "I will," as the words *as long as you both shall live* rattled through my brain.

"Abbie, repeat after me." Her eyes were wet, glassy and I wanted very much to take her away to a church, for a proper wedding. Abbie should have been dressed in white. Not denim and a white T-shirt. She should be dragging a long train, and flanked by fifteen sniffling girlfriends catering to her every need. There should be flowers spilling out of the church, an organ, a soloist, a man playing bagpipes, a priest with a long robe, flower girl, ring boy . . . But in every scenario I created in my head, her parents appeared. And when they did, Abbie's glassy-eyed smiled disappeared. Abbie would have endured it out of obligation and when we looked back on it, there would be no joy. The smile on her face, framed by that cheese-dog arbor and lit by yellowed decade-old lights, would never have occurred in anything in which her mother or father played a part.

Sometimes when I look back I think that maybe I should have stepped in, brokered a peace, but I wasn't strong enough then to face her folks. I didn't know how, and to be truthful, I didn't care about their peace. I cared about hers.

Abbie finished repeating her vow and there it was again, *keep only unto him, as long as you both shall live.*

Judge Fletcher motioned to me. "I, Doss, take you, Abbie, to be my wife. I promise to stand beside you and with you always, in times of celebration and in times of sorrow. In sickness and in health, I will live with you and love you, as long as we both shall live."

While my lips moved and my vocal cords made the sounds, my heart pushed a question to the surface. I don't know why, it just did. *How does she know I mean this until I've done it. I mean, how does she know?*

Abbie held my hands in hers. "I, Abbie, take you, Doss . . ." Her upper lip was sweating, a vein throbbed on her right temple, a tear was cascading down her face and her right hand was trembling. That told me two things: a migraine headache had just come out of nowhere and that, by itself, told me everything I needed to know. Abbie was all in. She was betting her life.

Judge Fletcher cleared his throat. "From earliest time, the ring has been a symbol of wedded love. It is a perfect circle to symbolize the unending love you promise." He poked me in the shoulder. "Son, have you got the rings?" Palm up, I held them out. "Good. Slide hers halfway on her finger and repeat after me." I slid the ring over her first knuckle and noticed that Abbie was absolutely glowing. That's when it hit me. She didn't need white. She deserved it, yes, but she didn't need it.

"This ring I give you, in token and in pledge"—I slid it over her knuckle and pressed it gently against the back of her finger—"of my constant faith and abiding love." Whoever owned that ring in the past had simply borrowed it for a time, because it fit like it had been made for her all along.

Abbie slid my ring over my first knuckle and began repeating after the judge. As she spoke, her eyes lit. Despite her public persona and the fact that she'd pretty much conquered the world at an early age, her private, emotional side was more guarded. But there beneath that arbor, she stepped out from behind the shell she had barricaded around herself.

The judge folded the printout and sighed. His nose hairs were long, curly and made a little whistle sound on the inhale. He looked at the two of us, shook his head and frowned. "And now, by the power of the authority vested in me and having heard you make these . . . pledges of affection, I pronounce you husband and wife." He raised his eyebrows. "Congratulations. You may kiss the bride."

~ ⚓

DESPITE OUR BEST ATTEMPTS at stealth, word spread quickly. We had yet to step foot out of the courthouse when Abbie's cell phone started ringing. When she didn't answer, mine rang.

She leaned against me. "Where can you take me where no one will find us?"

"I only know of one place and it's not too glamorous."

"I've had glamour."

So I took her to the only place I knew anything about. The river.

It's been fourteen years. My slave market ring is scratched, dull and worn thin around the edges. I don't know who wrote those vows, but they must have been married a long time because we have shared our joys and sorrows and we have known some health and much sickness.

And every time I look back on that day, I find myself wanting to change it.

20

JUNE 3, EVENING

Stokes Bridge is an almost attractive single-lane concrete structure that rises above the rotting stub remnants of old pilings now broken in two and poking up through the water's surface below. Rolling, bleached-white beaches span either side dotted with poplar, sprawling live oaks, dogwood and longleaf pine. Vacant during most of the week, that changes come Friday night. We rounded a bend, the bridge came into view and we could smell the campfires and hear the laughter. The beach was lit with a half-dozen campfires, the flash of aluminum cans and brown glass bottles and the sporadic red glow of cigarettes. Two dozen trucks with tires larger than the hood of a Buick lined the beach, their beds stacked with coolers brimming with beer. Evidently, everyone was tuned to the same XM satellite station. We passed underneath the bridge as a Kenny Chesney tune followed an old Hank Jr. song. Fifty or so shirtless good ol' boys and their scantily-clad girlfriends dotted the beach in circles around the fires. A few were swimming and off in the shadows a couple others were skinny-dipping. Three long-haired hippy types stood on the railing of the bridge, some ten feet above the water. They were howling at the moon and at the count of three, launched a Mountain Dew commercial plunge into the pool below. On the far bank, a guy and a girl were trying to hang on to a rope swing, while beneath the bridge a dejected-looking loner was halfway through a gallon-sized bottle of Jack Daniel's. We paddled through in the shadows, opposite the beach. One rotund fellow wearing a Georgia Bulldogs cap stood next to a grill, flipping burgers, dogs and what looked like sausage. Swinging her legs off the tailgate next to him sat a rather large bikini-clad biker chick who was nursing a coolie-wrapped longneck.

I waved but tried not to make eye contact. The guy at the grill hollered across the water, "Hey, ya'll hungry?" I shook my head, waved him off and hugged the far bank. He stepped back from his grill, out of the smoke, and tipped his hat. "You been paddling long?"

I nodded and kept dipping my paddle in the water. Another two hundred yards and we could disappear into the shadows. "A while."

He smiled and waved his beer at me. "Well, pull up and set awhile. What's your hurry?"

I shook my head with more finality. "Thanks, we're just passing." The moon was full and climbing high. "Thought we'd take advantage of the light while we had it."

The smoke from his grill wafted across the river, tugged on my nose and my brain started pumping out signals to my stomach. At that moment, a truck with more lights than an airport runway stopped in the middle of the bridge and turned up the volume on "Sweet Home Alabama" to a decibel I'd never heard rise out of an automobile. It sounded like a rock concert.

Without exception, every man on the beach or in the water stood, took off his hat, crossed his heart and hollered at the top of his lungs while many of the girls reached into their pockets, thumbed their lighters and swayed the single flames silently above their heads. I forgot to mention that, around here, this is known as the Redneck Riviera, that song is the redneck anthem and they were showing respect.

Some work the grocery store checkout counter, stock shelves at the auto parts store, sling feed bags at the local hardware, work for the forestry department or a master welder, shoe horses, deliver rural mail or sell cattle, real estate or, more than likely, pine trees. They talk slower, often stretching two syllables into five, use phrases that make little sense on the surface, dip Copenhagen and drink beer simultaneously, and have no desire to understand a New York minute. Admittedly, college degrees are not the norm, Ph.D.'s are few, and while outsiders drive across the bridge and see little more than a bunch of drunk rednecks, they'd do well to never confuse cultural difference with ignorance or stupidity. Beneath the twangy exterior, they value common sense, make do with less, laugh easily and will give you the shirt off their backs—they are the salt of the earth. When you're not in a hurry, pull up a chair and you will find your stomach full and that laughter has creased your face with wrinkles.

Abbie poked her head up. "You better stop this boat."

"Honey . . ."

"Don't 'honey' me. You stop this boat or I'm dancing with Chef Boyardee over there."

I beached the canoe just down from the sparks of the bonfires and lifted Abbie to her feet. She swayed as the dizziness eased. She hung her arms around my neck while nearly a hundred people danced in unison across the beach or in the water. She smiled. "I'll walk on the tops. You dance on the bottoms."

"Deal."

We danced along with everyone else through "Freebird,"

then Waylon and Willie's "Good Hearted Woman," ending with Don Williams's "Lord I Hope This Day Is Good" and AC/DC's "You Shook Me All Night Long." By the end, Abbie was laughing, singing along and hanging on me. I lifted her and we finished the dance carrying her along the beach. I hadn't eaten all day so when the airport truck finally cleared off the bridge, I laid her on the sand and collapsed next to her. Chef Boyardee appeared over my shoulder, stuck his hand out and said, "Name's Michael, but everyone around here cause me Link." He handed me a paper plate holding two of the largest, drippiest and best-smelling cheeseburgers I'd ever seen. He said, "Eat up. And welcome." He pointed at a cooler on the back of his truck. "Got sodas, beer, water, you name it. Make yourself comfortable." He took two steps away and then turned back. "Something wrong with your face?" Abbie laughed. I nodded. "Yeah, mosquitoes."

"Dang! That hurt?" I heard Abbie laughing behind me.

"A bit."

"You 'ont some medicine?"

"Yeah."

He slung open the diamond-plated toolbox atop his truck and pulled out a first aid kit. "Ought to be something in there."

I dug around and found two Benadryl. "Thanks."

Abbie eyed the box, her right eyebrow pulling up the edge of her lip. "You didn't happen to find a cure for cancer in there, did you?"

"No, fresh out, but maybe we could pick one up at the next Wal-Mart."

She leaned back and kicked her feet up. "That'd be nice. Let's do that."

IN THE NEXT THIRTY MINUTES, I downed four burgers and tried to get as much fluid into Abbie as she could stomach.

We kept to the shadows, watching the circus perform around us. Eventually, I asked Link, "You all do this every Friday night?"

He laughed, crushed a beer can single-handedly and quickly popped the tab on another. "Ain't you been watching the weather?" I shook my head. He pointed his beer toward the sky in a general southwesterly direction. "Hurricane Annie. She was stalled over the Gulf but it's looking like she's coming northeast and ought to be here in a couple of days. Thought we'd have us a welcoming party, seeing as how we got us a bull's-eye printed on our forehead."

He was quiet a minute. Chewing a bite of sausage, he said, "We heard of you."

That wasn't good. "You did?"

He nodded and took another bite—mustard and pork grease were smeared across the corners of his mouth. "Yeah. Seems some folks back upriver seen you slipping through. Thought it a might strange that someone would be paddling this far up. Most folks don't put in 'til St. George. Unless'n they know the river." He stared at me. "Which, judging you by the looks and"—he chuckled—"that hat, you been here afore."

I nodded. "Been down it a time or two."

"Given the time you're making, I'd say you've been down it more than just a time or two."

This could go one of two ways. Folks down on the river were rather protective of themselves and their privacy. They lived with an inherent distrust of anyone resembling a politician, salesman or journalist. That meant they didn't just invite everyone into their business, because they weren't all that eager to share it. Remember what my mom said. Folks come to this river for a lot of reasons. Those that are hiding wish to keep it that way. Drawing attention to themselves wouldn't help. Granted, we were an odd sight and to their way of thinking, we were intruding on what they thought was their private river, but I was hopeful that if we kept to ourselves and passed quietly through, when they spread word about us, they would do so in country-road whispers and not beauty-shop gossip.

I didn't say anything. He continued, "How far you headed?"

I had a choice. Lie or tell him the truth. I had a feeling that lying wouldn't get us any farther downriver while the truth might. "All the way if I can manage it."

He was in mid-bite. "All the way to St. Marys?"

"Unless something stops us."

He finished his sausage-dog and wiped his hands on his T-shirt. "You know if that hurricane dumps a bunch of rain on us that this river is going to change overnight."

I nodded. "Yeah, she will."

He pointed north toward Folkston. "I's raised up yonder. Never been down the length of her. Always wanted to. I'd like to see Reed's Bluff."

"It's worth seeing."

He stared off into the river. "Maybe I will." His eyes narrowed. "Folks say once you get up there that you can see where the river ends. That true?"

"Yes."

"She perty?"

A nod and a quick glance at Abbie. "She's . . . beautiful." Abbie's forehead was flush and the telltale blue vein had popped out on her left temple. I knelt down and she just moaned. I flipped open the Pelican case, discreetly cracked the cap on a dexamethasone syringe and pushed out the air. Then I slid it into Abbie's thigh. Syringe empty, I capped it and closed the case.

A minute passed. Link swallowed loud enough for me to hear it. Eyes wide, he glanced at his truck. "Ya'll . . . maybe need anything?" He said all this while rubbing his thigh.

I stared downriver. "Time and distance. And maybe a little more flow."

He raised an eyebrow and his voice lowered. "Have I seen her afore?"

"Probably."

"She famous? A model or something?"

"At one time."

"She alright?"

How exactly should I answer that? "She's been sick a long time. And . . . we needed some fresh air so I brought her where I knew she'd get it."

"Well . . ." He chewed on his bottom lip a minute. "I hope you make it. Both of you."

I spread a pallet on the beach beneath the low-lying limbs of an oak tree. They were thin, long and grew up out of the tree only to swoop down over the beach, brush the sand's surface, then rise back up above the water where they hung thick with leaves. Other than Link, we kept to ourselves.

Link had jowls the size of a bulldog and his fingers were three times as fat as mine, but that had little negative effect on his ability to play a guitar, because after he'd fed the troops, he lifted a Gibson out of the back of his truck and lit the strings on fire. I'd never seen someone's fingers move so fast across the strings of anything. I turned to Abbie. "Who is this guy? He ought to be on the *Grand Ole Opry*."

A fellow next to us heard and nodded. "He has been. And he's a regular at the Woodbine."

Woodbine is the South Georgia version of the Opry. He pointed his longneck at Chef. "Link there plays by ear, and he ain't never had no lessons." He swallowed, the foam dripping off his chin. "Perty good, huh?"

"I'll say."

Link played twenty to thirty songs with seamless transition, well-disguised improvisation and no rest. His music soaked the air with something I can only describe as resonance. He said very little because his hands were saying enough and he took every request without looking at a single note. Here was a guy who looked like he ought to be driving a tractor or mucking manure out of stalls and yet he was by far the most talented musician I'd ever seen. He blazed through blue grass, country, Southern rock and classical. If there were limits to his repertoire, we never saw them.

Around ten, a bunch of folks waded into the water, girls climbed onto the guys' shoulders and started a mixed-couples wrestling event. A king-of-the-river sort of thing. It was all fun and games until one girl ripped off another's bikini top and then all Hades broke loose. They were scratching, clawing, smacking. It looked like a catfight.

By midnight, three distinct groups had developed. The first had passed out and lay sprawled along the beach, a second group had retreated to their blankets and were snuggling around the fires—a few were making s'mores—while the third stood milling around, whispering, drinking or sitting in the water and letting the warm flow roll past them. All eyes were on Link. He hadn't said a word in nearly three hours. Finally, he stopped picking and began tapping the face of his guitar. His eyes were lost somewhere in the sand in front of him. Folks gathered in close. The guy next to me whispered, "Last song. Usually Zeppelin."

The crowd on the beach pulled in closer toward the fire—and him. Golden flames grew up out of white coals, chased the smoke and licked the air, lighting his face and the sweat that trickled down.

He tapped several beats, sounding out a hollow drum. Then he looked across the smoke and sand to me and Abbie, and his eyes lost themselves somewhere over my shoulder.

After a few moments, he spoke. "In 1991, Eric Clapton's son, Conor, fell from a fifty-third-story window. Forty-nine floors later he landed on the roof of a four-story building. A year later, Clapton released a tribute—'Tears in Heaven.' People wanted someone to blame, but at the end of the day, it was just a tragic accident." He shrugged. "Life is hard and sometimes it hurts. And sometimes those reasons ain't real clear."

A guy next to the fire pointed his bottle at the heavens and said, "I heard dat's right."

Link continued. "The song won most every award, as did his *Unplugged* album." He picked quietly. "It's difficult to pick the greatest tribute song. It's as if they have their own place outside auditoriums and awards dinners. They don't classify too easily. Critics nibble at them but I doubt it really matters. After 9/11, a lot of folks wrote songs but none captured what I was feeling like Alan Jackson's 'Where Were You.' " Couples around the fire leaned back-to-chest and melted into each other. "In 1977, Robert Plant's son Karac died suddenly of a stomach infection. Plant was on tour. Out of that, he wrote a song that many have said inspired Clapton." Link studied the neck of his guitar and his fingers delicately tapped the strings. "It's my favorite Zeppelin tune. It's called 'All My Love.' " He began playing an intro. "I don't normally dedicate songs. Just ain't my thing. The song speaks for itself, but . . . this one's for . . . everyone who's ever stood . . . where the river ends."

I lifted Abbie off her bed and swayed slowly above the sand, the water and the fire's reflection. She clutched my shoulders, pressed her head to my neck and held me as we twirled above the beach.

When he finished, even the woods around us were quiet. Abbie pulled on me and whispered, "How about an encore?"

The harmonics of his last notes were echoing off the river when I stopped him. "Link?" Everyone looked at me—the no-name stranger paddling the gaunt ghost downriver. I cleared my throat. "Would you play that one more time? Please?"

The crowd around him parted and somebody set a five-gallon bucket upside down in between us and the fire. Link rested his foot on the bucket, closed his eyes and poured himself into the song. The tail end of the last notes had yet to fade before they were met by the first.

When he finished, Abbie pressed her forehead to mine. I was drenched. Sweat was dripping off my nose and my shirt was vacuum-sealed to my back. We stayed there a minute. Finally, I walked down into the water and knelt in the flow. She pulled on my ear and managed a smile. "About time you learned to dance."

I laid her in the canoe, thanked Link, and we pulled off the beach at midnight. If people were talking about us, I wanted to get as much river under our belt after dark as I could. We could sleep in the middle of the day.

I dipped the paddle in the water while Abbie whispered, "I remember my first dance with Mr. Jake at the Dock Street. After the show, they dropped the curtain, but I was still so excited that he grabbed my hand and we danced backstage. I was so keyed up—I just . . . didn't want it to end."

Not long after my mom explained to me the meaning of an "easy woman," I decided to enact my own revenge on the big fat woman who started the rumor. She had this thermometer on her front porch that you could read from across the park. She had camouflaged it amongst all the stolen Coca-Cola and Burma-Shave signs. The thermometer was nearly as tall as me and hung on the sunny side of her trailer, which meant it read about five degrees hotter than it really was—which she thought made her special. It was like she'd cornered the South Georgia market on temperature readings. Things were a little slow around the park. Anyway, she drove out of the park one afternoon, leaving her place unattended. I never even hesitated. I grabbed a brick, walked straight up to the thermometer and smashed it into a thousand slivers. The glass exploded. I remember hearing this loud pop and when I looked again the ground was spotted with maybe a half-dozen large silver droplets that looked like warped chrome ball bearings. I poked at them with a stick and they jiggled. They pulled at my curiosity, so I pushed them back together and when I did they all rolled into one big, nearly egg-sized drop in which I saw my distant and distorted reflection.

The surface of the water clung to the paddle like a liquid mirror, then dripped off the tip in equal drops. Behind us, the moon climbed high and hung bright. Below, the drops pooled like mercury, drawing themselves into one long fluorescent flow.

She closed her eyes. "Guess we can check off number eight."

I never saw my reflection.

21

Her parents were livid. *Pissed* is probably a better word. Truer, too. They did everything they could to force a wedge between Abbie and me. They spelled out our differences, my failings, my lack of pedigree, my— You get the point. And if they did it once, they did it a hundred times. We suffered no shortage of Doss-bashing. Of the two of us, I probably understood it more than she.

In all the turmoil, I discovered something about their parenting. On the surface, I always thought that a family like hers had all their ducks in a row. They looked happy, therefore they must have been happy. Truth was, they were miserable. Her stepmom was pretty and had all the guys calling. Her dad was a rocketing political star. Seemed like a match made in heaven. Neither ever thought to ask if they actually loved each other. Love was an afterthought. But they learned to put on their happy face and show the world that they had it all together. So she became the ice queen and he, the face on TV. Then Abbie blossomed and they poured themselves into her in a style which said, "I know best, so buck up and pour your energy and passion into my vision for you." Not once did they think to ask Abbie, "What are you passionate about and how can I pour myself into your vision of you?"

As a result, Abbie lay in bed at night, listening to the arguments her parents promised her they never had, and she promised herself that—no matter the cost—she was going to marry for love.

So in a weird and twisted sort of way, I'm glad they fought. Otherwise, Abbie would have married some attorney who wore a seersucker suit and bow tie. Instead, she married me. I've never owned a seersucker suit and I couldn't tie a bow tie if my life depended on it.

Her parents drew a line in the sand—I was not welcome in their home, on their property or in their rearview mirror. On the other hand, Abbie was expected to attend every family holiday or political function. I said, "Honey, go. They're your family. You can't ignore them. I'll be here when you get back."

She shook her head and took the phone off the hook. "You are my family. So don't try pawning me off on them."

Abbie spent two more years doing the New York model thing and then hung it up and came home. She was never picked as the poster girl for Clinique or Estée Lauder but a lot of folks think she could have been. She looked at modeling a lot like climbers look at mountains. It was there so she climbed it, but once she got to the top, she looked around and discovered other peaks. When people asked why, she'd shrug and say, "Been there, did that." What she was really saying was that she'd proven her point and broken the tether to her dad. That didn't mean she didn't love him, but it did mean that when she came home, he couldn't control her with a noose through her nose. Modeling, traveling the world, opened her eyes to her real passion—design. So she returned to school in Charleston and finished a four-year interior design degree in two years and then went to work for a local firm. When it came to design, she had a knack for it. It didn't take her long to have her own clients. Abbie's sense of design was four-dimensional. She could see color and spatial design like everyone else, but her singular gift was that she saw opportunity and possibility when others saw bad lines, antiquated fixtures, a moth-eaten piece of furniture, wood rot or cracked and peeling layers of the previous owner's bad decisions.

I learned this firsthand after we'd been married about six months. Between her career as a model and what her father had given her from her deceased mother and his growing estate, Abbie had her own money. And a good bit of it, too.

One day she parked the Mercedes top down in front of this boarded-up house that looked like it should have been in a Stephen King novel. Paint chipped, windows busted, shingles missing, porch falling off one side of the house, it either needed to be dozed or blown up. Nearly four years earlier, in September of 1989, Hurricane Hugo attempted to rip Charleston off the map. A category-five storm, it caused $13 billion in damage, and much of that occurred in the Carolinas. In its wake, many of the homes it decimated remained untouched and rotting. Like this one. After four years of sitting, the city had tired of arguing with the owners and was in the process of condemning it. Evidently, Abbie had caught wind of it and bought it off the courthouse steps.

She led me inside, around the dry-rotted debris and up a spiral staircase that led into the master bedroom on the second floor. From there, we mounted a steep, narrow wooden staircase that led into a third story. Finally, she opened a window, pointed me through and said, "Close your eyes." I obeyed and she pulled me upward into the crow's nest. The platform shifted under our weight. I opened my eyes and she pointed out across the water. "I bought you something," she said. I scanned the waterline below for anything vaguely resembling an eighteen-foot fishing boat. I really wanted a Hewes, Key West or Pathfinder, but I'd have settled for a Carolina Skiff. I saw nothing.

"What?"

She stamped her feet and smiled. The iron platform rattled where a few of the bolts had wiggled loose.

I looked down, slowly. Pieces of the puzzle were sliding into place. While the house had weathered Hugo, it hadn't been touched since. We weren't just looking at a few missing shingle tiles, a little cracked and peeling paint or even a bit of wood rot. Not hardly. Entire sections of the roof were missing. Windows had disappeared leaving no trace that they'd ever been there. The front door was literally hanging on a twisted hinge. The basement sat stagnating in a foot of brackish water. Further, rumors told that the network of tunnels under this end of Charleston led from the old city, under this house, to the wharf. If that was true, and given the storm surge of Hugo, there was no telling how much water might have been in this house or how that might have eroded the foundations of this or any surrounding home. I leaned out over the railing and looked through the roof and down two stories into the kitchen. "You didn't."

Her eyes lit up, the smile stretching from ear to ear.

Months of nonstop weekends, long nights of work and ten thousand trips to Home Depot were piling up all around me. "Please don't tell me . . ."

She held out a hand, put her arm around my waist and pointed back to the view. Behind me, I could see all of Charleston—where, protected by those who loved her, nothing grew taller than her steeples. On the water side I could see well beyond Fort Sumter, and northeast, I could make out what was left of Sullivan's Island. She stamped her foot, demonstrating sturdiness. The ironwork rattled, sending reverberations throughout the hollow house. "Really," she said, "it's not that bad."

The house was one strong wind from collapsing. I shook my head. "Impossible."

She tapped me in the chest. "You function, me form." Which when translated meant: You do all the chipping, scraping, hammering, hauling, sawing and nailing and I'll decorate.

Function and form—a good description of us. And truth be told, if she had asked, I'd have built an ark in the desert. Which is about what we wound up doing. Not to mention, the view was pretty good.

Oddly enough, I hate to paint. I don't mean that I dislike it, I mean I despise anything that resembles a Tom Sawyer whitewash. Go figure. So when we first started renovating her hurricane fixer-upper, I told Abbie, "Honey, I'll pay anyone to paint whatever you want in whatever color you want. I'll hire da Vinci himself, but I'm not painting this house. At all. Ever. Deal?"

She nodded, 'cause she knew I had my work cut out for me and 'cause she thought she liked to paint. "No worries. I'll paint. I like painting." I knew better. After a few nights working in the house, hearing her mutter beneath her breath, and realizing I was going to have to hire someone to come fix her mess, she came to me. It was about midnight. I was leaning over a belt sander working on the floors. A dust cloud hovered around the room. I clicked it off, pushed my mask up on top of my head and waited for the ceiling fan to push out the cloud. She was covered in white primer. Head, hair, hands, arms, pants, feet. She looked like someone had rolled her in her own paint tray. She leaned against the wall, picked at some dried paint on one hand, raised an eyebrow and said, "You help me paint this house and I'll give you some loving." She dropped her wet brush. "Right here."

"I love to paint. I'll paint the whole house. Right now."

So we painted. The house, each other, neither of us was very good but we learned and more importantly, we laughed. A lot. Laughter filled our house from day one.

To become a member in ASID, designers must work under another designer for two years, then sit for and pass the NCIDQ exam. She put in her two years, passed the exam and, Christmas of 1995, hung up her shingle, opening her own studio. Doing so, she established a second name for herself. Her father was both proud and put off. And, in truth, she and her studio put me and my art on the map. Without it, I'd be very skinny, teaching art at a local high school.

Over the next decade, thanks in large part to the before-and-after pictures, Abbie's fixer-upper would be featured in *Southern Living, Architectural Digest* and a handful of regional and low-country magazines. Most of her girlfriends were jealous. When the articles appeared, her detractors gossiped beneath their breath, *Her daddy used his influence.* 'Course, those were the same detractors who cried *Nuts!* when we bought it, and trust me, her daddy wanted nothing to do with it. He, too, said she was nuts. But they didn't and do not know Abbie. She saw, and has always seen, what no one else could.

Meanwhile, during our first two married years, Senator and Mrs. Coleman didn't speak to me. But thanks to time and Abbie, they eventually warmed up. That doesn't mean they were kind or forgiving, but at least they weren't foaming at the mouth. Two things happened to soften them. First, Abbie's public persona of both successful model and designer surpassed that of her father. He could not deny that she was far more famous, and in some respects powerful, than he. Television personalities in and around South Carolina began introducing him as "Abbie Eliot's father." At the same time, they stopped introducing her as Senator Coleman's daughter. Secondly, I kept my mouth shut and nose to the canvas. My work output increased exponentially. Abbie had a grace and presence that attracted people like a magnet. Of course, she was beautiful, but beauty alone does not achieve Abbie's level of success. By default, that opened doors that I never could have opened on my own. I have no illusions—I did not get here on my own and hence, I am not responsible for my own success. In truth, I rode her coattails, and thankfully my talent was good enough to enable me to hang on. My growing success, especially in Charleston, put me—or rather my work—front and center every time the Colemans' walked into one of their friend's homes. Seems like they couldn't escape me. I took one project a month, and I was booking more than a year out. We had even started talking about a family.

Then Abbie forced me to take a year off.

22

JUNE 4, MORNING

The earth's surface over what we know as the State of Florida is essentially soft sand and a few rocks thrown over a thick layer of limestone. Once the river cut to the limestone, she had only one way to go: out. Her banks are continually on the move, meaning that the river was constantly changing its course—earning her the nickname the Crooked River. It might take years to see any visual difference, and only then if you were paying attention, but in areas of fast current or in times of increased flow, she could carve new boundaries at the rate of an inch or so a day. Beaches became beaches as the river cut itself further into the far bank. I'd been away for fifteen years, so to my eyes the river was transformed.

Few houses or people populate the river's banks between Stokes Bridge and St. George because most of that land has been acquired by plantation owners and paper companies. One such plantation sat on the Georgia side covering some twelve hundred acres. Spread Oak Plantation wound three miles along the river and served as a breeding ground for nocturnal corn-fed deer, territorial inbred turkeys, giant beavers, crafty red-tailed hawks, several dozen Tennessee walkers, spiraling pine trees and palm-sized bream, but her most famous "crop" was quail. The bobwhite. And those she grew by the thousands. My interest in Spread Oak centered on its protected beaches. Other than our extended stop at the Redneck Riviera, we'd been moving for nearly twenty-four hours and I was starting to ache in places I'd forgotten I had muscles.

With the sun just breaking the treetops and burning the steam off the water, we glided downriver. It was the first time since the bridge that I'd not had to paddle. The water was deeper here and the flow pushed us along at maybe a mile and a half an hour. Wood ducks flew single file down the center of the river. I looked up through the mist and saw a deer standing knee-deep next to the bank. Water dripped off his nose and his ears twitched in my direction. He was large-bodied, his stomach sagged and his horns were covered in golden velvet. They extended two to three inches beyond his ears and climbed high above his head. The light made it difficult to see, but I think he had six points on either side and the two directly above his head—brow tines—looked a foot long. I didn't hear him come, and I didn't hear him go. When I blinked, he was gone. A ghost. Leaving only ripples on the water. I didn't think deer like that still existed around here, but I guess he didn't get that big being stupid.

We pushed through the rising mist and listened to the earth wake around us. Dog barks, car doors, glass-pack mufflers, black crows, bright red cardinals. We spent the morning tucked beneath a birch tree on a Spread Oak beach. Other than the breeze whistling through the paper bark of the birch trees, bark that had curled like a twisted scroll, it was relatively quiet. Every now and then we'd catch the sound of a chainsaw or motorcycle and twice I spotted a bi-wing plane above us. On his second pass, he nearly brushed the treetops. As it flew away, I got a better look. Blue body, yellow wings.

Between the guys somewhere behind us, word spreading around about us and the plane above us, I was starting to get uncomfortable.

A funny smell rose up my nose. I looked down at Abbie and she was painting her toenails with clear polish. I chuckled.

"What're you laughing at?"

"Where did you get that?"

"You don't think I left home without it, do you?"

"No, but everything we had was made into a bonfire about twenty miles ago."

She smiled. "Not everything." She started on another toe. "Girl can't go around with dull toes."

I scratched my chin and found myself laughing again. She pointed her brush at me. "You're still laughing."

My face felt better, and while my eye was no longer swollen shut, my lip was still puffy. I tipped my hat and laid back. "When Gus first hired me, I guided these guys from Stokes Bridge to St. George. A good group—bunch of weekend warriors with wives at home—but they'd never really spent much time in the woods. After a long day, and then a longer night on hard ground, one of them came to me and said, 'What do we do about a bathroom?' I didn't know how much detail to give him so I handed him a small shovel, pointed to the woods and said, 'Just dig a hole and cover it up when you're done.' He looked at me and one end of his lip turned up. He glanced downriver. 'How long before we come to a public bathroom?' I shrugged. 'Maybe tonight.' A few minutes later, I looked upriver maybe a hundred yards and the guy was sitting on the beach reading a magazine. His shorts were at his ankles and his bare butt was pressed into the hole he'd dug. I just shook my head. Anyway, the others soon followed suit. Maybe I should've said something. That night one of the guys came to me and said, 'Ummm . . . hey, uh . . . do you have any bug bites? Like little red bites?' He was scratching himself as he talked. 'No. You?' He nodded without letting on. 'Where?' I asked. He pointed down. 'Everywhere.' He crossed his arms and whispered, 'Like . . . every square inch. And it's itching so bad I'm about to lose my religion.' I asked, 'Big red bumps?' He nodded. I reached in my bag and handed him a bottle of clear fingernail polish. 'They're called chiggers. You can't see them. They're little bugs that seek out hot spots, burrow into your skin and hang out for about two weeks unless you smother them. Put that on every one and keep it on there.' He looked at me like I'd lost my mind. 'You're yanking my chain, right? This is one of those rights-of-passage things that you river guides do to city boys like me.' I shook my head. 'No. I wouldn't kid around about chiggers. Come midnight, if you don't do something, you'll be itching so bad you'll . . . well, you'll be in a bad way.' He took the bottle and asked, 'Every single one?' I nodded. 'Yup.' I cleaned the breakfast dishes, broke down the tent and loaded the canoes. When I returned, all five of them were standing around the fire, pants at their ankles, fanning the polish dry. It's one of those images I could do without. One of them, a skinny guy that ran power plants around the country, said, 'What happens on the river, stays on the river . . . right?' 'Yeah, but you're going to have a hard time convincing your wives of that.' "

Abbie finished, spun the cap back on the bottle and blew on her little toe. "What in the world got you to thinking about that?"

"The smell."

"Well"—she waved the bottle in the air—"if you find yourself in need, you can get your own. I'm not letting you"—

she twirled her index finger in the air, making a circular motion and pointing it in my general direction—"paint yourself, and then expect me to paint my toes with it. A girl's got to have her boundaries. You're on your own."

"Can't say that I blame you."

23

Because of her travels, Abbie had seen some of the greatest art ever created. She'd stood right in front of it. Stared, laughed, cried. Hence, she understood it better and appreciated it on a level exponentially deeper than I did or could. While I might have understood the painters' lives, Abbie understood their work, and in a greater sense, them. Compared to Abbie, I didn't know squat. I'd be looking at an art book, turning the pages, and she'd say, "I've seen that," or "It's better in person," or "Oh, honey, you should see that . . . the way the light travels across . . ." I was always jealous.

We'd been married a year when she came to me. I was sitting in my studio, mixing paints.

She sat in my lap, arm around my neck. "I want to go on a trip."

"Okay."

"And I want to plan it. All by myself."

"Okay."

"And you'll go with me?"

"Sure."

She walked out of the room, grabbed a folder that was about four inches thick and came back in. She sat on the floor, patted the ground next to her and then unfolded a map of the world.

One of the great things she'd gotten from her father was the ability to think outside the box. Add to that the fact that she had money and Abbie could come up with some "out there" ideas.

We were gone nearly a year.

In a perfect world, we'd have started with the early Renaissance and moved forward linearly, hopping through a timeline of artists and their work. Instead, we hopped geographically, from city to city. That is, until the very end. But that, too, she did on purpose.

Our first stop on our way to New York was the National Gallery in D.C. I remember turning a corner and there hung Rubens's *Daniel in the Lions' Den*. I sat on a bench opposite the work and walked across it with my eyes for nearly three hours. The idealized grandeur reached down within me and touched something I never knew was there.

At the Art Institute of Chicago, we sat with Toulouse-Lautrec and his *At the Moulin Rouge*. Toulouse was the crippled outcast who hung out in Paris bordellos with prostitutes and other social outcasts and found comfort in the night world of Paris. If Toulouse had taught me anything, it was that it takes an outcast to paint the needy.

In London, Abbie rushed me to the National Gallery where I met Giovanni Bellini and his *Portrait of Doge Leonardo Loredan*. The face, the expression of the mouth, the facial wrinkle in the cheek matched by the neck and, most importantly, the eyes. Nothing prepared me for that.

We flew to Florence and met Giotto. Giotto had taken the flat two-dimensional creations of his predecessors and, using light and dark shading, added dimension. He gave solidity and weight where it had not existed before. In her role as my tutor, Abbie asked me, "Why is he important?"

I could see now. "He thought outside the box."

Second, she led me to Donatello's sculpture *Mary Magdalene*—the aged woman, her anguish imprinted on her face. Her torment stopped me. The way her hair draped across her face, her torn clothes, she wore her emaciated, withered soul on the outside.

In the Uffizi Gallery, I found Piero della Francesca and his one-sided portrait of Federico da Montefeltro. Federico was disfigured in that he'd lost his right eye in a sword fight, so Francesca painted him in full profile but only of his left side—to hide it. Oddly enough, while his contemporaries were idealizing their subjects, he showed the moles and crooked nose. Also there was Titian's *Venus of Urbino*. While her body is provocative, it is drawn in such a way that leads you time and time again to her face, the angle of her neck, the inviting drop of her shoulders, the playfulness in her eyes, the relaxed crossing of her legs. It's what a nude should be.

Then she took me to *Portrait of a Man (The Young Englishman)*. Whereas Bellini's *Doge* is stiff and wooden, Titian's *Englishman* is not, the youthful honesty of his face drips off the page. While his garment fades away, can even be described as washed out and nondescript, his gaze is almost verbal. He captures the viewer, pulls at your eyes and forces you to come to grips with the singular thought that this might just be the best portrait ever painted.

One afternoon, she wrapped a blindfold around my head and led me by the hand down a walkway, around a corner and sat me on a bench. I knew where we were. It's rather a famous walk, but then she took off the blindfold. There he stood. Michelangelo's *David*. I hit my knees. If there is anything perfect in art, that may be it. I cried. Cried like a baby.

Abbie knelt beside me. My tutor. "Why is he important?"

"He made his own box."

Halfway through our trip, I realized that Abbie had lifted my masters off the page, taken them out of the realm of gods and set me at a table where they were carrying on a rather lively conversation. She introduced me to them and slid my chair up to the table. It was a gift unlike any other. In doing so, she took what head knowledge I had of each of them and allowed it to sift down into my heart. Where it would take root.

In Rome we found Bernini's sculpture *Damned Soul.* It is the face of a tormented man facing eternal damnation. To get the face just right, Bernini scorched his forearm with a hot iron. It worked, because you can see the torment in the eye and cheek, the rise of the nose, the wild flaming hair—open mouth, wide eyes. I shook my head. How does he do that?

In Potsdam at the Neues Palais, I marveled with Caravaggio and his *Doubting of St. Thomas.* For so long I'd wanted to lean in close and study how the finger, up to the second knuckle, was stuck into the skin in Jesus's rib cage. In Rome, we found *Judith,* and I met the servant with the wrinkled, serious face.

At the Louvre in Paris, I met Raphael's *Baldassare Castiglione.* He was the clear-eyed and pensive man I'd met twenty years before on a page in the library with my mom. For the first time, I understood how the introspectiveness of the philosopher is seen through the eyes, and how such a somber mood is created with stillness and "quiet" colors.

We met countless others, but she saved my favorite for last. Rembrandt.

In an era when most who sat for portraits were posers, clothes horses, engaged in a costume drama where they believed their clothing identified them, along came Rembrandt. He didn't think twice about accurately depicting a crow's foot, a bulbous nose, the oversized scrotum of a chubby toddler, or Abraham's huge hand on Isaac's face—which we saw at the Hermitage in St. Petersburg.

Rembrandt looked for what described a person, what identified them, and he did not avoid it or shy away from it. He sought to uncover the personality of the person before him by taking off the mask that either he wore by choice or that society had placed on him. His fine motor skills caught the precise textures of fabric, like perforations in lace or the translucent layering of chiffonlike fabric. He used high finish and rough scraping within the same area, scratching back white paint with the stub end of a brush. In *A Portrait of an 83-Year-Old Woman* in the National Gallery in London, he gave us the droop of an octogenarian eyelid, where the skin hanging loosely over her lid had been made with jabbing strokes of the brush. Her tortoise face, the wetness of her eyes, the way she looked past you—the shadows give thoughtfulness, and her pink eyelids suggest nights without sleep.

Nobody does eyes like Rembrandt.

With Rembrandt, there were no grotesques. His naturalism—which some would say was uncompromising—jumped off the canvas. He read people emotively and looked through the mask to find the individual. Whether through the arc of an eyebrow, the angle of a chin, the rise or fall of cheekbones, a once-broken nose or the folds of a jowl. He listened to the pull on his insides and what that told him about someone. He found that singular thing, painted it and gave you a reason to look, and look again. I could not take my eyes away. Up close and in person, I saw levels and layers to his painting that didn't exist in any book. His craft did this, his technique, from finesse to broad strokes, his hand and brush were in perfect concert with his head, his imagination, and with this, he invited your sympathies. Even in something so simple as his *Slaughtered Ox* at the Louvre in Paris.

I had held it together until the end of the trip, but Rembrandt brought me to a crisis of confidence. Michelangelo would have, except that he's . . . Michelangelo. Abbie knew this—that's why she saved Rembrandt until last. I walked away from Rembrandt with a DNA-level desire to craft unedited human nature, in all its rumpled impurity.

Abbie tapped me on the shoulder. "And him?"

"Those people who sat for portraits . . . they didn't pose. Motionless, yes; but they nonetheless moved. They lived." I wanted to quit. To give up. Burn everything I'd ever done.

Abbie nodded. "What you see is human greatness. This is as good as it gets, as it's ever been, maybe as it ever will be." I saw what he'd done and I knew that I could not do that. Abbie wrapped her arm inside mine and said, "Come on, he's just a man. You can do that."

"You're out of your mind."

"You already do."

"But . . . he's *Rembrandt*."

She nodded. "And you're Doss."

"You're still nuts."

"No." She shook her head. "I believe."

Our trip was an education unlike anything I'd ever known. It was as if Abbie knew my incompleteness. My deficiencies. To combat them, she mapped out a course filled with precisely the art I needed to take in, proving that she knew instinctively which works I needed to see to become the artist I could be. To become the artist she knew I could.

I remember leaving the hall where *David* stands. Walking out, we passed by all the friezes he created. Nothing but huge chunks of granite with these forms of half-people climbing out of the rocks. It's like they're breaking free. Escaping. And when I walk back down that hallway in my mind, I realize that Abbie had done that for me.

Abbie led me to her river, and I drank deeply.

We returned home and I discovered that Abbie had given me a gift I had not anticipated. I stood before my easel and found that I saw beauty in the not-so-beautiful, even in the grotesque. What she had birthed with Rosalia, she had now shaped and matured. I looked at the paints piled in a bucket at my feet. Where before I had seen a few dozen, now I saw ten thousand.

24

JUNE 4, MIDDAY

The same railroad that runs through Moniac, just twelve crow miles away, passes along the south side of St. George. The A.E. Bell Bridge spans the river at St. George and is a favorite canvas for lovers with spray paint. Purple martins nest beneath the bridge by the hundreds on their return trek north after spending the winter in Brazil. Seldom stopping to rest, they eat and drink while flying. Each one cuts the air above and below the bridge like an F-16 in search of their daily quota of horseflies, dragonflies or June beetles. Then they drop to the surface and cut the glassy water with their beaks.

Compared to Moniac, St. George is a thriving metropolis. Population might top a hundred. Grammar school, restaurant, gas station with grocery store and butcher, auto repair shop, a four-way stop marked by a flashing caution light and a burger joint called the Shack by the Track.

I cut the paddle, pulled against the stern and steered us toward the bank. We swung around the skeleton of an old wooden boat. The keel and a few stubborn ribs were all that remained. I helped her from the boat and led her around the spare tires and the ten thousand shards of green glass. Up north, people spray paint boxcars or the back of billboards. Down here, we paint water towers or the underside of bridges. Abbie walked amongst the concrete pilings and read aloud, "Pie says hie." And, "Donna likes Robert." She reached down and pulled a discarded can from the rocks. She shook and mashed her thumb against the stuck depressor. It sputtered then sprayed green. She walked to an empty piling, reached above her and began spraying: "Abbie loves Doss."

She dropped the can to her feet. "You know, if you can't say it with Krylon, then you just can't say it."

She stood beside me, hanging her arm inside mine. She whispered, "Remember the Guadalquivir?"

THE GUADALQUIVIR RIVER in Spain is famous for several reasons. Columbus sailed it, as did Cortés, and in 1992 the World's Fair occurred on its banks. Huge, empty buildings—once the rave of the day that promised to attract tourists the world over—now sit empty, rotting and colored with mildew and cracked paint. A monument to stupidity. The river was rerouted years ago—sending it around Seville—but the stretch that remains is still very much in use. Because it's long, straight and has no current, Olympic crew teams come from all over the world to train year-round. A bike path, three miles long and wide enough for cars, lines one side. It's used by runners, bikers, skateboarders, rock climbers, fishermen, crapping ducks and kids shooting heroin. Abbie had brought me here. It was one more class in my education. We'd eaten tapas, drunk a bottle of vino just up from the Torre del Oro and needed a walk. It was getting dark and didn't look like the safest of places. I grabbed her hand. "What are we doing down here?"

We'd spent the last few weeks walking through museums. I was about museumed out. A concrete wall borders most of the river, lit by yellow streetlights that throw odd shadows across the walls. Some portions of the wall are a couple stories high and most every square inch is covered in graffiti. Huge scenes, thirty and forty feet tall and just as wide, cover long stretches. She ducked beneath an overpass and pointed. "Not all art is found in museums."

The drug culture seems to spur much of the content, as it's violent and has something to do with sex, somebody shooting somebody or needles and shooting up. It was angry, ripe with pain and reminded me of something I had begun to forget: escape is one of the miracles of art.

Abbie knew intuitively what I needed when I needed it. We had walked the length of it twice.

~⌁

I STEADIED HER and helped her sit next to a concrete piling where the smell of fresh paint hung in the air. I read her green note. "Yes, I remember."

I really wanted a hot veggie plate from the Shack by the Track, but prudence kept us hidden beneath the bridge.

With a circling tailwind, we continued past long, winding, bleached beaches, strands of mimosa trees—their purplish-pink blooms tickling the air—dogwoods, green and lush, and scrub oaks that anchored everything.

We passed beneath another railroad trestle that smelled strongly of creosote and diesel fuel, and around self-named places like Catfish Lane, Pond Fork Holler, and UGA Beach. The beaches here were longer, some a hundred yards long and covered in deer tracks and driftwood.

To the east was Conner's A-Maize-ing Acres—a pick-your-own farm that peddled to city slickers looking for that "farm experience." They raised pumpkins, watermelon and corn. A submerged sign in the river read "Poultry Fertilizer."

We passed Harris Creek, Johnson Cemetery and Dunn's Creek before passing Toledo, which is near the midpoint between St. George and Boulogne.

We passed the signature red clay of Tompkins Landing, where trash bags cluttered the bank and a man in a bathing suit lay sprawled across the sand like a beached whale. Given the number of empty Bud Light bottles strewn around him, the lobster tinge of his skin and the snoring, he'd been there awhile. The river widens here to maybe one hundred feet across. Lily pads have sprouted on the slower moving, sunlit Georgia side. At the landing, want-to-be rappers sucked on ten-cent stogies leaning against the mangled tailgate of a muddy red Toyota pickup. Tattoos, lip piercings, thick gold chains, chrome-sided sunglasses and pants worn below their buttocks seemed to be the local uniform. They paid me little notice and said nothing, so I pulled my hat down over my eyes and paddled quietly through.

I suppose that's the next generation of river people, but they bear little resemblance to the first.

A red-tailed hawk dropped out of a tree on my right, scooped along the bank and lifted an unsuspecting squirrel out of its hole in the sand. While the squirrel barked at the top of its lungs, the hawk flapped higher, struggled with the acorn-fat, hairy rodent and then lit on a tree limb and sunk its beak into the chest cavity, at which point the screaming stopped.

Trader's Hill was once a thriving port on the river. British and Portuguese sailors used to come this far inland to fill their casks with freshwater and rest in the cool waters. Later it served as a clearinghouse for lumber. There was even a treaty signed here. The U.S. and Spain signed the Treaty of San Lorenzo, or

Pinckney's Treaty, declaring that the boundary of Georgia and Florida would run to the start of the St. Marys River inside the Okefenokee. Today, Trader's Hill provides a much-used boat ramp because it's the first truly navigable place in the river for fishing boats and other watercraft. It's here that the tubers, wakeboarders and Jet Skiers begin to populate the water. There's a public phone and bathroom, camping hookups and several big blue Dumpsters covered in maggots, flies, blue-tailed skinks and fat lizards. Here, the river cuts deeper, grows bigger fish and even bigger alligators. Some as long as twelve feet. Reports say that sturgeon, too, grow here. Some as long as eight feet and weighing as much as two hundred pounds. Sightings are rare, but twice in the last year, kids on Jet Skis have been unseated and knocked unconscious by a sturgeon that wanted something its own size to play with. In both cases the kids survived, but when they woke up they had one heck of a fish story. Trader's Hill is also the first place we began to notice the tidal influence. Meaning, if I began timing our runs, we could hitch a ride on the outgoing tide, saving energy in the process. And if timed incorrectly, it would cost me dearly as I'd have to pull against a swelling incoming tide. Lastly, and most importantly, it was here that the river became recreational.

If I had grown "uncomfortable" between Spread Oak and St. George, the hair was really raised on my back now. I just could not shake the idea that the trees had eyes.

U.S. 1 runs across the St. Marys at a little border town called Boulogne. Gas station, bait shop, lottery tickets and beer are the hot commodities. We reached the bridge at nightfall where a hundred purple martins were engaged in aerial combat. The bridge sat on huge concrete pads and pilings the size of houses. A wooden ladder hung down off the center pad. I tied off the canoe and we climbed up the ladder to the platform some ten feet off the surface of the water. Every few minutes a truck or car would drive across the metal grate, sending echoes off the water. It was dry and safe, so I carried up Abbie's fleece sleeping bag and her towel pillow. I wrapped her up and then smelled the air. Yesterday's rest on the beach had allowed her to store some energy in reserves. She was awake and listening. I eyed the thick white clouds on the horizon. "I think it's gonna come a rain."

She turned up one eye. "Come a rain?" I nodded. She slid both hands under her face and pulled her knees up. "Where did you learn to talk?"

I pointed upriver. "About fifty miles that way."

A raised eyebrow. "Well, you can take the boy out of the country, but you can't take the country out of the boy."

Under the bridge, some local artist had written REPENT—JESUS IS COMING SOON and FOR A GOOD TIME CALL RHONDA, and then given her phone number with extension. On the bank, a thigh-thick wisteria vine climbed up the underside of the bridge where it met a Confederate jasmine that had come up from the other side. Both were in bloom and draping us in fragrance. Dozens of honeybees and five feisty hummingbirds flew from one bloom to the next, sucking in the nectar.

For us, U.S. 1 was significant. I stretched out alongside Abbie and took her into my arms. "Guess what?"

"What?"

"We're halfway."

25

Six years passed. Abbie handpicked only the design jobs she wanted her name associated with. I supported her, helped her manage a sometimes insane schedule and continued to dust off the canvas. Somewhere in there I bought a twenty-two-foot Hewes flats boat and taught Abbie how to bait her own hook. While Abbie had tried to put modeling behind her, it simply wouldn't go away. Unlike other teen-wonder models, Abbie aged beautifully, so New York kept calling. Occasionally, she'd accept a job if it meant a getaway for us. Given her success in two careers, we couldn't go out in public—at least in Charleston—without feeling like we were on display. Our boat, *The Empty Canvas,* became our escape. We'd motor back up into the flats or beach it on Dewees Island and disappear. Oftentimes, we'd overnight beneath the stars. I outfitted Abbie in her own fishing getup. Wide-brimmed hat, vest, she took to a fly rod like Brad Pitt in *A River Runs Through It.* Give her a flood tide and she'd spend all afternoon sight-fishing for reds. I'd stand on the poling platform, push us in close, point out the fins poking up through the water's surface, and she'd throw right on top of them. She'd roll the line, drop the fly and slowly pull the retrieve. I loved to hear her hook up, hear the bail peeling itself empty and then hear her howl at the top of her lungs as the fish headed for deep water. For Abbie, "wet a line" meant standing in knee-deep water and sight-casting.

Seems like I blinked and we celebrated our tenth wedding anniversary. Abbie had established herself as the premier designer in Charleston, which meant South Carolina. I quit guiding, began painting full-time, she decorated her studio with my art and once a month when her body told her it was "right now" time, we snuck away and tried to start a family.

It was better than Camelot.

Then we flew to New York for what we thought was a routine shoot. Some cosmetic line needed her face and shoulders. So we spent the day shopping and gazing at polar bears.

It was spring, most of Central Park was a wave of color and powdered in pollen. Ducks, birds, cyclists, double strollers, runners and lovers were everywhere. We had stolen a few hours between photo shoots and were shopping somewhere on Fifth Avenue. One of those high-dollar stores Abbie dreamed about and the kind I couldn't wait to get out of. Abbie leaned against the counter, sprayed some perfume onto a small sheet of paper, waved it dry, then held it to my nose. My nose has never been really good at smelling much of anything, so she was excited to have found something I not only could smell but liked. I paid the man, we walked across to the park, bought ice cream and spent the rest of the afternoon staring through the four-inch glass wall watching the polar bears swim. Every now and then someone would ask her for an autograph. Eventually, a small crowd gathered, so we slipped away and wandered the park, passing Balto and the brick fountain where Stuart Little flew his plane into the hawk.

Later that night, we found it.

Abbie had finished shooting and met me at the Ritz. We had a suite on the club floor that overlooked the park. I had just finished running and we were getting ready. Dinner at the Spice Market followed by the 8 p.m. of *Les Misérables*. I untied my running shoes and found her in the tub. She turned, lifted her hair off her shoulders and lifted the bar of soap above her head. "Wash my back."

After ten years of marriage, I didn't need a translator. It meant, *Wash my back, rub my shoulders, take that little pumice thing and rub the rough spots off my feet, then leave me alone. But only after you refill the tub with hot water. And if you're good, and don't turn this into something else, I'll let you shave my legs.*

Abbie wasn't selfish about much, except this. Tub time was her time. She might as well have hung a No Trespassing sign across the bathroom door. No matter how seductive the whole wet, bubbly, sweaty, hair pulled up picture might look. I sat on the edge and scrubbed her back. Abbie's problem is that she's a lot like a dog. When she doesn't want you to stop, she'll find places that don't itch.

I don't guess you need me to paint you a picture.

A little while later, we sat in the tub, having missed our dinner reservation and chances were slim for the show. I refilled the hot water and she lay back against me.

While the steam and heat spoke to us, I wrapped my arms around her waist. Her back to my chest. She placed my finger on her temple and said without a sound *Trace me.* So I did.

And there it was.

Just beneath the nipple on her left side. I pretended not to notice, but later that night, after the show, there it was again. There in the glow of the clock, my face betrayed me. She slipped her hand beneath mine, her face drained white and fear bubbled back up. And for some reason, amidst all the fear and horror of the months to come, when I look back on that moment, I remember smelling that perfume.

WE FLEW HOME the next day and her mammogram was the following morning. They took the pictures, brought her back to the waiting room and Abbie sat next to me, legs crossed, and quiet.

Twenty minutes later, three doctors walked in. Given Abbie's high profile, the hospital assigned us a team of three doctors. The senior doctor, Dr. Ruddy Hampton, was what you might think. Gray hair and a reassuring bedside manner. The other two, Dr. Roy Smith and Dr. Katherine Meyer, were younger and credited as being on the cutting edge of knowledge and technology.

They hung Abbie's images on the wall behind us and, for reference, hung up prints from a set of disease-free breasts. We didn't need the diagnosis. Dr. Hampton spoke first, "Abbie . . ." He pointed at the picture with a pencil. "These pictures confirm invasive ductile carcinoma." The clusters he circled looked like miniature Milky Ways. He drew imaginary lines on the films and said, "These are what we call satellite lesions. In English, this means that your cancer has invaded the milk ducts." As he spoke, I wrestled with the term *your cancer.*

While he explained the films, I realized that the bump I felt was just one of many, and even worse, it had spread to both breasts. If you doubt that cancer is evil, then why does it start in the milk ducts? Answer that. Abbie studied the films and turned her head sideways. "It looks like someone shot both my breasts with white paintballs."

Dr. Smith continued, "In oncology, there are three ways to attack cancer: surgery, chemotherapy and radiation."

Abbie interrupted. "Don't you call that 'slash, poison and burn'?"

He nodded. "Yes, but here's what's important for you two." He looked at Abbie. "We can address your particular situation with just chemotherapy and surgery." That's when I clued in to the fact that they intended to cut on my wife.

I scratched my head. "How's that?"

Dr. Meyer broke in. "Abbie needs a double mastectomy in order to give her the best chance."

"The best chance of what?"

"Beating this."

Somewhere in there, it struck me that the three of them were drawing a distinction between life and death.

Dr. Hampton had been quiet, but given the awkward silence, he spoke up. "This is an *advanced* form of cancer."

The word *advanced* floated around the room. Dr. Smith continued, "Before surgery, we will want to administer a strong and aggressive dose of chemotherapy—to shrink the tumors prior to surgery. Another aggressive course of chemo would follow—just to make certain."

"Will it get rid of the cancer?"

Everybody nodded. "Survival rate is ninety-seven percent."

I looked at the three doctors looking at us. "What about the other three percent?"

They reassured me, "We caught it in time. We'll look at the lymph nodes and make sure our margins are clear, but I wouldn't lose sleep over it."

Lose sleep? I wasn't worried about losing sleep. I was worried about losing my wife.

After outlining some breast reconstruction options, they left us alone in the room. "Honey. I'm so sorry. Maybe we should get a second opinion. I mean, they don't know everything."

She nodded, but there was no agreement in it. I compared the two sets of films.

We didn't need a second opinion.

She pressed her forehead to mine. "I'm glad you're in my corner."

"I wish I had a magic wand."

"Me too."

26

JUNE 5, MORNING

Just after daybreak, a mile south from Boulogne, we crossed Scotts Landing. A local boat ramp on the Florida side used mostly by fishermen. There's also a trailer park, rope swing and bait shop where they sell crickets, minnows, worms, artificial baits and absolutely no beer whatsoever. Lining the boat ramp a sign reads WARNING: IT IS NOT ADVISABLE TO GO SWIMMING AFTER IT RAINS, SUDDEN AND DANGEROUS UNDERCURRENTS OCCUR EVEN WHEN SURFACE APPEARS CALM, IN MEMORY OF SAM COVINGTON, 1/12/89 TO 4/30/04.

Undercurrents occur whenever too much water starts swirling between a river's banks. The increased volume changes how she flows. When she is full and overflowing her banks, she sucks down the surface and rolls it along the bottom, only to resurface it a few feet later.

The parking lot at Scotts was filled with people milling around, comparing baits and telling fishing lies, but we needed water and some food so I tied off the canoe and told Abbie to hang tight.

Somewhere somebody was frying sausage and eggs. I walked into the store and was immediately "Howdied" by four guys at the counter. I waved and tried to disappear among the grocery aisles. The wall above the cash register was decorated with locals' pics of their largest catch, first deer, biggest hog or senior prom date. Sort of a Wall of Fame. I was filling my arms with saltine crackers, a jar of peanut butter and a few bottles of Gatorade when the guy behind the counter raised his remote control and pointed it at the TV. "Hey, ya'll, shut up." He mashed the volume button several times. "Here it is."

The blue background of the weather channel flashed onto the screen with the words SPECIAL REPORT—HURRICANE ANNIE. INCHING CLOSER.

A reporter wearing a yellow rain slicker and standing in sideways rain said, "Five days ago, Annie strengthened and measured the fourth-lowest pressure ever measured in an Atlantic hurricane, tying with Hurricane Camille of 1969. On May twenty-sixth, Annie recorded sustained winds of a hundred fifty-five knots or a hundred eighty miles per hour, spinning itself into a class-five hurricane with winds gusting at over two hundred miles an hour. On May twenty-seventh, Annie moved west and then northwest with sustained winds exceeding a hundred and eighty, causing the governor to evacuate the Florida Keys, Miami and most everything south of Disneyworld." The weatherman smiled and shrugged. "Given the pictures we have been broadcasting, along with the radar pictures, folks didn't seem to need much convincing to evacuate." He held up a map of the state. "The three main routes out of Florida, I-95, I-75 and I-10, are little more than parking lots, prompting the governor to reverse southbound flow making all lanes northbound." The woman behind the desk in Virginia asked a few questions to which the reporter nodded and said, "She's acquiring energy and mass like the Tazmanian Devil. Through evaporation and sea spray, a hurricane in this stage sucks up more than two billion tons of water a day. Each whirling second, it circulates some two million metric tons of air in, up and out of itself. In doing so, it releases enough energy in one day to equal the energy of four hundred twenty-megaton hydrogen bombs. If scientists could convert all that energy into something they could shove down powerlines, it would supply the United States for six months." Satisfied with his science lesson, he paused to answer another question. He said, "Most of South Florida is a ghost town and will be for days to come as folks try to return to their homes. Problem is, Annie isn't finished with us yet. From midday on the twenty-seventh to early on the twenty-ninth, Annie hovered over Florida, tormenting Florida's west coast and bringing a definite stop to any highway traffic. Flooding is rampant. More to come after this . . ."

The man behind the counter flipped the channel and waved off his four friends. "Ya'll hush! Here it is. Four to one says the sucker killed her, dumped the body and is sitting on some beach in South America counting her money."

I looked up but something inside me told me I didn't really want to watch.

The commercial ended and the bottle-blond newswoman turned to the camera. "And in national news, former supermodel and Charleston designer Abbie Eliot is missing." Abbie's picture flashed upon the screen, followed by a running slide show of some of the images from her career. "Her husband and local Charleston portraitist, Doss Michaels, is being sought for questioning and is a suspect in what is described as 'possible foul play.' " On the screen, Abbie's picture moved left, making room for my face as it flashed upon the screen. I don't know where they'd gotten my picture but it looked like a mug shot. "Following a double mastectomy four years ago, Abbie Eliot, once widely thought of as one of the ten most beautiful women in the world, became the unofficial spokeswoman for breast cancer survivors when she invited the public to follow her through her radiation and chemotherapy treatments. But two years ago, the cancer returned. This time to her brain. We take you now to a press conference held by her father, the former governor of South Carolina and now in his fourth term in the United States Senate. Senator Coleman." The screen flashed to a live shot of the Colemans' house on the Battery. Senator Coleman, dressed down in jeans and a white oxford shirt, opened the front door, walked onto the porch and spoke over the railing to the cameras below. "Good morning. Thank you for coming." He panned the crowd of reporters. "Two years ago, Abigail Grace's cancer was found to have spread." He was never too comfortable with the way Abbie so publicly talked about her breasts or their absence once they were gone. He turned and pointed to the back of his own head. "The cancer traveled upward and took root somewhere in here. She has what is called a stage four central nervous system metastasis. These several lesions can be found in the back or base of her brain, which because of their sensitive location, exclude surgery as an option of treatment. Abigail Grace is a fighter, so like everything else in her life, she has fought this." He wiped his face with a handkerchief. "As many of you know, I was the donor for her second bone marrow transplant. But that, too . . . didn't take. Something I think about every day." He folded the papers in front of him. "Two weeks ago, we ran out of options, brought her home, circled the family and called hospice." He took a deep breath, back beneath the limelight. The sympathetic father—courting and counting the votes. He beckoned behind him to his wife— Abbie's stepmother—who stepped forward and put her arm around him. "We know that Abigail Grace would want to be here with her family." His practiced tone and measured cadence were near perfect. "She needs to be under the constant supervision of her doctors. We don't know Doss's intentions . . ." My picture flashed a second time onto the screen, filling the top right-hand corner. "He's our son-in-law and has been for nearly fourteen years, but certainly his actions cannot be in her best interest if he has taken her from her family and her doctors in what could very well be the last few days of her life." Senator Coleman looked directly into the camera and held up his right arm, beckoning someone off camera. A shorter man wearing a doctor's coat and a serious expression stepped into the frame, where the senator put his arm around him. The senator cleared his throat. "This is Dr. Wayne Massey."

It took me a second to recognize him. Television does funny things to a person. The senator was right. Wayne Massey was a good doctor. Had more plaques on his wall than he had space for them. He was a specialist studying the blood-brain barrier and had approached us hoping Abbie would join his study. The senator leaned forward. "Dr. Massey is one of the leading researchers in the country in studying conditions such as Abigail's." I noticed how carefully he chose his words.

Within the last month, we'd called him—we were covering all our bases. Dr. Massey listened to us, asked thorough questions and at the end of the day, he could only recommend a course of treatment that would not change the outcome, only prolong it a few weeks. And even that he couldn't guarantee. Those were his words, not mine. The choice not to enter into that course of treatment was Abbie's. The end of the phone call sounded something like, "The medical community I represent simply cannot help her. I am sorry."

At what point do you stop fighting? At what point does some quality of life take precedence over the possibility of a few more incoherent and painful, or at least more painful, weeks? I don't have the answer to this, but I do understand the question.

The senator knew that we knew Dr. Massey. And we knew

that he knew, because he'd arranged it through his office. He also knew that Dr. Massey could offer us nothing. Standing in front of the cameras, Dr. Massey was little more than a prop. A stunt. The public did not know. Hence, the reason he was there.

The senator continued, his face growing more pained: "Dr. Massey would like another opportunity to assess Abigail's condition and consider a new course of treatment. Possibly . . ." He held his hands out like the scales of justice. "Well, we just have no idea what is available or might be in the days to come." He patted Dr. Massey on the shoulder. "We're not finished fighting."

He was shrewd. In the span of a few seconds, the senator had raised an unspoken question: Was I—the sketchy, jealous son-in-law riding the coattails of the world-famous model—keeping Abbie from a possible treatment and cure? Was my kidnapping—because that's what this was—motivated by the intent to murder? In so doing, he was circling the edges of a bold-faced lie, yet what did he care? He knew that the best way to enlist the public's help was to dangle the question and create the perception. Because in the court of public opinion, perception equals reality. I might as well have had a rope around my neck.

The senator gathered his composure. "Doss . . . please bring my"—he placed his arm around Abbie's stepmom—". . . our daughter back to us . . . while there's still time."

Cameras returned to the newswoman, who tapped her pencil on the desk in front of her. She turned to her male counterpart who had been quiet throughout her report. "When I was fighting breast cancer, Abbie Eliot was a great encouragement to me. Even"—the woman's eyes glossed over—"writing me a note of encouragement when I lost my hair." The guy behind the counter mashed the mute button and threw it on the counter. "I hope they catch the son of a—" The ice machine dropped a tray of ice and drowned him out but I got the picture. A trial before the court of public opinion would not be lengthy. I quietly set down my groceries while the conversation ramped up. I slipped out a side door, walked down the boat ramp, untied the canoe and pushed off with unusual force.

Abbie sat up. "You okay?"

I dipped my hat in the water, soaking the brim, slid it back on my head and let it cool me from the top down. I nodded.

She pressed me. "What?"

"Your dad."

"What's he doing now?"

"What he's good at."

"Press conference?" I nodded.

She chewed on her lip. "That bad?"

"Denim shirt. Front porch of the house. Katherine standing behind him."

"You're not serious."

"Yep."

"You know . . . he really doesn't like you."

"Tell me about it."

To be honest, I'd be doing the same thing if some guy I didn't like had my daughter off on some river when she should be at home with me. Only difference was, I knew what was best for Abbie. He didn't. And deep down, he knew that, too. 'Course, he'd never admit it.

The problem with the senator tracking us down was that he would exert his will over ours. He'd stick Abbie in some sterile bed surrounded by people she didn't know in an environment she did not like. For some thirty-two years now, he had counted the votes of people who'd told him he knew best. After so long in politics, he had grown to believe that if he knew what was best for his constituents, then he obviously knew what was best for everyone. And that "everyone" included his family. No power on earth could convince him otherwise. I didn't doubt his intentions. The senator wasn't evil. In truth, he really didn't have a bad bone in his body. He was arrogant, but I knew he loved his daughter. But loving her and knowing what was best for her, or what she wanted, were entirely different things. "Honey, I think he's just trying to protect you."

"From what?"

That part was easy. "Me."

AFTER A LONG STRAIGHTAWAY, the river morphs again. Subtlety. Close your eyes and you'll miss it. The long, cool sections of bleached beach become fewer and shorter, giving way to darker mud and the occasional fiddler crab. Palmettos mixed with poplar reach over the bank and dip their fronds in the water, protecting the bank, making access more difficult and requiring you to pick your way to the bank. A twelve-strand powerline crosses the river, buzzing with currents strong enough to reset your wristwatch and make your hair stand up when you pass beneath.

The Ralph E. Simmons Memorial State Forest starts a half mile south of Scotts Landing and runs seven miles along the river. It's seven thousand–plus acres of sassafras, water hickory, yellow poplar and endangered plants such as hartwrightia, toothache grass and purple baldwinia. Sprouting up amidst the longleaf pine and live oaks are blueberries, blackberries, sweet pepperbrush, cinnamon fern, orchids and, along the riverbank, pitcher plant colonies. Wildlife is rather plentiful. Everything from otters to gopher tortoises, deer, bobcat, turkey and ribbon snakes—not to mention cottonmouth moccasins and eastern diamondback rattlers. Locals claim to have seen black bear and the endangered Florida panther. Inland, the ground is sandy, with patches of dark musky earth that give rise to gardenias, wild roses and the smell of turpentine.

For us, the Ralph E. Simmons brought rest because few people are found along its banks. We floated as much as the tide would let us.

~

CAMP PINCKNEY is a Georgia-side boat ramp a long way from nowhere. Regular visitors include kids on four-wheelers looking for a place to skim rocks or smoke dope. The tide is stronger here. And river tide is a lot like the flushing of a toilet—fast going out but slow to fill. Paddling downstream, we could easily manage four miles an hour. Five for shorter distances and only if I was focused. Against the incoming, we'd be lucky to average one and a half. Two would be a miracle. Add a headwind to the equation and we'd be backing up.

Abbie slept while I kept the paddle in the water and slung the canoe on the outside of the river where the current was faster. The less time I spent trying to steer, the more time I spent pulling. We passed Cooneys Landing, Elbow Landing and Horseshoe Island before rounding the last bend just north of Prospect Landing.

I pushed back my hat, scratched my head and watched the river slip beneath us.

If you've spent enough time in the river, you can tell the difference between when the flow pushes you along and when the tide pulls you out. Usually, if you're coming around a corner and your stern swings around—or fishtails—you're being pushed. If you come around that same corner and your keel cuts the water like it was on a rail, you're being pulled. The difference is key: you can fight the push, but you've got to ride the pull.

The river can be a magical place. As much as I've been here, I still don't quite get her. No matter how you hurry or how hard and fast you pull on the paddle, the river controls the tempo. She stretches every minute and steals back every lost second. Rivers do this naturally. They don't give two cents about the destination, only the journey. It's why they're crooked. Name one straight river and I'll show you a man-made canal. People make a big deal about how their watch automatically sets itself to atomic time from a tower somewhere in Colorado, but if we were smart, we'd set our watches to river time. We'd wrinkle less and wouldn't grow old as quickly.

Abbie knew this. It might have been the one thing I'd taught her. She had looked at her list and then chosen the river not because it was her favorite place in the world or because she was a closet river rat but because it was the singular place on earth where time slowed down. Where each second counted. Where, if you paid attention, the sun would stop long enough to let you catch your breath.

Near lunchtime, I lifted the paddle out of the water, lay down next to Abbie and counted the clouds that slipped overhead.

Then I tried to stop the sun.

27

Two days later, we drove to the oncology center—the last day of summer break before school started. We walked through the sliding electronic doors and into the chemotherapy waiting room. That first second did a lot to combat the two-day pity party we'd been having. People of all shapes and sizes were waiting. Old, young, pretty, heavy, skinny, healthy, sickly, bald—all of America was sitting in that room. The chemo room is a big circular room filled with comfortable rockers, colorful cushions, colorful walls, colorful nurses and pale and yellowy-looking patients. The healthy and the damned. It is a weird, parallel universe. The sick live one foot in here, one foot out there.

Chemotherapy is a systemic therapy, meaning it attacks fast-growing cells all over the body. So while it attacks the cancer, it also attacks the cells that grow hair, heal wounds, color your skin, etc. It's the reason why so many chemo patients look like the walking dead. Because parts of them are.

We signed in and sat next to a woman about Abbie's age. They began talking and their stories were similar. That's another thing we learned pretty quickly. While the types of cancer were different and in different stages, everybody's stories were similar. Their diagnosis surprised them and, depending on lots of factors, they either had been or were fearful. Fear is the primary mode of transportation for cancer because *cancer* is the one six-letter word none of us ever wanted to hear. And if I had any doubts before, a quick look around the room confirmed what I'd already suspected. Cancer is the ultimate identity theft. It's a vulture—it doesn't care how old you are, where you're from, who your daddy is, how much money you have or how important you think you are. It is no respecter of persons.

About half the women wore a hat, scarf or wig that some loved one had told them didn't look fake. Most had lied. Those who still had their hair looked around the room as if afraid that they were next. And because cancer is a vulture, most were. A few of the women wore baggy shirts that had not been baggy when they bought them. Some wore bright colors, some neutral. All wished they were someplace else.

We'd been going there a few weeks when it finally hit me. Admittedly, I can be a little slow. I thought to myself, Where are all the boyfriends and husbands?

Finally, I asked Abbie. She shook her head. It was one of those intuitive things that she knew without having to ask. "They left."

Apparently, some do. Not all, not most, just some. I did meet some super-dads who were wearing three hats and had soccer-mom stickers plastered on the backs of their Suburbans, but I never got used to that picture of a pale, skinny, gaunt woman wearing a scarf, baggy clothes and connected to a clear plastic line with the empty seat next to her. A powerful statement about them and a pitiful statement about the men who had left them.

So I asked Abbie. "Well . . ." She looked slowly around the room. "If you married a face, a set of boobs or a couple of curves"—she turned to me—"and those are gone . . ." She shrugged.

Behind Abbie's statement loomed a much larger question. One she was too afraid to ask. I had a feeling that the answer she was looking for might take months, even years, and was not verbal.

28

The distinguishing feature of Prospect Landing is not the elegantly sloped concrete boat ramp, the Florida Cracker houses that bookend either side of it, the cows or their pastures that lead down to it, or the manicured rows of cathedral pine trees whose needles have been raked and sold to the home mulch market, but rather the back end of the yellow 1957 Chevrolet station wagon that rises up out of the water like a channel buoy. Word has it that a disgruntled housewife had come home to find her husband entwined with the neighbor. In revenge, she backed his '57 Chevrolet out of the garage, punched the accelerator and in a move reminiscent of Sally Field in *Smokey and the Bandit,* tried to jump the river. It was his pride and joy and this was payback. Only difference was she had no bridge to launch her heavenward. Only incline she had was a mound of dirt next to the ramp. She hit it going about sixty-five, maybe seventy miles an hour, and pitched the hood upward only to quickly have the back end hit the same bump, which drove the front end downward. The car flew through the air like a plow, cut into the water and lodged into the pluff mud of the far bank, looking a lot like an errant Soviet-issued missile. It's been there ever since. Locals dubbed it the "butt-ugly" station wagon, but that didn't stop them from capitaliz-

ing on their neighbor's bad fortune and stripping it for parts.
Now it's a rusted shell, no glass, no taillights or hubcaps, no tires
and no engine. Somebody even took the steering wheel. Over
the years, the weight of the steel frame has driven it further into
the muck.

For me, the frame served as a marker. That may seem simple, but federal game and fish officers routinely used Prospect
as a launch for their twenty-two-foot Pathfinders. They fre-
quented it because it was seldom used, tucked out of the way
and gave them quick access up- and downriver. We slowed,
rounded the bend and I cut us in closer to the bank, skimming
across the tops of paper plate–sized lily pads to slow our speed
more. The rusted tailpipe of the station wagon came into view
first, followed quickly by the boat ramp. The game warden's
truck and trailer sat parked against the far fence. He was
nowhere in sight but his trailer was empty, which meant he and
his boat were touring the river. I said nothing to Abbie, but
started thinking about a place to spend the night.

We slipped past Walker's Landing, McKenzie Landing,
Colerain, Gum Stump Landing, Orange Bluff, Mallets Landing
and the Flea Hill boat ramp. The problem with all of this was
not our speed—in river terms, we were flying—but the number of people I'd seen. Houses rose up on stilts or were buried
into the bluffs in nearly every square inch of river frontage. And
down here, people expect you to wave. It's like two cars passing
on a dirt road. You wave. It's just the way it is. Boats on the
river are the same way. Wave and you're noticed little. Don't
wave, and you're noticed a lot. I waved without bringing attention, but sooner or later, somebody would put us together with
the news reports. If we caught the tide right and my body didn't
give out, we could be in St. Marys in thirty-six to forty-eight
hours. Miss the tides and it was anybody's guess.

LIKE TRADER'S HILL, Kings Ferry is a favorite among boaters, campers and joyriders. At its widest, it's maybe a hundred and fifty yards across. They have a large floating concrete dock— because high and low tide can fluctuate by as much as five feet—a store and several houses built up close to the ramp. I didn't want to pass it in the daylight. We floated until dark and passed through on the far side as the moon cracked over the treetops. That was both good and bad. Good because no one saw us. Bad because we missed the store and any chance at food.

Compounding the problem was the fact that I was deteriorating fast. I'd eaten sporadically and yet I was probably burning six to eight thousand calories a day. I'd long ago started eating away at my fat reserves. Not only was I growing weak, but huge blisters had come up across my palms, popped and were now raw and oozing. My sweat dripped down into the cracks, as did the water. And because the water was now tidal, it was also salty. Every time I dipped the paddle in the water, then flipped it over the opposite gunnel, the water trickled down and flowed across my hands.

While salt water hurt, it was not all bad. Salt water meant crabs. Blue crabs. And around here, blue crabs meant crab traps. It was a mortal sin to steal from another man's trap. People had been shot over such a thing. I spotted several numbered white floats down the center of the river, lifted them over the side and stole every crustacean I could dig out. Five traps later, I had twenty-eight crabs. Abbie poked open an eye and said, "Isn't that illegal?"

"Yep."

"If those things clamp onto my toe, I'm coming out of this canoe."

I took off my shirt, bundled the crabs inside and stuffed them behind my seat. They'd keep until the White Oak boat ramp at Brickyard Landing.

We slipped past Blood Landing and watched the moon reach full and high over Cabbage Bend. The moon lit the water in a hazy shade of blue and cast tall tree shadows across the water. The light brought out the water bugs, which in turn attracted the fish by the hundreds. We paddled through feeding frenzy after feeding frenzy. It was one of those rare occasions that would have been beautiful had it been any other time. Abbie climbed up, leaned against the side of the canoe and dangled her fingers in the water. All along the banks, the tree frogs croaked a summertime chorus that was answered by an occasional alligator and distant barking dog.

Years back, Mr. Gilman of the Gilman Paper Company donated several thousand acres of land for what is now the White Oak Plantation. It's beyond exclusive. There's a golf course, but you can't play it. You can't set foot on it unless you're a president or somebody real famous. Drive up to the gate and they'll instruct you in the finer points of a U-turn. Invitations are scarce and money won't buy you entrance.

Word has it that somewhere in the 1980s Mr. Gilman met Mikhail Baryshnikov. A friendship ensued and Mr. Gilman built a dance studio for what became the White Oak Dancers. Made up of the best dancers in the world, they are quite possibly the most elite group ever to perform, which they have done some six hundred times around the world. It always struck me as odd that the pinnacle of ballet achievement and performance trains at a plantation in the sticks of North Florida.

My interest in White Oak had little to do with Gilman or the dancers but rather Brickyard Landing. White Oak rolls out of the oaks and crawls up to the river's edge at a little concrete ramp and manicured landing tucked down in the woods behind a No Trespassing sign. Solitary needle-thin pine trees rise sixty feet high, swaying slightly in the breeze, but it's the smell of the marsh that gives it away. It is here that the river changes yet again. Sandy beaches, scrub oaks and poplar trees have given way to wiregrass, pluff mud and oyster beds. It's also the first place on the river where you can detect the tidal stain on the bank. Here it's just two or three feet, but closer to Highway 17 and I-95, the stain will color nearly six feet on the bank. The smell brushed under my nose, the trees spiked the night sky above us and Brickyard Landing appeared on our right.

I cut the paddle like a rudder, pulled the canoe up the concrete and steadied Abbie as she stepped out. When I was working for Gus, there was this older guy—maybe eighty years old—named Russ who came around every morning with his pipe, newspaper and coffee. He was lonely, widowed by both his wife and dog, so he talked to us while we gathered the boats, life jackets and paddles. His skin was real thin and both his forearms were covered in sailor's tattoos. He got them after he landed on the beach at Normandy and lived to tell about it. The skin had stretched and fallen in taut wrinkles and the voluptuous woman who had once stood there now drooped. Anyway, Russ was there most mornings, spinning stories and living vicariously through us. Every morning as we shoved off the bank, he'd push himself up out of Gus's rocker, wave us off and then stand there, hanging on to the side of the wall while his arthritic knees quivered beneath him. Then he'd stroll home, looking forward to tomorrow morning.

Abbie stood, her knees quivered, she hung on me and I remembered Russ.

Behind us lay a grassy lawn, ankle-high in Bermuda grass.

To our left sat a dark boathouse with a dock, screened-in porch and bathroom.

The power had been turned off, but I found a candle and began searching the porch, where I stumbled over a large pot and propane cooker. I boiled about three gallons of water, dumped the crabs in and then I spread an old newspaper across the picnic table while Abbie dug two lemon-lime Shastas out of a pantry in the back. I boiled the crabs, dumped them across the newspaper, and we gorged. I looked across the growing pile of shells on the table and Abbie was sucking one of the legs clean.

I cleaned up our mess while Abbie found the shower. The bathroom was new and relatively clean. The shower looked like four or five kids could shower at once. It was a four-foot by eight-foot area with six showerheads all shooting toward the drain in the middle. I turned on the shower and, surprisingly, warm water ran out. Abbie walked into the middle, grabbed the soap off the wall, sat down near the drain and patted the tile next to her.

I sniffed my shirt. "That bad, huh?"

"You don't know the half of it." We showered until the soap grew thin and the water ran cold.

The main portion of the boathouse was a large great room with vaulted ceilings centered around a fireplace and a moose head hanging above the mantel. I pulled the pads off some of the benches on the porch, making us a pallet on the floor while Abbie toweled off. I helped her into her dry T-shirt, slipped on her socks and then zipped her inside the fleece sleeping bag. Didn't take her long to fall asleep, so I rinsed out our clothes, washing them as best I could, and draped them over the railing to dry. That left me naked and tired, but not sleepy. I made some coffee and sipped in the silence while Abbie breathed heavily alongside me. The night air was surprisingly cool and damp on the concrete floor, so I lit a small fire in the fireplace and got lost in the glow of the coals.

Somewhere after midnight, a draft blew across the room, reigniting the coals and sending a small flame a few inches into the air. I stared into the darkness and let my eyes adjust. Behind me, a back door slid open and quietly clicked shut. Then I heard a footstep followed by a muffled whisper. I grabbed the revolver, back up against the wall and listened.

The first man walked into the room as if he was in a hurry. He stood about four feet from Abbie, staring down at her. If she knew he was there, she made no sign of it. The firelight reflected off his glasses and the oily shine on his face. The second man was taller and appeared to limp. The third man was broad-shouldered, thick-legged and walked like a troll. Their body shapes told me these were the same guys.

I pressed my right palm hard against the grip of the revolver and supported it with my left.

When the first man reached out and began to pull on the tarp covering Abbie's feet, I extended the revolver and put pressure on the trigger. The hammer was at half cock when something hard smashed down above my left eye. The blow slammed me backward into the wall and sent the bullet into the ceiling above me. I fell and landed hard on my back in what was probably a utility closet.

I tried to stand but couldn't. I couldn't see out of my left eye, my right wasn't much better and something warm oozed down my face. I tried crawling but could not force my hands to lift my own weight. The first man turned on a head-mounted light like a coal miner and ripped off the tarp, while a second began pulling on the sleeping bag. Limpy stood back and laughed in a high-pitched, devilish howl. Given the light from now two headlamps and the fire, I could see that a fourth man standing above me had just hit me with the butt of my own shotgun. He kicked me hard in the ribs.

Coal Miner said, "Look what we got here." Abbie's eyes were open but she made no movement and put up no fight. I tried to breathe but couldn't. Coal-miner man knelt between her legs while the Troll grabbed her by the head, ripping off the scarf. He held the scarf up like a scalp then looked in disbelief at Abbie. "Bufort, she bald as a peach. Ain't a lick o' dang hair."

Coal Miner knelt on top of her and began fumbling with his belt buckle. He laughed. "She ain't gonna need it." Limpy grabbed her T-shirt by the collar and ripped it down the middle. All three men sat back and stared at Abbie's pale, bosomless, concave white chest. Coal Miner's lamp lit her like a stage. "Well, I'll be a . . ." The second man poked him in the shoulder. "She ain't got no teets neither."

Limpy leaned in. "She flatter than you, Buf." Their laughter bounced off the vaulted ceiling. Troll turned his head sideways like a dog. "Looks like two puckering buttholes."

The three men had now multiplied to six, two of each of them. Another draft blew across the room, tugging at the fire and pulling more flame out that lit nearly the entire room. I lunged at the man over me, grabbed the shotgun and heard him click off the safety. I pulled, causing him to reflexively yank hard on the trigger. Two feet of flame shot out of the barrel as the percussion nearly burst my eardrum. The blast of number 8 birdshot cut through the house and ricocheted off the concrete floor. I turned toward Abbie just as the butt of the shotgun came down a second time on my left eye. I landed flat on the concrete in a puddle of something that smelled like oil and heard him jacking another shell in the chamber. My vision faded from black to blurry and back to black again. The fourth man was straddling me, pointing the barrel in my face, firelight reflecting off the whites of his eyes.

Coal Miner's hands were walking up and down Abbie. Limpy leaned in, squinting, and put his hand on Troll's shoulder. "Verl . . ." He pointed. "She ain't right."

Coal Miner sat back. "Wha' you talking 'bout?"

"Look at her. She looks 'bout dead."

Coal Miner adjusted his lamp, making him look like a Cyclops, and dropped his shorts. "She's alive enough."

Out of the corner of my right eye, I saw a bluish-reddish flash and then heard what sounded like the flip and flop of flip-flops. Half a second later, the shotgun man's head snapped back, he grunted and fell across me, shoving my face down hard against the concrete and back into the oil.

The man who now stood above me wore red and blue Hawaiian shorts, flip-flops, no shirt and he was holding a jagged piece of a two-by-four. Limpy leapt to his feet, only to be immediately met in the head by the swinging end of the lumber. Bits and pieces of teeth flew out across the room and scattered across the concrete. Somewhere, a small, furry, snarling thing entered the picture. It jumped off the ground—its nails scratching the concrete—latched onto Coal Miner's butt and hung there. Limpy hit the ground like a noodle, without so much as a grunt. Coal Miner had just gotten his pants below his butt, which was real hairy. I don't think he was wearing any underwear. Troll bounced like a cat, grabbed Hawaiian man around the neck only to get hip-tossed across the room toward me. He landed against the wall and I whacked him in the head with the side of the revolver. He moaned and I hit him again. He lifted his head and I slammed it down a third time. He lay on the ground moaning but not moving. I pulled myself across the floor toward Abbie. Coal Miner turned just in time to see Mr. Hawaii coming toward him. Coal Miner's lamp partially blinded Mr. Hawaii, but not the little snarling beast hanging on his butt. Pants still at his ankles, Coal Miner sack-jumped to one side and took three strides back, trying to shake loose the demon attached to his buttock. Coal Miner tripped and landed on the dog, momentarily shaking it loose, but when he stood it launched itself a second time off the concrete and latched firmly onto the man's crotch. Coal Miner began screaming at the top of his high-pitched lungs.

Incredibly, Coal Miner made it to the door and disappeared outside. I saw the reflection of his lamp as he jumped off the porch, tripped and began rolling down the grassy lawn toward the river. Mr. Hawaii looked at me, smiled, then disappeared out the door in the direction of the lamp and the sound of the snarling. I couldn't see out of my left eye, the world was spinning too fast and the edges were starting to tunnel inward. I crawled up next to Abbie as my own nausea came in waves. I lay across her, feeling her stomach rise and fall under mine. I forced my eyes open but I knew I didn't have long. I crawled back to the shotgun, press-checked the chamber with my finger and returned to Abbie. I pulled her up against the wall and then came to one knee, setting myself between her and the bodies in the room. Troll was moaning but his nose was spread across his face, so I doubted he felt like moving. Limpy had yet to twitch.

Sixty seconds later, we heard a loud crack somewhere outside followed by a loud splash. A single lamp returned up the hill and through the door. Its wearer was whistling and he was carrying something in his arms. I raised the shotgun, scattering my aim from the front door to the back. My arms were shaking but I wrapped my first digit around the trigger. The man with the lamp returned to the middle of the room, turned out his light and set the dog on the ground next to him. The dog sniffed across the floor to us. It licked my foot then wound behind me to Abbie. The man looked down at me but I was having a difficult time focusing. Finally, he dug a pack of cigarettes from his pocket, hung one from his lips and lit it with a shiny silver Zippo lighter. He drew deeply then slammed the lighter closed on his thigh. "Looks like you two have had some trouble."

I clicked on the safety and fumbled for the Pelican case. I grabbed two syringes, swabbed Abbie's thigh, cracked the cap on the dopamine and injected it, followed quickly by the dexamethasone. Then I leaned against the wall and my eyelids grew too heavy to hold open. The last thing I remember seeing before my eyelashes touched, was the red glow of his cigarette. A little while later, I remember feeling my stomach jump into my mouth, my shoulders press against a hard seat and feeling Abbie wrap her arms tight about me. I tried to wake but the fog was too thick. Abbie cradled me, locked her legs around mine and pulled me into her. She was trembling. Somewhere close I heard an engine roar, felt it rumble and somebody turned on a fan.

29

C hemo is a daily rug—three weeks on, one week off, four days a week, eight bags a day, six hours a day. It's like having a cold for a very long time. It also did a few other things. She bled around her gums and from her nose, had nonstop diarrhea, lost her appetite and hair, lived with nausea and tingling in her fingers and toes and vomited constantly for three weeks out of every month.

The first round of chemo did what the doctors were hoping. It shrank the tumors, but it did not change their recommendation. We checked into the hospital at 6 a.m. on a Friday morning for a 10 a.m. surgery. Minutes before they rolled her down the hall, she looked up at me out of the haze and fog of whatever sleepy medicine was dripping into her veins and she asked, "You be here when I wake up?"

"Yep."

"You promise?"

I nodded. "Tomorrow, too."

She closed her eyes, they wheeled her down the hall and I walked to the surgical waiting room where her stepmom and dad sat. After more than a decade of being married to their daughter, we'd reached an amicable truce. They didn't speak to me and I only spoke to them when spoken to.

I used to think I could win them over, but I'd made little

progress. In truth, none. Katherine sat there reading *Architectural Digest* while Abbie's father talked on the phone with offices in both Charleston and D.C.

During the five-hour surgery, a nurse gave us periodic updates. "We've finished with the right side, margins are clear, lymph nodes are good . . . now we're starting on the left." I noticed she didn't say anything about reconstruction.

At 4 p.m., the surgeon, Dr. Dismakh, appeared. He pulled off his mask and motioned for us to follow him into the private consultation room. He said, "We're finished. Abbie's sleeping and I'll take you to her shortly." He paused, telling me I didn't want to hear what he was about to say. "Her lymph nodes suggest the cancer has spread. We did not perform a reconstruction."

"Okay." I wasn't quite sure what to say. Seems a bit insensitive to ask why when cancer is still swimming around inside her.

"The cancer is . . . extensive. We've gotten what we could with surgery. In the months ahead, we'll need to attack it by alternating chemo with radiation." The words *months, chemo* and *radiation* bounced around the inside of my head like pinballs. He continued, "Physically, the reconstruction would hinder our future ability to see growth or reoccurrence of the disease. Further, the recovery from her reconstruction would delay our need to start treatments as soon as possible. As it is, she can begin soon."

They'd moved her to a recovery room and told me I could see her while we waited for a room upstairs. Prior to surgery, it was not uncommon for her to be at a function or anything where a bunch of women had gathered and for some lady to discreetly pull her aside, glance at her breasts and ask, "Tell the truth, who's your plastic surgeon?" I walked into her room, glanced at her gauze-covered chest and knew she'd never get that question again.

That's when I really clued in. The breast is not simply a body part. It's a part of the whole that says, *I am woman and I am beautiful,* but it's not on equal footing with the others. I sat in that room and realized that you can cut off a finger, cut off a hand, even cut off a leg, but if you take a woman's breast, you are cutting more than just a body part.

It requires an adjustment.

I slid my hand beneath hers and waited. When she woke, it was somewhere in the night and she was in a great deal of pain.

I didn't tell her until the next morning when the medicine wore off and the sun broke through the blinds. "Honey, the cancer was more . . . had spread further than they first thought. They got what they could. Now they're talking more chemo and alternating that with radiation." She glanced down at her flat chest. I shook my head. "Not yet. They didn't want that to get in the way of . . ." I trailed off. What did I know. Abbie was in a lot of pain and kept hitting the morphine button after it re-set every fifteen minutes.

Doctors Hampton, Smith and Meyer, along with Dr. Dismakh, her surgeon, stood in a semicircle around the foot of her bed. Dr. Hampton started. "Abbie, the lymph nodes we took from you tell us that your cancer has spread beyond what we call its organ of origin. The breast. At this point, it's systemic, meaning it could be anywhere. We know of one mass on the lining of your lung." We waited, listening but not quite comprehending. "We want to send you to M. D. Anderson in Houston. And maybe Sloan-Kettering. Both are on the cutting edge of this type of cancer."

I swallowed and then eked out, "What kind is that?"

Dr. Smith spoke next. "It's aggressive, fast-growing, known

for an insatiable appetite. The good news is that because it's fast-growing, it's also easier to kill. But that's also the bad news. It's fast-growing."

At this point, I didn't care if her breasts were ever recon-structed. We could live without them.

The doctors left us alone. When I looked up, Dr. Hampton had reappeared in the room. He sat next to us both. He asked, "Do you like to dance?"

The question came out of left field. "What?"

He smiled. "Do you like to dance?"

I shook my head. "What kind of question is that?"

"This"—he waved his hand across the room and looked at Abbie—"is a delicate dance. Because we must kill it without killing you . . . and before it kills you."

Two days later, they sent us home.

30

The sun was just cracking through the treetops when I tried to open my eyes. I lifted my head and found Abbie sleeping next to me and dressed in clothes I had not seen before. Curled up inside her arms was a Jack Russell terrier.

The smell of cigarette smoke turned my head. Mr. Hawaii sat in an Adirondack chair against the far wall, a mound of butts and ash at his feet. The room was a porch of sorts, wrapped in screen and at least as high as the treetops, because they rubbed gently against the screen. He was tall, handsome, had shoulder-length black hair, a mustache, blue eyes, was cleanly shaven, muscular and maybe late-forties.

He held a cigarette in one hand and a Popsicle in the other. He waved the cigarette at me. "I gave her the clothes and she dressed herself. Fell back asleep a while ago."

"How'd we get here?"

He laughed, puffed and sucked. "Well, you carried her to the Stearman and then passed out."

"What's a Stearman?"

"My plane."

"We flew in a plane?"

He nodded and turned the Popsicle in his mouth.

"I don't remember that."

239

"Seeing as how you weren't wearing any clothes, it's an image I won't soon forget."

"Sorry. I had washed our clothes, and . . ."

He waved me off and smiled. "You took a pretty good hit. She was worried about your head swelling, so she shot you up with one of those." On the table next to us lay the opened Pelican case. "She said it'd help with the swelling."

A single empty dexamethasone syringe lay on the table. Two remained. My heart sank.

The rhythmic ticking of the ceiling fan tapped out a lonely tempo above me. The piercing pain in my head was unlike anything I'd ever experienced. I lifted my hand to touch my eye, but Abbie stopped me. "Don't."

"Honey, are you—"

"They didn't take anything." She patted the corner of my head. "Easy, you'll tear the glue."

"Glue?"

She placed a cool rag on my face. "Superglue. We did our best but it's not pretty."

"We?"

Her voice lowered to a whisper. If he could hear us, he didn't let on. "If he wanted to hurt us, he'd have done it by now. Once we got back here, he disappeared for a while, trying to find what's left of the canoe."

"And?"

"Gone."

A quick mental inventory told me that we had the clothes on our backs, a shotgun, a revolver and the Pelican case.

I cracked a whisper, "Why did you give me one of the dex?"

She paused. "I wasn't sure about the swelling in your head."

"You should know better than to waste that on me."

She pressed her fingers to my lips. "Sleep. We'll talk later. Don't worry."

She laid alongside me, placing her head on my chest.

I reached across her, finding the patch. "How you doing?"

"I'm okay. We'll work on me later."

Sometime later, I woke to the smell of my own blood and the feel of a warm washcloth on my face.

The third time I woke it was dark and the pain in my head had morphed to a coming freight train. Complete with horn. Abbie and I were lying beside each other on what felt like two military cots. I groaned, a shadow crossed me and a large hand placed four pills into my palm. "It's ibuprofen." I stared into my hand, saw ten pills, swallowed them and then fought back the response to spew them across the porch. He leaned over me, a small flashlight wedged between his teeth. He shined the light into my eye several times, then clicked it off. "She wouldn't let me take you to a hospital, or call the police, but you should go. You both should." He paused. "But I got a feeling you already know that."

Abbie's hand found me beneath the blanket. She stretched it across my stomach, then searched higher, leaving it pressed flat across my heart.

31

The medical team in Charleston transferred us to the Mayo Clinic in Jacksonville. They could administer the chemo as well as anyone, but Mayo offered a radiation machine far superior to anything else. It shot a beam of radiation that was accurate to thousandths of an inch and it compensated for breathing. Meaning, if you inhaled deeply and your chest cavity moved a third of an inch, the beam moved with you. This allowed them to be more aggressive with the radiation they threw at the tumor. They had similar machines at Sloan-Kettering and M. D. Anderson, but Mayo was closer to home.

We'd been in treatment six months. Abbie had lost her hair, some twenty pounds and lived with twenty-four-hour nausea. She said it was a nonstop ride on Gilligan's three-hour tour. Treatments were four hours a day, Monday through Thursday. By Thursday night, she was usually so sick that she spent most of the night next to the toilet. We both did.

It was somewhere around 5 a.m. on a Friday. I don't really remember the month. Somewhere in there they all started running together. She'd been throwing up so long that all she had left were the dry heaves and her legs were cramping. Add to that the fact that she was weaker than I'd ever seen her and you can understand that her stomach muscles had pretty much given out. I was standing next to the toilet, a wet rag in my hand, she was heaving but nothing was coming out. I helped her into the shower, turned it on and just let her rest under the steam and heat. I got her cleaned up, and got her in bed. For nearly two days, I just changed the sheets.

Sunday afternoon, I called the doctor and told him that we were staying in Charleston—she was in no shape to start up again Monday morning. She needed a few days. He agreed. Sunday evening, I propped her up, laid some saltine crackers on the table along with some Gatorade and aimed the bed so she could look out over the harbor.

Despite the nausea medication—which cost $500 for seven pills—she couldn't eat or drink anything. I tried to monitor how close she was to becoming dehydrated by judging how many times she peed and the color. "Clear" and we were getting enough fluid. "Yellow" and we were getting close to trouble. Given the chemo routine, her doctor had inserted a PIC line into her chest. It was a direct dump line that allowed the medicine to flow through a clear tube and go directly through her heart and out into her bloodstream. This also helped keep her hydrated. I became the hydration king. I could swap, flush and hang a fluids bag quicker than most nurses. Without it, I'm not sure what we'd have done. So I swapped her bag and hung it on this stainless-steel pipe on wheels that Abbie had affectionately started calling Georgie. He was her six-foot, slender, quiet-type boyfriend that she kept on the side. With her "drinking," I took a whiff of myself. Given my maid duties, I desperately needed a shower and about twelve hours of uninterrupted sleep.

I turned on the shower, undressed and stepped on the scale. A hundred and seventy pounds. Abbie wasn't the only one losing weight. I'd lost twelve pounds. I stepped into the shower and let the hot water blast the backside of my neck. We have a propane hot water heater and a propane tank that holds a hundred and fifty gallons. That means I can take a hot shower for as long as I want.

After maybe thirty minutes, I cut off the water and stepped out. Abbie was sitting on the floor, Georgie stood next to her. I stood dripping.

The last six months had been a rodeo of monumental proportions. Abbie was either flat on her back trying to stop the earth from spinning or hanging over the toilet puking up her toes. During that time there had not been much time for us. Actually, no time. Nada. We'd tried once and the pain was so intense, we just stopped. So when I stepped out of the shower, it was rather obvious that I'd not been with my wife in quite some time. I'm not trying to draw attention to that—there's nothing special about me. It is what it is. That's where we were living.

It was probably the first time she'd seen me without my clothes in several weeks. She looked up, pulled the rag away from her mouth and looked through squinted eyes. "Maybe . . . maybe you could get a girlfriend for a little while."

"What?"

She nodded. "It's okay. You can't go walking around like that."

"What are you talking about?"

She pointed. "You could just . . . you know, get a girlfriend. I know you need . . ."

It was one of her lower points. I sat beside her, put my arm around her and pulled her to me without making her any more sick. "I have a girlfriend."

She started to cry and shake her head. She pulled off her robe, and sat Indian style in front of me. She was bald—all over. She was pale, her skin had yellowed, the scars on her chest had healed but had begun to pull in, drawing the skin tight and further concaving her chest. She leaned her head against the wall, tapped herself in the chest and managed, "How can you love this?"

"Honey, I didn't marry you for your boobs. Don't get me wrong, I miss them and once we beat this thing, maybe we can get them back, but . . . I already told you. I didn't marry the woman on the magazine cover."

She spoke between the sobs. "But why do you do what you do? Why? You have no life."

I held her hand in mine, turning her ring in circles around her bony finger.

I'm no expert on women and their feelings but I think they have two unspoken, fundamental wants that occur as soon as they open their eyes. They want to be pursued and they want to know that they are beautiful. Abbie had always been pursued by most men and everyone had always told her she was beautiful. She'd never been anything but. Then cancer. Surgery, radiation, chemotherapy. Slash, burn and poison. In her mind's eye, sitting on that bathroom floor, she saw a remnant of her former self. I did not see that. But how do you convince her of that? How do you tell her that she is not the sum of what she sees in the mirror? Starting with Rosalia, Abbie had taught me to see past the surface. I spent the next few days pilfering her scrapbooks. Abbie had never been one to keep every picture she had taken, but there were enough to get the job done. I found eighteen of my favorite pictures. I had some blown into life-sized posters, the rest I turned into eight-by-tens. I taped the eight-by-tens to every mirror in the house. Abbie couldn't look in the mirror without seeing what she once looked like. I hung the posters at the end of every hall, so every time she turned a corner, she was reminded of what her whole body once looked like. Then I walked her around the house. Abbie hated it. She hated seeing pictures of herself. She'd never been one to look at them before, and she waved her hand across the house. "Take them all down. I don't want them."

"Abbie, I don't care if you want them or not. They're staying."

"But . . . why?"

"The mirror lies."

32

I could smell eggs cooking and hear bacon sizzling but that's not what woke me. It was the laughter. Abbie's laughter. I blinked and the warm furball next to me crawled out from under the blanket, hopped up on my chest and started licking my face. About the size of a loaf of bread, its nose was cold, whiskers long and the pads on its feet were digging into my ribs. I sat up, put both feet on the floor and waited while the spin of the earth slowed.

The room was screened in, maybe twelve by twelve feet, metal roof, ceiling fan, fishing rods leaning in the corner. Cobwebs hung between the trusses along with two propane lanterns that rocked in the breeze. Spindly live oak limbs wrapped around both sides, giving shade and protection. A summer porch of sorts. Through the cracks between the boards I could see the ground, some thirty feet below. Stairs wound down to the river beneath me, while a walkway led toward the main house, the smell and the laughter. I fingered my left eye. Puffy and tender, I forced it open. My vision was fuzzy but I could see out of it. The Pelican case rested on the end of my cot. The revolver was there, too. I set the dog on the bed, flipped open the cylinder and found it loaded. I tucked it in the small of my back, heard Abbie laugh again and set the revolver back on the bed.

The dog jumped down, ran three circles around its stub of a tail, then pranced halfway down the walkway that led into the main house. Two more clockwise circles, followed by one counterclockwise and then it disappeared into the main house. I'm not too versed on dog-speak but I had a feeling that meant "Hey, food's this way. Follow me."

Abbie sat at a small table sipping something hot. A blue bandana covered her head, but not her ears, and she was wrapped in a terry-cloth robe that looked like it fit Mr. Hawaii. He stood over the stove talking both to a skillet full of eggs and what looked like a parrot perched on his shoulder. I walked into the room and all three looked at me. The bird—a brilliant red and blue—dropped off the man's shoulder, landed on the table, then climbed onto Abbie's arm, using its beak to pull itself up to her shoulder.

A small, muted television sat on the table next to Abbie. A talking head from one of the networks seemed to be rifling through the news of the day. The man turned to me, hung a towel over a shoulder and extended his hand. "Bob Porter." He pointed at the parrot. "That's Petey." Then he pointed to the dog. "That's Rocket."

"I owe you a lot."

He split the eggs between two plates and motioned for me to sit. On another eye of the stove he was browning diced onions. And on a third eye, he was frying grits. I turned to Abbie. "How you feeling?"

"Good. I actually slept."

The yellowish tint of her skin had receded in her cheeks to give way to some color I'd not seen in a while. She stood, placing her hand on my shoulder. "You two talk, I'm going to take a bath."

Bob pointed down the hall. "Towels are in that closet. And be careful, the water's hot."

She closed the door and I heard water running. A second later, she called for me. "Doss?"

Her tone of voice didn't say, "I need you," but rather sounded like "Hey, come take a look at this," or, "I want something." Live with a designer long enough and your ear can pick these things out. I pushed open the door and she sat chin-deep in one of those big cast-iron, ivory tubs with huge lion's feet. The edges rolled over the side and the back was high and made a pretty good headrest. Her left arm rested on the edge. She smiled, but didn't bother to open her eyes. "When we get home . . . I want one of these."

I felt the temperature of the water and said, "Deal."

When I walked back into the kitchen, Bob was hand-feeding his eggs to Rocket. "Thanks for what you did. I'd be in a mess if you hadn't come across us."

He nodded while Rocket licked the palm of his hand. "Rocket likes his salted. Petey won't touch them unless I load them up with cheddar cheese."

"How is it that you showed up when you did?"

"Gus." He shrugged. "I've known him a long time. He was kind to me when others were not."

"That'd be Gus."

He continued, "He knows I know the river and, given my occupation, I'm able to cover it, end to end, more quickly than most."

"Occupation?"

"I fly . . . a bit."

I looked more closely and put two and two together. "That was you at the gas station, in the rain?"

He laughed. "Yeah, thanks for the push. Gus called me the next day. Asked me to take a bird's-eye view of you from time to time. Make sure you were getting along. Wasn't too hard to spot a mango-colored canoe."

"Guess that explains why you've buzzed us every day for a week."

He nodded. "Once I clued in to how fast you were paddling, I could guess your progress to within a mile or so. You paddle well."

"Practice."

"That's what I hear."

More news about us. "I was afraid of that."

He raised an eyebrow. "You know Fisher's?"

Fisher's General Store was a public-access boat ramp on the Florida side. They sold beer, soda, candy bars, crickets, worms, life jackets, whatever somebody might need on the river. A handy little place. They also had public bathrooms, which weren't the cleanest in the world but when you're guiding folks, especially women, who've never squatted in the woods, it makes for a helpful stop. It was a routine stop on one of our legs downriver.

"I grew up guiding on this river, so I've been in a time or two."

"I stopped in to deliver a bill to the guy who owns the place. He owns a farm west of here. Anyway, these four guys were milling around out front, being a little too loud. Between their tone of voice and what Gus had told me, I had a feeling they were up to no good. So yesterday afternoon I took off and started looking south of Pinckney's."

"You did all that based on a tone of voice?"

"I've had a lot of practice. Once I caught sight of you, they weren't too far behind. The White Oak has a runway I've used once or twice. I set her down, made my way to the river and you came to me."

"Any idea who they are?"

He shook his head. "Four idiots looking for trouble."

"Why'd they choose us?"

"Hyenas always target the weak."

"How do you know they're not circling the house now?"

"They could be, but"—he smiled—"I highly doubt it."

"Speaking of house . . ." I turned in my seat. "Where are we?"

"You remember the river?"

I shrugged. "Sort of hard to forget."

"A few miles south of Trader's."

My heart sank. "South of the powerline?"

"You do know the river." He nodded. "Two miles." I did the math. We had just lost sixteen miles. Or rather, had them tacked back on. Now we were every bit of forty-six to Cedar Point and had to make our way back through real estate we'd already covered. It was a tough blow. He continued, "I imagine they're trying to figure out what they're going to tell the hospital when they ask about their injuries." He leaned across the table, pointed an ear toward the sound of Abbie in the tub and whispered, "I know it's none of my business, but I'm sort of curious to hear your side of why you're on this river with that lady."

"She's my wife."

"I understand that, but given her condition, why isn't she in a hospital?"

I sat down and forked my eggs around the plate. "I guess we can skip the small talk." He nodded. "That's a bit of a long story."

He checked his watch. "You been keeping up with the news?"

I shook my head. "Hadn't really had much access."

He flipped the channel on the TV, turned up the volume and leaned back in his chair, folding his hands across his stomach. The screen flashed: ABBIE ELIOT UPDATE.

Petey circled the table, stamping it with his feet. "Update. Update."

About there, it hit me that our trip downriver was over.

33

Spending so much time in treatment, Abbie got to know some of the other girls. All cancer patients stick together, but breast cancer patients share a bond that is unique. One of those girls was Deborah Fanning. Deborah, or Debbie as she became to us, was fighting a similar battle: double mastectomy, cancer metastasized, doctors were chasing it around her insides, too. Her husband, Rick, came with her for the first few months. They were both professionals, big house on the water in Miami, vacation home, yacht, seemed like they had everything. But over the months, we saw him less. Eventually, we saw him not at all.

Debbie just shrugged and said, "You know salesmen. Always traveling. Gotta pay that mortgage." She wasn't a very good liar. At Abbie's suggestion, I requested they put her room next to ours. They did and we ended up spending a lot of time together. Watching movies, eating when they could, sharing stories, talking about life after cancer. I used to roll them both around the parking lot. We'd hang two bags on Georgie and I'd push both chairs. Debbie was a beautiful girl, four years younger than Abbie. She too had lost her hair, and though she never said it, she was terrified. It didn't take Abbie and me long to pick up on the fact that her cell phone never rang. Rick wasn't traveling.

One afternoon, I walked into the room and Abbie was crying. She was also mad. Fuming. She said, "Are you going to divorce me?"

"What?"

"Tell me the truth."

"No. Abbie, what in the world are you—"

She threw a stack of papers at me. "Well, Rick did." She pointed next door. "He's over there now telling her how it's really for the best but it's all her fault."

I leaned against the wall and listened. She was right. I pushed open the door to Debbie's room, took three steps and punched him so hard it split all four of my knuckles. He lay on the floor, spitting teeth and foamy blood. I pointed down at him. "You don't deserve her." I picked her up, carried her into our room and that's where she stayed until she died three months later.

Now Rick's got that on his conscience. And to be gut-level honest, I hope it stays there a long time.

SO THIS BECAME OUR LIFE. Treatments, travel, staph infections, scans, more scans and still more scans, each one worse, this was the haunting fog we lived in and under. For us, the process of fighting became a Chinese water torture that weakened our expectation.

The months ran together. Because cancer is a morphing disease, the chemo chases it. Cancer knows this so it cloaks itself and morphs into something else, finally finding a way to break through the chemo. Much like a bacteria works its way around an antibiotic, eventually becoming resistant. It's the law of diminishing returns. The hope is to kill it before it breaks through.

You want to keep at it, not give the tumors a chance to breathe, but we seemed to always be one step behind.

We'd been in the hospital for weeks. Abbie was fighting an infection. My bed was a pallet on the floor. It was somewhere around seven in the morning and Abbie and I had finally fallen asleep, which was bad timing because it was shift change. Some alarm was going off above Abbie's head and in the haze of sleep I heard a nurse at the station outside say, "1054 needs a line flushed." A few minutes passed and I heard it again, "1054 needs a line flushed." I began thinking to myself, What is 1054? Then, Who is 1054? Finally, Who is in 1054?

I walked outside to the nurses' station where everyone had gathered for the day. About fifteen nurses and interns stood awaiting orders from the doctors. I whistled as loud as I could. Maybe I didn't look all that good, 'cause it got pin-drop quiet and everyone looked at me. I raised a hand and pointed. "Everybody! Follow me." I realize I wasn't making any friends, but I'd had it. Surprisingly, they followed. Maybe being a senator's son-in-law has its benefits. I mothered everyone into the room and we all gathered around Abbie's bed. Abbie's eyes were heavy and she was slowly waking up. I stood near the head of the bed and said, "I'd like to introduce all of you to my wife. This is Abbie Michaels. You can just call her Abbie." They looked at me a bit strangely. I held her hand. "She's a wife, a daughter, a friend, she has a tendency to talk with her hands, she likes Lucky Strike jeans and she sees beauty where others don't." I paused. "She is not and has never been '1054.' " The head nurse spoke up while a doctor shook his head and started walking out. She said, "Mr. Michaels, HIPAA law mandates that we not—"

I cut the doctor off and shut the door. He huffed, but I had everyone's full attention. I palmed the sleep off my face while the doctor stood a foot from me. "I know you all work hard. A lot harder than most give you credit for. I'm thankful for what you do and how you do it, but HIPAA's wife is not lying in that bed. I need to ask you to look at the woman in that bed and think of her not as a number. Not as a statistic. Hope is what feeds us. And, to be honest, it's running in short supply around here." I cupped my hands together. "It's like . . . like trying to hold water. Please don't take what little we have. Please . . ."

I looked at each of their name tags and shook their hands as they filed out: "Bill, Ann, Elaine, Simon, Dean, Ellen, Amy . . ." They got the idea.

Days later, I was walking past the nurses' station in search of coffee and heard one of the nurses nod toward our room and mutter beneath her breath, " 'High Maintenance' needs some sheets."

I shrugged. At least it was better than "1054." Then I realized she was specifically talking about me. I leaned against the counter, speaking to her and the other three nurses writing in their patient notebooks. "You're right. I am. And for that I'm sorry. But I'll gladly let you trade places with her."

They never really said much to me after that. I'm not proud of that. It wasn't cool or tough and it didn't really win friends and influence people. I'm just letting you know where I was. The bottom is an ugly place to be.

Problem was, I had a few floors yet to fall before I reached the basement of us.

34

Petey strutted around the table while Bob tuned the antennae for better reception and I tapped my fingers on my chin. The reporter narrowed her eyes, lowered her voice and seemed overly dramatic. "I'm standing outside the office of Dr. Gary Fencik, a primary care physician in the Charleston area. A lifelong friend of Abbie Eliot's, Dr. Fencik has actively followed her illness since the beginning. The Charleston police have just issued a statement saying that they have received video surveillance tapes showing Doss Michaels stealing large quantities of three different types of narcotics from a locked cabinet inside this building." The anchorwoman at the studio interrupted her, "Virginia, do we know how he got into the cabinet?"

"The authorities believe Mr. Michaels had access to both the keys and the combination."

"Do we know what amount of narcotics Mr. Michaels allegedly took?"

"Off camera, the office manager told me and I quote, 'enough to kill an elephant.' "

Bob clicked off the TV. He asked, "Any of that true?"

A deep breath. "Yeah."

"Which part?"

"Well . . . from a certain point of view, all of it."

He glanced at the windowsill where an electric panel read temperature, humidity, wind direction, barometric pressure, high and low tides and chance of rain indicated as a percentage. He frowned, checked his watch and then stood. "Personally, I think you're nuts, but I imagine you've got a pretty good reason or you wouldn't be out here. And you probably think you know what you're doing, in which case I'd also say you're nuts. Either way, you're nuts." He glanced at the readout again and the wind reading had dropped to two miles per hour. "I've got to get to work. I'll be back a bit after dark."

He pulled on a shirt and began walking out a side door. I hollered after him, "Hey, if you're going to get the police or call my father-in-law, there's not much I can do to stop you, but I'd like to know before they show up."

He stopped, put on his sunglasses and shook his head. "If the police show up here, it won't be because I had anything to do with it. But if you want some advice, you should call them. Picking the location of your own surrender is much better than letting them pick it." He smiled.

"Is that experience speaking?"

"Yup."

He turned again and I hollered one last time, "What do you do? I mean, for work."

Another smug smile. "Agricultural aviation."

That explains a lot. He waved his hand across the house. "Make yourself at home. Clothes are in the closet. *Mi casa es su casa.*"

"I have no idea what that means."

"My house is your house."

He whistled, Rocket ran after him and the two disappeared

down a well-worn footpath that led away from the river. I stood outside thinking, listening to Abbie do the dolphin-frolic in the tub. About five minutes later, I heard an engine crank then speed away. Ten seconds later, the sound of the engine returned. The Stearman brushed the treetops then shot upward, looped once, rolled, then returned—upside down. He was waving at me.

While Abbie bathed, I tucked the revolver behind my belt and took a walk around the house. If the four amigos came back, I wanted to have an idea of how and where. As for the revolver, I wasn't sure. I just knew I'd rather have it tucked behind my belt than sitting on top of the bed. Bob's house was an old river house, built up on a bluff on the Georgia side. I followed the footpath down which Bob had disappeared. It led to an airstrip and a makeshift hangar. The runway was dirt and short, which made me think that he must be a pretty good pilot. Two older Honda dirt bikes leaned against a far wall. One seat was less dusty than the other. Both needed a tune-up. The dirt road that led to his house ran for at least a half mile before it ran into another dirt road. Fresh tire tracks snaked along the soft sand. Feeling too far from Abbie, I turned around.

Beyond the house, further downriver and resting atop a small bluff, sat a one-room cabin. Like Bob's house, it was tucked up into the trees. If you weren't looking for it, you'd miss it. I walked around, peered in the windows and checked the doors but it had been winterized and was sealed up rather tight.

We seemed to be pretty well surrounded by woods without another house in sight or earshot. Even from the air, we were hidden beneath the trees. If I didn't know better, I'd say Bob was hiding, too. I knew the bend in the river, having passed through here a lot, but I didn't know much beyond the banks, because in all my passing through, I'd never ventured far from the water's edge.

I walked back in the house and found Abbie stepping out of the tub. She hung an arm over me and I helped her slip back into her bathing suit and cutoff shorts and then laid her on the couch while I searched for a shirt—seeing as how the last one I'd stolen from the yoga class had been ripped down the middle. I walked into Bob's room, pulled open his closet and started picking through the clothes. He didn't have much. Clothes were not his vice. I found a denim workshirt with snaps and slipped it off the hanger, thinking it might be easier for Abbie to get on and off. I was closing the door when I noticed the framed letter hanging inside the closet. It was partially hidden by a white coat. I slid the coat out of the way and read the letter. It was from the Diocese of Florida and dated 1988. It read,

The Rev. Robert Porter:

The purpose of this letter is to inform you that it is the decision of this Diocese that you are no longer a priest in good standing and are no longer a rector of St. Peter's. Having been hand-delivered to you, your receipt of this letter ensures your acceptance and compliance. In accordance with the canons of the Catholic Church and due to your admitted violations of the criminal code of the State of Florida and the admitted moral violations committed by you against your parishioners, and having abandoned the communion of the body elect, you are hereby released from the obligations of the ministerial office and are deprived of the right to exercise the author-

ity of a Minister of God's word and sacrament as con-
ferred in Ordination. Please vacate the premises of
St. Peter's immediately, and inform the office of the
Bishop of that date.

> In God's Service,
> The Rt. Rev. Phillip Turgrid, Ph.D., J.D.

I looked again at the white coat, but it wasn't a white coat at
all. Hanging alongside the robe was a clerical shirt with a collar,
three long pieces of fine white rope and several multicolored
pieces of fabric that looked like those things priests wore over
their robes.

I made Abbie some soup for dinner but I'd stolen so much
in the last week that I'd started feeling guilty and I couldn't
bring myself to steal from a priest. Even a defrocked one. Abbie
drank most of the broth and ate about half the noodles along
with a few saltine crackers. When she'd finished, I propped her
back on the couch, covered her in a blanket, then walked out
onto the porch.

The only sound was that of the metal rings of the hammock
rubbing against the metal anchors in the wall. Petey balanced
on a dowel above me that had been driven into the support
beam for the porch. He seemed happy enough, although if he
decided it was time to go to the bathroom, I was in trouble. I
stared out through the tree limbs, while the river moved along
without us. I'd watched the news on and off all afternoon. I
wasn't sure about the guys who'd jumped us, but if they saw the
reports of us, or heard the senator's news conference, they
might go to the authorities with a slightly altered story and hope
to capitalize on it. I wasn't quite sure where to go or what to
do. If I went home, the senator would intervene. That would

get ugly and I had a feeling that my time alone with Abbie would come to an end. If we showed our faces in public, we ran the risk of getting turned in, so I knew we'd need to be careful. Lastly, I knew that whoever had jumped us in the boathouse wouldn't let up so easily. We'd been lucky. The next time, I doubted we'd be that lucky.

Bob's plane landed an hour after dark. Ten minutes later, feet climbed the steps and entered the house. Wasn't long after that, Bob walked out onto the porch, a bottle of tequila in one hand, a cigar in the other. "Since you're now a guest in my house, why don't the two of us have a little come to Jesus meeting."

I lifted my head off the hammock. "Are you qualified to have those?"

He saw Abbie in his shirt and seemed to take notice of it. Then he nodded. "Used to be."

I knew I owed him an explanation. "We've been at this a few years. Abbie's and my struggle has, admittedly, narrowed our view of the world down to us. I rarely see much beyond our own needs. I'm not apologizing for that, but I know it's insensitive. And for that, I am sorry."

He shook his head. "Sounds to me like you've earned a little understanding."

"How'd you become a priest?"

"After college, I found myself in Rome. Worked four years in the Vatican. Thought I'd found my calling. Was assigned to a small parish in Mississippi. Then Florida. Finally, Georgia."

I nodded toward the closet. "What happened?"

"Oh, that." He smiled and swigged. "You want the honest answer?"

I shrugged. "Whatever."

"I stole too much of the parish's money and slept with too many of my female parishioners."

"That's honest enough."

"Twelve years in prison has a way of shaking you loose from the lies you hold dear."

He took another long swig and then lit the cigar. The breeze swept through the screen, caught the smoke and filtered it out through the other side of the screen before it hit the trees. He pulled long on the cigar, turning the end bright red, and said, "You thought about your options?"

"Not sure I have any."

He pointed beyond the screen with his cigar. "I've got a rental downriver. At the moment, it's empty." He laughed. "Actually, it's been empty awhile. Last guy to hole up there was some nut who ran a hedge fund. I think his name was Thad but, can't remember. He was something of a rock star for the better part of a decade, but then he made some bad decisions, the market turned against him and he couldn't cover his shorts. I don't pretend to understand all that, but at the end of the day, he was broke and so were his clients. While they were trying to put his head on a platter, he decided he had always wanted to be an artist. Only problem was, he had trouble selling his art." He nodded. " 'Course, that might be because he had trouble making any. Haven't seen him in a while. You all are welcome to stay in there as long as you like." He tapped his cigar, shaking off the ash, and then bit some dead skin off his lip. "Sometimes"—he tongued the skin around in his mouth, finally spitting it out—"it helps to let the storm blow over before you . . . venture out."

~❧~

THE MOON THREW our shadow on the beach as I carried Abbie to the cabin. I unlocked the door and pushed it open. It was clean, quiet and smelled of cedar. I fumbled for the light switch and clicked it on. The entire one-room cabin had been built from cedar. The room was broken up into two halves. The living side consisted of a four-poster bed pushed up against one wall, a dresser and a toilet, sink and mirror. Function ruled, because there was no form. On the other side, looking out over the river through a floor-to-ceiling window, sat an artist's studio. Three easels, several rolls of canvas, dozens of paints, brushes, knives and countless odds and ends needed by any artist. Evidently, the guy was a neat freak because everything was lined up and organized. All the paint labels were turned up and arranged alphabetically. I changed the sheets and tucked Abbie in bed.

I spent several hours picking through his paints and stacks of pencil sketches that had been filed in a plastic bucket in the corner. They were "snapshots" of birds, tree limbs, leaves, fish, whatever could be seen out the window of this studio. Fingering through the desk and drawers of supplies, I tried to remember when the last time was that I had painted . . . anything. It'd been over three years.

I stared out the window and tried to remember seeing this section of the river from the water. As many times as I'd been down it, I only had vague memories of passing through here. I could remember the S-turn upriver and the ninety-degree after that, followed by another long straightaway that ran for nearly a half mile before a hard left. I also remembered the way the water flowed faster along the Georgia side, but I had little recollection of seeing Bob's house or cabin tucked up in the trees. Which was good. If we needed a place to hide out, this would work.

Below the cabin, a blackwater creek flowed into the river. Abbie's forehead was wrinkled and a blue vein throbbed on her right temple. I pulled the covers up under her nose, grabbed a flashlight and stepped out onto the porch. I stared up at the moon, over at the creek and down inside myself. I didn't like what I saw so I climbed down the stairs and started walking up the creek bed.

While the moon had been bright a few hours ago, it was beaming now. The bank was narrow and the water deep. The water had been running out of here a long time and, given the depth and naked roots, probably fast, which indicated a spring. River guides were always looking for freshwater—clients liked everything from swimming in it to looking for buried pirate treasure, and we liked the taste of sweet cold water. I stepped in and the water accepted me, climbing to my waist. The flow pushed gently against me, pulling at my clothes. It snaked inland, cut through the bluff and into a covered area that looked like it was once a pond. Now dry, the bed of it was populated by twenty or so mature weeping willows and birch trees whose bark had peeled like paper and now dotted the pond floor. In the middle sat a building.

I ducked under the arms of the willows, its long green bows draping along my back, and made my way up a log walkway to the building. The logs had been cut in half and laid sideways, like railroad ties, spaced a short step apart. I shined the light onto the old wooden structure. The wood had darkened with age but I could tell it was pecky cyprus and that given the width of the planks, some eighteen inches in width, it had been cut a long time ago. Pecky cyprus is made when an organism like a worm gets into the wood and screws with its DNA. It makes for a beautiful and, some would say, psychedelic design. I walked around it trying to figure out why anyone would build a cabin here. The roof was made of cedar shingles and covered in a green spongy moss. Given the fading in the wood and the horizontal watermarks, the building flooded at high water. Which might explain why it looked like it'd been empty for some time. It stood about a foot off the ground, elevated on pilings that had been driven into the sand. They were two feet in diameter, hand-hewn and squared using an adze and an axe. Huge unequal planks made up the siding. The building looked to be a hundred, maybe a hundred and fifty years old. The windows were tall, and covered by shutters that were maybe three feet wide and six or seven feet tall. Hinged at the top, they opened at the bottom. I walked around the back, lighting the roofline and answering my question.

Maybe even pirates need God.

The front door hung on a huge rusted iron hinge that looked like it could have come off an old sailing vessel. A carved dowel had been wedged through an iron ring, making a crude latch. I knocked it loose with the flashlight and leaned against the door. Inside, a dozen or so benches with no backs sat in equals rows and faced forward. Standing and sitting room, the place might hold fifty people if they didn't mind getting close. Everything was worn, dusty, tacked together with cobwebs and hadn't been used in decades. Equidistant drill holes lined the walkway down the middle. I stood there dripping, wondering why somebody would mess up a perfectly good floor. The water fell off me, filled the cracks, then disappeared. *Drain holes.* They were large enough to let a lizard in but would keep out most snakes. On the back wall, above the window, somebody had carved intricate lettering into a single beam that supported the roof. The carvings had faded, but I ran my fingers through the grooves I could reach. *"When you pass through the waters . . ."* The passage continued but my arm was too short.

35

Her doctors said we needed to be "more aggressive," so they scheduled her for accelerated treatments first thing Monday morning—giving us the weekend to ourselves. Mid-morning Friday she wrapped a blindfold around my head, led me to her car, drove four hours—talking nonstop about everything and nothing—then parked in a gravel lot, slid me down into a canoe and paddled for more than an hour while I leaned against the seat back, twiddled my thumbs and threatened to swamp the canoe. The sounds and smells—along with the taste of the water—told me, generally, where we were, but I didn't know for sure until sundown, when she beached the canoe, sat me on the sand and whispered in my ear, "I want you to promise me something."

I didn't need to open my eyes. I stretched my feet into the sand and felt the St. Marys River flowing gently through my toes. We'd spent the last night of our honeymoon here, camped beneath the cedars, the smoke from our campfire filtering up through the limbs and the smell of us painted on each other. Cedar Point is the southeasternmost point of real estate in the state of Georgia. Maybe an acre in size, the little finger of dry land rises up out of the marsh like an oversized pitcher's mound. Surrounded by marsh, and hidden in palm trees, cedars, scrub oaks and wiregrass, the small island rests untouched and unknown—even to most of the locals. A few hundred yards west, or upriver, sat the historic town of St. Marys. Nearly a mile across the river sat the state of Florida. Off to our left, or southeast, maybe five miles, lay Fernandina Beach. Just north of it, and due east, sat Cumberland Island. Between the two stretched the Atlantic Ocean. It was the island of endless possibility.

She was trying to be so strong. She popped the cork herself and poured my favorite wine, Writer's Block, into two plastic Solo cups. "What's that?"

She touched her cup to mine. "Say, 'I promise.' "

"But I don't know what I'm promising."

She sipped. "Say it."

"But—"

"Say it."

I sipped. "I promise."

"That was heartfelt."

"Well, if you'd tell me what I'm promising, maybe I could put a little something behind it."

"But you promise?"

I raised my hand in the air. "Yes, I promise."

She hesitated, staring at the water. In the distance, a dolphin's dorsal fin broke the surface of the water, rolled over the top of it, then disappeared. A second later, several more rolled behind it. "If, for some reason, I ever get to the place where . . . where something's happened, maybe I'm not me, and even worse, we're not us . . ." I tried to stop her, but she can be pretty headstrong. She waved me off. "I want you to bring me here." She placed her hand on the blindfold. "Right here." The silence blanketed us. "No matter what."

She tugged on my arm. No more games. I squinted against the sun. "I promise."

She lay back, her left foot resting atop her bent right knee—a character straight out of *Tom Sawyer*.

She stared at the red polish chipping and peeling off her big toenail. "One more thing."

I raised an eyebrow. "Didn't we just go through this?"

She stared up through the smoke-charred limbs swaying above us. "One of these days, you'll come back and buy this place."

Even then she believed.

"I'm not even sure this place is on the map. Any map."

"Then it won't be too expensive. Now, say it."

I stared out across the water. "I promise."

Following the mullet, the dolphins passed within a few feet of shore, rolling and disappearing only to reappear a few feet downriver. One shot up into the air, spun, shimmered, then splashed and popped the water with its tail. Abbie screamed with delight, shook off her fear, took three steps and dove into the water where the dolphins circled her and one bumped her thigh with its body.

36

It was dark and overcast when I woke. The sky threatened rain with an occasional drop that rippled the river. A bamboo fly rod leaned against one corner. I lay in the dim daylight. Abbie had thrown her right leg over mine and my left foot was asleep. Her leg was smooth, and warm. An hour after daylight, the Stearman engine cranked, rolled out of earshot, then zoomed back into it and overhead.

The sound woke her. She responded by rolling into me. She had something on her mind because she wasted little time. She pointed into the corner. "Does it work?"

"Yeah."

"What size?"

"Maybe a four weight. Could be a two. It's pretty old."

"Flies?"

"A few."

"Leader? Tippet?" She could be focused when she wanted.

"Might be dry-rotted."

She stepped out of bed, slipped on her cutoff shorts and looped the top of her bikini over her neck. "Tie me." I tied both ends, thinking there was a lot of slack left over.

She shook her scarf loose of the knot and popped her bikini top like suspenders. "Didn't used to be that much slack."

270

I faked a slow smile. "Nope."

She grabbed a straw hat off one shelf and then licked the end of the line, feeding it through the eyelet of the fly. Five minutes later, Abbie was wading into the river. "It's cold."

"Rain does that."

Waist-deep, she peeled the line and stood, drying the fly. She waved it through the air like a lasso, then released it, letting it roll across the top of the water. She started a slow retrieve. Whenever she fished, she bit her bottom lip. If she fished all day, she'd rub it raw. The water swirled with a flash of bronze and red, followed by the quick sound of suction, and the fly disappeared. I closed my eyes and waited. The reel wound backward, the drag singing just a bit. Abbie howled and let the fish run. She lifted the rod tip and followed it to deeper water. Gently, she pulled it in and laid it on the beach. The perch, also known as red-breasted bream, lay flopping on the sand, its gills opening and closing like an accordion.

I pulled out the fly, slipped the fish back in the water and held it while the river filtered through its gills. Spurred by cold water and oxygen, it jerked loose and shot toward the bottom. Abbie had moved on, slowly wading upriver, casting into a dark hole on the opposite bank.

She fished through lunch.

By three in the afternoon, I'd released forty-seven bream and eight smallmouth bass. Finally, she laid down the pole, sat down and dug her toes into the sand. Her face was flush so I handed her a cup of water and one of her lollipops. A bald eagle flew upriver and perched in a tree above us, some fifty feet away. White head and gold beak shining in the sun. It scanned the water, jumped off the limb, shot toward the water and sank its claws beneath the surface. Its huge wings slapped the water, cut the air and pulled it higher. He reached the treetops, circled and returned to his limb, where he began methodically tearing at the fish. Abbie closed her eyes and smiled. "That takes care of number six."

"Yup."

"That's five down."

She lay back and closed her eyes. The finger-sized vein in her neck told me her heart was beating fast. "What's next?"

Bob buzzed the trees overhead, circling his runway before landing. Abbie clung to me—breathing deeply but not catching her breath. I helped her up the bank, laid her in bed and walked out onto the porch, where the rain was smacking the palmetto fronds with an irregular rhythm.

BOB'S PLANE TOUCHED DOWN in the field. Minutes later, he, Rocket and Petey appeared on the riverbank. He climbed the stairs and found me sitting in the artist's chair, staring at an empty canvas. It was dusty and I'd done a poor job of stretching it across the frame.

He carried a canvas bag slung over one shoulder. He set it on the ground and pulled out two bottles of red wine. He popped the cork on one and then pulled two Styrofoam cups out of the bag. He filled both and offered me one. I took it. He didn't say anything, but stared downriver, occasionally glancing over his shoulder at Abbie lying in the bed just a few feet away.

He gulped from the cup—taking half. "How is she?"

"She fished through lunch, and now she's sleeping it off. That much activity takes a toll on her."

"She catch any?"

"Fifty-five."

He nodded approvingly. "The media is starting to whisper

words like *assisted suicide* and *mercy killing* followed by questions to the senator if he'd consider unleashing the National Guard." Another gulp. Cabernet dripped down the right side of his mouth.

"I wouldn't put it past him."

"Your story is filling all the networks. Actually"—he sat back and crossed his legs—"her story is. Yours is simply thrown in to give the viewer someone to hate. Pretty girl, riddled with cancer, lot of pain, taken from her home and family when she needs them most."

"I know how it looks."

He raised both eyebrows. "You sure?" I nodded but didn't look at him. "I doubt it," he said, " 'cause if you did, you'd hightail it home."

"Perception is not reality."

"You don't have to convince me, but you're swimming up current."

"Tell me about it."

He sloshed his glass at me. "More?"

"Yeah."

We sat in the dark awhile. The only light was the red tip of his cigar. He placed it in his mouth, drew on it until his cheeks pressed against his teeth and the end turned a bright red.

The river has an uncanny way of drowning out ambient noise. Anything outside two hundred feet off the river's bank is quieted by the canopy. The exception to the rule is a clear night when the sound seems to bounce off the skyline and shoot like stars onto the river's surface, where it floats upriver, carrying every second or third note. I bent my ear toward a noise I couldn't place.

"What's that sound?"

"Local carnival."

"What? You mean like with a Ferris wheel, people guessing body weights and somebody barking at the yak woman?"

He chuckled. "Just a bunch of gypsies running from the law."

"We ought to fit right in." I was quiet a minute. "You know if they got a carousel?"

"Yeah. Don't know how well I'd trust it. Kind of old."

"They got a head gypsy?"

"If that's what you want to call him."

"You know him?"

"Not too well, but we've spoken."

"You think you could get us in . . . after hours?"

"What do you have in mind?"

37

Two years passed. Abbie's health became tidal—it ebbed and flowed. A tug-of-war between chemo and cancer with her caught up in the middle. Some days she could get out of bed, maybe once a week I'd push her down the Battery in her chair, but for the most part, she was bed- or couch-ridden and withering away in front of me.

Somewhere in here, it struck me—the truth in all this. Normal cells have automatic self-destruct buttons that they punch after they've served their purpose. They live, do what they were made to do, then pull the cord. Suicide is expected. At the end of the day, cancer is nothing more than a cell or group of cells that refuse to die. And to make matters worse, cancer cells are not foreign. It's not like they come from somewhere else. Our bodies make the very thing that kills us.

I have a difficult time with the logic in all of this.

It's strange. I know my wife has cancer because they told me, but I've never actually seen it. Never touched it. I don't have any real connection to it other than it's killing my wife.

Cancer hurts beyond the pain. It is a cycle of diagnosis, prognosis and scan. We live not paycheck to paycheck, but scan to scan. Every time we stand in the doctor's office and hear the scan results, we think, It's getting bigger and I can't do a single thing about it.

That may be the single worst feeling in the world.

Any positive report is tempered by our experience, and the knowledge that no matter what the doctors do, we will always believe there are still cancer cells in her body. We feel as though we're always just one scan away from hearing the word *metastatic,* which is often followed by, *I'm going to miss you.*

Riddled with fear, sadness and stress, our imaginations run wild like they did when we were kids and the monsters camped out in the closets. What's worse, we listen like Captain Hook, haunted by the ticking of the clock. Cancer-free moments are the exception, not the norm. We have progressed from beating it, to living with it . . . to just living. I have become more defensive in posture, building walls to insulate us from the bad news. Because there's always more. Life and death are always on our mind. Idle thinking is no longer idle. I wanted so badly to think in future tense, to talk about summer movies, buy two tickets to the next Superbowl, plant a garden, put off something, schedule an appointment to get her teeth cleaned, plan a vacation, but then would find myself standing in the produce aisle and asking myself, Should I buy green bananas?

If there is one plus, it is this: For someone with cancer, life is more real. They *feel* more. It's like having the senses of a blind and deaf man and yet you can hear and see just fine. Abbie says it's like the difference between a six-inch black-and-white TV and an IMAX.

38

JUNE 8, EVENING

At 10 p.m., I woke Abbie and fed her some eggs, an RC cola and a Kit Kat—her favorite. "You feel like getting up?"

"Foooooor you?" The slurring struck me, pile-driving my spine down into the earth. "Yyyyyeeeeessss." Her eyes were glassy and swimming around the room. She too heard the slurring. She pressed her forehead to mine. "I'mmmm sorrrry." She pressed a finger to her mouth in an effort to shut herself up.

"Come on." I helped her stand and held on to her while the blood rushed to her head. "I've got a surprise for you."

We walked down Bob's dirt trail to the airplane hangar. He rolled out the bike and I straddled it. It was an older Honda 250cc. He said, "You know how to ride these things?"

"I didn't always paint."

"Good. Third gear sticks, so pull hard."

I cranked it, and gave it some gas. It backfired, spat white smoke out the muffler, then quieted and purred. He thumbed off the choke. "Give her a minute and she'll warm up." Abbie threw a leg over, pressed her chest to my back and leaned on me, wrapping her arms around my waist.

She whispered, "I'm wiiiith yewww."

The clock was ticking.

I patted her on the thigh, eased off the clutch and followed Bob's taillight through the night. We swerved through soft sand down dirt roads, crossed a hard road and then down a wider dirt road that was lined with a ditch on either side. The lights of the Ferris wheel turned counterclockwise across the treetops in the distance. We came through a tall stand of old pines, probably thirty-plus years old and then turned right, into a grass lot where most of the grass had been replaced with mud. Four-wheel-drive trucks sitting on top of mud tires that were four feet tall, bookended by chest-high bumpers and capped with silver roll bars, dominated the parking lot. Most were circled by kids holding a cigarette in one hand and an aluminum can or spit cup in the other.

The carnival was closed but either nobody had bothered to tell the kids or they didn't really care. We rode around the trucks, through the gate and down a long row of booths vacant of people.

Trash, most of which had been heeled into the ground, was strewn from one end to the other. It reminded me of Templeton in *Charlotte's Web*.

We rounded a corner, Bob stopped and leaned his bike against the side of a trailer. A short, squatty man with little beady eyes and a hat that covered most of his face walked out of the shadows next to the carousel. I heeled down the kickstand while Bob helped Abbie slide off the seat. Bob might be gruff, may even tend to push people away with his callous exterior, but there was a deep tenderness about him. Abbie felt it, too. She leaned on him while she caught her balance.

Bob spoke to the little man in Spanish. When he finished, the man looked around Bob, tilted his hat back and waved us closer. "You want to ride my carousel?" His Mexican accent was thick.

"Yes."

He extended his hand. *"Mi llamo es Gomez."*

"Doss. And my wife, Abbie."

Behind him stood what looked like a very old carousel. He waved his hand across it. "Dentzel, 1927. My pride and joy. Two rows, forty horses." He flicked a switch behind him and ten thousand lightbulbs lit half the county around us. He stood aside and waved at his horses, "Take your pick."

Abbie looped her arm in mine and we shuffled like an old married couple toward the horses. Her steps were slower, shorter, more uncertain. Her heels dragged the ground. I helped her up the steps, and she walked between the horses. Each horse's name had been painted across its saddle: *Fancy, Dreamer, Spicy, Flame, Untouched, Wild Angel, El Camino.* Abbie walked alongside each, stroking their wooden manes. She ran her hands along the windswept tails, the thick manes, then grasped the pole that connected their head to the ceiling and the feet to the floor. Finally, she chose Windswept.

The horse had no stirrup, so I formed one with my hand. Fortunately, Windswept had ended his last ride closer to the floor than the ceiling. Abbie swung her leg over and I lifted her into the saddle. She sat gently, one hand on the neck and mane, and one hand on me. I stood alongside and nodded to Gomez. He thumbed his cigarette, pushed a button and the music started. Then he slowly palmed a lever forward and we began the slow circle.

Windswept slid up and down, lifting Abbie closer to the ceiling, then lower toward the floor. Gomez watched, slowly increasing our speed to match that of the music. Abbie closed her eyes, and leaned on the pole that raised and lowered her horse. We rode around ten, eleven, then twelve times. After the twelfth pass, Abbie said, "Uh-oh." She picked her head up off the pole, turned past me, and spewed eggs, RC cola and Kit Kat in a long arc across the walkway that circled the carousel. I braced her as she lurched to one side, trying not to soil the man's carousel. He slowed us quickly, cutting off the music and the spinning horses. He jumped onto the platform and stood next to me. "*Señor,* I am sorry."

I shook my head. My hands were wrapped around Abbie's stomach, which told me a second wave was coming. When it did, she let go of the pole and slid off the saddle. I caught her and held her while she heaved over the edge.

Eyes closed, she spat. Her forehead sparkled with sweat. She wiped her mouth and said, "Ferrrrgottttt how dizzzzzzzy these . . . make mmmme."

I turned back toward Gomez. "If you'll show me where I can get a hose or a mop, I'll clean up."

He waved me off. "No, no. Me do. I do every night. No problem." Abbie straightened, some color returned to her face and Gomez pointed to the Ferris wheel. "Please. You ride? Much slower. No dizzy."

"Sir, I'm not sure she's—"

Abbie spoke up, "I'm okay."

He opened the small iron gate and we sat in the seat of the Ferris wheel. He whispered to me, "Very slowly."

Abbie leaned against me as the wheel lifted us higher. It was a tall wheel. Much larger than it looked from a distance. When we got to three o'clock we cleared the treetops. When we reached the top, he stopped the wheel. I looked down and he gave me the thumbs-up along with a shrug.

I returned his thumbs-up. Abbie opened her eyes and wrapped her arms across me. "Sorrrrry aaaabout that."

The night was clear. Above us, ten trillion stars lit the universe. The moon, half full, shone like a spotlight. The oblong shadow of the Ferris wheel laid out across the ground like a giant clock face with us sitting at the stroke of midnight. In the distance, the river snaked out of the trees—dross from the silversmith's ladle.

Abbie laid her palm across my chest. "Howwww far?"

"As a crow flies, almost thirty to Cedar Point. As the river flows, forty-five plus."

She held up her hand and started counting to herself. "We've checked off . . . six."

After a few minutes, she pointed behind us at a growing mass of clouds that spread from one end of the horizon to the other. Then she turned and pointed at the lights of St. Marys shining in the distance, and the river that flowed into her. "I wish we could finnnnish."

I nodded. It was all I could do. Everything else hurt. The words came hard. "I wish I could take your place."

39

Early in this entire process, Abbie tested positive for an ugly little gene called VBRCA-1. The presence of the gene meant she had a really good chance of also developing ovarian cancer. The problem, or one of the problems, with ovarian cancer is that there is no good or effective screening for it so it's difficult to know that you have it until it's too late. By the time you present symptoms, the cancer is usually stage four, which is metastatic. The best defense against it is the prophylactic removal of the ovaries. This came as a bit of a blow. Our remaining option was in vitro, so the doctors stimulated ovulation, forcing Abbie's body to produce several eggs which they harvested and quickly froze. Then, with the casual demure of sipping a Starbucks and nibbling on a bear claw, they cut out her ovaries and pitched them.

Because they planned to dump enough poison into her system to kill the abnormal cells, they also ran the risk of compromising her bone marrow. The marrow produces white blood cells that fight infection that occurs when your body is weak— like after chemotherapy. If you're starting to think that fighting cancer is a lot like a dog chasing its tail, you'd be right. To increase her chances, doctors harvested Abbie's own marrow in preparation for what's called an autologous bone marrow transplant. The marrow held in reserve would enable Abbie's doctors to treat her disease as aggressively as they could—giving them unlimited license to pummel her with every treatment at their fingertips.

Given the choice of the possibility of life or the guarantee of a slow painful death, we chose the pummeling. And the evening after her third surgery—the removal of her own marrow—we watched Reese Witherspoon in *Sweet Home Alabama* on my laptop in the hospital.

They had intended to be aggressive and they were. The chemo wiped her out again, annihilating her white blood count. Doctors quickly recommended the bone marrow transplant. After her fourth surgery—putting the marrow back in—she was laid up about a month. We were living at the Mayo Clinic in Jacksonville. Abbie had a room in the recovery ward while I had a small one-room in what they call the family wing. It's an apartment complex built by Mayo for the family members of those in treatment. It was a pretty close-knit community and everybody was on a first-name basis. We'd eat together, share stories and compare diagnoses and suggested treatments. Abbie was exhausted and usually fell asleep about 6 p.m., so most nights, I ate by myself. I'd stay with her until her eyes started rolling back and forth behind her eyelids, then I'd walk over to the cafeteria or go for a drive and find some dinner.

It was a lonely time.

I'd had about all the cafeteria food I could handle, so I walked across the parking lot to the Jeep and started to get in.

Another couple in the community was Heather and John Mancini. He was a feisty Italian, she a fiery redhead. Heather and I had met in the cafeteria one Saturday during lunch about three months ago. I was just starting a Clive Cussler novel and she sat at my table. She eyed the novel. "You a Cussler fan?"

"Yeah . . . only one Clive."

She reached into her shoulder bag and pulled out a paper-back. "I'm a Patterson person myself."

I shuddered. "He gives me the creeps. I can't read him without making sure all the doors and windows are locked tight and that some firearm is loaded and within arm's reach."

She laughed, we talked and I never made it to the second page.

Heather was a stewardess for a major airline and, like me, spent a lot of time alone. After John had been diagnosed and they saw that he'd be spending a lot of time at Mayo, she asked that her hub of origination be moved to Jacksonville so she could spend her nonworking time with John. John was not re-sponding well to treatment, so I did what I could to cheer her up. Which brings up another thing. You play this treatment game long enough and, sometimes, there's just not much that can cheer you up. Sometimes, you just need someone to listen to how bad the situation really is, nod their head so you know that they've heard you and that's it. Nothing more. We all know there's no magic wand. If there was, we'd be passing it around like a group of high-schoolers with a case of stolen beer.

So there I stood, getting in our Jeep when I heard some-body call my name. I knew who it was before I turned around. Heather waved. She said, "I think I've had about all the light blue walls and hollow metal tubes that I can handle."

"Yeah," I said, scratching my head, "me too. The walls, that is."

Her red skirt matched her hair, which had been pulled back in that I'm-grown-up-but-still-a-kid-at-heart style. She pointed toward the treatment center. "John's sleeping. How 'bout you let me buy you some dinner?"

"Sure."

So, with my wife fighting for her life, I drove some strange woman, whose white oxford had been unbuttoned down to the third button, to the beach and strolled Third Street in search of a place to eat. We landed on Pete's. Glad to be out of the compound, we sat through seven innings of a Red Sox baseball game and one period of a hockey match. Somewhere during dinner, another button slipped through its hole and her skirt climbed halfway up her thigh. With every sip, it climbed further. It didn't hit me until halfway through my third beer that people don't visit hospitals dressed like that. Admittedly, I can be a little slow on the uptake.

We ate hot wings until the snot dripped out of our noses and drank enough beer to numb the hot sauce on our lips. To walk off the buzz, we strolled down the boardwalk next to the beach and told each other how we'd met our respective spouses. I didn't realize until we were headed back, walking up the beach, that she held her shoes in one hand and had her other looped through mine. I told myself, It's just the sand. It's too soft. Right?

We walked to the Waffle House and downed a pot of coffee. It was nearly midnight by the time we got back.

We stepped onto the elevator, the door shut and without a word or a moment's notice, she pressed me into the corner. It had been a long time since anyone but my wife had kissed me. The little guy on my right shoulder sounded with the measured cadence of an ESPN commentator, "He might go all the way!" Both his arms shot into the air like an end-zone referee. "Score!" And the little guy on my left shoulder was standing there quiet as a church mouse. In his hand he held the picture of my Abbie that I kept in my wallet.

I tried to wriggle free and feed some oxygen to my brain, but that was not in her plan. When the elevator bell signaled the fifth floor and the doors slid open, she stepped through and, as she did, she reached up with her right hand and began uncon-sciously twirling the hair at the base of her neck. When she turned, an inviting smile had creased her face.

I watched her loop her finger through the thin, short hair behind her ear, then straighten it and let it go. She never should've done it.

It wasn't the kiss, or her leg that she had wrapped around mine as the elevator lifted off, or even the pressure of her chest, taut stomach and narrow hips against mine. No, it was that fin-ger twirling the hair at the base of her neck. And in that split second, her spell had broken. Like crystal on a marble floor, sliv-ers shattered everywhere. Abbie, who'd taught me how to love, used to twirl the hair at the base of her neck as she stood at the sink cleaning dishes or standing in the shower while the hot water poured down her back or while she studied one of my paintings. It was a telltale sign that she was thinking.

In truth, I don't know much about women, but I knew bet-ter than to get off that elevator. Inexperienced? Yes. Stupid? Not yet. Tempted? Just a little. My decision not to get off that elevator was a combination of knowing better and just plain cowardice. I placed my hand across the sensor that held the doors open and watched her walk backward toward her room. She had already unbuttoned and untucked her shirt and was dangling the room key in front of me.

Between treatment and exhaustion, cancer had robbed me and Abbie of any real physical relationship whatsoever. That's not to say Abbie was ever unkind. She wasn't. She did what she could, but there came a point at which my physical need had to take a backseat to her need to not be in pain—to be left alone. I stood in the elevator watching Heather undress in front of me. She backed up to her apartment doorway and by the time she slid her key in the door, her skirt had fallen to the floor. And whereas for the last six months my wife had worn granny-panties designed to hold the adult pad that assisted in the loss of bladder control, Heather had no such problem. The white lace thong was proof of this.

The little guy on my right shoulder had changed his tune. Instead of screaming, he was whispering. "Go ahead. No one will ever know." Quiet man on my left shoulder hadn't changed one bit. He simply stood, holding that wrinkled and faded picture and tapping his foot.

Love might leave, but the memory of its touch and the hope of its return doesn't. Ever. It's like that street in Hollywood where all the stars press their hands in the wet concrete. Abbie had long ago pressed her imprint into my heart. There on that elevator, Heather tried to place her hand into the dried form but it wouldn't fit.

I shook my head. "Heather, I . . ." What could I say? Abbie had long ago taught me that people wear their inside hurts on their outside self. Heather was no different—a beautiful girl, a good heart. Even a tender heart. How else does someone survive as a stewardess? Think about it. She served pretzels and Diet Cokes, handed out pillows and blankets and offered connection information to cranky air travelers, day after day after day. Compound that with John's decline and she lived in a bleak present with the prospects of a dismal future. All that hurt had to go somewhere. I'm not excusing her, and I'm not blaming her. It is what it was. For my part, I didn't see it until it was too late.

I took a deep breath, pushed the button for the seventh floor and watched her roll the sides of her thong off her hips. I rode the two floors to my room wishing I could pull that cool steel out of my back and turn it on my demons, but I'm no King Arthur. I unlocked the door and tied on my running shoes while the phone rang off the hook.

Running had become my narcotic. There were times that I would have preferred something more passive like scotch or bourbon, but I'd never developed a taste for it. Running had become my escape.

I usually ran between three and seven miles. Any less and I don't feel like I've run. Any more and my knees start aching. I climbed downstairs to the fitness room, jumped on the treadmill, set it for an eight-minute pace and tried to run that lace out of my mind.

Given that my mom had died and I was more or less raised by the people who populated my trailer park, I didn't have much of a fatherly role model. Hence, knowing how to treat a woman was something Abbie alone had taught me. The instincts were there, but Abbie had honed them. The way a man speaks to a woman who's alone in a parking lot after locking her keys in her car, the way he holds the door for an older lady with an armful of groceries, the way he asks a question of a female police officer, the way he stops to pick up the movie ticket that the college co-ed dropped, the way he orders for his date, the way he walks her up the sidewalk fifteen minutes before her curfew because he knew her dad was counting the minutes, the way he asks her father's permission to drive her to the lake on Saturday for a day of skiing—the way a man treats a woman is intangible. It is like a baton in a relay race—handed off and given from one to another. Abbie passed that baton to me. My learning curve with girls had been steep and mistake-riddled, but until that moment, not regret-laden.

After an hour, the treadmill had done little good so I hopped off, ran out to the parking lot, took a right turn on San

Pablo and ran under J. Turner Butler Boulevard. A half mile later, I crept around a security gate and snuck out onto the golf course of a private club commonly referred to as "Pablo." Pablo Creek is one of the more exclusive and less well-known golf clubs in the country. Membership is capped at two hundred and fifty, and if you have to ask about the initiation fee, you can't afford it. The course makes the Masters course look like kiddie Putt-Putt. I ran all eighteen holes beneath the moonlight. About 3 a.m., I hobbled back to the clinic and walked straight to Abbie's room.

The pain of her transplant was rather intense, so most nights, they gave her a sedative. Basically, it forced her into a twelve- to fourteen-hour coma—which was good. That meant she only hurt half the day.

I walked into the room, took one look at my wife and felt the pang of dinner at the beach. She was deep in sleep, eyes rolling back and forth behind her lids. Sweat caked across me, I rolled the silver stool up next to the bed, slid my hand beneath Abbie's and started at the beginning. I told her about the parking lot, how Heather had been dressed, Pete's, the buttons and skirt, then the beach and, finally, the elevator. Then I told her I was sorry and that I loved her.

It was little consolation.

I walked back to the apartment building, climbed seven floors to my room and stood in the shower nearly an hour. Daylight was breaking through my windows when I walked out of the bathroom wearing a towel. I cracked the blinds, staring out over the marsh and the Intracoastal Waterway, and that's when a lump between my sheets moved. I turned on the light, and Heather sat up in my bed.

And no, she wasn't dressed.

My heart jumped into my throat. She smiled a sleepy smile,

pushed her hair out of her face and stared at me. She really didn't need to say anything. Being in my bed said enough.

"You left your door unlocked," she said.

I nodded. "Look . . ." I was about to say something when there was a strong knock at the door. I knew who it was. The knock told me. I also knew that he never waited. He pushed the door open and strode in. He took four steps, saw me in a towel, and then saw Heather wearing nothing.

I would have said something, but I didn't figure it would do any good in this lifetime or the next. He stared at me a long moment, a vein popping out on his neck. He shook his head and walked out.

"Who was that?" she asked.

I stared into the mirror hanging on the back of the door. "My father-in-law."

She chewed on a fingernail. "Senator Coleman?"

"Yeah . . ." I nodded. "He's that, too."

She shook her head, pulled the sheets up and let her hair fall over her eyes. "I'm sorry."

I dressed, walked back up to Abbie's room and found him standing there. "Sir, can I talk to you?"

"My only daughter is lying here, fighting for her life. And you're up there—" He backhanded me hard across the face. The acrid taste of blood spread across my mouth. "Don't ever speak to me again."

"Sir, it's not what you think."

He turned and swung a fisted blow to my face. It spun me and cut my lip. He pointed a shaking hand at me, the spit gathered in the corner of his mouth. "Get out of my sight."

"I'm not leaving."

He looked at Abbie and rubbed her toes. He checked the time, then walked toward the door. He turned. "She's too weak

WHERE THE RIVER ENDS

right now. This . . . would devastate her. She'd lose her will to fight. But . . . when she beats this . . . and she will . . . I'll tell her the truth. What you do between now and then is up to you."

"Sir—"

He walked out and never looked back.

When Abbie woke up, the transplant had thrown her body into a tailspin. She smiled, her eyes glassy beneath the 103-degree fever. "Hey you . . ."

Two months later, Abbie's father became the donor for her second bone marrow transplant—a process that some say is more painful for the donor than the recipient.

It didn't take, either.

40

JUNE 9, MORNING

I walked into Bob's kitchen and found him, Petey and Rocket watching the Weather Channel. The screen showed a guy standing in the rain. He was wearing a yellow rain slicker and the wind had peeled his comb-over up and held it in the air like a rooster's feathers. He was mid-broadcast. "Hurricane Annie stalled over the Gulf, fattening herself on the warm water. Hemmed in by opposing fronts, Annie held there for a week. On June sixth, Annie started a slow crawl across North Florida and South Georgia, where she has dumped more than twenty inches of rain." The swirling green and red mass now filling the screen told me that the worst of the storm would miss us but it would not miss the Okefenokee. We were on the southeastern side. The side that would get little rain but lots of tornadoes. The reporter continued, "After a head-fake to the northwest, she sidestepped, twirled and tiptoed northeast." He mimicked the storm's path with dance moves I'd never seen before. "Climbing out of the Gulf, she slowed yesterday, weakening to a tropical storm. Given that she's just bumped into a colder front moving down from the north, it could be a while before the rain disappears. With her massive size and bulging waistline, her three-day, four-knot crawl across land is a lot like a walrus bellying across an ice sheet." He stepped closer to the camera and lowered his voice. "Noisy, not very pretty, threatening and almighty slow. Folks might want to start thinking about trading their cars in on boats, because we are projecting record floods across North Florida and South Georgia." The weatherman was quite proud of his report and stood there with an ear-to-ear smile while the rain peppered the side of his face.

Bob stared through the window at a cloudless, sunlit deep blue sky and mumbled something to himself. He pulled on his cap and began walking outside. "Think I'll check on the storm."

"Isn't that sort of dangerous?"

"Depends on how close you get."

Abbie pushed open the kitchen door carrying a syringe. She leaned on the table while Rocket licked her toes and spoke around the Actiq filling her cheek. "Cannnn weeee goooo?"

Petey walked in a circle on the table. "We go? Hell no. We go? Hell no."

Bob shook his head. "I've tried teaching him some new words but . . ." He shrugged. "He's very religious. Always talking about heaven and hell. Aren't you, Petey?"

Petey flapped his wings. "Hail Mary. Hail Mary."

I whispered to Abbie, "Honey, there are only two left."

She pulled the cap and handed it to me. "Let's hope it lassssssts a llllllllong timmmmmmme." She looked again at Bob, the wrinkle hard creased between her eyes. "Cannn weeeeee?"

He tried to make light of it. "You been drinking?"

"I wwwwisshhhh."

"You can be rather determined, you know."

I piped in. "She gets it from her dad."

"It can get bumpy. If you thought the carousel made you woozy . . ."

I pulled the cap and she nodded as I injected the dexamethasone into her thigh.

"You sure?" Bob asked.

She nodded and lifted the lollipop. "Yyyyyes, on one connndition."

"Name it."

"I want to do a llllllloopty . . . loooooop."

He smiled. "I think I can handle that."

We stood next to his plane. He said, "You know much about planes?"

"I know it's bright blue and yellow, has a propeller, four wings and a couple of wheels."

He ran his hand affectionately along the part behind the engine. "This is a Stearman Kaydet. During World War Two, they served both the Navy and the Air Force and saw aerial combat in several theaters. Manufactured 'til 1945, about ten thousand were made."

Abbie put her hands on her hips. "Youuu donnn't saaaayyy."

Other than the slurring sound of my wife's voice, the year 1945 bothered me a bit. "Doesn't that make her rather old?"

"Rebuilt every square inch myself."

"Didn't that take a lot of time?"

Bob smiled. "That's something I've had a good bit of. A priest with no collar is . . . questionable. Up there, I'm a man flying a plane. Folks don't care as long as their crops grow." He continued, "It's a two-seat biplane. Part wood, part fabric, part steel. Landing gear is nonretractable tail-wheel type. After the war, the government surplused thousands of Stearmans. Some were used for aerobatic competitions, some served in the air forces of other nations, while most of the rest were converted to crop sprayers." He walked toward the rear and ran his hand along a weird-looking pipe with a whole bunch of little nozzles sticking out of it. "When converted with crop-spraying bars and hoppers, the standard issue two-twenty horsepower Lycoming engine didn't measure up." He tapped the nose. "Many, like this one"—he stroked her as a middle-aged man touches his Ferrari—"were re-engined with brand-new war-surplus R-985 Wasp junior radials. About four-fifty hp—or twice the original power. We fly about five feet above the ground, so it helps to have good control and response."

To me, it looked like something out of *Peanuts*. But I kept that part to myself. He continued, talking as much to the plane as to us. "Empty, she weighs a few pounds shy of a ton. About nineteen hundred thirty-six pounds. She's got a wingspan of thirty-two feet and a length of twenty-four feet. Initially her max speed was a hundred and twenty-four miles per hour, but I can do a good bit better now. She'll fly to just over eleven thousand feet with a range of five hundred and five miles."

Abbie smiled. "I've heeeard modellllls, descrrribed wwwwith lllessss affffection."

I raised a hand. "You ever crashed?"

"Not in her." There was more there but he didn't offer and we let it go.

Abbie looked at me, the dexamethasone kicking in. "I don't think I want ttttto know anymmmmmmore."

"Why?" Bob asked. He was wearing both his priest and pilot hats. "You afraid of dying?"

She shook her head. "I made peace with that long ago." The dexamethasone had taken effect. "We all die. Some just sooner than we want." Abbie stared at me. "I'm afraid of leaving him."

We climbed in and Abbie tapped Bob on the shoulder. "Listen, I don't handle things like this very well, so unless you want this little cockpit to turn into the vomit comet, you'll get up there, do the loop and get me on the ground. Got it?"

Bob half nodded. "Not really, but . . ."

I tapped him on the other shoulder and pointed out across the grassy field he used as a runway. "What are all those dark green mounds?"

He yelled above the grumble of the engine. "Animal bones."

There must've been a hundred mounds covered with dark green grass. "That's a lot of bones. Where'd you get them?"

He shrugged and continued our taxi. "Roadkill, mostly."

"Any human bones out there?"

He throttled the engine, pulled down his goggles and yelled above the roar, "Not yet."

He left off the brakes, we sped down what seemed like at most a hundred feet and then Bob pulled back on the stick, lifting us skyward. We had just cleared the treetops when he slammed the stick back further, rocketing the nose toward the sky. We climbed and climbed and climbed and just when I thought I couldn't take it anymore, he rolled us over, let the stick fall forward and we spiraled toward the earth. To add insult to injury, he started rolling. I thought we'd been shot down. Abbie howled with excitement while I tried not to crap in my pants. We shot earthward, then without notice, we leveled out and rolled six or eight times on our own axis. Abbie braced herself on both sides of the plane, laughed at the top of her lungs and babbled uncontrollably. Evidently, that was just a warm-up, because no roller coaster at Busch Gardens can do what came next. We skidded across the treetops—I think I remember seeing the reflection of the river off to my right—and then we shot heavenward again, but this time we just kept rolling over. When I could see the earth below us and we started falling, Abbie realized that she was at the top of her loop. She began screaming, "Yes! Yes! Do it again! Do it again!"

I lost count after the sixth loop.

In front of us, Bob had taken to singing at the top of his lungs. The words were off-key but washed over us just the same. With one hand on the stick, the other conducting the air around him, he sang, "I'll fly away old Glory, I'll fly away . . ."

Later, when the wheels touched down, Abbie laid her head against me and I checked her carotid pulse—her heart was about to jump out of her chest. Bob cut the engine and rolled to a stop beneath his hangar. I lifted her out and lay her flat on the ground. Knees bent, one hand braced on a post, the other spread flat across the ground, she was half smiling, half moaning and her shorts were wet where she'd peed in her pants. "Oh, please stop the earth from spinning."

I sat down next to her and used my shirt to dab the mucousy blood trickling out of her nose.

41

We traveled to M. D. Anderson in Houston, Sloan-Kettering in New York, Mayo Clinic in Rochester, then back to Jacksonville. Each diagnosis, although worded differently, was the same. "Your cancer has metastasized and we are chasing it." Although she'd never smoked, it went into the lining of her lungs. Next we found spots on her liver. Though the drugs were effective and the cancer seemed responsive to treatment, it was always a step ahead. In the meantime, Abbie grew weaker. Pretty soon, I knew her ability to fight a sniffle would be compromised. She couldn't take much more.

I, on the other hand, hadn't painted in more than three years. Leonardo da Vinci once said that "where the spirit does not work with the mind, there is no art." He was right. Given the fact that nobody wanted to hire Abbie and that her remaining contracts had been canceled upon failure to deliver what she'd promised, i.e. herself, we were rifling through our savings. I sold my flats boat and had started eating into our home equity line of credit.

We participated in two trial studies that increased our hope, but while CAT and PET scans showed decreases in the size of the tumors, the tumors were still there. I investigated experimental and, according to some, radical treatments in Mexico, but that was a Hail Mary pass I was not willing to throw.

Six more months passed, we finished another trial run and then started the month-long wait before we could have more scans to determine if the drugs had worked. At the end of that month, I didn't need the scans.

It started in the kitchen. She was trying to say *apple* and turned it into about five syllables. Then she murdered *spaghetti* and completely gave up on *refrigerator.* Slurring her words was a bad sign.

CAT, PET and blood scans confirmed inoperable brain metastasis. If there was any good news in this it was that this was the worst possible news. This was the basement. Dr. Hampton explained, "The tumor's location rules out radio frequency ablation, which is highly successful . . . except when it scrambles your brains. We can't go sticking an eight-hundred-degree probe into your noggin and expect you to wake up."

"What about more chemo?"

He shook his head. "Chemotherapy is largely ineffective against brain lesions because the lining of the brain is quite effective at protecting itself against any sort of toxin. It's called the blood-brain barrier and thus far, chemotherapy has not found a way through or around it."

I sat there listening but not listening. Dr. Hampton described her condition—and our final option. Abbie never blinked. She said, "I want the maximum dose that you can give me." We drove to Jacksonville, checked into Mayo and I just sat there twiddling my thumbs while they shot Chernobyl into my wife.

For fourteen weeks, Abbie endured the near-crippling effects of two six-week doses of radiation. She slept much of the time, which from a certain point of view, was good. It gave her less time to think or feel the effects of either the cancer or the radiation. I didn't fault her. I missed her madly but sleep was the only hole she could crawl into. The only escape she had left. Every other avenue had been taken away.

When she was awake, we were limited in that the slightest noise, light or movement contributed to further nausea. This forced us to sit in dark, still silence. Just being together. It was about all we had left. Fortunately, they gave Abbie whatever she wanted for the pain, proving that lunacy can be a luxury.

Following her last treatment, they ran one final series of scans. Given her condition and the fact that she'd "earned" the right to go to the front of the line, they fast-tracked her results and that afternoon found us waiting. I needed a walk—something I'd been doing a lot of lately. I felt like a traitor leaving Abbie, but she was always asleep and I needed to clear my head prior to Ruddy walking in with the news. I whispered, "Honey, I'm going to go hunt a muffin or something." I left and walked down the hall. When I returned, one of the nurses had slipped her file—and results—into the plastic box on the door. I stared at it and I thought of my wife, sitting in there dreading more bad news.

Watching my wife die was killing me. I was sick and tired of being absolutely and completely useless. I was engaged in a battle, a life-and-death struggle, that I could not win. In my estimation, the only thing worse would be watching your child fight disease. I know this because I had lied and said I was hunting a muffin when in fact I was searching for a parent's face, which when I saw it would tell me they were suffering as much if not more than I. When I had found one and felt the sick consolation of knowing someone else on this planet was hurting as much as me, I returned.

I know that's wrong. I know that is absolutely twisted. And I'm sorry for it.

I flipped open the chart and found the letter sitting on top of the stack. It was from the radiation oncologist who'd read the scans:

> Dear Dr. Ruddy Hampton,
>
> I have reviewed Abbie Eliot Michael's most recent CAT scan. I understand that she has completed her second course of six weeks of palliative radiation. Having just returned from the radiology department, I personally reviewed her films along with Dr. Steve Surrat, Chief Radiation Oncologist. He is convinced that the metastatic lesion in her brain is no smaller. In fact, it has grown measurably. I concur. At this point, my field has nothing further to offer. It is my professional opinion with cases such as this, Hospice is the only remaining option. Thank you for allow-ing me to share in the care of this nice young woman.
>
> > Sincerely,
> > Dr. Paul McIntyre
> > Radiation Oncologist
> cc: Dr. Roy Smith
> > Dr. Katherine Meyer
> > Dr. Raul Dismakh
> > Dr. Gary Fencik

I read it once and more slowly a second time. Whispering aloud to myself, I read it a final time—hoping that I could hear it differently than I saw it. But each time I pronounced the words in my head, I heard glass breaking.

Only remaining option . . .

I closed the folder and leaned against the door. At thirty-five years old, she had physically exhausted her body, emotionally spent her soul and spiritually lost her hope. We had hit bottom—the fight was over.

I walked in and found the room was empty save the bed, dirty linens and the empty electrolytes bag hanging above her head. The clear feed line snaked down Georgie's one-inch, stainless-steel chest. I looked around the room and wondered how many white-coated, Harvard-trained optimists had rained poison into her veins through the ever-present needle that stuck to her skin like a leech.

I stared at the Christmas cards taped to the wall and realized we'd been added to the list of most every oncologist at Mayo. I knew as much, probably even more, about the cancer in her as the interns who stood stone-faced at the foot of her bed, nodding, scribbling notes and thanking God it wasn't them.

Heels clicked on the hard floor outside the door. The long gait and hard-soled wingtips told me it was Ruddy. His question echoed in my mind: *Do you like to dance?*

Ruddy walked in, set the folder on the bed and sat opposite me at Abbie's feet. He gently patted her toes and put a hand on my shoulder. "The CAT scan . . ." He shook his head. "It's replicating, too . . ."

Abbie opened her eyes. "How long do I have?"

Ruddy was hurting. "I don't know if you have a week, a month or . . ." He was quiet a minute. "Hard to say." He smiled. "You're the toughest fighter I've ever met, so . . . I give you longer than the textbooks do."

I asked, "What do the books say?"

"They say she shouldn't be here now."

Ruddy continued, "I've recommended you for a spot in a trial study out of M. D. Anderson. You don't quite fit the parameters but I . . ." He shrugged. "I've asked anyway. And we have yet to see the results of your other two scans, but they'll be a few days.

"I recommend you go home. We'll give you whatever you want to keep you comfortable, and in the meantime, let's see what happens with Anderson and these other scans."

"When will we know something?" I asked.

Ruddy stood. "Couple of days."

I shook my head. After all that we'd been through, we were down to waiting on two phone calls.

I turned to Ruddy. "And if the phone calls don't offer us anything?"

Ruddy palmed his face. "We make you as comfortable as possible."

I stared up at the ceiling, then looked down at Abbie's arm, the thin blue vein slightly visible. I thought of that scene in *The English Patient* where the nurse finally shoots Ralph Fiennes full of about eight vials of morphine.

Abbie climbed out of bed, and kissed Ruddy on the forehead. She pulled at the tape, slid the needle from under her thin, translucent skin, retaped it quietly around Georgie's single leg and whispered, "Georgie, meet Lilith. Been nice knowing you." Her voice was scratchy and dry. She turned her ear toward Georgie. "Nope . . . won't hear of it. I really think it's time we start seeing other people." She held out a stop-sign hand. "I know . . . I get it all the time, but our careers are taking us different places, and you need someone who can stand by you, support you in your work and offer you more than just a few hours a week. Really . . ." She grabbed Georgie about his "waist" and pushed him, rolling him against the far wall.

I extended my hand, Ruddy hugged me, kissed Abbie and walked out. He had fought hard, too. They all had.

Given the movement, the familiar nausea returned. Abbie

rested her head on her hand and closed her eyes. With her other hand, she rubbed her legs, begging for blood flow. She sat in the chair and I pushed her across the room. She whispered over her shoulder to Georgie, "You deserve someone better than me. Someone who can appreciate your commitment to your work."

The afternoon sun breaking through the window was harsh and direct. Squinting, I rolled her to the closet where she stood and stared inside. Her gown, untied in the back, flapped under the flow of the oscillating fan on the floor. I offered to tie it but she waved me off. "I don't care. Not much left to see anyway." She let it slide to the floor and stood there in her birthday suit— which was baggy and two sizes too big. She pointed and I pulled down a pair of jeans and a T-shirt. She leaned on me as I helped her slide into a pair of panties. They too sagged, hanging loosely off her hips. She looked over her shoulder and realized her butt was pointed toward the hall where two male nursing assistants stood staring in. She whispered, "Free advertising." She leaned against me while I helped her guide one foot into her jeans. "I used to work so hard to sell that space. Now I can't give it away." I buttoned her jeans and pulled the T-shirt over her arms. She didn't need a bra. She slid on a baseball cap, and I slid her flip-flops onto her toes. One last time, I pushed her up against the windowsill where she let her eye follow the marsh from the Intracoastal Waterway to the ocean, shimmering in the distance. Shrimp boats dotted the horizon along with one gray aircraft carrier headed north to Mayport where Navy wives waited for their Davys with handheld flags and babies dressed in blue.

Getting dressed had taxed her equilibrium. The nausea climbed up her legs, shook her knees, gained strength in her stomach, launched into her throat and exited out her mouth like a rocket blast. I held her over the sink and wiped her mouth as the sound of footsteps grew closer. A young man stood in the hall. We'd met him several times—he was the acne-faced teenaged grandson of a patient next door. He stood some four inches shorter than me. Abbie opened her eyes. "Yes?" she managed.

He looked away, tried to say something, but couldn't quite get it out, so he pointed next door and walked away without looking back—something few men would have done two years ago. But we'd grown accustomed to that, too.

We rode the elevator down—Abbie vomiting again between the sixth and fourth floors. We crossed the parking lot, I laid her in the front seat and then started the car. Four hours later, we were home.

We'd come full circle.

42

After our flight lesson, we returned to the cabin. While Abbie napped, I ran through the rain to Bob's to ask for some coffee. When I got there, he pointed at the TV. "Looks like your buddies caught on." He turned up the volume. On the screen, a reporter stood in a hospital room and held the microphone in front of a man with raccoon eyes, whose face was black-and-blue and whose nose had been taped up. His voice was nasal and he sounded as though he had a bad cold. It was Verl, the broad-shouldered, thick-legged troll that I hit in the face with the revolver. Next to him stood Coal Miner, or "Buf." He was the first guy to walk in and stand over Abbie. I remember his face being shiny and he was wearing glasses. They hung on his face now, bent and held together with tape. Last time I saw him he was running out of the room with Rocket attached to his crotch. His voice at the time had been rather high-pitched. Currently, all he could muster was a cracked whisper. "Yeah, he come out of nowhere. Like a tiger or something. I never seen nothing like it. He was swinging shi— I mean stuff, and he was like a crazed badger or something."

The reporter interrupted him. "What were you doing on the river when you encountered Mr. and Mrs. Michaels?"

Verl spoke up. "We'uz frog gigging."

The reporter waved the microphone in front of a third man. It was Limpy, the tallest of the four with the high-pitched, devilish howl—the one Bob smacked in the face with the lumber. She asked, "Is this something you've done before?"

Limpy nodded. His mouth was a mess. One tooth up front was badly cracked and several others were missing. He whistled when he spoke. "Aw, yes, ma'am. Lots of times. Me and Buf here, we's grown up doing it." The camera panned across the three men. The only one missing was shotgun man—the guy that had hit me with my own shotgun.

She continued, "And how many frogs had you gigged by the time Mr. Michaels allegedly attacked you?"

Limpy scratched his head. "Done what?"

Verl, the self-appointed spokesperson, piped in. "Shut up, dummy." His hands accentuated his mouth. "See, they'uz a storm coming and so the frogs felt the change in the baronmetic pressure and so we had us like fi'teen or twenty. And we wuz coming round this bend when we heard this screaming . . ." He snapped his fingers. "Sounded like a woman in distress."

Bufort tapped her on the shoulder. "Dat's right. Di'tress."

Verl continued, "Anyway, we wuz paddling up 'er near Brickyard—not the racetrack but the ramp—and we seen dis feller and dis woman. She didn't have no clothes on, and she looked real sick, you know, and he didn't have no clothes neither. We thought maybe they's part of that resort upriver. So we paddled by, uh . . . and then got on the cell phone and dial 911 . . . cause, uh, she look sick, and then we wuz coming in close to the bank, about to get out of the boat when he come running off the bank like a . . . like a Ninja Turtle."

Bufort's eyes grew wide and he karate-chopped the air. "Yeah. A Ninja Turtle."

Verl pointed at his face. "Smacked me in the mouth, broke Buf's nose and it was just an awful mess."

She held the microphone to her mouth. "So, he attacked the three of you."

Bufort nodded, then shook his head. "Yes. Well . . . no. I mean he jumped us'n three and Pete." He counted on his fingers. "That makes four."

She stared at the three of them. "Tell me about Pete."

"He got knocked out when Mr. Michaels hit him upside the head with a . . . a iron pipe."

"Is he in this hospital?"

Bufort shook his head. "Naw, he's home drinking beer."

She nodded. "I see."

Bob laughed. "This is better than reality TV."

She placed the microphone in front of Verl. "And what about the frogs?"

"Oh they, uh . . . they jumped back in the water when he done tumped the boat over."

She raised both eyebrows. "I thought you said they had been speared."

Bufort poked her in the shoulder. "Gigged."

Verl thought a minute. "Uh . . . yeah. See we gig 'em just enough to sting them so they's knocked out. We're sort of like sniper-giggers. And, uh . . . when the boat tumped, they come to and runned off."

She said, "What do you do with them?"

Verl nodded. "We eat them. They taste like chicken."

Bufort elbowed his way into the picture. "And ya'll need to be careful 'cause he's armed and dangerous."

Verl pointed at the camera. "That's right. Armed and dangerous."

"I see. Thank you, gentlemen." She returned to the camera. "Back to you, Sam."

Sam spoke to his teleprompter. "Barbara, any idea where Abbie Eliot and Doss Michaels are now?"

Barbara shook her head. "If, in fact, these gentlemen encountered Abbie Eliot and Doss Michaels, then the best guess is that they are making their way down the St. Marys River." She shrugged. "But given the storm, exactly *where* is anybody's guess."

Sam narrowed his eyes and spoke to a second camera. "We take you now to Senator Coleman's home in Charleston. Senator, any word on the location of your daughter and have you had any contact with her?"

The camera showed her dad in the front hall of their house—eight microphones stuffed in his face. Oddly enough, Rosalia hung quietly behind him on the wall. She was looking down on him. The senator cleared his throat. "We're zeroing in on their location. Getting closer, but Doss grew up down there, so he's a step or two ahead of us. The storm isn't helping much. As for contact with Abigail Grace, no. No one that we know of has had contact with Abigail Grace or Doss in over a week and a half." I guess that means he hadn't received Abbie's letter yet.

Bob clicked off the TV. "What's with the double names?"

"It's a Charleston thing."

He continued, "I don't think anybody in their right mind is going to believe the story of the three stooges, but they just pinpointed you. And put it on national television. Listen closely. The helicopters are probably outside now."

"You don't know the half of it."

43

We'd had hundreds of tests, each one confirming further improbabilities, but throughout that, there was always the hope of another test, another new medical development, another something possible that strung us along. Breakfast, lunch, dinner, midnight snack, we fed on hope.

While Abbie slept off the residue of chemo and radiation, I walked laps around the house and realized that something had changed. Something was gone. We'd stopped feeding. The buffet of options had been slowly taken away—one by one—leaving only empty stainless-steel trays and spent Sterno cans. Dying is one thing. Knowing you're dying and having to sit there and wait on it is another. And having to sit there and watch someone who's having to sit there and wait on it is yet another.

A few days passed. I circled the inside of the house, waiting on two phone calls while Abbie slept some of the toxins out of her system. Late in the evening, I walked out of my studio, climbed up into the crow's nest and stared out across the expanse. The moon cast shadows on the water and the lights of Fort Sumter glistened in the distance. Moments later, my phone rang. I checked the faceplate and saw the Texas area code. "Hello?"

"Doss Michaels?"

"Speaking."

"This is Anita Becker, assistant to Dr. Paul Virth."

"Yes?"

44

JUNE 10

When I walked back into the cabin, Abbie was gone. I checked the bed but only the stain remained. The fly rod leaned in the corner and her clothes sat on the end of the bed. I scratched my head. A few seconds later, the steps creaked. Abbie walked up onto the back porch wearing only the top sheet as a sarong. She sat next to me. I said, "Bob says the outskirts of the storm should pass through tonight."

"Yeah." She held a spotted tissue. Her temple vein was throbbing, visually enlarged. She slid a trembling hand under mine. "I want you to do something for me."

"Anything."

She led me down the stairs to the river's bank. She walked carefully, stopping every few steps to catch her breath and not aggravate the pain between her eyes. She'd not napped long, because she had it all set up. She sat me in the chair, the easel at my fingertips. Pencils sharp and canvas white. She had aimed me downriver. A few feet beyond me, a cedar tree lay fallen—water-beaten, sun-bleached and smooth—stretched across the bank. The top side of the trunk rested about bench height. The stub of a single branch stuck two feet into the air, making a natural niche to stretch out and watch the river. Untouched and unbroken.

"Honey, I don't feel like—"

She pressed her finger to my lips. "Shhhh . . ."

She kissed me, walked around in front of me, and sat on the cedar, crossing her legs. She let the sheet fall. It slipped down around her hips, exposing her scars, and lay across the tree trunk like a tablecloth. She untied the scarf and hung it on the tip of the branch stub where it flagged in the breeze. She dabbed her nose and stared into the tissue, turning it in her hands. Another whisper, "I've learned something in all this." A single drop fell from her nose and landed on her thigh. "You don't have to be beautiful . . . to *be beautiful*." She raised her chin, inhaling, filling her chest cavity and flaring her pink nostrils and whispered, "Breathe on me."

I STARED A LONG TIME. With my eyes and without. I took a deep breath, closed my eyes, held it a long time, found the one thing that made me want to look again and started.

Slowly, the image took shape. A charcoal outline on canvas. Like heavy fog lifting off the ocean after a storm. The sun burned it off. The way her toes curled into the sand, the right foot turned slightly in more than the left, the slim legs, long calves, knotty knees, drawn thighs, hollow hips, the hand clasped around a bloody tissue, the scars that barbwired around her chest, the yellowed, thin skin draped across her collarbone, the throbbing vine-thick vein on her neck, the flaky and cracked flaring nostrils, the purplish-blue vein pulsating on her temple, the white head, deep eyes, gray skin, the fatigue. Silhouetted against a backdrop of storm clouds, thunder and the river.

The hours passed.

I'd been painting long enough to know that each piece, if made well, can take on a life of its own. This piece had done something I'd not intended. It etched both her smallness—her shrunken, pale, sickly frame, the protrusion of her collarbone and the indentation of every rib, the matching cavities in her chest—while also capturing her enormity and her magnificence. Her larger-than-lifeness. Her I-am-not-my-cancerness. I sat back and looked at my sketch—the structure of what would become the one piece she'd always thought I could make. And there, beneath the tears, beneath the realization of what she'd just given me, it came to me. She whispered it from the canvas—the word that is my wife.

Indomitable.

At dusk, I carried her from the bench. She glanced at the canvas. "Took you long enough."

"Sorry. Couldn't get my subject to sit still."

She tied the scarf back around her head. "Gee, that's sort of a letdown. I thought you were just enjoying seeing me naked."

"Well . . ."

Her breathing was labored and raspy. I set her on my seat, my feet sinking into the sand. She stared at herself, following each stroke, each shadow with her finger. After a minute, she nodded. "Not even Rembrandt . . ."

Her eyes were slits. She cracked a smile and fought the pain, pushing her lids upward. I asked, "Scale of one to ten?"

Her eyelids fell and she leaned against me as the rain began to smack the river.

45

JUNE 10, DUSK

Abbie lay on her back, her stomach rising and falling with short, shallow breaths. Posing had wiped her out. Her face was white and pale. Eyes rolled back and forth behind her lids. Bob sat with a shot glass in one hand and a bottle of tequila in the other. I stared out over the river. Bob said, "You don't owe me anything and you have every right to your own privacy, but . . . how'd you two get here? Really?"

I started at the beginning and told him the story of us. Of jogging along the Battery. Of Rosalia. Of asking the senator's permission to marry, eloping and buying our house in Charleston. I told him about our nearly year-long trip. I told him about finding the lump, and of the last four years. Every detail. The surgeries, treatments, hopes and discoveries. Finally, I told him about Heather.

While I talked, Annie rolled through in gentle sheets beyond the glass. She had weakened to a tropical storm, but every few minutes, we felt a gust followed by the muted pop of a pine tree snapping in half. Toward dark, the river had swelled with debris—muddying the water.

I stared through the window, speaking softly. "Growing up on the river, we found rope swings at every bend. Climbing and swinging were just part of what we did. A paper mill, located about a mile or so through the woods behind our trailer park, used to pipe their discharge into a pond behind the mill. In times of heavy rain, the pond would fill up and any discharge would overflow into these concrete holding tanks which would then 'spill' the water down into the river. The tanks helped reduce the erosion on the river's bank. To prevent kids like me from playing in them, they welded metal grates over the holes. Problem was, the temptation was too great. Being an asthmatic, I was relatively small, so I tied my rope to a grate, climbed through the hole and started swinging around like Tarzan. It was all fun and games until I slipped, the rope burned my hands, and I let go. I splashed in the chest-high water, set my feet on the bottom and reached for the rope. The hole was about eight feet deep, which was about two feet too much for a four-foot boy with a two-foot reach. Fortunately, the water flushed itself every day so it wasn't like I was swimming in an Indiana Jones den of snakes or a malaria melting pot. Other than stand there and shiver, I could not do a single thing to help myself. To compound the problem, I had no inhaler. My own fear was clamping down on my lungs, cutting off my air and my head was growing light. If I passed out, I'd collapse into the water and drown. I stood there for hours, concentrating on one thing. That next breath.

"After quitting time, the paper mill blew a huge Flintstones-like whistle, signaling both a shift change and the let-off of its discharge, which overflowed the lake which poured into the hole. I stood off to one side until it climbed high enough to float me, which was only a couple of minutes. Then it floated me some more and I grabbed the rope. I pulled myself up, crawled out and stood there scratching my head.

"That feeling of helplessness doesn't hold a candle to sitting next to a hospital bed watching chemical poisons drip into your bald, pale, chestless, gaunt, sickly, vomiting wife."

I was quiet for a while. "I don't understand how a God who"—I waved my hand across the river and Abbie—"can do all this . . . can let something so bad happen to her." I sat shaking my head. "I mean, why?"

Moments passed. He turned up the bottle and polished off all but the last sip. His eyes were red and tequila dripped off his chin. He walked across the floor to where Abbie lay. He knelt next to her, placed his hand on her forehead and whispered, "Do I wonder why God is silent?" He nodded. "Can I explain the existence of suffering and evil?" He shook his head. "Do I sometimes despair at this world?" He was quiet a moment. "You damn right." He turned up the bottle, grabbed the worm with his tongue, held it between his front teeth, bit it in half and swallowed. He turned to me. "Nevertheless, I believe."

I stared at the river. The night was clear, and the moon had returned. The river stared back at me. Forty-six miles to go. A day and a half if I gave all of me. I wanted to finish, to steal back time.

I placed my hand across Abbie's tummy. "Can I ask a favor?"

He nodded. "Name it."

"You'll need your collar."

I shook Abbie and her eyes cracked. Heavy and hazy. It took her a second to come back. "Hi," she managed.

"Hey. You feel like checking off something that's not on the list?"

"Anything."

"Will you marry me . . . again?" I pointed at Bob. "Properly?"

She lifted her head. "Love to."

WE WADED THROUGH the swirling current. Walked up what was once the creek and into the old pond where the old wooden building sat. I pushed open the door and carried her through. Where the boards beneath me once creaked under my weight, now they were silent. Currently, the water was pew-high and rising. I waded up the narrow center aisle while Bob set Rocket on top of the altar and then pushed open a few windows to let in some light and air. The old building swayed on its foundation—one strong wind or current from crumbling. A house of cards. Next stop would be the ocean. Rocket walked around the altar considering his options while Petey stood on Bob's shoulder studying the glassy floor below him. He said, "Hell in a basket. Hell in a basket."

The rear of the church had been demolished by the storm. And there had been nothing delicate about it. A tree limb had fallen across the supporting timber where I'd traced the letters with my fingers. Both the tree limb and the old timber were gone. Downriver. It had taken part of the roof with it. Every few seconds, the breeze would peel up several loose cedar shingles and then let them go, where they'd flap several times before falling quiet.

Bob stood before us. Dressed in a white robe tied with a white cord and draped with a purple vestment that looked like a poncho. A large cross hung down to his stomach. Petey hopped onto his right shoulder. Bob was sweating and the skin of his neck had slightly folded over his collar. He ran his finger along the inside to loosen it, tucking the skin inside as he went. Bob looked around and laughed to himself. "Fitting."

The river shone all around us. In the time we'd been standing there, it'd risen another few inches.

Abbie rested her head on my shoulder, her arms around my neck. She came to and whispered, "I can stand."

"You sure?"

She nodded, so I set her down. I unfolded the sheet I'd carried down from the house, folded it in half then wrapped it around her and tucked it inside itself like a towel. The blue bandana hung loose around her head so she retied the knot then looped her arm inside mine. Her sheet-train floated behind her. We made a motley crew.

Bob held a small red leather-bound book. He turned a few pages, stared at us, then back at the book. Finally, he closed the book and set it on the altar behind him. Rocket stared at it, then sat obediently.

I nodded at the book. "Don't you need that?"

He shook his head. "I remember."

Bob cleared his throat. "You have come here today to seek the blessing of God and"—he looked around the dim room—"his Church upon your marriage. I require, therefore, that you promise, with the help of God, to fulfill the obligations which Christian marriage demands."

He turned to me. "Doss, you took Abbie to be your wife." He whispered out the side of his mouth. "How long ago?"

I leaned forward. "Fourteen years."

Bob cleared his throat a second time. "Fourteen years ago. Having here expressed a wish to recommit your vows, do you promise here in the presence of God and"—he glanced over his shoulder at Rocket and Petey—"these witnesses, to love her, comfort her, honor and keep her . . ." I saw his lips moving but his words sounded somewhere down deep within me. I watched Abbie out of the corner of my eye. She had straightened. Chin high, her face reflected the light off the river. He paused, then continued, "In sickness and in health, and forsaking all others, to be faithful to her as long as you both shall live?"

I rewound the tape of the last four years. Playing and re-playing the video in my mind. It was difficult to watch. We'd known good, bad and the unthinkable. His echo disappeared off down the river.

I grabbed both of Abbie's hands. "For as long as I shall live."

Abbie exhaled, leaned against me and tucked her arms in-side mine. Bob nodded. "That works, too."

Petey fluttered his wings and began bobbing his head up and down. "Hell yes. Hell yes."

Bob looked at Abbie. "Abbie, you have taken Doss to be your husband. Do you promise to love him, comfort him, honor and keep him, in sickness and in health, and forsaking all others, to be faithful to him as long as you both shall live?"

She nodded. "I do."

Bob crossed us and raised his hands. "Lord, please bless . . ." He started to say something else, but shook his head. He tried to recover and couldn't. Finally, he closed his eyes, squeezing tears out each side. He whispered, "Amen. You may kiss your wife."

Petey flapped his wings and settled back on Bob's shoulder. "Kiss the bride. Kiss the bride."

Abbie stared up at me. There was a lot I wanted to say and do. A lot I still wished for. But none of that would come out of my mouth. She nodded and said, "I know." I placed her narrow cheeks in my palms and pressed my trembling lips to hers.

Abbie turned in the water and spoke to the empty pews. "I'd like to thank you all for coming. Especially on such short notice." A lizard on the windowsill bobbed its head up and down. Then she turned to me and poked me in the chest. "Af-ter fourteen years, I finally got married in a church." She stared through the hole in the roof and laughed. "At least, what's left of one." She looped her arm inside mine, hanging as much as standing. "Come on. You owe me a honeymoon."

We waded out through the front doors and swam back through the trees to the cabin, where we spent the evening wrapped up in a blanket, staring out the window at the rising water.

Annie floundered north of us, dumping her guts and un-loading more than four inches of rain—per hour—across the "First Coast." During her five-knot crawl, counties from Tal-lahassee to Jacksonville to Savannah averaged twenty inches of rain. The Weather Channel said that even in the Smoky foot-hills of Tennessee and Georgia, mountaintop outposts recorded record rainfall. Reaching the East Coast, Annie hugged the shoreline and moved north again. By midnight on the tenth, Annie dissipated along the northeast coastline and faded back into the North Atlantic Ocean where she finally took a swan dive and disappeared.

The problem left in her wake was not the wind, downed trees or erased homes, or the tornadoes that spun angrily off her heels or the cost of the damage. No, it was the several million cubic feet of rain that had rolled off her shoulders as she saun-tered across land.

And all that rain had to go somewhere.

~✦

MIDNIGHT BROUGHT CALM, clear skies and the brightest moon that had ever shone. Bob's canoe was sixteen feet, made of aluminum and had been painted dark green somewhere in the past. It wasn't the most comfortable thing, nor was it for-giving, but she was fast and we needed speed more than com-fort. I rolled up *Indomitable* and slid her into a PVC tube with

watertight screw caps. Bob handed me a rainbow-colored um-
brella and said, "To keep the sun off her." I wedged both next to
the seat and then laid Abbie on a foam pad along the bottom of
the canoe.

Dressed in fraying cutoffs and half a bikini, Abbie looked
like she did the first time we made this trip. Bob was still
dressed. He lifted off his purple robe and laid it across Abbie like
a blanket. I extended my hand. "Thank you."

He nodded. "You know they've probably got people
camped out on all the bridges."

"Yeah."

"Can you get around them?"

"Don't know."

"I don't think you'll get very far."

"Never thought we'd get this far."

Bob said, "Call me anytime. I can land her on a dime." He
pushed us off the bank, I reached deep into the water and
pulled, staring forty-six miles and a lifetime in the face.

46

JUNE 11, 1 A.M.—THE LAST DAY

On the Florida side, the river had overflowed its bank by a wide margin. What was once a hundred feet across might stretch out a half mile now through pine trees and palmettos. It reminded me of pictures I'd seen of the Everglades. Given my experience with the river, and limited knowledge of how it drained, most of that rain had yet to hit the river. It would do so in the next twenty-four hours. By morning, the river would be unrecognizable. Even to me. The further we went, the faster it would flow. That meant I couldn't necessarily judge our progress by known landmarks. Some yes, but I'd have to rely on the flow.

With enough flow, we could average as much as eight miles an hour. In a canoe on the river, that's like breaking the sound barrier. The good news was knowing that much water would shut down the bridge at Highway 17. That only left the overpass at I-95. If we could slip beneath that, or around it, we had a shot. I knew they'd have people looking for us, but I'd worry about that when we got there. We could always travel under the cover of night, and with enough debris in the water, maybe we had a chance.

'Course, the debris could slow us, too. With the water rising to new levels every minute, it was picking up limbs and trash and sucking it all into the main flow of the river. In some places, where the water circled and swirled, the trash would accumulate, forming a mangled patchwork the size of a football field. Or several. While it might camouflage us, it could also hide the surface of the water. And if we ever got turned over—swamped—I wasn't sure that we'd ever get it right again.

We'd been in the water two hours when I heard the motors coming. Along the Georgia side, somebody had planted eight palm trees in a row. They were older, mature and their fronds dragged the surface of the water. I ducked in behind the fronds, pulled hard and snapped two of them in half, letting them fall behind us. Two Pathfinders, moving at a good clip, raced upriver, spotlighting the banks and water in front of them. Their light washed over us, but the palms broke our outline. They disappeared, their wake shook the canoe and I backed us out. Things just grew more complicated.

An hour before daylight, we passed what I thought was Coopers Neck Road, but between the darkness and the water, it was difficult to tell for sure. We slipped beyond the roofline at Mount Horeb Baptist Church. It, too, was underwater. Oddly enough, the baptismal was not. Painted white, made of cement blocks stacked eight high and surrounded with a lead pipe railing, it sat on a higher grassy hill. Currently three wood ducks floated in circles behind the railing.

The last several hours I'd paddled at close to ninety percent. The river had transformed overnight and flowed unlike anything I'd ever known. I did what I could to keep the bow pointed downriver, but the constancy of that spent me. In paddling terms, I was cooked.

Before daylight, we reached Brickyard Landing and slipped by on the other side—recapturing the sixteen miles we lost when Bob took us back to his place. The increased flow of the

WHERE THE RIVER ENDS

river had negated the incoming tide. I couldn't tell if it was coming in or going out because so much water was flowing out. Normally, along this part of the river, a black stain registers along the marsh grass indicating how high or low the tide had risen or fallen, but the water was several feet above what was once considered high tide.

While I felt we could slip by White Oak and its seven miles of shoreline, we still had two remaining hurdles. The bridge at Highway 17 and the bridge at I-95. The senator was no dummy. He'd have people on both bridges. Probably news cameras, too. If we got lucky and slipped beneath the first bridge, we had only five miles to go before we reached the bigger bridge—and bigger problem—at I-95. The interstate bridge was tall, giving them a clear view upriver long before we got there. Further, the water was wide and the bank was muck, marsh and oyster bed, allowing no place to hide and no place to rest. To make it, we'd have to shoot the center, which meant we'd be silhouetted against the reflection. A lot like those ducks circling the inside of the baptismal pool.

But twelve miles on the other side lay Cedar Point. Given the fact that I was sure he'd received Abbie's letter by now, I was pretty well assured he'd be in St. Marys. Maybe even Cedar Point, if he could find it. I was so tired, I really didn't care.

Sitting there staring over the water, paddle resting across my legs, I realized that I was way past tired. Tired beyond my bones. For some reason, all of it, everything, chose right there to press me into my seat. It was the first time I'd ever sensed the presence of the revolver at my back for a purpose other than those outside of me.

It was a dark place.

So many times I'd wanted to tell her. To explain how Heather got into my room and what had happened. I had convinced myself that she was better off not knowing. Unless, of course, her dad had already gotten to her. In which case, she had lived in doubt of me and we were living inside a cat-and-mouse mind game in which we pick at each other's scabs. But if he hadn't and I brought it up, and it was all news to her, then I was cutting her when there was no cut before.

I had no easy answer.

"Abbie?"

She cracked her eyes and smiled at me. "Hey, Band-Aid."

"I need to tell you something."

She shook her head. "No you don't."

"But . . . you need to know that . . ."

She opened her eyes. They were glassy and bloodshot. She shook her head and held out a stop-sign hand. "You mean Heather?"

"You know?"

She nodded. "Heather came and saw me. Told me about dinner. Apologized. We had a good cry over it. She said you were"—Abbie rested her head on her hands and pulled her knees into her chest—"everything she'd ever wanted in a husband." She swallowed and reached for my hand, placing it on her chest.

"But, honey . . ."

Her whisper fell. "Doss, you've never wounded me." The words were hard to come by. "No scars."

∽

RESTING PEACEFULLY on the Florida side, a long-bed Ford sat backed up to the water where a buzz-cut kid dangled his toes, a cane pole and a frantic cricket. On the beach next to him, he'd lit a fire and was slowly smoking the fish he was catching. While the world flooded around him, he didn't seem to have a care in the world—a picture of me twenty years ago.

He was drinking an RC cola, eating a MoonPie and listening to an old Keith Whitley tune: "When You Say Nothing at All." It was one of our favorite songs.

Abbie heard it, too. She stirred, tapping the side of the canoe with her toe. I flagged him and cut the canoe toward the river's edge. "Caught anything?" He nodded and glanced at the fire. He tipped his hat back and scratched his chin, sizing me up.

I beached the canoe and lifted Abbie. The nosebleed trickled again, so she pulled the scarf off her head and dabbed her nose. When she did, his expression changed. He reached in his cooler, twisted off a top and handed me a soda. I lifted it to her lips and she sipped. She smiled, the cola dripping off her chin. "Mmmm . . . good."

The kid picked at his tooth with a toothpick and whispered, "You that guy? The one on the news?"

I pushed my hat back. My left eye was still puffy, swollen and tender to the touch. "Yeah."

He tilted his head sideways. "You don't look dangerous."

"Don't feel it."

"You seen them two Pathfinders?"

"Yeah."

"I reckon they looking for you." He looked south toward Highway 17. "I hear they got folks camped out on the bridge at Highway 17. And I been hearing helicopters, but they sound fu'ther off. Maybe the in'erstate."

I nodded, thinking to myself.

"You got a plan?"

"Not really."

He said, "You know Miller's Creek?"

Miller's Creek used to run up around the south side of the

bridge, through the marsh, and skirt just under the lowest section of the bridge on the Florida side. But when they finished the bridge, the construction crew dumped all the used rebar and concrete into the middle of the creek, protecting the base of the bridge but blocking off the creek. I nodded. "Used to until they dammed it up."

He shook his head. "Not anymore. The tree-huggers found out. Said it wasn't eco-friendly. Whatever that is." He swigged and chewed. "Gov'ment came in and cleaned it up." He stared at the canoe. "You might give it a try, get to the other side without nobody knowing."

I didn't know whether to trust him or not, but I didn't have many options. Given the look of him, chances were good that the kid knew this part of the river better than me.

"Many thanks."

47

JUNE 11, MORNING

Abbie was snoring quietly. I wanted to wake her, but sleep was good. When she slept, she felt no pain. The water was alive around us—a combination of water rising rapidly through the oyster beds and game fish feeding on the fiddler crabs driven from their holes. On the shoreline, four rows of neatly planted cornstalks rose above the surface of the water. I don't know how tall they were, but they had tassled and corn floated above the water's surface. In the air above us, a great blue heron glided silently. He flapped his wings once over the span of the river, landing somewhere in the marsh beyond. Further in the distance, I heard the whine of a chainsaw and the buzzing of a tree cutter.

Here marsh leads from the river's edge for nearly a half mile before it reaches dry land. It's a flooded wasteland. Nothing but wiregrass, pluff mud and muck. Even the treetops flatten out. The smell of the marsh was thick and pungent mixed with a whiff of pine and salt.

From underneath the blanket, Abbie stirred. She pulled it down off her face, dabbed her crusty nose and faked a smile. "You tired?" The slurring had faded temporarily, but the blood had returned.

Every inch of me hurt. I shook my head. "I'll paddle you to China if you keep talking to me."

She closed her eyes. "I'd like that." Along the bank, the cicadas tuned up, singing their singular psychedelic tune. She raised her hand above the gunnel of the canoe and pointed at the noise. "Any chance you can get them to be quiet? It's starting to match the ringing in my head." Not twenty feet away, a male cardinal quietly hung on a single blade of wiregrass.

The sun came up bright and piercing over Cabbage Bend. The glare was painful. By midmorning, we had reached the railroad trestle at Highway 17. Fortunately, the river had flooded the banks and now flowed across the road. The water covered the concrete columns of both the trestle and the bridge and was washing through the huge gears that turned the trestle. An orange light was flashing quietly at the top. Beyond the trestle was an old fish house. It sat up on stilts and two old cars had always been parked beneath. Draped in fishnet and made mostly from cedar logs, the house was octagonal and shot full of holes. If the cars were still there, I couldn't see them, because the water had reached the underside of the floor. Every few seconds a wave would reach the house, rise up through it and send water streaming out the bullet holes. A deer carcass had become wedged in the rafters beneath the house, its head bobbing with the water. An alligator was locked onto the hind quarter of the carcass, spinning and ripping off large chunks.

Above us, wedged into the gears of the trestle, was a black pig carcass. Its legs had been crushed or cut off, eyes gouged out, one tusk had been broken off, its stomach was bloated and ten trillion flies were swarming the air around it. The air beneath the bridge was thick with dirt daubers by the thousands, pigeons, purple martins, and the sound of chimney sweeps—though I didn't see any.

I paddled slowly, watching the water around me as much as in front of me. A dragonfly sputtered next to us. A second later, a fish popped it from beneath, flipping it over where it lay motionless—belly up.

We slipped by Scrubby Bluff, where the water had flooded the marsh and spread around us for miles. The old homes built on the bank—those built before code required stilts—sat flooded with water flowing in the kitchen windows and out the front doors.

Before us, the river wound south, then turned back hard north and ran due east under the bridge at the interstate. I hugged the Florida bank for almost four miles and cut into Miller's Creek when it opened on my right. It carried us away from the main flow of the river, maybe close to a mile to the Florida bank where the pines rose up. We hugged the bank, padded with pine needles that muffled the sound, and then slipped along the rocks that formed the foundation for the interstate. Flashing lights lit the apex of the bridge. There were men on top with what looked like cameras, and men in uniforms were directing traffic on the southbound lane. They'd closed off one lane, causing what looked like a nasty traffic jam north of the bridge. I brought the canoe up under some trees and tied her off, thinking. Above me, on my right, some thirty feet up the bank, sat the interstate. We had maybe a hundred yards to go before a hard right turn would shoot us under the bridge. If they had people under the bridge, they'd be on the Georgia side, because the Florida side was too narrow. No place to stand.

People used the bank beneath the bridge at I-95 for all sorts of purposes, most of which weren't legal. Trash covered the bank, outlined with palmettos, tall dead oaks and a sandy beach, and at the far end sat a stone circle around a much-used campfire.

In the sky north of us, along the highway, towered a sign for a truck stop and cheap gas. It was a landmark we could see for four miles before the bridge and five miles after. If you were with a slow group, you could paddle nearly a whole day in the shadow of that one sign.

I tied off and found myself dozing. I don't know for how long. The crumple of metal and the shattering of glass woke me. I looked up and saw a small plume of white and black smoke. The men standing along the bridge stepped away from the rail. I didn't wait. I pushed out of the trees, pulled hard on the paddle and sprinted. I paddled fifty yards. Then seventy-five, and finally, when the water opened up on the right, I cut hard into it and shot the canoe back into the flow that carried us under the bridge. We drifted under the southbound lane, then the northbound and back into the sunlight that silhouetted us against the river. I turned back, afraid of what I'd see. Standing on the bank was a kid about four years old. Cowboy hat, Spider-Man T-shirt, two-holster belt, a plastic sword wedged in the belt, knee-high boots, pants at his ankles, peeing a high-arcing stream out into the water. His dad was bent over his shoulders, struggling to hold his pants under the flow. Hoping he'd just be quiet, I waved. Guess I was wrong. Tells you what I know about kids, because he said, "Look, Daddy."

His dad shook his head and didn't look up. "Not now, son. Just pay attention to what you're doing."

We'd come twenty-eight miles. My skin was sunburned, hot to the touch, and my hands were raw. Most of my fingers were bleeding around the nails where the constant pressure had split the skin. Touching the paddle was excruciating, much less pulling on it. I watched the kid grow smaller while the wind swirled around us.

We snaked through the S-turn, slipped through the tips of

the marsh grass, passed out of the shadow of I-95, cut the corner and headed for Crandall—a public boat ramp tucked up into the woods and owned by Georgia Power. If I kept my head and paddle down, we could skirt the edge and not be seen from the bridge, because at this point the river was a half mile to even a mile wide. In the distance, southeast of us, white smoke poured from the tops of the smokestacks of the paper mills in Fernandina. The smoke billowed then faded south. At night, the stacks send sparks shooting up through the smoke. When I was working for Gus, we called it the light at the end of the tunnel.

While Crandall is public, few know about it. It's a wide, deepwater ramp made of crushed oyster shells. Huge oaks tower above a grassy bluff where years back somebody built a stone picnic table and drove a four-inch, free-flowing well deep into the aquifer. I wanted the water. Another half mile and we slid onto the ramp. The water was whipping through her, so, steadying the canoe, I lifted my right foot onto the ramp and was nearly crippled by a piercing pain. The pain brought up a wave of nausea and a black circle crept in around the edge of my eyes. I gabbed the bowline, stepped out of the boat and pulled as I fell. The boat swung into the current, then slid quietly onto the shells. Fish skeletons littered the ramp. Some were three feet long and other than the heads, had been picked clean. I tied off the bowline, lifted Abbie from the boat and limped her to the table. My foot was throbbing and staining the grass behind me. I laid her across the table, propped up her head on a red plastic inner tube and then turned on the spigot at the well. Around us, forearm-thick bamboo grew up through the live oaks and water oaks competing for the same sun. Growing wild amongst the trees were camellia, azalea and mimosa trees. Above us, shading Abbie, spread a crepe myrtle in half bloom. Its branches were heavy with hundreds of berries that would soon burst and bloom in pink bouquets. Under pressure, the well coughed air, bubbled then shot sideways some eight feet, making a decent shower for an Oompa Loompa. The water flowed rusty for several seconds, finally turning cold and clear and smelling of eggs. I drenched my head, then filled a water bottle, returning to dab Abbie's lips and bathe her face. After she'd sipped, I sat on the bench and looked at my foot. A four-inch fish bone was sticking up through the center of my foot. It was thick, maybe three millimeters, and had pierced the sole of my Tevas. I un-velcroed the sandal and lifted my foot, pulling out the bone. The hole bled and painted the bottom of my foot and sandal red. I held it beneath the water and pulled the bone out of my sandal. I drank long and deep and soaked my hat, letting it drip on my sunburned neck and shoulders.

The sun was falling and I knew we didn't have much time. I placed Abbie back on her pallet and pushed the bow into the current. It caught us and we shot off the bank. I tried not to look at my foot. The bleeding had slowed but the skin was sticky.

Northeast, the red-brick chimney of the deserted iron factory rose some hundred feet or more into the air, marking the north side of town. Between it and me, swaying above the mirage of the marsh, the masts of a hundred or more sailboats moored at the marina shimmered in the sun. If the senator's people were anywhere, they'd be standing on the dock, binoculars poised to spot us.

From Crandall, the river winds around five S-curves to Reed's Bluff, where the water flows deep and dangerous. Beyond the bluff, the river stretches nearly a mile before it is joined by Burrell's Creek. The two merge, forming a narrow mess called Devil's Elbow. Once through the elbow, the river flows past the marina, past the fish houses and restaurants and then to Cedar Point, where she slingshots to the ocean.

I looked behind us. Fourteen years had led to this. Seven miles were all that remained. Seven impossible miles.

The sun, once high and hot, now sat low in the west, threatening to slip behind the treetops. And though I tried, I could not stop it.

48

An hour later, we reached the bend that flowed into Reed's Bluff. The water was moving faster than I'd ever seen it. It was the worst kind of water. Not rapids above but undertow below. The water here was forty feet deep and the volume was squeezing through, ripping a fast current. I threw the canoe into the flow, it caught us and began pushing the back end around. I dug the paddle in, fought it and pulled, but it was no use. The undertow swung the stern around, then the bow, then the stern again. The water swirled, billowing up from the bottom, and threw us into the mix. All the debris, the trees, logs and trash, had gathered in a hole just north of the bluff, swirling like in a blender. The canoe rammed the center, climbed onto the pile and I grabbed Abbie's hand just as water spilled over the stern. The river flooded in, angry and violent, swamped my seat and then shot us airborne like a canon. I hit the water and began pulling upward, but the water pulled us down and apart. It flipped us, tumbled us, and then wrapped us together in a knot. I struggled for air but could not break through the blanket of debris that held me beneath the water. My lungs were screaming and when I reached for Abbie, she was gone. I clawed at the water, pulling and kicking, but I could not break free. Locked in a somersault, I desperately needed air. The bottom sat some forty feet below me. The surface only a foot above. But I could reach neither. My lungs closed in and the familiar stars returned.

Had it all come to this?

From below me, a swirl of water caught my foot and righted me. It lifted me like a bobber and freed me. My eyes broke the surface and I saw a flash of bathing suit. I took three strokes, grabbed Abbie's foot, and dug my arms beneath hers, pulling her toward the air. She sucked in a breath and hacked, coughing. The bank was only ten feet away. A fallen tree reached out across the water. A single, leafless limb stretched through the air above me. I lunged, caught it and it broke. The two of us spun, flipped and twirled through the water. My shoulder slammed into the bank and the water flipped us again, but I held fast to the broken limb and Abbie. We turned a cartwheel and when my arm came down I slammed the limb into the soft bank. The splintered end spiked into the sand and momentarily anchored us. I looped an arm around Abbie's chest, pulled and threw myself at the bank. The sand was soft, gave way beneath me and the water sucked us down again. I dug my fingers in, kicked with my toes, and inched onto the beach. Slowly, I pulled Abbie toward me. She was spitting blood and water—both of which had smeared across her face. Her breathing was short, raspy and the effort not to drown had exhausted her. She was a rag doll. I combed the beach but everything was gone. The canoe. The purple blanket. The revolver.

Only we remained.

Sixty feet above me towered Reed's Bluff. It's a sand dune that, for no apparent reason, rises straight up out of the water and runs east and west for nearly a mile. At the top, it might be five feet in width and the backside falls off as fast as the front rises. It's dotted with scrub oaks and enough wiregrass to hold the sand together. It's steep, but once at the top, you can see for miles. More important, you can see St. Marys. I needed to show Abbie. She needed to know we were close.

I cradled her and threw her arms around my neck. Her arms fell. "Hold on to me." She made no response.

I dug my toes into the sand, pulled on the wiregrass and crawled up. Every few feet, the sand gave way, spilling away beneath us and forcing me to dig in further and pull harder. Climbing up took several minutes. Finally, I laid her on the narrow ridge, caught my breath, sat her up and let her lean against me. "Honey, look." I held her arm out and pointed her index finger. "St. Marys. Just five miles. That's all." She couldn't breathe through her nose without coughing.

"Hey . . ." I was reaching. Grasping. "When we get there, I'll call the folks at M. D. Anderson. Maybe something's opened up. We could have dinner tonight at Sterlings and fly out tomorrow."

Her eyes cracked. She leaned toward me and patted my chest. "Doss . . ." Her whisper was faint and gurgled with fluid. "I'm dying. Not stupid."

"You know about that, too?"

She nodded and spat. "Uh-huh." Cracking a smile, she said, "You're not a very good liar." She locked her arms around me, kissed my cheek and whispered, "No scars."

I stared out across the expanse. The wind blew in two directions, meeting in the middle. In front of us, the wind blew in from the northwest, rolling across the marsh grass that ran for several miles out in front of us. It blew southeast, bending the grass and trees toward us. Behind us, the wind rose up over the bluff from the southwest and moved northeast, pulling the limbs, branches, wiregrass and Spanish moss, laying them out across the water like hair. We sat in the middle, looking out upon a world that had come to pay its final respects.

"Abbie . . . look. Everything is . . ." The world was bowing down, but she never saw it.

Her eyes were rolling back and her tongue grew thick and white. I checked her pulse and it was faint. Barely there. I slid back down the bluff and scoured the bank for the Pelican case, but it was nowhere. I ran up and down the bank, looking. How hard can it be to spot a yellow plastic case? I ran a quarter mile down the bank to where a tree had fallen from the bluff into the water. The current stripped it of its foliage but left the thin twigs: They poked into the water like fingers, slowing the flow. Tangled in the middle, floated a yellow box.

I dove in.

When I surfaced, I grabbed the box and fought the current back to the bank. I anchored a hand in the soft sand, pulled and spiked the other hand. Three pulls and I'd freed myself from the current that sought to wash me out to sea. I ran back up the bank, clawed and scrambled back up the bluff and dropped next to Abbie. I flipped open the case, cracked the seal on the last of the dopamine and shot it into the inside of her thigh—into her femoral artery. Then I cracked the dexamethasone and slid the syringe into her arm. "Abbie, please come back. Don't go. Not yet." Finally, I dug around through the discarded syringes and found one last Actiq. I read the label, *800 mcg.*

I pulled off the wrapper and placed it just inside her cheek. The three medications went to work quickly.

She stirred. "Have you ever broken a promise to me?"

I stared off down the river. She traced the lines of my face, breathing as deeply as she could. "Then don't start now." I cradled her on my lap and we slid tandem down the sand. When we reached the bank, I laid her down and scrambled through the debris, looking for anything that would float. A piece of plastic, an old cooler, a chunk of Styrofoam. If I could keep her afloat, I could swim alongside and we'd make it. We could still make it.

I thought about a makeshift raft, but a raft would never make the turn at Devil's Elbow. I ran a half mile one way, then a half mile in the other. I rummaged through every piece of trash and fallen limb along the beach. That's when I found it.

Rammed into the sand on the south side of the bluff lay a squared log. It looked weathered, was tunneled along one side by worms, was rough hewn—maybe even by hand—and looked about twelve feet long. Most important, it was bobbing.

It was heavy, which would be needed in about six miles, so I ran back to Abbie, picked her up and carried all that I held dear back down the beach. We reached the log and I laid her onto it, draping an arm around each side, and we shoved off. I latched on to the front and kicked us into the current. It picked us up, straightened us and led us out.

From the front, I could steady the log, keep Abbie afloat and make minute changes to our direction. It also allowed me to look at Abbie. We'd been in the water a few minutes when she stirred. Blood dripped off her face and trickled onto the log where it mixed with the water and trailed behind us.

The river had overflowed on every side. The volume was unlike anything I'd ever imagined. As was its speed. Even without a paddle and with me dragging in the water, we were making five to six miles an hour. In normal tides, dragging like this would pull me across the top of razor-sharp oyster beds, slicing my legs and back to shreds. But the volume had changed that. The only problem with our speed was Devil's Elbow.

The current and weight of the log kept us in the middle. Actually, we didn't have much of a choice. The further we flowed, the more whitecaps we encountered. Soon, they were rolling over the top of Abbie. The good news was that they couldn't swamp us. The bad news was they were nearly drowning me. I clung to the front and kicked with little effect. The waves crashed across us, tearing at my hands.

We floated a mile, then two, made the wide southward turn at Rose's Bluff and, finally, headed due east into the last straight stretch before Devil's Elbow. Around us, the bank was a feeding frenzy of redfish and tarpon. On each side, the water had covered up the pluff mud and driven the fiddler crabs from their holes. Some clung to the wiregrass with their one large claw while others floated helplessly along the water's surface.

I heard it long before I saw it.

Devil's Elbow is the last bend before you reach St. Marys. When the waters collide, the river makes a muted roaring sound like rapids. The waves grow two to four feet and foam with whitecaps—enough to swamp any canoe. When I was guiding, we learned to skirt the elbow by paddling wide south and slingshotting around it. The problem with the log I was currently holding on to was control. I couldn't paddle wide and we'd miss the slingshot.

The sound woke Abbie. She grabbed my hand and continued to straddle the log with her legs. The water swept us up, pushing us through the center of the elbow. Water rolled over the top of us, crashed down on the center of us and pulled at me from all sides. I hugged the log, trying to keep it upright, but I'm afraid I had little effect. Fortunately for us, the log was so long and heavy, it rode through the elbow as much as over it. I gripped the log and felt finger grooves on the far side. I moved to the side, threw an arm around Abbie, dug my fingers into the grooves and hung on. We passed through the chop, turned left or northeast and for the first time, saw St. Marys in the distance. All the buildings were white and the masts of nearly a hundred moored sailboats soared into the air. I swam to the other side of the log and that's when it hit me. The timber. The grooves were actually letters—carved into the wood. I looked a second time at the log, finally recognizing it. *Even pirates need God.* I retraced the grooves, finishing the sentence. *". . . I will be with you."*

I kicked and pulled on the log, steering us toward the Florida side and pulling us wide of St. Marys. In the distance, news trucks with telescoping satellite antennae sat parked along the dock. News personalities and their cameramen were set up on the dock, aiming out across the water. Mixed in with the debris, we floated some half mile away, relatively camouflaged. We drifted along the Florida bank, Abbie's fingers locked into mine. It was dusk, and the sun had long since fallen.

Abbie lay her head on the timber and stared at the far bank. "Look at all those people."

"Yeah."

She coughed. "I think we caused some trouble."

"It was no trouble."

~❦

ST. MARYS SLIPPED BY. Seagulls strutted along the docks and pelicans perched on rooftops waiting for the shrimp boats to return and empty their nets. Cedar Point appeared on our left, so I kicked into the current, cut us across the water and slid us across the top of the marsh grass and through the schools of mullet that had gathered there. They, too, were seeking safety. The water nudged us inward, gently lodging our one-log raft onto shore.

We'd done it. All the way from Moniac.

I lifted Abbie, walked up on the beach and knelt, laying her head gently on the sand. Rising above us stood thirty or so sunflowers, some eight feet tall and in full bloom. They had followed the sun as it had fallen behind the trees, and now they were aimed down at us.

Abbie pushed her feet down into the sand, her toes resting in the water. She took a deep breath and her face relaxed—telling me that she remembered. "Honey . . . Abbie?" A helicopter sounded in the distance. "Honey . . . Abbie . . ." Her eyes fluttered. "We're here." I could hear men running toward us in the marsh. Her father's voice in the background.

She turned toward me and wrapped her arms about my waist. I wiped her face with the scarf but the bleeding soaked through. I cradled her head. Words came hard. "Abbie . . . ?"

She pulled my hand to her face, placing my index finger just above her ear and closed her eyes.

A few minutes later, she was gone.

49

THE FIRST DAY

The sun broke through the bars of my cell and landed on my face, warming my skin but little else. It was the same sun that we'd woken to yesterday morning. Bright, lonely and now hollow. The kid next to me chewed on what was left of one of his fingernails while both his legs bounced like popcorn.

A dozen or so men crowded the cell where they held me until my hearing with the judge. Given that it was Sunday, I imagine the judge wouldn't be too happy about it. Strike one. The kid leaned in. "What 'choo in fo'?"

I hadn't slept in four or five days, so I pushed the words around my mouth before getting them out. He was skinny, and his eyes never seemed to land any one place. *Where do I start?* "Uh . . . umm . . . murder."

His eyes lit. "You bust a cop?" The walls around me were littered with graffiti, but I don't know where they got a pencil given the cavity search they had given me before they walked me in here. I shook my head. He spat a nail sliver. "Who?"

A man next to me stood, walked to the wall urinal and peed everywhere but in the urinal. It ran down the wall and trickled into a drain on the floor. "My wife."

He quit chewing on his finger, his eyes settled on me and then grew wide. "You da dude dey been talkin' 'bout on TV.

344

You da one done kilt the sen'tor's daughter. That model." He snapped his fingers. "The one on all the magazine covers. What her name?"

Most of the faces in the cell turned toward me. I whispered, "Abbie."

"Yeah, da's it. You da dude that kill Abbie." He shouted across the room, "Hey . . . dis da honkey that shot the swimsuit model."

"I didn't kill her."

He shrugged, legs bouncing again. "Well, she dead."

I shook my head. A large, smelly man lying in the corner lifted his head off his arm and said, "Nervy! Shut the hell up."

The kid sat quiet a minute and nodded at the big man. He whispered, "He call me Nervy cuz he say I got nervous legs." A minute passed. "And if he tell you to shut up, you better do as he say. He big." Another minute passed. "You shoot her?" I shook my head. "But dey say dey foun' a gun. A fo'ty-fi'." I tried to translate but couldn't. He whispered more slowly. "A forty-five." I nodded. "Wuz you gunna?" I looked at him and frowned. "Well, CNN say you want the family money." I made no response.

The big man climbed off the floor, swayed back and forth, took three steps and grabbed my nervous friend, lifting his head to the ceiling, his shoes four feet off the floor. He banged his head twice against the bars, then carried him to the urinal, where he submerged his head against the porcelain and pulled the flush handle. The kid sputtered and whined, which caught the dutiful attention of the napping guard down the hall. He banged his stick against the bars and said, "Hey, shut up!"

Swaying man returned to his bed on the floor while the kid sat next to me. This time closer. Dripping, he leaned in. "Wuz it the money?"

I looked at the man on the ground and then the kid, wondering if he'd lost his mind. His eyes narrowed. "Look, man, you da one been on the news for two weeks. You crazy. Not me." He had a point. He held his hands out, palms up. "So?" I shook my head. He turned his slightly. "It wadn't da money? You tell me wher' dey hid it?"

"No."

"Shi . . ." He trailed off. "You dumb as a bag of hammers. You shudda took the money and runned off." He waved his hand through the air like a kid hanging his arm out the window of a car on the highway. "Skee-daddle."

Despite the fact that my friend next to me was murdering the English language, he did get his point across. Most of the heads in the cell were pointed at me. My eyes were heavy with sleep. My shorts had dried, as had Abbie's blood on my shirt and hands. The Superglue stitching above my left eye was itchy and infected. He pointed. "She do that?"

The walls were cold, concrete, trimmed with steel and rivet—rising up out of a world bordered by razor wire and the possibility of speeding lead projectiles. The hard part is not this. I'd only been here a few hours but prison seemed like paradise compared to the possibilities. To hurt, to know punishment, you must be living and I am only half alive. Given that, the pain in my head hurts half as much. Pain in the heart is another matter.

I looked at my hands. The palms were bright red, badly blistered, and the knuckles had been rubbed skinless. He pointed. "Shi . . . dat hurt?"

I turned them over. "I don't know."

"Well, it look like it hurt like hell."

Hell. There's a thought.

He asked again, "She do that, too?"

The big man on the floor didn't move, but I kept quiet and shook my head. "Who den?" His face had broken out in ten or fifteen sores and many of his teeth had rotted out. Based on the maggot-breath coming out of his mouth, I'd imagine rotting was an ongoing process. I'm no drug expert, but he looked like the pictures that I'd seen of folks who were hooked on crystal meth.

"Some men we met . . . on the river."

"You shoot dem, too?"

"No, and I didn't shoot my wife either."

"Da's wha' dey all say."

A few of the other men in the cell laughed, and one of them slapped his leg and said, "Dat's what I be talking 'bout." Three seats down, a graying man with a two-day beard, wearing a dirty blue suit, sat leaning against the wall. One eye was purple, swollen shut, and he reeked of alcohol and vomit. His shirt was half untucked, the front of his pants was wet and he was missing a shoe, but oddly, his Windsor knot was snug against his neck. I doubted it would help.

The guard unlocked our cell and began leading us one by one to a table where two other guards cuffed our wrists and ankles. The twelve of us paraded down three flights of stairs to courtroom number 4. My scabby-faced friend whispered up at me, "Dis ain't good. No good at all. Da's Judge Fergy's bench and dey's a nor'easter comin' in."

"So?"

"Dat means da surfin' be good and he be stuck here wit' us." He nodded toward the bench. "Bettuh get yo' story skrait."

The bailiff stood and said, "All rise." We did, the sound of hungover grunts and uncomfortable chains echoed across the chamber. A balding man with a dark tan and draped in a black robe walked through a door in the back. He sat quickly, tapping his foot, reading through a stack of papers. He nodded to the bailiff. "The court calls . . ." He looked down and shook his head. His eyes narrowed on Nervy. "Ellswood Maxwell Lamont Augustus the Third."

Nervy stood up. The judge dropped the papers in front of him and folded his hands across his desk. "Nervy, I thought I told you I didn't want to ever see you in my courtroom again."

Nervy smiled. "I missed yo' comp'ny, Yo' Honuh."

Judge Ferguson looked down at his desk, then back at the kid. "Looks like you're still cooking in your backyard."

Nervy shook his head. "No suh." He pointed at the large man who'd flushed his head in the urinal. "He be."

The judge frowned. "Then what's that crap on your face."

Nervy shrugged. "Skin cancer?"

"You're trying to tell me that those leper-looking sores on your face were caused by the sun?" Nervy nodded enthusiastically.

The judge sat back. "And let me guess. You're innocent."

Nervy smiled. "Abso-frickin-one-hunrid-percen-lutely."

"Is that your plea?"

He pointed at the big man. "He guilty. Not me. I was minding my own bit'ness. Watching TV. *American Idol.* Thinkin' 'bout trying out, when—"

"Nervy, have you been to the city morgue lately?"

Urinal man to my left whispered beneath his breath in a voice that rivaled James Earl Jones, "No, but he keep dis up and he be going real soon."

Nervy's eyes grew wide. "Judge, um . . . Yo' Honor, he be threatenin' me."

Judge Ferguson leaned across his bench. "It's full of kids just like you. My patience has run out." The judge rolled his eyes and turned to the bailiff. "Set a date, get him an attorney. Bail is set at twenty thousand."

Nervy sat down, nodded his head and smirked. "He in a good mood."

The bailiff said, "The court calls Stephen Doss Michaels."

I stood.

Judge Ferguson looked at me, chewed on his lip then spit whatever it was off the end of his tongue and out across his bench. Nervy leaned forward. "He do that sometime when he be thinkin'."

I tried to find my voice. "Yes, sir."

He leaned back, his chair squeaking, and rocked a minute. "Looks like they finally caught up with you."

"Yes, sir."

"Must be hard to outrun the television. What with all the helicopters." I made no response. He tapped himself in the chest. "I, like most every other person in this country, have been following your story. CNN. Fox. All the biggies." He paused. "Where'd they catch you?"

Good question. "At the end, sir."

"You being smart with me?"

I shook my head. "Sir?"

He frowned. "Do you understand the charges made against you?"

"I'm sorry, sir?"

"Do you understand why you're standing in my courtroom on a beautiful Sunday morning while six-foot swells spill gently across North Jax Beach?"

Nervy nodded, legs bouncing. "Oh, he be pissed now."

The judge reached behind him and clicked on an oscillating fan that circulated out across the room. I suppose it was his way of fending off the smell of us. Mr. Windsor Knot–no-shoe-wet-pants had started to hiccup. He gagged once and we all heard it coming. He leaned forward, hiccuped one last time and blew last night's party all over the judge's floor. The judge shook his head and motioned to one of the four officers sitting in the courtroom. While the man wiped his face with his tie, something he'd done repeatedly over the last few hours, the officer led him from the courtroom.

The fan blew gently, wafted the fragrance under my nose and carried me to the court reporter. She was maybe mid-fifties, her fingers tapping almost as fast as Nervy's legs.

I stared at the reporter, but my mind was sitting on a bench in Central Park and asking, What is the name of that perfume?

Judge Ferguson pounded his gavel, and raising his voice, said, "Excuse me, Mr. Michaels. Am I keeping you from something?" He sat back, eyes narrowing. "We'll just wait until you're ready."

Nervy sat back and scooted away from me. "Oh, you don' did it. He be really pissed now."

The cuff on my left hand was tight, and my fingers tingled. My hand felt stiff from the caked blood. The edge of the cuff was rubbing off red flakes embedded in my wrist. I opened my hand and stared at the four busted blisters. He pounded his gavel again.

"I'm sorry, sir."

What is the name of that perfume?

He took a deep breath. "Do you understand the charges made against you?"

I shook my head. Nervy scooted a few more inches away. "Nope. Don' do that neither. He 'spect you to speak when spoke to. When he aks, you ansuh."

I looked at the judge. "Not . . . not really, sir."

The judge raised an eyebrow and spoke mostly to himself, "What is it with me, northeasters and idiots?" He leaned forward. "Mr. Michaels, you are being charged with . . ." He eyed the stack of papers on his desk. "Kidnapping. Breaking and entering. Tresspassing. Larceny. Grand Larceny. Possession of a controlled substance. Resisting arrest. Assault. Battery of an officer. Illegal administration of a drug. And last but not least, first degree murder." He tapped the desk with his index finger. "Down here, Mr. Michaels, 'euthanasia' is just a sophisticated name for murder. And a premeditated one at that."

Nervy nodded and looked up and down the row of men next to us. "He good."

I swallowed. The judge continued, "Do you understand these charges as I've read them to you?"

"Yes, sir."

"How do you plead?"

"Well, I mean . . ."

"Mr. Michaels." Sweat beaded on his forehead and trickled down the ridge of his nose. "The charges made against you are either true . . . or not. Yes? Can we at least agree on that?"

The fan made a ticking noise as it turned. The name of the perfume hung on the tip of my tongue.

"Son." The judge waved at me. "Are you guilty or not guilty?"

I turned to the recorder. "Ma'am? Excuse me, ma'am?" She stopped tapping long enough to look up. "What is the name of your perfume?"

The judge stood and slammed his gavel on the desk. "Mr. Michaels! I will find you in contempt of this court if you do not answer my question. Now"—his forehead was starting to glisten—"while there's still an ocean to surf in. Guilty or not guilty?"

The tape of the last two weeks ran across the backs of my eyes. Sorrow, laughter, deep-down hurt and a touch I could not reach tumbled together. Raindrops in the river. I stared at the judge—my mind miles from his oaken courtroom. "Sir, I didn't kill my wife. Least not intentionally."

"There are some people in very high places who believe otherwise." He scribbled something on the desk in front of him. "I'll take that as 'no contest.' "

"Sir, you can take it however you want, but—" He held out his hand, but I spoke over him, "I'd do it again."

He shook his head and sat down. "Mr. Michaels, do you have counsel?"

"Sir?"

"Do you have an attorney?" I shook my head. "Can you afford one?"

"I don't think so."

He studied me. "Given your popularity over the last two weeks, I doubt you'll have trouble finding one. And do you know that I have personally received calls from both the governor and senator this morning—neither of which like you very much." He turned to the bailiff and was about to open his mouth when the senator stormed through the doors. "Your Honor, may I see you in chambers?" He didn't wait for a reply but walked through the swinging wooden half-door and around the bench, where he and the judge disappeared through the judge's office door. We waited while the whispers grew louder up and down the bench.

The judge reappeared by himself, sat, swung his gavel and said, "Set bail at two hundred and fifty thousand dollars."

Nervy whispered beneath his breath. "He def'ny don' like you."

I sat down, my nose bobbing in the air.

The tape rewound. Two years. Then three. Ten. Fifteen. I walked back through the moments. Some good. Some not. All hurt. I looked around and found myself flying somewhere between Central Park, the Battery and Cedar Point.

50

THE THIRD DAY

Two days had passed. They'd moved me to the Duval County jail while I awaited trial. Because most of my "crimes" occurred on the border between Florida and Georgia, and because Florida has a death penalty and is pretty good at using it, the senator pushed for Florida to retain jurisdiction. Which it did.

Jesse was the guard assigned to cell block E. Mine. We didn't cause him too much trouble. Sometimes, late at night, he'd slip past the cameras and he'd tell me of his wife and kids. He was about six foot two, weighed probably two-twenty, and, I think, got a job working in the penitentiary when his college football days ran out and the pro scouts didn't come calling. He's never told me, but my guess is that he was too slow. Beneath his muscles—of which he had many—was a man who sketched animals on cafeteria napkins. Maybe he figured I was safe.

Spend any time at all down here and you learn to differentiate people by the sound of their walk—the weight of their step, the length of their gait, the type of shoe they wear. Jesse tapped on the door with his stick, but that's only because he'd seen it done in movies. A hand grenade wouldn't knock that door off its hinges. He nodded to the guard behind the glass at the end of the hall, who punched a button numbered "217" and my door slid open. Jesse motioned with his stick. "Picasso, some people here to see you. Come on. You got twenty minutes."

The senator walked in first, followed by three men in suits. Attorneys, I guessed. They set a tape recorder on the table. He spoke without looking at me. "I'm going to ask you some questions and you're going to answer. If you don't, you can go to hell."

"You really think that matters to me?"

He laid a single-page printout on the table. "That's my daughter's toxicology report. There was enough narcotic in Abigail Grace's blood system to kill each man in this room. Based on that alone, I can build a prison on top of you."

"I happen to agree with you."

"That's all you have to say?"

"You walked in here with your mind made up. I can't change that. You're a pollster politician. Unlike you, Abbie never paid attention to the polls."

"I'm suggesting they lead with the euthanasia charge."

"Whatever helps you sleep at night, Senator."

He pointed at the recorder. "You could expedite this entire process by making a statement."

"You mean a confession?"

"If that's what you choose to call it."

"I don't really expect you to understand, but let me put it this way . . . For four years, I watched my Abbie shrink, grow, lose her hair, grow hair, get sick, vomit, bleed from her gums, bloat and gain fifty pounds on steroids, then vomit it all off. I saw her get stuck with more needles than I care to think about. And half of those needle pricks came under my hand. I watched more poison drip into her veins than any one person should have to endure. So, bring your threats and your lawyers. You could bury me under this place and it wouldn't touch the hurt I feel inside." The pain comes in waves. It, too, is tidal. I turned my wedding band around my finger.

A long silence.

"Cancer can do a lot. It can wreck your life, steal that which you hold dear, shatter dreams, crack your confidence, sever your soul and leave you wasted and wrung out. It can rob you of hope, whisper lies you learn to believe and dim the lights along the river. It'll rob your voice, your health and your image of yourself. It'll feed you with nausea, and cause you to know the difference between tired and fatigued. And when you think you can't cope, and can't think, it pours despair in like a blanket. Soon, it covers and colors everything. It's an absolute bona fide hell. But—" I found myself standing, pounding on the table.

I sat down and spoke softly, "Hopelessness is a disease, more powerful than the one that stole Abbie's life. Because it affects the heart . . . There is no vaccine, no one is immune. And only one weapon can battle it." He looked up at me. "It is the weapon that says I will walk through hell with you—no matter what." My echo settled across the room. "In the end, cancer only steals what you give it. I may die right here or in some prison not too far away, but I'll die knowing this: I never gave it Abbie. And I never gave it us. Senator, there are worse things than dying."

He laughed, the anger palpable. "Like what!"

"Like . . . living dead."

"What's that supposed to mean?"

I shook my head. "Abbie didn't die knowing her pain alone. The seat beside her was never empty. You may be angry at me for taking her away. Tough. Your loss. I'd do it again." I met him eye to eye. I had said enough. I was finished talking.

He stood up and walked out.

Two DAYS LATER, he returned. This time alone. No tape recorder, no tie, a blue sport coat unbuttoned and a PVC tube tucked under his arm.

He sat down, slowly folding, unfolding and refolding his handkerchief. Finally, he spoke. A painful admission. "I've doubted you for a long time. The . . ." He shrugged. "The discovery at Mayo . . . cemented in my mind your betrayal of Abigail Grace."

"Sir, her name is Abbie. And no matter how it looked when you walked in, I never betrayed her."

He nodded slowly. "Your friend, the flying priest, came to see me. Shared with me your confession."

"Is that what he called it?"

"He did."

"Whatever happened to confidentiality?"

"He said that since he'd been defrocked, that no longer pertained to him."

"Funny, he didn't say that to me."

He tapped the table with his fingers. "I thought I could make . . . Abbie . . . see, but she knew you better than me."

He set the tube on the table. "We found your canoe. This was wedged beneath the seat." He unscrewed the cap and rolled the canvas across the table. He stared at the drawing several seconds. "I always thought she'd beat it." He let go and it curled itself into a loose scroll. He shook his head. "No man is good enough for another man's daughter." Staring at the ceiling, a single tear cascaded off his cheek. "After I lost her mother, I decided no man would ever be. Then she met you. And you were . . ." He laughed, shrugging. "Not what I had in mind."

"Sir, may I ask you a question?" He raised an eyebrow.

"What'd I ever do to you? I mean, just what did I do to hack you off?"

He wiped his eyes. "You gave Abbie what I never did. You gave her yourself."

"Yes, sir. Every day." For the first time ever, I saw him as a man. Even a father. "Sir, with all due respect, the fact that her second transplant didn't take had nothing to do with you. You did what you could."

He glanced at me and almost nodded. Flipping open his cell phone, he dialed a number from memory and waited until somebody picked up on the other end. He cleared his throat and said, "You sign it?" He nodded, waiting. "I'd be obliged if you faxed it to me at this number." He gave the number and hung up. A few minutes later, a guard walked in, laid a single sheet in his hands and walked out. The senator read it, placed it on the table and stood. "The murder charges have been dropped. I can't do much about the narcotics charges, but if you plead guilty, we can get your sentence reduced to probation. Maybe some community service. Like . . . teaching old, stubborn politicians how to paint." He stood—his back to me—pulled a wrinkled letter from his coat pocket and laid it gently on the table. His fingertips slowly skimmed the surface of the letter like a blind man reading braille. He swallowed, managing a whisper. "You're free to go."

He walked out, slowly, almost limping. I unfolded the letter. Her New York perfume flowered into the room and laid across me like a blanket.

May 30th

Dear Dad,

It's late and my morphine is wearing off, which is both good and bad. Hospice is downstairs, shuffling around. Doss is up in the crow's nest. I can hear it creaking under his weight.

In the last several years, I've learned to listen to my body. Right now, it's telling me that by the time you get this, I'll be gone. Whatever cancer is going to do to me, it's done it. New treatments, specialists, opinions, and medications along with all the power of the Senate won't change that. Only one thing remains. Don't cry. Pressed between the memory of Mom and now the thought of me, I can see those big broad shoulders beginning to shake. Crocodile tears welling up. Dad, don't hold it back. Even senators cry. As for me—I'm a big girl now. Of course, it's not my choosing. If I had anything to do with it, I'd stick around another fifty or sixty years, learn to cook like Rosalia and run my fingers through Doss's handsome gray hair. I'd like to have seen that. I think he will age well.

If you're thinking Doss stole me away, don't. He didn't. Few respect you more than he. This trip is my idea. I have one thing left to give him and I need the river to do this. Please understand. He is gifted unlike any I've ever known and I don't want that gift to die with me. So please leave us to the river. Remember this when you get mad, hire lawyers and start scheming. Just let it go. Doss didn't kill me. Cancer did. Blame it. Sending Doss to prison won't bring me—or Mom—back. I have lived well. Now let me die well.

When I was a little girl, you held my hand and walked me down to the Dock Street on the opening night of Annie. I was so scared. But once in the theater, you pulled me aside, knelt and pushed the hair out of my eyes. You said, "Abigail Grace, you weren't made to sit in those seats." Then you pointed my eyes at the stage and the spotlights. "You were made to stand up there . . . under them. Go take your place." Dad, Doss is a lot like me. Remember that. He's worth it, he needs you and we all need him. Trust me on this one.

I'm leaving you a present. But there's a catch. It's held for safekeeping in the chest of my husband. Unwrap him, and you'll find me. I gave him my heart a long time ago and I don't need it where I'm going. If you swallow your pride long enough to see past your own private pain, you'll find that you two are more alike than you think. And that you can learn from him.

I know this will be hard for you to hear. If you read this letter and think I'm just trying to have the last word, don't. I'd gladly trade it.

I love you.

> Yours,
> Abigail Grace

AFTERWARD

I went home, climbed up into my studio, unrolled my scroll and started at the beginning. My life with Abbie. I let the tape roll, walking down each sidewalk of pain—each anchor line—and when the hurt got to be too much, I stopped the tape and dove in—sketching that one single frame. I've cried more in one year than the rest of my life combined.

Tears on the canvas.

The only difference now is that I no longer paint the world I wish I lived in. I paint this one.

THE SENATOR STARTED coming to see me on the weekends. At first, he just followed his toes around my studio. We didn't talk much. But slowly the words came. He'd ask questions about style, form, process. Good questions, too. I think in another life, he might have had an artistic bent. Finally, I set up an easel for him and taught him how to work with charcoal. Not too bad, either. Surprisingly, the senator had a soft side. He hated the Yankees but after a few weeks, he ran his fingers along the frame of my Nat Fein print. He shook his head and said, "I suppose it's coming for all of us." I reached into my closet, pulled out my dusty attempt at Babe's face and handed it to him. While the photo evokes emotions of sadness few words can create, my picture shows Babe, eyes staring up through baggy eyelids, cheeks fallen, staring out across the house he built. Yet beneath the shell of the skin he once trotted around the bases, he's smiling. He's still Babe. The senator liked that. I handed both to him. "Please. They're yours."

A single tear trickled off his cheek. Finally, he said, "Abbie once told me that nobody paints like God, but"—he waved a hand across the studio—"you get pretty close."

Not a week passed that we didn't sit in my studio, quietly making art. It was what we did. Together. You'd think Washington might miss him, but he could slip out when wanted.

A year passed.

⤝

HE HAD BEEN THERE all morning, the two of us easy with each other's company and lost in the smell and color of paint. Not talking had become easy. Which told me a lot about us. At lunchtime, he was walking out. I'm not sure why, other than time, but he finally stopped to ask me the question that had been on the tip of his tongue for almost a year. He pointed at *Indomitable*. I'd finished her several months ago and let her hang there, staring down at me. He said, "May I . . . please?"

It was his olive branch. The senator had forgiven me. More important, he had forgiven himself.

"Yes."

A deep breath, big enough to fill his barrel chest. "You sure?"

"Senator, our trip downriver was not my gift to Abbie. It was her gift to me—and I have a feeling that she'd been planning it a long time." I studied my work. "I didn't paint her to imprison her. I painted her . . . to set us free."

Abbie's death had shattered his tough exterior. Now he lived with his emotions close to the surface. Sewn on his sleeve. "She teach you that?"

The hurt reminded me of what was, and is, beautiful. Of what I'd known, and lost. Of love given. And taken away. The more it hurt, the deeper the ache, the sweeter the memory. So while I mind the hurt, I live with it.

I smiled.

The senator hung *Indomitable,* and many others, in Abbie's design studio, which he turned into my gallery. Or rather, *our* gallery. We call it "Abbie's." He named it. He hung the Fein print in his bathroom, where it's his alone to see. He stares at it when he's shaving. The interest in my work has been overwhelming. It's funny. Now New York is coming to us. Two weeks ago, he called to say we'd gotten six figures for something I painted a few months ago—a picture of me walking back across that lawn at the Bare Bottom with Abbie laughing so hard it hurt. The buyer said something about that laughter, something about Abbie's face, how it tugged at him and wouldn't let him go. How it spoke to him.

That pleases me in places that words don't reach. The senator told me that a philosopher named Ludwig Wittgenstein once said, "That which we cannot speak about, we must pass over in silence." I've known silence my whole life. I'm okay with that, too. Only difference now is that my hands are screaming at the top of their lungs.

Last week, I pulled my cap down, slid on my sunglasses and mingled around the gallery. Sort of eavesdropping. Nobody knew me. I got to talking to this lady and she said she'd been there for four hours. Said she'd been doing that once a month for six months. She tapped her chest and said, "Something about it satisfies me." I asked her which one was her favorite and she quickly pointed at this little eight by ten. It was the picture of me and my mom on the river, sitting on that bench. I pulled off my hat, slid off my glasses, lifted the piece off the wall and gave it to her. When I left she was still crying. Maybe my mom was right. Maybe some people just need to dive in and drink deeply. Maybe we all do.

~✻

THE SMELL OF PAINT filled my studio. The painter's high. The light over Fort Sumter was gentle, even golden. I stared at the vase on the shelf to my left. She'd been there every day, watching. Reminding me of my last promise.

The eleventh wish.

It was time.

I set down my brush, picked up the phone and dialed the number. When he picked up, I asked, "Can you land that thing on a dirt road?"

I could hear him move the cigar from one side of his mouth to the other. " 'Pends on the road."

I put in a call to my probation officer. While the district attorney had dropped all charges against me related to Abbie's death, they couldn't let the drug thing slide. In truth, I did steal a rather large amount of drugs and transport them across several state lines. I admitted it. The evidence would have been difficult to hide. But given that they found none in my system, they gave me twenty-four months' probation. Any time I leave the city, I need to register it with a guy behind a desk in Columbia who likes my painting.

I made a stop at the senator's house. He was in his study. Yesterday, he'd made the announcement that he would not stand for reelection. He saw the vase in my arms. "You decided to keep your promise?"

I nodded. "I can put you right alongside her."

He smiled. We'd come a long way. Abbie would have liked that.

He nodded and began unfolding and folding his handkerchief. "I'd like that. I'd like that very much."

BOB PICKED ME UP outside of town and we flew south, hugging the coastline. When we reached Cumberland Island, he banked hard west and we buzzed the town of St. Marys. We circled it once and Bob landed on a dirt road not far from the point. I walked down the dirt road, hopped the ditch and slogged through the marsh. I held Abbie in a backpack slung over my shoulder. I stepped out onto Cedar Point, talking. "Won't be long now." I walked through the cedars, the knee-high grass, around what was once our campsite.

It was a tough place.

The river moved by, sliding across the earth's surface like a sheet of polished slate. I stepped in and it tugged on me. I waded in waist-deep and pressed her to my chest. I missed her. And standing in that water, I missed her a lot.

An osprey glided above me and a pelican floated by some hundred yards away. Downriver a shrimp boat's horn sounded. I lifted the lid, held her, turned her over and watched as Abbie took a swan dive.

AFTER ELEVEN DAYS on the river, we had reached Cedar Point and, unbelievably, we had checked off all but one. Nine out of ten. I pulled her halfway up the shore. A helicopter sounded in the distance. "Honey . . . Abbie . . ." Her eyes fluttered. "We're here." I could hear men running toward us in the marsh. Her father's voice in the background.

She swallowed and tried to catch her breath. I didn't know what to say. She nodded but didn't open her eyes. "We'll save the dolphins for another day."

I patted her cheek with my hand. "You should have wished for more?"

She lifted her hand and touched my face. "I got all I ever wanted."

I was stalling. "Hey, you . . . you said you wanted to give me something. Didn't you? An anniversary present?"

She nodded. "Already gave it to you."

"But . . . ?"

She tapped me in the chest. "It'll be there when you need it."

Her eyes were starting to roll back. She sucked in a deep breath. Eyes closed, she placed her hand behind my head and pulled me toward her, pressing her forehead to mine. "Don't keep all that to yourself. People need what you've got. So you give it away. Invite them to your island." She closed her eyes and lay back. Her face was on fire but her hands were clammy and her breathing was shallow. She pulled my face to hers and whispered, "When you wake up and discover the hurt places, don't run. Sink your paddle in and ride the river." She tapped me hard in the chest. "Every time. Dive in, let the river take you, and you'll find me." She pointed toward the ocean. "I'll be waiting." The tears began to flow. Her arms fell limp and breathing all but disappeared. I held her head in my hands. "Abbie? Abbie?"

Her body tensed, she inhaled—filling her stomach—and focused somewhere ten thousand miles behind me. "Abbie?"

She pulled on me. "Promise."

"But . . ."

She smiled and her eyes returned to me. "Doss?" I couldn't look. She pulled again. "Life is a series of hellos and goodbyes. This . . . is goodbye. But not our last hello." She tapped me in the chest. "Say it."

My voice was broken. "I promise."

She sucked in hard, blood draining out of each nostril, and pointed toward the ocean. "I'll be there. Waiting. So bury me . . . where the river ends."

She lifted my hand, placed my finger between her temple and her ear—and then she was gone.

HER ASHES SPREAD across the water. There were so few. They spread out covering the surface, stretching from ripple to ripple. The outgoing current tugged at them, then strung them out single file in a long stretch toward the ocean. A hundred yards away, I saw the flash of a tail. A bottlenose dolphin rose up through the ashes. Then another. And another. Four of them rolled slowly through, painting their skin in white ash. The water was warm and clear. I whispered softly across the ripples on the water, "Abbie . . . wait for me. Wait for me where the river ends."

She passed out of view and I walked up on the bank. Dripping.

I stood on the beach, watching a fiddler crab crawl across my toe. I crossed the point, through the marsh and headed back up the dirt road. A man I didn't know approached. Long hair, short-cropped beard, pad of paper in his hand. A second man with a video camera perched on his shoulder was following him. The first said, "You're that artist? The one that made the trip downriver . . . with Abbie." I nodded. He crossed his arms and stood between me and the end of the road. "It's been about a year, hasn't it?"

He was no dummy. He was here for the story. "Yeah."

"Why'd you come back?"

I scratched my chin. "We had one thing left to do."

He nodded like he knew. "Still checking items off your list?"

I stared at him. "Something like that."

He stood off to one side while the cameraman got a better view. "Public record says you bought this piece of land. That true?"

I shaded my eyes, staring downriver and nodded.

"You got a name for it?"

I shook my head, remembering what Abbie had said, *I didn't tell that paper man everything.*

"Okay, tell me this . . . would you do it again?"

I've given that a lot of thought. Sometimes, in weaker moments, I can second-guess myself. But then I remember. I nodded. "In a heartbeat."

He scribbled in his notebook and walked backward. "You've been rather quiet the last year. Word is you've spent most of your time painting in your studio. That right?" I nodded. He shrugged and stepped in front of me. "So . . . I mean, what's the reason? Why all the trouble?"

I considered him. "Take a deep breath."

He looked at the cameraman, shrugged, then back at me with an uncomfortable smile. "What?"

"Take a deep breath."

"Okay."

"Now hold it."

He spoke like a man who'd just taken a long drag off a joint. "How long?"

"Just hold it."

He looked into the camera and shrugged. A minute passed. His face turned red. Another ten seconds and his face turned the shade of a beet. Finally, he let it out. He caught his breath, stared at me and held the microphone in my face. "That's the reason."

I walked to Bob's plane, where the wind kicked up the dust and tickled my nose.

He leaned against the wing, watching the breeze rattle the marsh and shift the color from green to brown and back to green again. After several minutes he whispered, "You ever think about remarrying?" The look on his face was not one of pilot, or crop duster, or thief or adulterer, but of priest. Bob was taking my pulse. It was an honest question.

I shook my head and spun the wedding ring around my finger.

In the distance, a bell sounded, and then as if launched from a canon, dozens of dirty seagulls and ragged-looking pelicans appeared out of the marsh and headed en masse to the dock at St. Marys where, evidently, a shrimp boat was unloading. The bell continued ringing in the distance.

He leaned across the wing. "What now?"

Months ago, I had started carrying a copy of Abbie's wish

list in my wallet. I pulled it out, unfolded it and read back through each one. "It's simple, really. I paint what my talent will allow . . . and every now and then Abbie visits me."

"Sounds painful."

A long silence followed.

I folded the article and slid it into my wallet. "Yes . . ." I filled my chest, sucking in deeply. "Hurts like hell. And that's good."

When I woke up, the floodwaters had risen and the undercurrents tore at me in ways I could not defend. It flooded my banks, spread wider and threatened to swamp my island.

But time does heal. Not like we think it does, not like we would—from the front—but more from the back or side or someplace we can't see it coming. It bubbles up beneath and rises all around. All of a sudden I dried my eyes long enough to look up, look beyond myself, and discovered my pain had become the sinew that held me together. I stood on the bank, stared out across the vast epicenter of me and faced a choice— do I risk the river? So I cut the water, paddled out of my own black hole and discovered that the river was not one but many, and like it or not, they all merge. Each turn, each bend, led to something beautiful, something whole, something worth remembering. Why? How? I can't answer that. I just know she kept her promise. She was waiting. And there in that Devil's Elbow, I found the glue that connects the pieces of me.

Tides ebb, rivers flow crooked, and love uses pain.

Bob waved his hand back across the river. "After I got out of jail, I wanted a place to hide. Some place with no past. A short time later, I bumped into Gus and he befriended me. And unlike others, he didn't hold *me* against me. I asked him why and he told me something I've yet to forget. He was standing in the water and pointed at the flow. He said, 'Once this water hits the ocean, the sun lifts it up and collects it in clouds until they get full enough, the wind blows, nudges them back over land, where they empty themselves across the continent.'"

"Meaning?"

"The river never ends."

We climbed in, he taxied, if you can call it that, and then he took off, pulling the stick back hard. Up front, my defrocked river-priest sang at the top of his lungs. A couple of chords out of tune, he conducted the clouds as we sliced through them. And while my ears listened to his beautiful song, my heart heard laughter. We circled the town, then followed the river, past Point Peter, around Cumberland and the ruins at Dungeness and then out over the waves breaking across the shoreline where the tide was just beginning to turn.

The last time I looked down, Abbie was still swimming with the dolphins.

ACKNOWLEDGMENTS

This book is my sixth novel to find its way to the shelf. I have yet to pick a favorite or say, "This is my best stuff." I simply can't. It's like asking me which of our three boys I love the most. But each story has required from me a certain amount of sweat equity. A certain measure of physical, emotional, and spiritual gut-wrenching, or pouring out of myself. When I submitted this book in August 2007, I knew that this story had required more of me than any I'd written to date. Maybe more than any two. Just ask Christy. It took nearly a week before we could hold an adult conversation.

Take that for what it's worth.

Along the way, I had much help—more than I deserve. The following "thank yous" touch on a few and in no particular order.

John Trainer, M.D.—once again, thanks, Doc, for pointing me in the right direction. You truly are a genius. Still glad you're not a lawyer.

Kathryn Pearson-Peyton, M.D.—for allowing me to spend a day with you, for introducing me to your work, along with the pleasures and dilemmas you face daily. You are gifted at what you do, and the women of Jacksonville are fortunate to have you.

Elizabeth Coleman—for opening my eyes to your side of Charleston, then coloring it with your grace. You're a blessing. I'd have never seen it without you.

Kim Neitzel—for your candid e-mails and honesty. One day I hope we get to meet face to face.

Laura Wichmann-Hipp—for your tour of Charleston that gave me insight and history I'd never have found on my own. Can't thank you enough.

John and Kay Miller—for sharing your story with me, for introducing me to Misty, and her life, and for the afternoon we spent at her graveside. Please hear me when I say that this book never could have occurred in its present form without your honesty, your laughter, and your tears—of which we shared many.

Carol Fitzgerald—You "discovered" me six books ago and have not stopped talking since. Many thanks.

Virginia McNulty—from changing my diapers to here, we've come a long way. Thank you for introducing me to John and Kay and for sharing my stories.

Jon Livingston and David Flory—for broken paddles, soaked sleeping bags, and for the laughter that echoed across three days on the river.

David Wainer—thanks, pal. You're a rock.

Todd Chupp—for the river, the miles of portage, for coming prepared with your space blanket, glow stick, and mosquito repellant, and, most important, your friendship. Psalm 144. Oh, and, yes, I do have enough research for my book now.

Chris Ferebee—for your friendship, your counsel and . . . for this. Oh, and for future reference, you sit on the seat-looking thing and the flat side goes down.

The Doubleday Broadway team—to all the folks I've yet to meet who have done so much already. From marketing to publicity to foreign sales, you all have exceeded every expectation. My deepest thanks.

Michael Palgon—thank you for taking a chance on me, for tirelessly running with this story, for letting me work with Stacy and . . . for this.

Stacy Creamer—you took a relatively good story and made it far better. I'm grateful. Thank you for your excitement, enthusiasm, your encouragement of me, your friendship and . . . for this. I simply cannot thank you enough.

Band-Aid, Scoop, and Sportmodel—Don't ever sell your dream at the altar of convenience, money, laziness or, worst of all, fear. One day you'll understand this. Probably about the time you need to hear it. Forgive me if I ever get in the way of that. I love you.

Christy—for fifteen years, for letting me do this, for loving me when I'm not lovable—which is more often than I care to admit, for forgiving me when I'm wrong . . . and for giving me the freedom to dream.

Lord—*Son of David . . . I want to see.*

READERS' GUIDE

1. What does Doss's mother teach him in the novel's opening scenes? What gift does she give him through the words "if you ever find your well empty, nothing but dust—then you come back here . . . dive in and drink deeply"?

2. Doss recalls overcoming his suffocating asthma and growing up without a father figure. Abbie had to cope with the death of her mother and life with a domineering father. In what ways did Doss and Abbie heal each other through love?

3. Discuss the Saint Mary's River as a character in *Where the River Ends*. What "personality" is reflected in the variety of scenes depicting the river? How does the timeless symbolism of water—as cleansing, life-sustaining, and ever-changing—shape its power in the novel? Where does the river ultimately take Doss and Abbie?

4. What versions of beauty are presented in the novel? What does Doss discover about himself by painting Rosalia in Chapter 15? Why are some able to see inner beauty, or unconventional physical beauty, while others are not?

5. What makes Charleston and South Carolina appropriate settings for this novel? How do the region's beautiful landscape and complex history, encompassing the grim slave trade as well as the rise of an exceptional aristocracy, shape the families depicted in *Where the River Ends*?

6. What does the novel indicate about modern medicine and its limits? What was Doss able to do for Abbie that no doctor could?

7. Doss's first up-close encounter with Abbie occurs when he fends off her attacker. During their river journey, they must again defend themselves against other threatening characters. What is the nature of such evil in the world? What determines whether victims remain optimistic, like Doss and Abbie, or descend into a quest for vengeance?

8. How does Doss and Abbie's journey down the river compare to their fantasy of it? What does it say about them that, despite the lack of creature comforts or security, they are able to savor every moment of the voyage? Why was Abbie better off without traditional hospice care?

9. Which of the wishes on Abbie's list seemed the most difficult to achieve? Which one would have been the most exhilarating for you?

10. What does Bob's history as a defrocked religious leader say about the frailty of human beings, and the power of second chances? How did the marriage ceremony he performed for Doss and Abbie compare to more lavish nuptials you have witnessed?

11. How was the storytelling enhanced by the author's use of flashbacks? In what way did the timeline mirror the way memories are woven into the present?

12. Were you surprised by the scene of forgiveness in the end? What did Doss and his father-in-law ultimately have in common?

13. Describe the most important farewell you have experienced. Have you ever served as the navigator for someone who had to endure a difficult journey?

14. If you were faced with Abbie's prognosis, what unfulfilled promises and unfinished wishes would you make haste to experience? What would it take to accomplish the dreams on this list even if you were not faced with Abbie's fate?

AN EXCERPT FROM

The Mountain Between Us

Coming in June 2011

PRELUDE

Hey . . .

I'm not sure what time it is. This thing should record that. I woke a few minutes ago. It's still dark. I don't know how long I was out.

The snow is spilling in through the windshield. It's frozen across my face. Hard to blink. Feels like dried paint on my cheeks. It just doesn't taste like dried paint.

I'm shivering . . . and it feels like somebody is sitting on my chest. Can't catch my breath. Maybe broke two or three ribs. Might have a collapsed lung.

The wind up here is steady, leaning against the tail of the fuselage . . . or what's left of it. Something above me, maybe a branch, is slapping the Plexiglas. Sounds like fingernails on a chalkboard. And more cold air is coming in behind me. Where the tail used to be.

I can smell gas. I guess both wings were still pretty full of fuel.

I feel like I want to throw up.

A hand is wrapped around mine. The fingers are cold and callused. There's a wedding band, worn thin around the edges. That's Grover.

He was dead before we hit the treetops. I'll never understand how he landed this thing without killing me, too.

When we took off, the ground temperature was in the single digits. Not sure what it is now. Feels colder. Our elevation should be around

11,500. Give or take. We couldn't have fallen more than five hundred feet when Grover dipped the wing. The control panel sits dark, unlit. Dusted in white. Every few minutes the GPS on the dash will flicker, then go black again.

There was a dog here somewhere. All teeth and muscle. Real short hair. About the size of a bread box. Makes angry gurgling sounds when he breathes. Looks like he's jacked up on speed. Wait . . .

"Hey, boy . . . Wait . . . no. Not there. Okay, lick, but don't jump. What's your name? You scared? Yeah . . . me too."

I can't remember his name.

I'm back . . . was I gone long? There's a dog here. Buried between my coat and armpit.

Did I already tell you about him? I can't remember his name.

He's shivering, and the skin around his eyes is quivering. Whenever the wind howls, he jumps up and growls at it.

The memory's foggy. Grover and I were talking, he was flying, maybe banking right, the dash flashed a buffet of blue and green lights, a carpet of black stretched out below us, not a lightbulb for sixty miles in any direction, and . . . there was a woman. Trying to get home to her fiancé and a rehearsal dinner. I'll look.

. . . I found her. Unconscious. Elevated pulse. Eyes are swollen shut. Pupils are dilated. Probably a concussion. Several lacerations across her face. A few will need stitches. Right shoulder is dislocated and left femur is broken. It didn't break the skin, but her leg is angling out and her pant leg is tight. I need to set it . . . once I catch my breath.

. . . It's getting colder. I guess the storm finally caught us. If I don't get us wrapped in something we'll freeze to death before daylight. I'll have to set that leg in the morning.

Rachel . . . I don't know how much time we have, don't know if we'll make it out . . . but . . . I take it all back. I was wrong. I was angry. I never should've said it. You were thinking about us. Not you. I can see that now.

You're right. Right all along. There's always a chance.

Always.

CHAPTER ONE

The view was ugly. Gray, dreary, January dragging on. On the TV screen behind me, some guy sitting in a studio in New York used the words "socked in." I pressed my forehead to the glass. On the tarmac, guys in yellow suits drove trains of luggage that snaked around the planes, leaving snow flurries swirling in their exhaust. Next to me, a tired pilot sat on his flight-weathered leather case, hat in his hand—hoping for a last chance hop home and a night in his own bed.

To the west, clouds covered the runway; visibility near zero, but given the wind, it came and went. Windows of hope. The Salt Lake City airport is surrounded by mountains. Eastward, snowcapped mountains rose above the clouds. Mountains have long been an attraction for me. For a moment, I wondered what was on the other side.

My flight was scheduled to depart at 6:07 p.m., but given delays was starting to look like the red-eye. If at all. Annoyed by the flashing Delayed sign, I moved to a corner on the floor, against a far wall. I spread patient files across my lap and began dictating my reports, diagnoses, and prescriptions into a digital recorder. Folks I'd seen the week before I left. While I treated adults too, most of the files on my lap belonged to kids. Years ago Rachel, my wife, convinced me to focus on sports medicine in kids. She was right. I hated seeing them limp in, but loved watching them run out.

I had some more work to do, and the battery indicator on my digital recorder was flashing red, so I walked to the store in the terminal and found I could buy two AA batteries for four dollars or twelve for seven. I gave the lady seven dollars, replaced the batteries in my recorder, and slid the other ten into my backpack.

I had just returned from a medical conference in Colorado Springs where I had been invited to join a panel on "The Intersection of Pediatric Orthopedics and Emergency Medicine." We covered ER procedures and the differing bedside manners needed to treat fearful kids. The venue was beautiful, the conference satisfied several of my continuing ed requirements, and most important, it gave me an excuse to spend four days climbing the Collegiate Peaks near Buena Vista, Colorado. In truth, it was a business trip that satisfied my hiking addiction. Many doctors buy Porsches and big homes and pay for country club memberships they seldom use. I take long runs on the beach and climb mountains when I can get to them.

I'd been gone a week.

My return trip took me from Colorado Springs to Salt Lake for the direct flight home. Airline travel never ceases to amaze me; flying west to end up east. The crowd in the airport had thinned. Most folks were home by this time on a Sunday. Those still in the airport were either at their gate, waiting, or at the bar, hovering over a beer and a basket of nachos or hot wings.

Her walk caught my attention. Long, slender legs; purposeful gait, yet graceful and rhythmic. Comfortable, and confident, in her own skin. She was maybe five foot nine or ten, dark-haired, and attractive, but not too concerned about it. Maybe thirty. Her hair was short. Think Winona Ryder in Girl, Interrupted. Or Julia Ormond in Harrison Ford's remake of Sabrina. Not a lot of fuss, yet you could find the same style up and down Manhattan with girls who'd paid a lot of money to look like that. My bet was that she had paid very little. Or she could have paid a lot to make it look like she paid a little.

She walked up, eyed the crowd across the terminal, and then chose a spot ten or fifteen feet away on the floor. I watched her out of the corner of my eye. Dark pantsuit, a leather attaché, and one carry-on. Looked like she was returning from a business overnight. She set down her bags, tied on a pair of Nike running shoes, then, eying the terminal, sat on the floor and stretched. Based on the fact that not only her head, but also her chest and stomach could touch her thigh and the floor between her legs, I surmised that she had done that before. Her legs were muscular, like an aerobics instructor's. After she stretched a few minutes, she pulled several yellow legal pads from her attaché, flipped through pages of handwritten notes, and started typing on her laptop. Her fingers moved at the speed of hummingbird wings.

After a few minutes, her laptop beeped. She frowned, stuck her pencil between her teeth, and began eyeballing the wall for an outlet. I was using half. She was holding the swinging end of her laptop's power cord.

"Mind if I share?"

"Sure."

She plugged in and then sat cross-legged with the computer on the floor, surrounded by her legal pads. I continued with my files.

"Follow-up orthopedics consultation dated . . ." I studied my calendar, trying to resurrect the date. "January 23. This is Dr. Ben Payne. Patient's name is Rebecca Peterson, identifying data follows. Date of birth, 7-6-95, medical record number BMC2453, Caucasian female, star right wing on her soccer team, leading scorer in Florida, highly recruited by teams around the country, at last count she had fourteen Division I offers; surgery three weeks ago, post op was normal, presenting no complications, followed by aggressive physical therapy; presents full range of motion, bend test 127 degrees, strength test shows marked improvement, as does agility. She's good as new, or in her words, better. Rebecca reports movement is pain free, and she is free to resume all activities . . . except skateboarding. She is to stay off the skateboard until she's at least thirty-five."

I turned to the next file. "Initial orthopedics consultation dated January 23. This is Dr. Ben Payne."

I say the same thing each time because in the electronic world in which we live, each recording is separate and, if lost, needs to be identified.

"Patient's name is Rasheed Smith, identifying data follows. Date of birth, 2-19-79, medical record number BMC17437, black male, starting defensive back for the Jacksonville Jaguars and one of the fastest human beings I've ever been around. MRI confirms no tear in the ACL or MCL, recommend aggressive physical therapy and that he stay off the YMCA basketball court until he's finished playing professional football. Range of motion is limited due to pain and tenderness, which should subside given therapy during the off-season. Can resume limited strength and speed training with cessation in pain. Schedule two-week follow-up and call the YMCA and tell them to revoke his membership."

I slid the files into my backpack and noticed she was laughing.

"You a doctor?"

"Surgeon." I held up the manila folders. "Last week's patients."

"You really get to know your patients, don't you?" She shrugged. "Sorry, I couldn't help but overhear."

I nodded. "Something my wife taught me."

"Which is?"

"That people are more than the sum of their blood pressure plus their pulse divided by their body mass index."

She laughed again. "You're my kind of doctor."

I nodded at her pads. "And you?"

"Columnist." She waved her hand across the papers in front of her. "I write for several different women's magazines."

"What kind of topics do you cover?"

"Fashion, trends, a lot of humor or satire, some relationships, but I'm not Jane Doe and I don't do gossip."

"I can't write my way out of a wet paper bag. How many will you write in a year?"

She weighed her head side to side. "Forty, maybe fifty." She glanced at my recorder. "Most doctors I know loathe those things."

I turned it in my hand. "I'm seldom without it."

"Like an albatross?"

I laughed. "Something like that."

"Take much getting used to?"

"It's grown on me. Now I couldn't live without it."

"Sounds like a story here."

"Rachel . . . my wife, gave it to me. I was driving the moving truck to Jacksonville. Moving our life back home. Joining the staff at the hospital. She was afraid of the schedule. Of finding herself on the couch, a doctor's widow, a gallon of Häagen-Dazs and the Lifeway channel. This . . . was a way to hear the sound of each other's voice, to be together, to not miss the little things . . . between surgery, making rounds, and the sound of my beeper at two a.m. She'd keep it a day or so, speak her mind . . . or heart, then pass the baton. I'd keep it a day or two, or maybe three, and pass it back."

"Wouldn't a cell phone do the same thing?"

I shrugged. "It's different. Try it sometime and you'll see what I mean."

"How long you been married?"

"We married . . . fifteen years ago this week." I glanced at her hand. A single diamond decorated her left hand. Absent was the wedding band. "You got one coming up?"

She couldn't control the smile. "I'm trying to get home for my rehearsal dinner party tomorrow night."

"Congratulations."

She shook her head and smiled, staring out across the crowd. "I have a million things to do, and yet here I am making notes on a story about a flash-in-the-pan fashion I don't even like."

I nodded. "You're probably a good writer."

A shrug. "They keep me around. I've heard that there are people who buy these magazines just to read my column, though I've never met them." Her charm was magnetic. She asked, "Jacksonville still home?"

"Yep. And you?"

"Atlanta." She handed me her card. ASHLEY KNOX.

"Ashley."

"To everyone but my dad, who calls me Asher. He wanted a boy, was mad at my mom when I appeared with the wrong equipment, or lack thereof, so he changed the ending. Instead of ballet and softball he took me to tae kwon do."

"Let me guess . . . you're one of those crazy people who can kick stuff off the top of other people's heads."

She nodded.

"That would explain the stretching and chest to the floor thing."

She nodded again, like she didn't need to impress me.

"What degree?"

She held up three fingers.

"I worked on a guy a few weeks ago, put a few rods and screws in his shin."

"How'd he do it?"

"Kicked his opponent, who blocked it with an elbow. The shin kept going. Sort of folded it the wrong way."

"I've seen that before."

"You say that like you've been cut on."

"I competed a lot in my teens and early twenties. National championships. Several countries. I broke my fair share of bones and joints. There was a time when my orthopedist in Atlanta was on speed dial. So is this trip work, play, or both?"

"I'm returning from a medical conference, where I sat on a panel, and . . ." I smiled. "Got in some climbing on the side."

"Climbing?"

"Mountains."

"Is that what you do when you're not cutting on people?"

I laughed. "I have two hobbies. Running is one . . . it's how I met Rachel. Started in high school. Tough habit to break. When we moved back home we bought a condo on the beach so we could chase the tide in and out. The second is climbing mountains, something we started while attending medical school in Denver. Well, I attended, she kept me sane. Anyway, there are fifty-four peaks in Colorado higher than 14,000 feet. Locals call them 'fourteeners.' There's an unofficial club of folks who have climbed them all. We started checking them off in medical school."

"How many have you climbed?"

"Twenty. Just added Mt. Princeton. 14,197 feet. It's one of the Collegiate Peaks."

She thought about that a minute. "That's almost three miles above sea level."

I nodded. "Close, but not quite."

"How long does something like that take?"

"Normally a day or less, but conditions this time of year make it a bit"—I shifted my head back and forth—"tougher."

She laughed. "You need oxygen?"

"No, but acclimating helps."

"Was it covered in snow and ice?"

"Yes."

"And was it bitter cold, snowing and blowing like crazy?"

"I'll bet you're a good journalist."

"Well . . . was it?"

"At times."

"Did you make it up and down without dying?"

I laughed. "Evidently."

One eyebrow rose above the other. "So, you're one of those people?"

"What type is that?"

"The 'man versus wild' type."

I shook my head. "Weekend warrior. I'm most at home at sea level."

She stared up and down the rows of people. "Your wife's not with you?"

"Not this time."

My stomach growled. The aroma from the California Pizza Kitchen wafted down the terminal. I stood. "You mind watching my stuff?"

"Sure."

"Be right back."

I returned with a Caesar salad and a plate-sized pepperoni pizza just as the loudspeaker cackled.

"Folks, if we can load quickly, we might beat this storm.

There aren't too many of us, so all zones, all passengers, please board Flight 1672 to Atlanta."

The eight gates around me read DELAYED. Frustrated faces populated the seats and walls. A mom and dad ran the length of the terminal hollering over their shoulders at two boys dragging Star Wars suitcases and plastic lightsabers.

I grabbed my pack and my food, and then followed seven other passengers—including Ashley—toward the plane. I found my seat and buckled in, the attendants cross-checked, and we began backing up. It was the fastest load I'd ever seen.

The plane stopped, the pilot got on the intercom: "Folks, we're in line for the deicer, and if we can get them over here, we might beat this storm. By the way, there's plenty of room up front. As a matter of fact, if you're not in first class, it's your own fault. We've got room for everyone."

Everyone moved.

The only remaining seat placed me next to Ashley. She looked up and smiled as she was buckling her belt. "Think we'll get out of here?"

I stared out the window. "Doubtful."

"Pessimist, are you?"

"I'm a doctor. That makes me an optimist with realistic notions."

"Good point."

We sat for thirty minutes while the attendants served us most anything we asked for. I drank spicy tomato juice. Ashley drank Cabernet.

The pilot came on again. His tone did not encourage me. "Folks . . . as you all know, we were trying to beat this storm."

I heard the past tense.

"The controllers in the tower tell us we've got about an hour's window to make it out before the storm closes in. . . . "

Everyone breathed a collective sigh. Maybe there was hope.

"But the ground crew just informed me that one of our two deicing trucks is inoperative. Which means we have one truck attempting to service all the planes on the runway, and ours is the twentieth in line. Long story short, we're not getting out of here tonight."

Groans echoed around the plane.

Ashley unbuckled and shook her head. "You got to be kidding me."

A large man off to my left muttered, "Son of a . . ."

The pilot continued, "Our folks will meet you at the end of the gate. If you'd like a hotel voucher, please see Mark, who's wearing the red coat and flak jacket. Once you reclaim your baggage, our shuttle will take you to the hotel. Folks, I'm really sorry."

We walked back into the terminal and watched as each of the Delayed signs changed to Canceled.

I spoke for everyone in the terminal. "That's not good."

I walked to the counter. The female attendant stood staring at a computer screen, shaking her head. Before I opened my mouth, she turned toward the television, which was tuned to the weather channel. "I'm sorry, there's nothing I can do."

Four screens over my shoulder showed a huge green blob moving east-southeast from Washington, Oregon, and northern California. The ticker at the bottom of the screen called for snow, ice, single-digit temperatures, and wind chills in the negatives. A couple to my left embraced in a passionate kiss. Smiling. An unscheduled day added to their vacation.

Mark began handing out hotel vouchers and ushering people toward baggage claim. I had one carry-on—a small daypack that doubled as my briefcase—and one checked bag in the belly of the plane. We were all headed to baggage claim whether we liked it or not.

I walked toward the baggage claim and lost Ashley when she stopped at the Natural Snacks store. I found a place near the conveyor belt and looked around. Through the sliding glass doors, I saw the lights of the private airport less than a mile away. Painted on the side of the closest hangar, in huge letters, was one word: Charters.

The lights were on in one of the hangars. My bag appeared. I hefted it atop my free shoulder and bumped into Ashley, who was waiting on hers. She eyed it.

"You weren't kidding when you said you got in some climbing on the side. Looks like you're climbing Everest. You really need all that?"

My bag is an orangish Osprey 70 backpack, and it's got a few miles on it. I use it as a suitcase because it works, but its main function is best served hiking and it fits me like a glove. It was stuffed with all my overnight and cold-weather hiking gear for my climbs in the Collegiate Peaks. Sleeping bag, Therm-a-Rest pad, Jetboil stove—maybe the most underappreciated and most valuable piece of equipment I own, next to my sleeping bag—a couple of Nalgene bottles, a few layers of polypropylene, and several other odds and ends that help me stay alive and comfortable when sleeping above ten or eleven thousand feet. There's also a dark blue pin-striped suit, a handsome blue tie that Rachel gave me, and a pair of Johnston & Murphy's, which I wore once, for the panel.

"I know my limitations, and I'm not made for Everest. I get pretty sick above fifteen thousand. I'm okay below that. These"—I hefted the pack—"are just the essentials. Good idea to have along."

She spotted her bag and turned to run it down, then turned back, a pained expression on her face. Apparently the idea of missing her wedding was starting to sink in, bleeding away her charm. She extended her hand. Her grip was firm yet warm. "Great to meet you. Hope you can get home."

"Yeah, you—"

She never heard me. She turned, threw her bag over her shoulder, and headed toward the taxi lane where a hundred people stood in line.

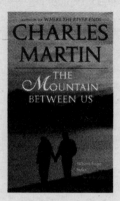